By MARGUERITE LABBE

NOVELS
All Bets Are Off
Ghosts in the Wind

THE TRIQUETRA TRILOGY
My Heart Is Within You
Haunted by Your Soul
Our Sacred Balance

NOVELS WITH FAE SUTHERLAND
Bee Among the Clover
Lotus in the Wild

Published by DREAMSPINNER PRESS
http://www.dreamspinnerpress.com

GHOSTS
IN THE
WIND

Marguerite Labbe

Dreamspinner Press

Published by
Dreamspinner Press
5032 Capital Circle SW
Ste 2, PMB# 279
Tallahassee, FL 32305-7886
USA
http://www.dreamspinnerpress.com/

Ghosts in the Wind

Cover Art by Reese Dante
http://www.reesedante.com

ISBN: 978-1-62380-052-9

Printed in the United States of America
First Edition
October 2012

eBook edition available
eBook ISBN: 978-1-62380-053-6

For my Uncle John and all of those who were abused and taken from us too soon.

Chapter One

DEAN MARSHALL savored the rare morning when he got to linger in bed instead of having to be out the door before the sun rose. Especially mornings like this, with the sun streaming through the window and with his partner, Andrei Cuza, curled against his back. Andrei's calf had slid between Dean's legs sometime in the night, as usual, and his hand splayed against Dean's stomach. Dean smiled sleepily and let his eyes drift shut again as he burrowed back into the warmth of Andrei's body. Now this was the only way to wake up right. He drank in the sun on his face, the scent of fresh brewed coffee in the air, and the feel of Andrei stirring behind him.

Breath brushed the nape of his neck followed by a kiss to his shoulder. The hand on Dean's stomach shifted and long fingers stroked his skin. "Morning, *iubito*," Andrei said in a sleep-husky voice that made desire stir Dean's blood. He loved the dark timbre of his tone, the quiet manner he had that made people listen without him ever having to raise his voice.

"Hey, babe," Dean murmured back, turning his head to graze his lips along Andrei's stubbled jaw. As he shifted, cool cotton sheets caressed his skin, and he longed for Andrei's hands to do the same. "Tell me you don't have anywhere you have to be in the next hour."

"I have a pile of paperwork waiting for me on my desk." Andrei smiled, his dark eyes lighting up with teasing. "She's a cruel, demanding mistress."

"Leaving me naked in bed for paperwork is a cardinal sin." Dean's breath caught as Andrei slid his hand lower between Dean's thighs to cup his morning wood. He reached behind him and burrowed his fingers into Andrei's thick hair. "Stay and play with me, Andrei."

"You make it sound like I have any chance of resisting you. We both know the truth about that," Andrei replied, trailing his lips down Dean's neck to linger at his pulse. "Besides, I'm not the one with an oh-so-important meeting in DC today."

Dean cursed and his eyes flew open as he untangled himself from Andrei's embrace to lean over to check the time on his cell phone.

Andrei started chuckling. "You should've seen the look of horror that crossed your face."

"Ass, you knew I didn't oversleep." Dean whacked him with a pillow and leveled an accusing glare at him.

Andrei, the sheet tangled around his waist and a gold crucifix gleaming against his bare chest, seemed unbothered as he grinned back at Dean. "It's so much fun to fuck with you. I rarely get the chance. Think of it as retaliation for all those times you messed with me on the big days." Andrei took Dean's hand, lifted it to his lips, and kissed the knuckles before turning Dean's hand around to kiss the inside of his wrist as well. The look in Andrei's smoky, dark brown eyes turned warm and seductive as he continued to rain kisses along Dean's arm.

Dean fought a smile and tried to hold on to his glare, but the teasing lift of Andrei's lips beat him. He grinned and sank back into Andrei's arms, determined to relax instead of triple-checking and making sure he had everything for his proposal ready before heading out. He already knew he had it together, and obsessing would only get him all worked up for nothing. Dean wanted to lose himself in the taste and feel of Andrei as they moved together.

"And you call me evil. I didn't think retaliation was your style."

Andrei's black hair lay in a tumbled mess from sleep, and the sun highlighted his swarthy skin that he got from his Romani blood. He looked more rugged than beautiful, with his too-strong nose that bore a kink from being broken more than once, and his chiseled jaw, which had a cleft that gave him a rough-hewn appearance. Dean thought that those features were what made him so very sexy. Andrei's smile widened into a devilish grin as he tugged Dean on top of him. "You do have your moments."

Dean brushed his lips along Andrei's jaw again, savoring the familiar sensation of Andrei's long, lean body beneath him. After all of these years, it didn't get old. The hot rush of teenage hormones had settled somewhat, and he found the familiarity between them to be a comfort. Dean knew every inch of him, knew how to drive him crazy in slow degrees. If anything, he wanted Andrei more now than when they'd first fallen for each other.

Their tongues tangled in a slow, lazy kiss, and Dean sighed in pleasure as Andrei ran his hands over him in a lingering sweep from his shoulders down to the backs of his thighs. It was easy to dismiss his excitement over the possibilities later on that day in favor of making love to Andrei. He wrapped his arms around Dean, holding him closer as he broke the kiss and bared his neck.

Dean chuckled and nuzzled Andrei's throat. "Now where's that spot?" he murmured, as Andrei's breath caught.

"Tease." Andrei thrust his fingers into Dean's hair, guiding his mouth to that place on Andrei's throat that made him shiver. "Oh yeah, right there," Andrei whispered and shifted restlessly under Dean as he traced the spot—just behind and below his ear toward the nape of his neck—with his tongue before giving it a gentle bite.

"I think I could get you to agree to anything if I lingered here long enough." Dean nibbled again with teeth and lips interspersed with tiny licks as Andrei's cock came to life against him.

"Good thing for me you have a short attention span." Andrei danced his fingertips over the small of Dean's back, making him shiver and arch. "And I know your own spots."

Dean grabbed Andrei's wrists, mock growling as they wrestled, kicking the tangled sheets and blankets onto the floor. His cock throbbed, filling him with a welcome ache as they rubbed against each other during their bout. Dean was stronger, even if Andrei was taller by a good few inches. A nice side effect from working out on a daily basis at the gym he owned, and he needed all the advantage he could get.

Andrei got one of his hands free, and Dean squawked, loosening his grip as Andrei went for the pressure point on the inside of his elbow, making his arm tingle. "Sneaky bastard."

"You started it." Andrei snickered as he wrapped his arms around Dean again and pulled him down. There was nothing he liked more than feeling Andrei's naked skin all along his body. "And I'm finishing it. Stop playing around and kiss me."

ANDREI'S heart flipped when Dean's hazel eyes darkened as he lowered his head. Dean still had the power to do that to him, to make him weak inside with need, to make him forget all the ugliness outside their home, because with him Andrei had a security that he hadn't felt anywhere else. He sank into the kiss, arching against Dean's cock throbbing between his thighs. He wanted more of that, needed to feel it throbbing inside of him.

Heat rose and Andrei slid one leg up to hook over Dean's hip as the kiss broke. He rocked his hips up, sighing in pleasure as Dean's cock nestled against his ass. "I think I like you, maybe just a bit."

Dean chuckled at the old running joke between them and reached over for the lube they'd tossed onto the stand last night. "You still won't let me live that down."

"You'd be crushed if I did." Andrei had understood Dean's response when he'd first told his best friend how he'd felt about him in college. Dean hadn't been at all prepared for his feelings, and the uncertain expression on his face, the worry there, had told Andrei all he needed to know. He'd taken a step back, given Dean the space he needed to figure things out. And his patience had finally won what he'd wanted since he'd first seen that handsome boy who'd befriended him after Andrei had been abandoned. And when Dean had been ready, those words, those stumbling, awkward words, had been the sweetest he had heard in a long time.

"I love you," Dean murmured, his slick cock pushing at Andrei's entrance as his lips brushed Andrei's own. "I always have, even if I made you wait for me."

Andrei's breath caught at the familiar sensation of Dean sinking into him. Hard and hot and slick, he filled that aching emptiness inside Andrei. "I know, I was just teasing."

He slid his legs high around Dean, groaning as Dean began rocking his hips in a slow, sensual pace that stoked the fire hotter bit by bit. Their gentle murmurs and soft sounds of passion mingled in the morning air as the urgency built. Andrei's heart beat faster, and he lifted up to meet each thrust with a moan.

Sweat darkened Dean's hair at the temples, dulling the golden highlights. Andrei slid his fingers into Dean's short hair and drew him down again. Andrei wasn't always the best at expressing how he felt, and he was far more comfortable with just showing him. So he kissed Dean, letting hands and exploring tongue do the speaking for him. Somehow, Dean always heard him anyway.

Dean thrust his hips faster, driving away everything but Andrei's need to come and to feel Dean do the same. Andrei dragged his mouth down to Dean's throat with a rough groan as he gave him a gentle bite. "Almost there." He slid his hands down to Dean's ass, feeling the flex of muscle with every thrust, and it brought him that much closer.

Dean slipped his hand between their stomachs and began stroking Andrei's cock. "Let's see what I can do to get you all the way there."

It didn't take much, not with the electricity they generated together. Andrei felt the sizzle in his blood and tasted the heat on Dean's lips as their breath mingled. He came, clenching hard around Dean's cock so he wouldn't miss one moment of it throbbing inside of him with his partner's orgasm.

Dean groaned, kissing him hard, stealing his breath as they ground together until the last ripples faded from their bodies. Andrei panted, pressing his forehead against Dean's for a moment before letting his head fall back onto the pillow. "Now that's the way I like to wake up. None of this already out the door and at the gym for a 6:00 a.m. class bullshit, trying to disturb my rest."

"Oh really?" Mock outrage crossed Dean's face as he grabbed Andrei's wrists again and pinned them to the mattress. "What about the not coming home till two bullshit and looking for a little action? Hmmm, what do you have to say about that?"

Andrei jerked his arms free and rolled them both over so Dean lay under him. "I think that as two men who own their own businesses, we really need to coordinate better."

"Good point." Dean leaned up and stole a quick kiss. "So less midnight stakeouts for you, and I let Zack take over some of the morning classes like he's been wanting to. Deal?"

Andrei liked the sound of that. Quite frankly he was tired of the whole spying on cheating spouses game. It never ended well, and the ugliness of it all could be downright depressing at times. It was no wonder that when he returned home, he wanted to be as close to Dean as he could. To remind himself that not all relationships were like that. If Dean wanted out, he'd tell Andrei so to his face, not go around behind his back.

"Deal."

"Damn," Dean sighed, dropping his head back on the pillow. "Do I really want to split my time between DC and Baltimore? What was I thinking?"

Andrei eased onto his side, amused by the worried expression on Dean's face. Dean rarely let nerves get the best of him. He stroked Dean's stomach, watching the play of emotion in his hazel eyes. "I mean seriously," Dean continued. "Why did I decide it was a good idea to brand myself out and try to open a second gym? I'm a personal trainer, not a businessman."

"You're worrying about it too much. I'm the brooder, not you." Andrei laid his head down on Dean's shoulder before he gave in to the smile that threatened. "Besides, I know why you did it. You just can't sit still or ignore an opportunity as it goes by."

"Stop laughing at me." Dean poked him in the ribs. "This is serious."

"You're going to do fine." Andrei lifted his head and gave him a warm smile. "You've proven you can run a successful business and have the paperwork and statements to back it up. Just turn on your charm and let all your hard work speak for itself."

"That easy, huh?" Dean cast Andrei a skeptical glance. "Just brazen my way through the presentation?"

"Don't you do that with everything?" Andrei teased as he dropped a kiss on his lips and then rose from the bed. As much as he would love to linger, he had to check his e-mail and get moving. "Trust me, you will kick ass and win them over. Relax."

"I THINK you're getting me and you confused. I don't brazen or charm my way through anything," Dean called, ogling Andrei's naked, tight ass as he walked away. It was a nice distraction from the presentation awaiting him later on in the day.

Andrei snickered and cast him a "yeah right" glance over his shoulder. "Keep telling yourself that, Marshall."

Once the view of that lean, muscled ass disappeared, Dean's nerves over the rest of the day returned. The idea of talking figures, spreadsheets, and accounting with bank execs made him sweat worse than he did when marathon training.

Several minutes later, Dean heard the sound of the shower running. He contemplated trying to catch a bit more sleep or horning in on Andrei's shower with the offer of a back wash. The scent of coffee tantalized him as well, luring him toward the kitchen instead.

Dean tugged on a pair of track pants and paused in the bathroom long enough to pull back the curtain and land a satisfying, wet smack on Andrei's ass. He danced out of the way laughing as Andrei spun with an indignant squawk to take a retaliatory swipe at him. "Ever vigilant! Dude, after all these years you'd think you'd have learned. Be happy I didn't toss in cold water this time."

Andrei jerked the shower curtain closed again. "You should be happy I've got too much shampoo in my hair to chase you down and beat your ass."

Dean snickered and paused at the mirror to run a comb over his cropped hair. "Got me shaking there, babe. Seriously, I'm terrified."

He was on his second cup of coffee and contemplating breakfast when Andrei came into the kitchen in jeans and a T-shirt, his hair lying in wet tangles about his face. Andrei needed a haircut. He was getting shaggy, and he hadn't shaved as he usually did, though the stubble that still covered his cheeks and jaw was rather sexy.

Dean frowned as Andrei laid his ankle holster and pistol on the counter. "I thought you said you had paperwork to do." Andrei rarely took a gun out on routine investigations. That he had picked this particular gun and holster told Dean that Andrei planned on going into a dangerous place instead of dealing with a possibly touchy, angry spouse, insurance scam, or reluctant witness.

"I always have paperwork to do. It's vile and never-ending." Andrei poured himself a cup of coffee and sipped it straight black. It made Dean shudder; he had to have lots of cream, lots of sugar. Any other way was downright gross. "However, I've got to go into West Baltimore today. A lead came in on that missing teenager."

Dean knew he shouldn't worry. Andrei had been taking care of himself since he was fifteen, rarely letting anyone help him. Still, he hated it when Andrei went among the crack houses with the drug dealers, spaced out addicts, and prostitutes. It didn't take much for something to get ugly. Like trying to pull a kid out of there who didn't want to be found or who had someone with a vested interest in seeing that the kid stayed put.

"You heading over there now?"

"Yeah, I don't want to risk the trail going cold again, and the lead is solid. If you call my cell and I don't answer, then it's 'cause I'm still in the middle of it all." Andrei propped his foot on the chair and strapped the holster at his ankle, then slipped the gun in place and checked to make sure it was secure.

As much as Dean didn't like the sight of him with a gun, he couldn't deny the satisfaction Andrei got out of solving cases that reunited kids with their families over the other bullshit. So even though he worried, he never said a word against him going. Andrei could not look away from a kid in trouble, and it would be unfair of Dean to ask him to, no matter how dangerous the case or how nonexistent the backup.

"You look like a hood rat, babe."

Andrei glanced over at him and gave Dean a toothy grin. "Nice to know I'll blend right in."

"It's giving me all kinds of ideas. Can I use your handcuffs on you later? I could be the upstanding guy making a citizen's arrest."

"You've got to get them away from me first." Andrei's gaze heated as he raked his eyes over Dean, making his pulse skip a beat. "And if you lose, oh buddy, I'm going to be doing the interrogating, not you."

"Oooh, a wrestling match." Dean pulled the carton of egg whites from the fridge and raised his brow as Andrei grabbed his wallet and keys. "Hey, what about breakfast? I'm cooking."

"I'd love to take you up on that, but the timing on this may be critical." Andrei looked around the counter and swiped an apple. "See, I'm all set. It's even healthy, no Pop Tarts this morning."

Dean gave up with a shake of his head. Trying to get a real meal into Andrei was an exercise in frustration sometimes. "Go out and save the day, mister hotshot private detective," he said, smiling at him. "Again, 'cause you're like that."

"You have this image of heroism and me in your head that just doesn't exist, *iubito*." Andrei paused, a faint line appearing between his brows. "I spy on cheating spouses for the most part."

"Yeah and then there are the days like this. I think these are the days you live for." Dean slid his hand around the nape of Andrei's neck and drew him in for a kiss. "I'll call you later after I've won over the bank execs with my enthusiasm and charm."

"You'd better." Andrei smiled. "I'm proud of you."

"Yeah, yeah, yeah. Go on, get out of here. Be careful, okay?" Dean said, allowing that small part of his concern to show.

"I promise, Dean. I'm not going to let anything happen to me."

"JUSTIN, I'm telling you, dozens of kids are being held captive here," Andrei said urgently into his cell phone as he crouched on the rooftop near the fire escape. There wasn't one bit of shade to shelter him from the August sun that beat down on him. Combine that with the heat trapped in the hardened tar on the roof and it felt like he could bathe in his own sweat, and the humidity made it a struggle for every breath taken.

He kept one wary eye on the access door, prepared to duck behind the dying AC unit if it opened. "I haven't spotted that many guys running the operation, but still more than I can handle." After the tip he'd gotten this morning, he'd expected one guy holding at the most two kids, Marco being one of them. One pervert, not a fucking gang of them.

"Are you out of your mind?" Detective Justin Mansle roared at him from the other end of the line. "The chief is going to have my ass this time if you escalate things. Just stay put and let us handle it, okay? We're on our way."

"Hurry up, will you? I'm not joking when I say these kids are in immediate danger." Andrei hung up the phone before Justin continued to rail at him. He scanned the other nearby rooftops, most of them just as derelict as this one, covered in graffiti, with broken and boarded up windows. He caught a quick glimpse of a young girl in a cheerful red-and-yellow sundress. She lifted her hand in a wave and disappeared.

Andrei forced his thoughts back to the problem at hand, away from that brief vision and the familiar prickle of guilt tinged with bittersweet. He should stay put, just like Justin had ordered. Only, he had wasted enough time already. If those creeps noticed that some of the kids were missing already, things would get nasty real quick. It wasn't like he could've left them behind after finding them locked up in that room. There were some things that shouldn't be stomached.

"Justin had better fucking hurry," he muttered under his breath. It wouldn't take long for the girls' hiding place to become intolerable in this heat.

Andrei's heart pounded from adrenaline as he made his way back through the abandoned, boarded-up flophouse right in the heart of the worst of what Baltimore had to offer. He blinked at the sudden dimness as the access door shut behind him, and he savored the relief from the sun before the stuffiness of the air inside made its presence known. So much for that AC unit.

Dean would have a heart attack if he knew the stunt Andrei was pulling. It had been sheer luck that let him get up the fire escape in the first place, but now the lookout had returned to the alley, and Andrei would never be able to get the kids out that way unseen. He'd just have to figure out another way in the time he had left to him before the cops arrived.

He encountered no one on the stairwell and narrowly escaped another lookout as he emerged onto the next level. The creak of footsteps on the rotting boards alerted him, and Andrei slipped into an empty room. He waited for the sound of footsteps to pass before coming up behind him and catching the guy in a choke hold.

Andrei squeezed as the man clawed at his arm and kicked his shins. The jackass mustn't have noticed that those girls were missing, or the alarm would've been raised. But just the thought of what might've happened if he'd looked into the girls' empty room made Andrei's blood run cold.

The man went limp, and Andrei listened intently to see if the sounds of the scuffle alerted anyone before dragging him back into the room. He left the man handcuffed and gagged with his own shirt. Crude, but he had little time for finesse.

Andrei could feel time slipping away from him with every beat of his heart. "Stupid, stupid, stupid...." He'd gotten lucky this time. Another encounter like that and he could escalate the whole situation. He should've listened to Justin and remained on the roof or in that room on the empty top floor where he'd stashed the girls.

Only, once again, the thought of what might happen to the remaining kids when the assholes realized they were being raided wouldn't let Andrei stay still. They'd been through enough horror. They didn't need to lose their lives at the moment of rescue. Men like these didn't leave witnesses behind.

The next door down from where he'd found the girls was locked as well, but it was cheap and it didn't take Andrei long to pop that one open either. Eight faces turned toward him with expressions ranging from terror to masks of stony indifference. The youngest of the boys couldn't have been more than seven. Unlike the girls, each one of them had been shackled to one of several beds stuffed into the room with them, but like them, their eyes were glazed from drugs.

Hot fury rose up in Andrei's throat again as they all drew back as if a living monster had entered the room. In their eyes, one probably had. The scent of fear lay heavy in the sweat that appeared on their faces and in the quick pants of their breaths. Bile rose in the back of Andrei's throat. Hopefully, that rush of fear and adrenaline would help burn off the effects of the drugs. It had seemed to work some with the girls.

"The police are on their way," Andrei whispered, shutting the door behind him again and twisting the lock. "I'm going to get you free, but you have to remain very quiet. We don't want anyone to come looking, and it's going to take some time to get those cuffs off of everyone."

"Bullshit," the oldest one hissed, his indifference giving way to anger as he positioned his body between Andrei and the two others on the bed with him. "You're just going to drag us off someplace different. How do we know we can trust you?"

Andrei held up a soothing hand and met the young man's gaze. He recognized that face. His cap of dark curls had been cut short and his eyes were far older than in the picture Andrei had, but this was who he'd been looking for. "Because you're Marco Orsini. Your parents hired me to find you."

For a second hope came alive in Marco's face, and then he looked away, his cheeks flushing in shame. "I can't go home."

"I wanna go home," another voice piped up.

"I'm working on that," Andrei said, bringing his finger to his lips and looking around at each expectant face. "But I need you all to keep quiet, okay?"

Seven heads bobbed and Marco bit his lip. Andrei crossed over to him, careful not to crowd him when the young man stiffened and pulled back. "Let's concentrate on getting out of here first, then we'll worry about the rest."

Marco looked up at him, searching Andrei's face, and then he nodded.

"Good. Now how many more rooms are there like this? Do you know?"

"No, not for sure," Marco whispered. "At least four rooms, I think. They lock us up in the rooms up here and use the rooms downstairs for—for other things."

Andrei clenched his jaw until his teeth ground together. Marco didn't have to say what he already knew. He would have to recount it enough to the police and the courts innumerable times before he could finally start to put those memories behind him. He pulled out his handcuff keys and popped open the shackle around Marco's wrist.

"Help the others stay calm and quiet while I work. Keep the beds between you and the door."

While Andrei was unlocking the last cuff, alarmed shouts rang up from downstairs. A chill gripped his stomach as the kids cried out in fear. "What happened? Why are they yelling? Are they gonna hurt us?"

"They're freaking out because the police are here," Andrei hastened to reassure them before the boys panicked. "Just stay quiet."

He drew his gun and got between the kids and the door, praying that the bastards would be too busy scrambling to get away from the cops to worry about their victims. Then he bit back a curse as footsteps pounded up the stairs. No such luck, when they needed all the luck they could get. The reek of gasoline wafted under the door, and Andrei cursed under his breath. Rage and horror hit his blood with another punch of adrenaline.

Andrei turned to the kids and pointed at Marco with an intent stare. "Marco, when I yell run, you grab those kids and haul ass up the back stairs to the roof."

"What about the others?" Marco asked, his expression sick with anxiety.

"You let me worry about the others. Your concern is the boys with you. Got it?"

"Yes, sir." Marco grabbed the hands of the two youngest, his eyes huge as he gave Andrei a look that begged him not to leave them.

Andrei steeled himself against that expression and shoved his gun back in the holster. He didn't have time to give them the reassurance they needed. He barreled out into the hallway, his heart in his throat. Two men whirled around, and the one closest to Andrei dropped his gas can and jumped back. "Who the fuck?"

Andrei leapt forward, punched the guy in the nose, and shoved him into the other man, tangling them together. "There's more up here," the bastard roared, trying to shove the other guy off of him to come at Andrei.

The other gas can dropped, spilling onto its side, and Andrei bent to right it before the entire hallway became saturated. A kick caught him hard in the thigh, buckling his leg and making him stumble into the wall.

"Light 'em up, dammit. Hurry!"

Andrei spun around with a snarl, yanked the gun from the man's waist, and whipped it across the fucker's cheek as the man reached for his pocket. He went down with a howl of pain, right in the biggest puddle of gasoline, his clothes soaking up the liquid. "Light them up and you get yourself, asshole. Go ahead."

He spun again, kicking the door closest to him open as startled shrieks rose from within. More girls. Good, they were unbound. "*Run!*"

"Stop them." The other thug crashed into him, knocking them both into the wall. "They're getting away, dammit!"

Andrei doubled over, gasping as his breath rushed out from the knee to his stomach. The gun clattered to the floor, followed by the more welcome sound of rushing bare feet heading toward the back stairs. Fuck, how many more doors were there? How many kids trapped? Just one spark was all those bastards needed, and the ones still locked up would be lost.

He wouldn't let that happen.

Other hands grabbed him, yanked him around. "Ya broke my nose," the guy snarled and then punched Andrei in the face. "Go get the brats. Make sure none of them can talk. I'll take care of this one."

"Some help would be appreciated, Justin," Andrei shouted, barreling the both of them into the wall. A section of it crumbled as they exchanged blows, and Andrei barely registered the pain of them under the urgency of the situation. Andrei jabbed his elbow into the other man's face twice, hard, and then kicked him for good measure as the thug went down. Andrei turned and pitched him down the stairs, scattering the police coming up.

"Freeze," one of them called out, raising a gun.

"Don't shoot, can't you smell the gas?" Andrei dropped back out of sight before the cop decided he was one of the perverts. "There might still be some kids locked up on this level." With that he bolted toward the backstairs after the other guy.

Hurry, hurry, hurry. He couldn't let Marco and the other kids face that thug alone.

The perv turned around at the top of the stairs, a kicking and screaming girl in his arms. "Stop right there or I break her neck."

"You hurt her and I swear I will punt you off the fucking roof before the cops can save you from me," Andrei snarled.

The guy's face paled as Andrei advanced up the stairs, his hands out to each side. "Stay right there."

"You will scream the whole way down before your brains spatter on the asphalt," Andrei promised, staring him down.

"I want my mom," the girl sobbed, tears streaking down her terrified face as she continued to fight.

"You're not a cop?"

Andrei shook his head as the guy stumbled back from a kick to his shin. "No, so you'd better believe I'd do it and think it's more than worth the jail time if you die screaming."

The guy must've seen the truth in Andrei's face, because he set the girl down, and she ran up the stairs wailing as Andrei breathed a sigh of relief.

"Everybody on your knees, now." Andrei froze at the steel-cold voice behind him, and his skin prickled. He had no idea how many guns were trained on him, but even one was one too many.

He lifted his hands higher and slowly sank down on his knees, putting his hands on the back of his head. The bastard at the top of the stairs fell to his knees too. Police pounded up toward him as more hands grabbed Andrei and wrenched his arms behind his back to cuff him tightly. "Easy, I'm the guy who called you. Get Detective Mansle. He can ID me."

His gun was yanked out of its holster. "Do you have a permit for a concealed weapon?" a deep bass rumbled in his ear.

Andrei looked over his shoulder to glare at Justin. "You know I do. Now will you get these cuffs off me?"

"Hell no, not yet." Justin dragged Andrei up by his arm, his dark brown face tight with anger. "You almost killed that guy you tossed down the stairs, and you threatened another right in front of half the squad."

"I was just trying to get him away from those gasoline-soaked doors before his desperation to get rid of the evidence overcame self-preservation. Same with the other, I had to scare him into letting her go. I wasn't trying to kill anyone." Not that Andrei would mourn if either fucker had broken their necks. "There's a locked room on the top floor with a bunch of girls barricaded inside. I told them not to let anyone in unless they identified themselves as you. So why don't you go fetch them before they suffocate in this heat?"

"What part of stay put did you not understand? See this is exactly why you got kicked out of the academy. You don't follow directions for shit." Justin pushed him up the stairs toward the roof, not bothering to take the cuffs off. He really was pissed this time.

"No, I got kicked out for decking the jackass in charge," Andrei retorted as they emerged on the top floor. He jerked his chin toward a room at the end of the hall. "They're in there."

"You wouldn't have decked him if you'd listened to me in the first place."

Andrei dug in his heels and turned to look his friend in the eyes. "If I'd listened this time, I'd be telling Marco's parents, hey, I found your son, but he's dead, so sorry. They were going to burn them alive, Justin, and you wouldn't have gotten up the stairs in time. Not to save them all."

Justin sighed and unlocked the cuffs. "Don't leave the scene until I give the okay. I will lock your ass up this time if you don't listen. So stop pushing your fucking luck, 'cause I'm itching for a reason to arrest you and let you cool your heels in lockup for a day or two."

Chapter Two

DEAN headed back home, elation bubbling inside of him. After years of planning and saving, months of agonizing, it wasn't going to be a dream any longer. The second gym would be a reality, right in the heart of Dupont Circle. He'd tried to get ahold of Andrei to give him the news and then tried not to think about where Andrei could be and what he was doing when he didn't answer.

There were days when Andrei's job gave him the heebie-jeebies, and today was one of them. There had been a hard bleakness in Andrei's eyes when he'd left in the morning, and Dean just hoped that bleakness would have eased by the end of the day. Andrei always took it extra hard when he hadn't been able to save a kid. No matter how much he insisted that he didn't have a soft heart.

Dean was crooning along to Stone Temple Pilots' "Big Empty" when he saw the minivan pulled over onto the narrow shoulder of the Baltimore-Washington Parkway. A black woman held a baby in the crook of her arm, a little girl hovering near her knees as the woman examined her rear tire.

He didn't even consider not stopping to help. He slowed down and pulled to a stop behind them. The woman shooed the little girl back into the van and turned to face him with a tense body and a wary expression on her face. She was pretty, with delicate features, smooth, dark skin, and her hair done up in sassy, coiled curls. She angled her body so she was between him and the baby in her arm as he got out of the car.

"Anything I can do to help?" Dean asked with a friendly smile as he approached. He glanced at the tire and couldn't miss the bolt lodged deep in the tread. The baby wailed with the outraged tone of a hungry and tired child. He knew that sound well from all the times he'd watched his sister's kids.

Apprehension and relief warred on her face as she jiggled the baby with a soft, soothing sound. "Could you? If I put Tristan back in his car seat right now, he'll cry himself into fits, and like an idiot I left my cell phone at home."

She was desperately afraid of something, that much Dean could tell, and he strove to reassure her as he crouched to look at the tire. "Well, you can borrow my phone and call your insurance company for roadside assistance, or if you have a spare, I can change it for you. Won't take long."

"No, Inez, you stay put," the woman said as the van door opened. "This isn't a neighborhood street."

Dean smiled at the little girl who peered out. She had the paler, warm-cream complexion of a mixed-race child, and her gray eyes were alight with avid curiosity. He gave her a wink that started her giggling as the woman looked between the flat tire and the back of the van loaded down with suitcases and boxes.

"I don't want to impose, but I don't have anyone I can call for help. Would you mind? My mom's expecting us soon, and if we're too late, she'll start to worry."

"It's not a problem," Dean said as he rolled up the sleeves of his dress shirt. Oh well, it had served its purpose. Dean didn't plan on dressing like this again anytime soon. In fact, if he ruined it, he'd have the perfect excuse to bury it in the trash.

"The tire and tools are in the compartment under the suitcases. I can pay you for your trouble."

"Money isn't necessary, glad to help. I'm Dean Marshall, by the way."

"Robin," she said tersely, looking away.

Just scared Robin with no last name and her two kids. Dean was pretty sure he knew what Andrei would say about the situation. It didn't take a genius to figure out she was running from something, probably a man, and he hoped it worked out for her. At least she had family she could go to. "Why don't you show me what needs to be moved to get to the compartment, then you can borrow my phone to call your mom."

"I don't know how to thank you." Robin shifted the baby, who couldn't have been more than a few months old, onto her shoulder. She gave Dean a tentative smile, some of the fear and tension disappearing from her face. Her smile turned her from pretty to beautiful.

"Don't worry about it. I'm happy to help."

Robin laid the baby back in his car seat and returned to help Dean shift and move boxes as he began to wail again. Dean smiled as he saw Inez lean over, giving her pinky to the baby as she sang "Hush Little Baby" in an off-key lilt, and he quieted. By the time they got the compartment open and the spare tire out, Inez's distraction had ceased working, and once again the baby's voice rose in a furious cry.

"I need to feed him before he makes himself sick," Robin said, already taking a step toward the van door before she hesitated and glanced toward him.

"Yeah, he sounds pretty pissed." Dean set down the jack and spare tire. "You can sit in my car with them if you want. You can't be in the van while it's jacked up."

Robin gave him a dubious glance, all of the tension coming back to her in a rush. Dean wasn't sure what he could do to reassure her past acting like everything was normal and continuing to be friendly. He knelt down on the asphalt and laid out the tools. "The jack's flimsy," he explained. "If you're moving about in there, it could slip. That would cause more damage to the van and possibly hurt somebody too."

Like him. He didn't mind playing knight errant to help a lady out and earn good karma, but he didn't want to waste time arguing over common sense either. To his relief, Robin nodded and lifted Inez out first before collecting the baby.

The little girl sidled closer, lifting her hand in a wave. She showed none of the hesitancy of her mother, and when she smiled, her entire face lit up. Her grin had a gap, showing off a recently lost tooth. "My name's Inez. What's yours?"

Dean grinned back at her. What a cute kid. He loved children, wanted to adopt enough to make their own basketball team, but Andrei was adamant that he wasn't father material. Which was utter bullshit. Dean just thought that he was too afraid of making his parents' mistakes to give it a try.

"I'm Dean."

"The car got tired, Mr. Dean," Inez said solemnly as she crouched down next to him. Her dark brown braids bobbled, the ends adorned with pale green ribbons that matched her dress. She pointed toward the flat and then examined the tools curiously. "It no wanna go no more."

"Ah, so that's why it happened." Dean started wrestling with the lug nuts as soon as Robin shut the door, juggling the baby and a diaper bag. She looked worn out, not the van, and to make matters worse for her, Tristan's wails had only gotten shriller in the last few minutes.

"Come on, Inez."

"Can I stay with Mr. Dean? Please, Mommy? I swears I listen."

"He's doing enough for us right now. He doesn't need you pestering him with endless questions, too."

Inez's lower lip stuck out in a stubborn sulk, and between that expression and Robin's frayed nerves, Dean hurried to intervene before he ended up in the center of a female meltdown. "You should listen to your mom. The side of the parkway isn't a safe place."

If anything, her pout increased, but Inez let Robin pull her away without further argument. Dean returned to wrestling with the lug nuts that refused to give way. *Note to self, check our own damn tires and make sure we have a better jack in the trunk.* Dean let out an explosive breath as the first lug nut loosened. The others weren't in much better shape.

Dean eyed the scissor jack and sighed. It was going to take forever to get the wheel off the ground. Irritation turned to frustration as the rod kept slipping out of the jack and the van rose one painstaking quarter inch at a time. *Damned Mickey Mouse jack. Whoever designed this piece of shit is an idiot.*

He was mounting the spare tire when he heard the car door again, the sound of the baby's crying mercifully stopped. He looked over to see Inez skipping toward him. A quick glance at his car showed Robin fast asleep in the passenger's seat. Poor woman. He kept a careful eye on Inez, making sure she didn't edge toward the parkway or the cars that zipped by at speeds that made him jumpy.

"You're going to give your mom a heart attack," he said as she neared. "Stick close, sweetheart. This is a busy road. You don't want to make her worry, do you?"

"Nope, she sleepin' and so's Tris. She always says be quiet, don' wake the baby. If I with you, I can't 'sturb her."

Dean contemplated sending her back. Only the thought of her possibly slipping out again, maybe this time on the side of the parkway, stopped him. "Are you going to listen to me?"

He almost laughed out loud as Inez considered the question seriously, sticking the tip of her finger between her teeth as she inched toward him. She studied him with curious eyes and then crouched beside him again. "Yeah, I listen. Why's the tire still broked?" she asked, pointing to the flat.

"I think it's past fixing, sweetheart." Dean flicked his finger against the spare tire. "This will get you back on the road so you can get to your grandma's quickly."

Dean began to tighten the lug nuts, answering Inez's many questions, when the scrape of a shoe on the asphalt drew his attention. He looked over and caught a brief glimpse of a blue camper truck parked behind his car. A man in worn jeans, a faded T-shirt, and a trucker's hat walked toward them. There was something about his stance, the way he kept his head ducked down, as if he didn't want them to see his face, that made Dean uneasy.

He paused at Dean's car long enough to peek in at Robin and the baby before continuing on toward Dean and Inez. "Run into some trouble?"

"Thanks for stopping, buddy. We've got it taken care of," Dean said as he turned his attention back to the lug nuts. He was letting his imagination and concern for Andrei get the best of him. "Looks like someone else wants to help, but we're all done, aren't we?" Dean said in an aside to Inez, giving her a wink, but all of her attention remained on the man as she gripped Dean's shoulder.

"Very fucking neighborly of you," the man snarled. "Just what are you getting out of it?"

"Daddy?" Inez whispered and then suddenly burrowed into Dean's side throwing him off balance. Confused, he twisted around as the man's footsteps quickened, and he came up beside him. Dean's eyes widened on the gun pointed at him. The sudden, hot rush of fear became an acid taste in his mouth, and his heart hammered. What the fuck was going on?

"Whoa, whoa, just wait a second. Whatever you're thinking, you're wrong." Dean held up a hand as he pushed Inez behind him. Andrei would know what to do in a situation like this. Dean had never been confronted with a crazy man or a gun in his entire life. Inez's little fingers dug into his shirt, and he felt her breath on his back from where she had her face pressed against him. She trembled all over, and it raised all of Dean's protective instincts.

No little girl should ever be that afraid when she looked at her dad.

"You have no idea what I'm thinking, asshole. Now give me my daughter. She belongs with me."

It all clicked at once in Dean's head. What Robin had been running from had caught up with her. Dean slowly stood up, hands out so he wouldn't appear threatening. He didn't dare look toward his car to see if Robin had woken up. Besides, she couldn't run while this man was distracted, not if Inez was with him. "Put the gun down and we'll talk. I don't want any trouble."

Maybe somebody from the parkway would see the situation and call the police. Then his heart sank. Not likely, with the van blocking most of the view. *Fuck, what would Andrei do?* Something badass, no doubt. Only Dean couldn't think of anything badass with Inez clinging to his leg. She peered around to look up at the man confronting them, whimpering under her breath.

The man glanced down at her, and his expression hardened. "Too fucking late for that," he snapped.

Two sharp bangs pierced the air, and Dean crumpled, stumbled back, and fell to the ground. Inez screamed as Dean struggled to draw a breath through the sudden pain in his chest. It felt as if he'd been punched in the sternum, and his heart labored. He stared down at the rapidly growing bloodstain on his only good dress shirt, his mouth working, though no sound came out.

Oh God. I've been shot.

It was the middle of the day. People didn't get shot in the middle of the day on the parkway.

The heat from the asphalt burned into his back as Dean tried to push away his shock and numbness to react. "Inez!" A woman's shriek jerked him out of his circling thoughts. He rolled to his side and fought to rise, but his legs didn't seem to want to work as he lurched onto his hands and knees. "Blake, no!"

Robin ran toward them, her face distorted with fear. Whatever she shouted was now lost in the roaring in Dean's ears and the faltering sound of his own heartbeat. Dark droplets of blood fell to the ground, splattering the dust and gravel that littered the shoulder of the road. The little girl stood a few feet away from Dean, staring at him, her dark gray eyes huge in her face. What was her name?

"Run, sweetheart," Dean croaked. They were along the parkway. Someone would stop to help a little girl. How could this be happening right along the parkway? The pain worsened, seizing his lungs and making it almost impossible to draw in a breath. *Oh God, Andrei.*

"Mommy!" the little girl screamed, her hands coming to her mouth as the gun roared again. The sound of a baby wailing came from somewhere far off. Robin stumbled to a halt, her hand coming to her chest as an expression of astonished horror crossed her face. She fell face down on the ground in a limp sprawl, and Dean flung out a hand, grabbing Inez as she tried to run to her.

The bastard was going to kill all of them. Dean had to do something before he passed out.

"Run!" Dean gave her a push in the opposite direction and groped for the lug wrench as Inez bolted. Somehow he managed to lurch to his feet, brandishing the makeshift weapon. The man started to turn to follow his daughter but faced Dean instead, his eyes widening. Dean staggered toward him, swinging the lug wrench.

The man howled in pain as it struck his left shoulder. The impact jarred Dean's shaking hands, and the strength flowed out of his arms like water. The lug wrench clanged to the ground along with the gun, and Dean fell trying to get to it first.

"Stupid fucker," the man snarled, booting him in his ribs. Dean's vision went white with pain. He crumpled, detritus from the road digging into his cheek. Through the ground, he could hear small feet running, the sound fading. He breathed a prayer. Someone would find her. She'd be safe.

A baby wailed. Tristan. How could he forget about him? Dean willed past the pain and groped for the gun as a shadow fell across him. He cursed, lifting his head, tasting grit and blood on his lips. A rough foot rolled him onto his back, leaving him gasping. The edges of his vision were going dark as the monster leaned over him, the sun blazing behind him and the gun back in his hand.

Andrei. Andrei, I'm sorry.

"Tough bastard. Wrong place, wrong woman. You shoulda minded your own business."

"Asswipe," Dean spat. *Run, Inez. Run, sweetheart.* Tristan's cries haunted him, and the sound of the gun cocking again was unnaturally loud in the sudden stillness between heartbeats.

Andrei. Dean clung to the thought of him as the third shot tore through his chest, dragging him down into darkness. *I'm sorry.*

MARCO hovered near Andrei, his dark eyes needy and his face pinched with anxiety. He kept looking at Andrei like he had all the answers and could magically make everything better, and then he'd get defensive again and become a prickly wall of teenage attitude. Andrei preferred the attitude, because there was nothing more he could do for Marco now. The rest remained with his parents, counselors, and Marco himself.

The police station bustled around them, punctuated by happy cries and tears as families were reunited with their kids. Andrei just wanted to get home. He still stank of gasoline, and it gave him a headache even though Justin had loaned him a clean shirt that hung too large off his lean frame. His ribs ached and he hoped there wouldn't be any bruising to make Dean worry. Until Marco was ready, though, he wouldn't budge.

"Are they really here?" Marco asked, staring down in misery at his hands.

"Yeah, Detective Mansle put them in a waiting room for you."

Marco bit his lip and looked away. "You must think that I'm the worst pussy asshole on the fucking earth."

Andrei remembered how Marco got between him and the other kids in the room when he'd found them, and shook his head. "I think you've been through one brutal ordeal and things are going to be pretty messed up for a while for you, but you've got the guts to work it through."

"What would your parents have said if, well you know?" Marco asked with a tense, sideways glance.

"My parents aren't the best to judge this by, Marco. They left me in a church when I was about your age. I haven't seen them since." After all of these years, it still brought up a dull, distant pain whenever he said those words, though Andrei had come to the point where he didn't blame himself anymore. Marco turned toward him, his eyes widening. "They would never have paid for a private investigator to bring their son back to them like your parents did."

"Why would they do that?"

A picture of a young girl, her black hair in twin braids and mischief on her face, rose up in his mind. It ate at him, not knowing if his parents had been right, if his big sister would've been better off if he'd ignored her. There was no telling what Ileana would've done. Maybe she would've moved on like they said she would.

"I broke the rules once too often. And it all kind of fell apart when they caught me kissing another guy." It certainly hadn't helped that the boy had been a *gadje*, an outsider. Though by that point, Andrei didn't think the outsider part made much of a difference. Bad enough that he talked with ghosts. Bad enough that he kissed another boy. A *gadje* boy was just another finger in his parents' eye after breaking yet another cardinal rule.

"They kicked you out for that?"

"Well there was a lot more to it than that. The family had always been sticklers for tradition, and ever since I was little, I rebelled against them. It didn't make a comfortable environment for anyone."

"I don't understand," Marco said, shaking his head as he shot Andrei an accusing look. "You sound almost like you're defending them."

"No, I'm not. I get why they did it. I disagree with what they did. But that's not really the point." Andrei caught and held Marco's gaze. "I've met with your parents several times, and you and I both know that no matter what happened to you they still love you."

Marco's cheeks flushed scarlet, and his eyes glittered with tears. "But every time they look at me they're gonna think about it, about—"

Andrei shook his head and refrained from a casual touch on his shoulder that he would've given a kid not in Marco's situation. "Not every time. And I guarantee you that the first time they see you all they're going to be thinking about is thank fucking God their son is alive and is coming home."

"You really think so?" Marco asked in a small voice, and the flicker of a new light appeared in his eyes.

"I know so."

"You'll go with me, right? You won't make me walk in there alone?"

"I'll be with you every step." Andrei handed Marco a card. "And if there's any time you need to talk, you call me, okay?"

Marco took it and fingered the edge. "You mean that?"

"I do." Andrei rose and nodded toward the door. "You ready?"

"Yeah, I guess so." Marco stuck the card in his pocket and rubbed his palms on his jeans. At first his steps lagged until eagerness overcame shame, and when his mom saw him coming and emerged from the holding room, the young man broke into a run and flung himself at her.

Andrei looked away from the reunion, his throat tightening up.

"You did a good thing today," Justin said, coming up beside him.

Andrei shrugged, grimacing under the flash of discomfort at his words. "I just did what I had to do," he said gruffly. Now Marco hugged his dad, and all three of them were crying. The sight eased the tight ache inside of him. It would take time, but they would be okay.

"You know, you should really take Joshua Norton up on his offer. You're wasted investigating petty shit. It still irks me that you didn't finish the academy."

"Let it rest, Justin. You and I both know that it wouldn't have worked even if I'd finished."

"What about Norton?" Justin persisted. "Just call the man back and hear what he has to say. You still have his card?"

Andrei took another look at Marco's face. He didn't know if he could handle working kids and the pervert trade on a day-to-day basis. Even when he won there was heartbreak. Then again, on days like today, he couldn't see how he could say no either. He'd talk it over with Dean and Dean's dad. Get their take on it.

"I'll think about it, I promise. Now if you'll excuse me." Andrei wanted to have a chance to talk to Marco and his parents one more time before he let his friend lecture him some more about interfering with a police investigation. There wouldn't have been an investigation if it hadn't been for him. And he had no doubt that the Feds would want to talk with him now that they were taking over the investigation.

Andrei joined the family, shook hands with Marco's dad, and let his mom hug him several times. Marco's anxieties about his parents seemed to have disappeared as he hovered by his mom's side instead of Andrei's. It eased his heart to see that.

He told Marco's parents of their son's heroism and how he had not let his fear get the best of him. And when he finally left them, he left with confidence that Marco would have the support and environment he needed to heal.

By the time he finished talking with the Feds, Justin was nowhere to be seen, and Andrei took advantage of that fact to slip away. He wanted another shower and a hot meal, not to rehash the same pointless argument over again. Andrei turned on his cell phone, and the little icon appeared telling him he had a message.

He grinned as Dean's warm baritone filled his ear.

"Babe, it's time to celebrate. Break out the good shit and get in your boxers. I'm on my way home."

Andrei grinned and tried to call Dean back, but his cell just rang until it went to voice mail. He must still be on the road then. Perfect. Andrei had enough time to pick out a nice bottle of champagne and get home to shower before he arrived. He could be waiting for Dean on the couch when he walked through that door.

Chapter Three

DEAN sat up and stared around in confusion at the sea of emergency lights illuminating the shoulder of the road. A number of people milled about him, talking and examining the ground and van as the sun sank lower in the sky, casting long shadows on the ground.

Andrei. Dean had to call him. He was late getting home, and his partner would be very worried by now. He checked his pockets only to discover that his cell phone was missing. What the hell had happened? Why was he on the ground? His last memories before he passed out were a muddled blur.

"Do you mind telling me what's going on?" Dean scrambled to his feet as a cop approached.

The cop ignored him as he crouched and dropped a plastic number on the ground next to the lug wrench. "The vic might've had a chance to fight back. He looked like a fighter, took more shots than the woman. The perp could be hurt," he said to another man taking notes.

"Or the perp saw him as the bigger threat." Neither of them looked at Dean as they carried on their conversation.

A memory emerged from the chaos in his head. The sound of little feet running away from a monster that chased her. Dean tapped the side of his head, struggling for a name that finally surfaced.

"Hey, I'm talking to you. Did you find Inez, the little girl? What happened to the baby?" Dean peered into the van, steeling himself for the horror of blood and small bodies in the thickening shadows, but to his relief it was empty. He ran to his own car, which remained just as he left it except for the pacifier lying on the passenger seat and the door being wide open.

Dean's confused thoughts bombarded him as he walked back toward the cops who were still talking as they took pictures. What was wrong with them? They couldn't spare two minutes to talk to a witness?

Then those last few horrible moments came rushing back in a montage of terrible images. How huge the gun had seemed when it had been pointed at him. How Robin had jerked and crumpled when she'd been shot. The sickening fear on Inez's little face.

Dean stooped to pick up a bit of green hair ribbon and clutched it in his fist. He swallowed hard against the rising bile as he finally noticed the shrouded body lying on the ground next to the van and the other body being loaded into the back of an ambulance. Both adult-sized. Not child.

"Look, you have to listen to me. Inez called the guy Daddy. He's the one who shot me and Robin. I think maybe I need to go to the hospital, and I need to borrow a phone, my…." Dean's words faltered as neither cop glanced at him. "Fucking look at me."

Dean reached out to grab one of the cops on the shoulder, stealing himself for a shove or a punch, and gaped in disbelief as his hand went right through the man. Warmth spread across his chest, and a chill raced through his body as he stared down at the growing red stain on his dress shirt. It was ruined. He'd never be able to get the blood out.

"Will somebody please help me?" Dean pressed his hands to his chest, trying to staunch the blood. Something was wrong. This whole situation was even more surreal than being shot. Why wasn't he being tended to? Having his statement taken? Andrei should already be here trying to take charge of the investigation.

"You died." The stark words struck him as forcefully as the bullets had.

He couldn't be dead. He didn't feel dead. A dead man wouldn't tremble like this. Dean shook his head, trying in vain to ignore that voice.

"The blood will go away if you stop thinking about it."

A young girl stood several feet away staring right at him. She was older than Inez by several years. Her long black hair was caught back in two braids, and there was something familiar about her face, though Dean couldn't place where he'd seen her before. She wore a red-and-yellow sundress and battered sandals and clutched a stuffed turtle to her skinny body. His confused mind picked out those little details and latched on to them. They were concrete, real, and somehow more vivid than the other people around him.

"Wait, you can see me. Tell the cops what I said. It's important." Dean moved toward her, practically vibrating with urgency. He had to remind himself not to scare her away and tried to summon up a reassuring smile, only he wasn't sure that he succeeded.

"They can't hear me, either. Most people can't hear or see the dead." A sad expression crossed her face. "Some can but don't want to, so they block us out."

"I am not dead!"

Dean stared down at the blood that now saturated his shirt and shook his head in denial. Somewhere in the back of his consciousness he could feel his wounds throbbing along with his heartbeat. Shouldn't they hurt more than that? He'd been fucking shot for godsake. Maybe the EMTs had already given him something for the pain. This couldn't be happening.

"There has to be some kind of mistake. I can't be dead. They're going to resuscitate me at the hospital. I'll get better and Andrei can go after the bastard and get those kids back," he insisted, too aware of the sheet-shrouded figure on the ground behind him. The sensation crawled across his skin with little fingers. Fucking creepy.

Dean ignored its intrusive presence by concentrating on Inez and Tristan. He fingered the bit of ribbon in his pocket. They were what was important. He had to find out if they were okay or not. That bastard wouldn't shoot his own kids, would he? Their mother was horrifying enough, but they were just babies.

The understanding, sympathetic expression in the girl's familiar, dark eyes drove it home far more than words could. Her gaze was older than her appearance, and Dean felt a shout of denial and rage lodge in his throat. *No, no, no... Andrei, oh God....* "I'm not dead, damn you," he snarled.

"I'm sorry." Tears glimmered in her eyes, and she hugged the stuffed turtle to her. "Please don't be mad at me, Dean."

Great, good job Dean, be an ass and make a little girl cry. He sighed and tried to summon up a smile through the frustration, anger, and fear. "No, I'm the one who should be sorry. I shouldn't have yelled. Now, don't start crying on me, okay? Please?"

The girl threw herself into his arms, and Dean let out a startled yelp as she pressed her cheek against his blood-stained shirt and squeezed him tight in a hug. "I'm glad Andrei picked you. I'd never liked any of the other guys he kissy-faced with. You made him happy."

Dean's mind spun as he tried to absorb the implications of that statement out of everything else that had happened. Reality began to sink in past the denial and confusion. The way he couldn't touch anyone and how no one would even look at him, much less talk to him. They were looking *through* him. The way the pain seemed nebulous, like it really belonged to someone else, or something else outside his body. And how everything seemed washed-out and unreal. Everything except himself and the young girl with him.

He didn't want to admit that it was over. He couldn't. All those plans with Andrei... *God, Andrei, he would be all alone now.* Dean's throat closed up in grief at the thought. Even more than missing Andrei already, feeling as if an integral part of Dean's being had been cut from him, the thought of Andrei being alone to deal with this sent a surge of fury through him. He had a powerful need to hurt someone. Inez's daddy. Blake... that's what Robin had called him. He'd get his hands around the man's throat and choke the....

"Stop it!" The strange girl tightened her arms around him. "No, no, no. You can't think that. Even toward the bad man. You'll bring the Jackal Wraiths. Please, stop thinking the bad thoughts. You can't help Andrei if you get eaten."

Dean put his hands on her shoulders and gently pushed her back. To his surprise, her cheek remained clean despite being against his shirt. "Okay, who are you? You seem to know an awful lot about Andrei and me." He'd never heard of a spirit guide being a young girl who carried a stuffed animal. Where were the bright lights, the feeling of peace, and all the other mumbo-jumbo he'd heard from those who'd had near-death experiences?

"I'm Ileana. Andrei's big sister." Her face took on a stricken look. "Didn't he ever tell you about me?"

Dean smiled in recognition. He should've realized it sooner. Andrei had a battered picture of the two of them taken just a few weeks before she had died of pneumonia. Ileana had had a protective arm slung around her baby brother's shoulders, and Andrei had been leaning into her, his dark eyes lit up with joy. That picture had been sitting on Andrei's desk for as long as Dean had known him. Ileana and Andrei shared the same eyes. He should've recognized that if nothing else.

"Yes, he did. He had quite a few stories about you and mentions you often. Though I'm surprised by how well he remembers you. He was only five when you got sick." From the way Andrei talked, it sounded sometimes like they'd grown up together. But whenever Dean would start asking questions, Andrei would stop talking about her for a while, so he'd learned to leave it alone.

"That's because he knew me for a long time after I died. Andrei used to play with me all the time. It upset Mum and Dad something awful. They used to yell at him whenever he'd talk about me." Her dark eyes were solemn as she looked up at him. "They thought I was a *mulo*, a bad spirit, for staying behind. But I wanted to play with him."

Dean looked at her in astonishment. She really was serious. "You aren't joking. Andrei can hear and see you?" Andrei had never told him that. Not in all the years they'd been friends even before they became a couple.

"Not as often anymore. Andrei got old and then got distracted looking at boys. I don't think he knows how to play anymore." Her eyes, so like Andrei's, were sad and confused. Dean knelt down to give her another hug, and she leaned into him with absolute trust. Despite the fact that she had been around for almost forty years, she still seemed to have the mind of an eight-year-old. "Him and Mum and Dad fought all the time, and he stopped being any fun. He became so serious."

"He never forgot about you, though. That I do know." Dean sat back on his heels and lightly gripped her shoulders. His mind raced; Andrei could hear spirits. If he chose to. Or at least he had. There had to be a way to get through to him. Ileana could help.

An unnatural shiver raced through him, and Dean turned to see the body in front of the van being loaded onto a stretcher. His body. It might make it more real if he'd seen his face, but at the moment he really didn't want to. It was too fucking freaky already.

He couldn't have Andrei find out about this alone. Even if Andrei couldn't hear or see him, Dean wanted to be there. He needed to be with Andrei.

"Andrei already knows. Well, he's scared and knows something's wrong. He got worried when you were late and wouldn't answer your phone, so he listened to that radio thingie he has. He asked for you at the hospitals, and now he's at the police station."

Dean's eyes narrowed on Ileana. "How do you know what I'm thinking?"

"You think very loud." She gave him an impish grin, a dimple appearing on her cheek. "And your face gets all grrrr, then sad, then confused. Makes it very easy."

"And how do you know what Andrei's doing?"

"I always know when he's upset, so I went to check on him, and when you still hadn't come back yet, I went looking for you. I thought maybe Andrei would feel better if I could tell him where you were." She took his hand in both of hers and gave it a squeeze. "Then I couldn't let you wake up alone."

Dean listened to the murmur of the cops' conversation all around him, and his heart plummeted. "They didn't find the kids?" He didn't want them to have been murdered or left behind with their mother's body, but the thought of that little girl and baby in a monster's hands made him ill.

One thing at a time. Andrei might be able to hear and see him. He could give the police the answers that only Dean knew. His partner was a private detective. He'd know how to approach them. But even if Andrei couldn't hear him, right now Dean needed the comfort of his presence more than anything else.

"Okay, Ileana, what's the magic trick? If I'm... if I'm, well, you know, I'm not like stuck in the place where I was shot, am I? Because I've got to get to Andrei."

"Don't be silly. Of course you're not stuck where you died or else I wouldn't be here." Ileana wrinkled her nose and rolled her eyes. "And all the hospitals would be so crowded. We'd be tripping all over each other. At least, those who chose to stay. Boring."

"Okay, stupid question, fine. How do I get to Andrei without having to put one foot in front of the other or catch rides in random vehicles?" Dean tugged lightly on her braid and gave her a tense smile. "Come on, Poppet. Help me out here. What do you do when you want to see him?"

"I just think of him. Close your eyes and think of Andrei and how much he needs you. That's what's worked for me. If you picture him real hard, it's easy."

Dean closed his eyes, trying to block out the emergency lights flashing, the cops talking, the scent of blood and death. He thought of Andrei, wished for him, but when he opened his eyes, he was still kneeling on the side of the road with Ileana looking at him curiously.

He bit back a curse. "Now what?"

Ileana shrugged, the kind of pitying look in her eyes only a child could have. "Try again, silly."

Try again. Dean bit back his frustration with a concentrated effort. He did not have time for this bullshit.

"Maybe you aren't tied to Andrei," Ileana said suddenly.

Dean's eyes flew open again as a chill struck him. "What?"

"A very bad man hurt you. He could be the reason why you're here. Or the other kids. Why don't you try thinking of them instead? They might be easier to reach until you get better at this."

"There is no way in hell I'm tied to that f—" Dean took a deep breath. "I'm not tied to a monster." But Inez and Tristan, that was a possibility. Even if it was Andrei he wanted to see, he couldn't deny the possibility that concern for the kids had been uppermost in his mind when he'd died.

No. His last thought had been of Andrei. Dean closed his eyes and cleared his mind. He brought up memories. Simple things. How Andrei's face softened when he slept, the rough edges becoming more open and vulnerable. The scent of his hair after he'd showered, and the little rumble in his voice when he laughed. The way Andrei liked to come up behind him to slip his arms around Dean's waist and lay his chin on Dean's shoulder.

The ground lurched sideways, and the change of temperature from summer evening to artificial, chilled air told Dean he'd shifted. He could no longer sense the flash of lights through his eyelids, and it was eerily quiet. Too quiet.

His heart thudding hard, Dean opened his eyes, and his skin crawled as he realized he'd shifted into a medical examiner's office. The clock on the wall showed just after 9 p.m. And he was utterly alone. No Andrei and no Ileana. Great. Now what? He was really sucking at this ghost business.

It was strange. He was supposed to be dead, but he didn't feel dead. He still had all the sensations he would have if he were still breathing. Well he wasn't on the side of the road anymore, though, so that was progress. Ileana's trick had worked. Now he just needed to figure out what he was tied to and why he'd showed up here instead of with Andrei. And how was he going to do that with no Ileana to guide him. He must've fucked it up somehow.

The room was cold and unnaturally clean. There wasn't a spot of gore or the clutter of tools anywhere. One wall held a bank of stainless steel lockers, and there were several pristine examining tables, deep sinks, and neatly arranged instruments that Dean did not care to look at too closely. Yeah, definitely the wrong place. Ileana had said that Andrei was at the police station. Dean closed his eyes and was ready to try again when a slither of intuition had him turning around.

A sheet-covered gurney sat between an examination table and an observation window. Dean swallowed hard as an icy chill raced through him. He knew. Somehow he just knew that was his body under there. *God please, don't let me be fettered to my own body.* That would just be sick.

Dean's head jerked around as the door opened and a young woman in a lab coat came in leading Andrei. Dean's heart lurched at the sight of him, and he took an involuntary step toward Andrei, relief and a terrifying sorrow warring in him. "Andrei."

Andrei looked terrible with a haunted look in his dark eyes, his hair mussed instead of neatly groomed, and deeply etched lines of tension on his brow and around his mouth. He had changed out of the clothes he'd left in that morning. Dean never had a chance to talk to him, to find out whether or not he'd been successful in searching for the missing teenager.

An awful realization hit him, shaking him out of his shock. "Oh no. *No!* Get him out of here. You can't ask him to do this," Dean snapped, rushing forward to block them from the gurney.

It was the strangest sensation, to be talking, looking right at Andrei without a flicker of recognition crossing his face. Whatever ability he'd once had to see ghosts must have faded. A cold feeling settled in the pit of Dean's stomach, and his eyes burned as they stopped in front of his body.

"Andrei, I'm right here, babe." Dean started to reach out to touch him and then let his hands fall. He didn't know if he could handle seeing them go right through Andrei. The woman paused, her hands hovering over the sheet.

"Are you sure, Mr. Cuza?" the woman asked in a gentle voice. "Detective Mansle already ID'd him. You don't have to do this."

"I have to see him with my own eyes," Andrei said tersely.

The woman nodded. "If you're ready, then."

What kind of an asinine statement was that? Dean raged in his head, his eyes locked on Andrei's face as his partner shoved a hand in his pocket and nodded. To those that didn't know him, it seemed as if Andrei's expression didn't change when she folded back the sheet. But Dean knew every nuance of him. And to have to watch the last, desperate hope die in Andrei's eyes hurt far worse than those gunshots had.

"Yeah, that's Dean." Andrei's jaw clenched as he forced the words out.

"Andrei," Dean said, his voice hoarse. "Please, babe, you've got to hear me."

Andrei's eyes lifted, and their gazes clashed. Dean's breath caught as a lump hurtled up into his throat, choking him. He tried to speak, but no words would emerge. Andrei's eyes widened. Oh God, Andrei could see him. Ileana had been right. Dean blinked back the burning in his eyes as he tried to smile.

And just as quickly as the hope hit, it died again when horror replaced the surprise in Andrei's expression. Andrei looked away, his shoulders tensing and drawing in, his jaw clenched tight enough to shatter bone.

In all the years he'd known Andrei, even when they'd just been friends and Andrei had been a bitter teenager angry at the entire world, Andrei had never rejected him with such utter finality. It was a punch to the gut that Dean had never expected, and once again he found himself unable to speak. Not even to say Andrei's name. What kind of a fucked-up nightmare had he fallen into?

"I've seen enough, ma'am. Thank you for your time," Andrei said, his voice so faint that Dean barely heard him. In some way that Dean didn't understand, it was as if finding out he'd become a ghost had been an even bigger blow than hearing about his death.

Before Dean found his voice again, Andrei left, practically running through the door as the woman covered Dean's face again. He jumped, realizing that he hadn't gotten a chance to see himself, before being pathetically glad he hadn't. The woman wheeled him away, and Dean drifted toward the door that Andrei had disappeared through.

Dean could see him through the little window. Andrei had his back to him, fist clenched against the wall as he leaned into it. Dean watched him, his emotions a confused whirl. It made no sense. Andrei would talk with Ileana, but not him?

There was more than one mystery to figure out, and if Andrei thought Dean would just go away if he ignored him, he had a thing or two to learn. Apparently he still had things to learn about Andrei too.

"This is far from over, babe."

THE more Andrei tried to get himself under control, the more he thought he was about to lose it altogether. He pounded his fist against the wall to keep from screaming. Dean had been murdered. His thoughts jerked back to that one cold, hard truth. He still couldn't believe that, much less that Dean was still hanging around. Stuck. Just like Ileana.

Fuck, he couldn't go through that again.

He should have listened to his parents and not encouraged Ileana. The dead needed to stay dead. They had to move on. And the living had no business interacting with them, making them believe in something no longer real. He'd dealt with that guilt every day and would continue to do so for the rest of his life. He couldn't let that happen to Dean too.

Andrei bowed his head, grateful that the lab technician hadn't followed him into the hallway. He needed to get himself together, and he didn't trust himself with anybody right now. Not with the need for violence running through him. Not with that raw, screaming place inside.

Dean. He couldn't get the image of his partner's face, leeched of all color and animation, out of his mind. It wasn't right. If there was anybody destined to end up in the morgue one day, it was him, not Dean. Blinking rapidly against the stinging in his eyes, Andrei started shaking as bile rose into his throat.

The door behind him opened, and Andrei stiffened. A low murmur sounded in his ears, and the susurration filled him with a strange warmth, the sound wearing down the sharp edges of his grief. For a split second, he thought he felt the touch of fingers in his hair, and a light breeze slid up his arms. Andrei shook his head and jerked away, his heart skittering. He couldn't encourage Dean; as much as it tore him apart to turn away, he had to give Dean every reason not to stay.

And if Dean considered him a coldhearted, cruel bastard for it, at least Dean would be safe. Though, fuck, hurting Dean in any way, especially now.... A hot, acidic ball of grief blossomed in his chest, squeezed his lungs, and tears filled his eyes.

Oh God, Dean. What the fuck? What the fuck? Andrei couldn't stop the litany in his head. His whole fucking world had bottomed out and shattered. He forced himself to take several deep breaths to get himself under control again and blinked the tears away. Losing it wouldn't solve anything. He didn't have time to grieve. Dean's murderer was out there somewhere, and every minute that the bastard walked free was one fucking minute too long.

Andrei stalked out of the medical examiner's anteroom and bore down on the detective waiting in the hallway. Justin straightened and the expression of sympathy that crossed his face had Andrei's hands balling into fists. "Andrei, I—"

"Don't," Andrei bit off before Justin could tell him how sorry he was. He didn't want to hear it, not even from a friend. "Just fucking tell me you know who did it." Andrei stopped in front of Justin, his chest tightening as soon as he'd ceased moving. He squeezed his fists until his palms stung from his nails biting into them. "What happened?"

"Come on, let's go somewhere a little more private, and I'll tell you what I know."

Andrei nodded shortly, even though frustration threatened to strangle him. The sooner he had answers, the faster he could find Dean's killer. He'd known Justin for years, though, and he knew he wouldn't get one word out of him until Justin wanted to.

Soon they were in a booth at one of the bars around the corner. "Let me buy you a drink." Justin started to gesture for the waiter, and Andrei grabbed his hand, shaking his head.

"I don't want a drink. I want answers."

"This is just between you and me, Andrei. It can't go any further for now." Justin leaned in close, his gaze intent. "I want your promise. I'll trust that."

"You've got it," Andrei replied without hesitation. At least Justin hadn't tried to get him to agree to not investigate on his own. That was a promise he couldn't give.

Justin searched his face, and then, apparently satisfied with what he saw, he sat back with a tired sigh. "As far as I know, Dean stopped to help someone change their tire on the Baltimore-Washington parkway and was shot."

Andrei closed his eyes as his stomach clenched spasmodically. Dean had always been far more trusting than Andrei. Out of anybody else Andrei had known, Dean had always been the first to give a helping hand to another without one question. And to lose him through such a senseless, random act of violence... it was perverted in its wrongness.

"Was he robbed?" Andrei asked through stiff lips.

Justin waited until after the waiter came and went before responding. "His wallet was taken. Would he have had a lot of cash on him?"

"Not enough to motivate a murder. He may have had a couple twenties. Neither of us carry cash often." Andrei picked at a piece of lint on his shirt, rolled it into a ball between his fingers, and set it on the table before searching for another piece. The task helped to keep his tenuous hold on his rioting emotions. "What about the person he stopped to help? Do you know who it is?"

"She was killed too. And I'm not giving you a name until we've informed her family," Justin cut in before Andrei could ask. "It looks like she may have had kids with her. Young ones, but they're missing. The Feds are now involved with the search for them."

Andrei's took his eyes off the lint he was rolling and cut a glance at Justin. That explained quite a bit. Dean would've done anything he could have if there had been kids in danger. "Do you think they're dead?"

"It's too early to say, but I have hope we'll find them. We're trying to move as fast as we can on this."

Andrei's mind raced, thinking of all the reasons why the children had been taken instead of killed out of hand. His plucked another piece of lint and started rolling it with the others until Justin reached over and stopped him by laying his hand on top of Andrei's. "Don't bother getting involved; you're staying out of this."

Andrei wouldn't respond to such a ludicrous statement. Nothing could impel him to drop it and leave it to the police and their politics to handle. Justin was a good detective, and he knew the other man would try, but Andrei wasn't bound by the same rules as Justin. The difference in their personalities was why Justin had excelled in the police academy and Andrei hadn't.

Andrei eyed the whiskey that the waiter set in front of him as Justin picked up his beer. The rawness inside of him craved the numbness it would give. The oblivion he'd sought out when he was younger and he had lost everything. Ironically, it had been Dean who'd pulled him back from that edge with his friendship. Dean and his family.

He didn't think Dean had ever known what that had meant to him. How could he ever really understand? Dean's family had never been anything but accepting and loving with him, and that had extended to Andrei as well, both when they had become friends and then, much later on, lovers.

Andrei's throat tightened to the point of pain, and he pushed the whiskey to the side. "You know more than you're telling me."

"We're chasing leads. I'll be all over it, Andrei. I swear to you. We won't let this bastard walk." There was no way the guy would walk, because Andrei had every intention of hunting him down first. "I hate to ask this, but I need to cover all possibilities in case this was deliberate. Do you know of anyone who would want to hurt Dean?"

"Sweet Jesus," Andrei swore, going hoarse as his throat tightened again. "No. He's a good guy. He got along with people. And if he had an issue with anyone, I would've known about it."

"How about you?" Justin persisted. "You had to have pissed somebody off. An ex looking to get back at you for photos you took? Someone who didn't get their insurance claim? What have you been working on lately?"

Andrei forced himself to consider the possibility despite the horrifying implication that he may have been the reason Dean had been killed. Once again that warm murmur filled his ears, melting away the ice that had seized his spine, and Andrei knew Dean hovered close, even if he couldn't see him. Knowing was both a comfort and a cause for more pain, and the comfort brought guilt. He couldn't allow himself to indulge in that consolation and tempt Dean to stay. No matter how much he wanted to. He kept his concentration on the table instead of looking around for another glimpse of him.

"My gut says that it wasn't a client, an ex-client, or somebody that got burned because of evidence I turned up," Andrei said, shaking his head. "How would they know Dean was going to be on the parkway at that time? It's a pretty elaborate trap, a woman on the side of the road with a flat? Come on. Give me a fucking break. So if it's not Dean, what about the other victim? Did someone sabotage her tires? Give me something, Justin."

"You know I can't share that with you. What about that business deal Dean went to today? Could someone have followed him?"

Andrei took a deep breath, trying to tamp down the seething frustration and rage that gripped him. He had to consider every angle. "I'll look into it, but the last message he left me…." A lump slammed into his throat, making it impossible to speak. Andrei swallowed around it, his eyes stinging.

"Babe, it's time to celebrate. Break out the good shit and get in your boxers. I'm on my way home."

On his way home.

"It sounded like everything had gone very well," he said when he trusted his voice would be steady. "It was a huge deal for Dean, but we weren't talking a lot of money. Not the kind of money that people get killed over. He met with some people to discuss plans for opening a new gym in DC. That's it."

Justin frowned and Andrei held his breath. His friend had to drop some small clue, give him a direction to go in. Anything. "You're right, it doesn't sound like much of a motive. We'll find the guy, Andrei. I swear to you. I'm going to look at everything personally."

Andrei felt a hand on his own as his fist balled, but when he looked down, he couldn't see anything, and the sensation faded like a ghost on the wind. *Dean.* So close and still impossibly far. "Tell me what you know," he said, his voice becoming hoarse again despite his best efforts. *Not again, please, not again.*

"You know I can't."

With supreme effort, Andrei suppressed the white-hot spurt of rage that threatened to choke him. "Bullshit. Give me something. The other victim's name. What was the caliber of the gun that was used?

Anything. At least tell me when you're going to release Dean so I can give his parents that, right after I fucking crush them when I tell them he's been murdered."

"As soon as I hear that they're done with him, you'll be the first person I tell."

Andrei did not want to think of a bunch of strangers poking and prodding at Dean's body. His logic and training said it was necessary. His upbringing screamed that it was unnatural.

"Go home, Andrei. Let us take care of it. Come on, I'll drive you."

Justin reached out to touch him, and Andrei jerked back violently. Justin meant well, but Andrei did not want company in their home or to feel like someone was babysitting him. "Don't bother, I'll be fine."

"What are you going to do?" Justin asked as Andrei rose from the table and dropped some money down for his untouched drink. "Please don't do something fucking stupid, and stay in town. You know some people are going to want to talk to you. Don't make me sic someone on your ass."

"Yeah, I got it. They'll want to rule me out as a suspect. I'm going home and grabbing my files, and then I'm heading down to St. Mary's City to talk to Dean's parents." He fixed the detective with a hard look. "I'm the one who's going to talk with them, got that?"

"Don't worry. No one's going to take away your prerogative. I already took care of it." Justin's brow furrowed with worry as he studied Andrei. "I don't like the thought of you being alone right now."

"Well that's just something we're all going to have to learn to live with, isn't it?"

ANDREI'S heart lurched as he pulled up in front of their house still blazing with lights. He almost kept going to drive on to St. Mary's City. Though he hated the thought of disturbing Dean's family this late at night and destroying their peace. All of his files were here, however, and he needed them if he was going to rule out one of his cases being the cause for Dean's murder. So he had to come home. And Dean's dad would want to go over them with him.

He pulled his old Volkswagen van around to the back of the house and descended the outside steps to his basement office. He hadn't been able to sense Dean since he'd left the bar, and he wasn't sure if that was a good sign or not. His worry over Dean becoming a ghost and his anger toward Dean's killer dulled the sharp edge of his loss.

There was just too much to do. Too much to concentrate on. He experienced almost a sense of relief when he entered his office and flipped on the lights. His office had order, this made sense, and he had a job to do. Andrei tossed his keys on the desk and went immediately to his file cabinet and took out the stack that represented the most recent cases. Most he could dismiss immediately, like routine insurance investigations that had turned up no fraud. Or cases where he'd been able to reunite a family.

A lump rose in Andrei's throat. Andrei tossed the files on his desk, sat down, and fisted his hands in his hair. The house was too silent and still. At this time of night, he should be hearing Dean moving around upstairs, or calling down to him that it was time to close shop and eat some dinner. His eyes burned as he stared at the ink spots on his desk blotter.

It had to be just a nightmare. He'd go up the stairs, and Dean would be waiting for him with that mischievous smile on his face, some smart-assed comment on his lips, and a wicked promise in his eyes. He'd never get to see that again, and their time together when they woke up, that rare morning they got to linger in bed, felt so far away. Now their bed would be empty and cold.

Grief seized his throat as he felt familiar fingers on the back of his neck and the warm murmur sounded in his ears. The sound hovered on the edge of his understanding, and he thought that maybe, if he concentrated a little harder, he'd be able to hear what Dean said. Andrei had to stop himself from reaching to understand.

"Dean, you can't stay." Andrei closed his eyes, swallowing convulsively. He couldn't ignore him any longer. Dean had to understand. "Please, *iubito*, I know it doesn't make sense. And maybe one day I'll have the chance to explain it to you, but you've got to leave me behind."

The murmur became insistent, and Dean's hands slid to his shoulders, giving him a little shake. A thought cut through the haze in Andrei's mind, and he gathered what reserves he had left and slowly straightened and turned in his chair.

Dean stood behind him, his warm hazel eyes grave as they stared at each other. He looked so vital and solid. So goddamned fucking real. He could be selfish and let Dean stay, and at first it would be wonderful, until it became obvious that Dean was like an old-time LP caught in the same skipping loop over and over again.

Andrei blinked rapidly. "Why are you here? Is it to be with me? Is it to help you find your killer?"

Ileana had stayed so he wouldn't be alone, but the cost had been too high for her.

A helpless look crossed Dean's face, and his lips moved, though Andrei still couldn't make sense of what he said. "I don't understand." Andrei swore in frustration, shoving up from his desk. He pulled a dusty bottle of vodka down from a shelf and poured a glass with a trembling hand.

Dean snatched the glass away, his gaze hard and intent. Inexplicably, Andrei heard the sound of a bird singing—a songbird of some kind, cheery and bright with the promise of spring and sun-filled days. A breeze tugged at his shirt; then far off in the distance, a baby began to cry, the sound rising and falling, melding with the bird into a strange melody.

Andrei opened his mouth to ask a question, but the fierce look of concentration on Dean's face stopped him. A picture appeared in the middle of the air, fluttering to the floor. Frowning, Andrei scooped it up and saw a little girl with dark hair and smiling eyes. "Is this one of the kids Justin told me about?"

Dean shook his head and a line appeared between his brows. A dozen more pictures fell, all of different little girls with dark hair, all about the same age. Andrei shuffled through them, mentally noting the similarities. "Okay, so you're saying that one of the missing children is a girl about four or five, maybe bi-racial, with light eyes?"

Dean beamed at him, excitement lighting up his face, and Andrei's stomach clenched. This had to have been the look on his face when he'd left Andrei that last message. Andrei memorized it, not knowing when he'd ever see it again, fighting the urge to reach for him, because if his arms came up empty, he might just lose it.

"What else can you tell me?"

More pictures began to litter the floor, pictures of babies, of robins, pictures of slim white men in trucker hats, ads of camper trucks. More and more pictures fell, striking Andrei's face and the back of his head; crying babies, laughing babies, until Andrei thought it would never end.

"For godssake, Dean, stop it!"

The pictures rose up in a whirlwind, and Andrei lifted his arms up to protect his face as they slashed and beat at him before they vanished. When Andrei looked up, Dean had gone too.

Chapter Four

THE road heading into Southern Maryland was empty at this time of night. Andrei passed mile after mile of old tobacco fields that had been left empty as the demand had died or been converted to corn crops. Will-o-the-wisps drifted over the road, providing momentary pockets of cooler air as Andrei passed through them. The heat of the day had passed, and Andrei had the windows down to take in the familiar scents and sounds of the quiet county. This was the first place that he'd truly called home.

A streetlamp briefly illuminated the seat behind him, and Andrei's hands tightened on the wheel as he caught a flash of red and yellow from the backseat. How long had Ileana been sitting there?

"For a little bit. I wanted to be super quiet and not spook you."

Ileana had always loved that game, coming in silently behind him and finding a place out of the way until Andrei noticed her. "You did a very good job. How's Cougar?"

She held the stuffed turtle up, making his head move and her voice squeaky. "I'm fine."

Andrei hadn't seen or heard his sister this clearly in months, and every time he passed under a streetlight, his eyes flew to the rearview mirror to catch a glimpse of her. She hadn't changed at all, and the thought brought with it the ever-present regret.

"Is Dean here too?" Andrei couldn't see him, but that didn't mean anything, and maybe Ileana could help him explain all those pictures. And she could get Dean to see the danger in staying.

"Nope, he's popping about somewhere. I don't think he knows what he's doing. I like him though. He called me Poppet, and he gives great hugs."

It took several moments before Andrei could speak. "Yeah, he does, Illy."

Ileana crawled into the front seat with a stir of air and set her stuffed turtle between them. "He might be with his mommy and daddy already. He knows that's where you're going."

Without thinking about it, Andrei reached out his hand and felt the slight pressure and warmth of Ileana's fingers slipping against his palm. It wasn't like how it used to be when she felt as solid as if she still lived; it was more an impression of slender fingers. He wondered what had made Ileana so real then and how Dean had a hard time making himself seen or heard.

Maybe because, as an adult, Dean understood what death meant far more than a little girl who had been sick for weeks. So his death was more profound. Or it could just be that when Ileana had died, he'd had a child's accepting imagination. The same kind of imagination that Ileana still had, where possibilities were endless and magic was real.

"Illy, I need you to speak to Dean for me."

"'Bout what?" Andrei glanced at her and found Ileana watching him with curious eyes. Well at least she was paying attention.

"I need you to tell him that he can't stay, okay?" Ileana's lower lip stuck out in a pout. "This is important. He has to move on before it's too late. Tell him that for me."

"But I like him." Ileana pulled her hand free and hugged Cougar to her, squishing his shell. "He can play games with me since you're too busy all the time. I tried to go visit Sergey, but Mum and Dad got so mad, and they brought the scary man with the burning eyes."

Andrei pulled over to the side of the road and twisted to look at Ileana sternly. "Ileana Therese Cuza, you promised me that you would never go back there. Not ever."

Tears welled in Ileana's eyes, and her pouting lip trembled. "But, I missed you and I thought... Sergey is younger, maybe he would want to play. I don't like being alone all the time."

Andrei drew in a deep breath, going cold inside. At one time his parents had tried to exorcize Ileana, and she had gotten so dangerously weak. That was when he realized that he could never dare speak of her again. Not to anyone. Probably the only thing that had saved her was that she wasn't a malicious spirit. But how would a suspicious Romani priest know that? To his people, all spirits who lingered were malicious.

"Illy, I know you're confused and scared and lonely. I'm so sorry about that. And I know I got all big and boring on you, and it's hard for you to find me and talk to me sometimes. But this is very, very important. Stay away from our family. They don't understand and will try to hurt you because you scare them."

Andrei's heart sank as Ileana just stared at him in confusion, clutching her turtle hard enough to squeeze the stuffing out of him. How could he explain to an eight-year-old that everything she knew had changed? He'd been trying for thirty years.

"If I tell Dean to go away, who will stay with you?" Ileana clutched at his shirt. "I can't always find you, and a Cuza's not supposed to be alone, Andrei. Even I know that."

Until Andrei was fifteen, he'd never understood what it was to be alone. He grew up constantly surrounded by family, not just his parents, but aunts, grandparents, and second cousins too. He'd had family everywhere he turned, and they'd all traveled together, up and down the East Coast.

"Hey, I've been without the clan longer than I've been with the clan." Andrei tried to smile at her, not sure if he wanted to convince her or himself. "And I'm not alone. I still have Dean's family."

Which reminded him, it was getting late, and he wanted to be at Dean's parents before they went to bed. Or worse, heard about Dean from someone else or the news. Ileana's brows came together in a fierce frown. "How come ya gotta always do something?"

"Because that's what adults do. Doesn't mean I want you to go away." Andrei kissed the top of her head. "Strap yourself in, big sis. You, me, and Cougar are going for a ride."

Ileana rolled her eyes and said with all the bluntness of youth, "Don't need a seatbelt, Andrei. I'm dead, 'member?"

"Yeah," Andrei said hoarsely as he pulled back onto the road. "Yeah, sweetie, I remember."

"Sing me a song."

Andrei almost started to protest. His singing was terrible. He couldn't find a note on a scale even if he had a gun to his head and his life depended on it. He cast a quick glance at his sister and saw that she'd curled up, her cheek pressed against the seat with Cougar cradled in her arms. She had such a look of hope in her eyes that he couldn't deny her request. At least no one but her would hear him butcher the song.

"'Nani, Nani.' That's my favorite."

Andrei smiled and stroked the top of her head. "I know, that's the one Mum used to sing to us every night." It had been the last thing Ileana had heard. As angry as Andrei was toward his parents, he couldn't deny that there had been far more good times than bad. They probably would've continued to have been good if Andrei had had any skills at conforming.

He sang the old lullaby, finding an aching comfort in it as he did. Without her having to ask, he started it again. By the time he reached St. Mary's City, she had appeared to have fallen asleep and disappeared once again on him. He missed her already, but he didn't want her to witness this conversation anyway. It would only upset her to see him and Dean's family grieving.

His heart beat faster, and his stomach churned with dread as he pulled the van up to a small Cape Cod house overlooking the Chesapeake Bay. Andrei sat in the van for a few minutes, gripping the wheel as he studied the peaceful house. He was such a fucking coward.

How the hell was he going to tell Phil and Carole that their son was dead? Dean had been so close to his parents.

It was only the thought that they might hear it elsewhere that drove Andrei from the van. He shoved his hand in his pocket, steeling himself as he went to knock on the door. Andrei's heart caught when Phil opened the door, dressed for bed. Dean stood behind him, his hand on his dad's shoulder, raw emotion on his face. Andrei had to stop himself from reaching out to comfort him.

"Andrei." The surprise and welcome on Phil's face immediately changed to alarm. "What is it?"

He looked over Andrei's shoulder toward the van, looking for Dean, and Andrei drew in a deep breath, struggling to keep the emotion out of his voice or else he'd break down. "Is Carole awake? I need to talk to you both."

"Come on in. I'll go get her." Phil stepped back to let him in and clapped him lightly on the shoulder. As always, Andrei immediately felt surrounded by the love within these walls. Dean's family had gone out of their way to make him feel included, a fact for which he'd always been grateful. They had become his family.

And now he was going to have to break their hearts. Andrei followed Phil and Dean to the kitchen, his thoughts whirling as he tried to come up with the gentlest way he could tell them that they would never see their son again.

WHEN the entire Marshall clan gathered together, it reminded Andrei of what it was like growing up, surrounded by chattering family, each doing their own thing and still remaining part of a whole. Dean's mother and sisters cooked while Andrei sat at the table with Dean's dad and brother, the stack of files in front of them. Aunts and uncles had been streaming in and out all morning, pulling Carole aside and giving her a chance to weep before she busied herself again.

Andrei longed to be busy too. To be out there searching, finding Dean's killer so he could make him pay for what he'd done. He glanced down at the list of his clients with possible grievances against him, the careful notes that he and Phil had compiled. It was a sheer fucking waste of time. Justin had given him busy work to keep him out of the way. Murder was simple ninety percent of the time. This revenge scenario was entirely too convoluted.

"You're not going to find answers there, son." Phil's voice echoed his thoughts. "You're better off finding out who the other victim is to see if there's a connection there."

Andrei trusted Phil's instincts, and besides, he agreed. If this wasn't a random killing, then the who and why lay with the other victim and her missing kids.

He nodded and sat back, looking around the room, exhausted from his efforts to hold back the onrush of emotion. His parents would've given into it. His mum with a wild storm of weeping and his dad with his raging anger, and they would've torn at each other until they were spent. Here, they comforted each other, cried on each other's shoulders, and murmured words of love.

The other major difference between his old family and Dean's was that in this gathering, Andrei felt completely included instead of how he'd always been shunted off to the side. He hadn't realized how much he had subconsciously braced himself, expecting their utter rejection now that Dean was gone. Instead, they treated him as they always had, as one of their own. And the experience of shared grief, while heart-wrenching and raw, had given Andrei a chance to bury his own sorrow and anger down deep so he wouldn't break down.

"I just don't understand it," Rachel said, still sounding dazed as her mother slipped an arm about her shoulders. Andrei didn't understand it himself. Every time he thought that he'd processed the awful truth, his mind would wrench back to that stark statement: Dean had been murdered.

It played over and over, a litany in his mind that he couldn't quite grasp. The best were always taken early, which meant he'd be around for a very long time indeed.

"What're you planning now?" Phil asked, cutting through Andrei's exhausted thoughts as the other man returned to the table with his refilled coffee mug.

Andrei blinked at the diagram he'd drawn in his little notebook. A robin, baby, little girl, camper truck, with lines drawn between them and notes on the side. He'd been trying to figure out what Dean had shown him, but as the hours wore on, his brain made less and less sense.

"At this very moment, nothing. I'm waiting for them to release the name of the woman that Dean had been with. If I tried to leave here right now—"

"I'd brain you," Carole said, dropping a basket of hot biscuits down with butter and jam. "You're not in any condition to be driving right now. Do you hear me?"

Andrei tipped his head back and looked up into her red-rimmed eyes. Normally when someone tried to give him an order in a tone like that, his immediate knee-jerk response was to dig in his heels, but Carole had always been different. "I promise, I won't hit the road until I've laid down for a few hours."

Lured by the aroma of food, all of Andrei's nieces and nephews came thundering into the kitchen and were soon leaving again, following the oldest, who carried a tray of treats out to the picnic table outside. All except for the youngest, Caleb, who remained sound asleep on his dad's lap, thumb stuck in his mouth.

"You're going after this guy, aren't you?" Joseph asked after his mother left again. He shifted Caleb on his lap so he could reach for a biscuit. He spoke low with a quick glance at the women gathered around the kitchen island.

Phil's brows furrowed, the silver in his hair standing out more than normal. The lines on his face deepened. "Don't encourage him, Joseph." He sighed and rubbed his temple. "Don't get me wrong, son," he said gravely, meeting Andrei's eyes. "You've got everything it takes to find him. You know I've always believed in you. It's your temper that concerns me."

Andrei took a sip of his tea and broke open a biscuit before Carole noticed his lack of appetite and forced more food on him. He understood where Phil came from. He had good reason for his worry, and Andrei didn't know how to reassure him. "I know how proud you were when I got into the police academy, and I screwed that up. I do better on my own, Phil. All those rules, people looking over my shoulder and judging me, it just wasn't a good fit. I think everybody heaved a sigh of relief when they kicked me out."

"I'm not saying you haven't done a fine job on your own because I know you have." Phil's gaze sharpened, reminding Andrei that the man had spent over thirty years as a detective in DC. "But this is personal, and personal gets ugly. Investigate on your own. I know you have to, so keep your head on straight and keep it legal. You may not be a Baltimore cop, but you have to work with those guys in the future, and they can make it difficult or easy for you."

A flicker of movement out of the corner of Andrei's eye caught his attention. Dean had returned, leaning against the doorframe, watching everyone with sad eyes. Andrei's hand started trembling, and he set the teacup down harder than he meant to, splashing the hot liquid on his fingers.

Dean had disappeared on him after seeing Andrei get settled with his family. When he'd squeezed his shoulder before going, Andrei had thought it had been good-bye. A rush of forbidden relief went through him. It wasn't good-bye. Not yet. How could he be so selfish? He knew the stakes.

"I'm sorry about that," Andrei muttered, grabbing a napkin to mop up the spill.

Joseph rose, cradling Caleb to him. "You need to sleep, man. Before you fall over and scare everyone. Everyone's had their snatch but you. Here, you can put him down, too."

Andrei started to protest, only to find his arms full of sleeping child. Caleb didn't stir, his limbs heavy as Andrei tucked his nephew's head against his shoulder. Dean gave him a stern look, pointing back toward the bedrooms, and Andrei bit back a sigh. He was outnumbered on this one, and arguing with Dean would only make him look like a crazed wreck.

He paused at the doorway and looked back at Phil. "I'll keep it together. I promise."

Some of the tension eased on Phil's face. "That's all I ask for. I'll come wake you if anything new develops."

That promise allowed Andrei to relax a little bit, enough that he thought he might be able to at least close his eyes and rest, if not sleep. He laid Caleb down in the playpen that Phil and Carole kept for the little ones and covered him with a light blanket. When he straightened and turned around, Dean was waiting for him, pointing toward the guest bed with an insistent look on his face.

Andrei's eyes stung as he looked at the empty bed. At least it wasn't their own, though that was scant comfort. "Talk to me, Dean," he murmured in a low voice as he sat down on the edge of the bed and kicked off his shoes. "What is it that you're so desperate to tell me?"

Dean shook his head and stabbed his finger toward the bed again.

"Fine, I get it. Sleep or I get nothing, right?" Andrei sighed as Dean nodded. He squeezed his eyes shut tight as he lay down, his arms achingly empty. "I can't do this without you, *iubito*," he whispered, the storm welling up. "How the hell am I supposed to do this?"

The bed dipped as a weight settled on it, and Andrei felt warm lips against his temple. His heart slammed up into his throat. "Don't," he said, his voice strangling in his throat. "Don't, it's not real. It can't be real. Don't you understand?"

A finger brushed against his lips, and then, from very far off, Andrei thought he heard Dean's voice. Just for a moment, he almost understood him. It seemed as if heat and energy poured off of him in that touch, and Dean's gentle murmur dissolved his will, sending Andrei into a troubled sleep.

DEAN lay down next to Andrei, watching him sleep, so wrung out that he didn't even stir when Caleb woke up, climbed out of his playpen, and went to join his cousins. He'd breathed a sigh of relief when the door closed without Andrei waking. He needed all the rest he could get, because once Andrei started hunting, he ignored sleeping except for quick naps, or eating regular meals. And Dean wouldn't be there to make sure that he took care of himself anymore.

Hot tears streaked down his cheeks. He didn't bother wiping them away. Who would see him cry other than Andrei, and he would be out for a few more hours at least. Dean didn't belong here. Not anymore. It had been torture to walk amongst his family, to see them mourning him and to be unable to tell them that he would be all right. He could see himself going on for years as just a shadow. Even if he could get Andrei to eventually hear him or figured out how to really touch him, his partner was right. It wasn't real. It would only be an imitation of what they'd had.

Dean looked up, startled, as light fell across his face. The door to the bedroom stood wide open and instead of the hallway beyond, a bright golden glow surrounded a figure in the doorway. He surged to his feet, his heart slamming in his chest in awe and yearning.

The figure stepped forward, a smile on his face, and Dean shook his head in confusion, stumbling back to fall on the bed again. He stood in the doorway or another version of him. Freaky.

"W-what the… oh hell."

The other Dean laughed. "Hardly."

He was dressed in the clothes he'd worn to his commitment ceremony with Andrei. They'd had it on a warm June evening on the shores of the Chesapeake Bay not far from here. To this day Dean could remember the feel of cool sand between his toes, the sound of the gentle surf, and the joy in Andrei's eyes as they faced each other.

"It's time, Dean."

Dean swallowed hard and tore his eyes away. It was unnerving to see himself like that and to feel that strong pull tugging at him to go through the doorway. He stared at Andrei's drawn face, trying to commit it to memory. "I can't. Not yet."

"You know in your heart what you need to do. You were just thinking on how you don't belong here. There is no purpose to staying."

Dean shook his head stubbornly, laying his hand over Andrei's and digging the other hand into his pocket to finger the hair ribbon there. "There's something I've got to do first."

"He won't thank you if you get stuck in limbo. You're only going to have so many opportunities to cross over before you're trapped here. That thought is a nightmare for him."

Dean's thoughts flew to Ileana as he turned to face himself. "Is that what happened to his sister?"

A breeze came through the door, and Dean swore he could taste summer and salt water on it as it wrapped around him. His other self shook his head with an amused smile. "I can't tell you that. There are no answers in limbo, buddy. But I will say this, be careful of Ileana. You can't trust everything she'll tell you. She has her own motivations." He glanced over his shoulder at the light behind him as if responding to some inner call. "Time's running short for this round, Dean; you coming or going?"

The call came even stronger this time, and Dean found himself taking a step toward him. He started to reach out for the hand extended out to him when a distressed moan had him looking back toward Andrei.

"He has to stand or fall on his own now, Dean. You can't walk with him anymore. Not in the way you both want."

"How can you say that?" Dean glared at him, taking a step back. "If you're supposed to be me, then you love him. I don't understand how it can be so easy for you to dismiss him."

He let his anger and confusion fuel him as he surged forward and shut the door in his own face. Immediately, the glow disappeared, taking the yearning with it, and Dean gasped in relief as he began to shake in reaction. Oh God... oh God, what had he done?

"What's wrong?"

Dean nearly jumped out of his skin at the sound of a voice near his elbow. He gasped and looked down to find Ileana watching him curiously. "For the love of God, Poppet, don't sneak up on people like that."

She slipped her hand in his and smiled up at him. "Will you play a game with me?"

"Now's not the time for games," Dean said, thinking on what his other half had told him. He couldn't picture Ileana being evil, though. Not Andrei's sister who looked at him with trust and disappointment in her eyes. "We have to help Andrei find those missing kids."

"Andrei can do that on his own. He's super good at finding things." She clung to him with both hands now. "Please, Dean. I haven't had anybody to play with in so long."

Dean bit back a sigh. He knew from his nieces and nephews that Ileana was not likely to give up. "Why don't we do both?" he suggested. "We can make a game out of helping Andrei."

Ileana looked at him with a dubious expression. "Maybe... what kinda game?"

Dean racked his brain, trying to come up with something that would sound like fun to a little girl. Then the door flew open again, passing right through them, and Ileana disappeared with a soft, startled cry.

Andrei immediately sat up with a questioning expression as Dean's dad came into the room. "They've released the name of the other victim. Robin Olsen."

All trace of exhaustion disappeared from his face as Andrei's gaze sharpened. "Did you dig up anything on her?"

Despite the circumstances, a little thrill of excitement went through Dean. He'd always wanted to accompany Andrei on one of his investigations, but Andrei had never allowed it. He wouldn't be able to keep Dean away now. Andrei's gaze swept unseeing over him as he rose and raked a hand through his hair.

"She's got a mom just outside of Baltimore, a house in Richmond, and a missing ex-husband. I managed to get both addresses. I take it you're going to visit them."

Dean shook his head frantically, trying to get Andrei's attention, but his partner still didn't see him. Dammit, how could he warn him if he couldn't figure out how to communicate? A headache started to throb at his temples. Yet again, Ileana was gone, and he'd forgotten to ask her some critical questions.

"Yeah, but I'll head to Baltimore first. How is her ex missing? Did he abandon them?"

"I'm not sure," Phil admitted. "The details are sketchy, but she did file a missing person's report a month ago."

Andrei put his shoes back on. "I might be able to get more out of Robin's mom. Exes are always tricky situations. I'd like to get a feel for what I might be walking into before I head to Richmond."

"You find him, Andrei. You find whoever did this to my boy."

Chapter Five

ANDREI took the time to shower, shave, and change before heading out to Evelyn Acosta's house in Timonium. At least there was a bathroom and spare clothes in his office. He was not ready to go upstairs and face an empty house. He hadn't seen Dean in a couple hours, not since he'd left St. Mary's. He hadn't sensed him either, and it made him antsy inside, not knowing whether or not Dean had moved on or if he haunted his parents.

Now all those pictures made sense. They had been for Robin and her two kids, though it would help to know what the children really looked like. All he knew at this point was a baby and a little girl were missing; that didn't narrow things down at all.

The street that he turned onto looked quiet, nothing appearing to be out of place as he parked outside of the small, neat home. Humid heat struck Andrei when he opened the door, reminding him of how miserable this area was at the tail end of summer. The sun beat down on him and sweat trickled at the small of his back as he crossed to the porch and knocked on the door.

It opened a crack, and a young woman peered out. She had to be in her late twenties, so not the woman he needed to see. Another daughter, maybe. "We're not making any statements," she said in a flat, angry voice. Tearstains marked her warm brown cheeks, and more tears strained in her voice.

Andrei's heart panged in sympathy. There had been reporters waiting for him too when he'd gotten home, and he hadn't been in the mood to address them either. "I'm not with the news, ma'am. My name's Andrei Cuza. I'm a private detective working for the family of the other victim," he said, almost stumbling over the last word.

He pulled out his wallet and lifted it up so she could see his license. She opened the door a little wider, encouraging Andrei. At least she hadn't slammed it in his face. "We've already talked to the FBI and the police."

"Detective Mansle of the Baltimore PD can verify my identity if you need him to. He knows that I'm working this case." Justin should know that Andrei wouldn't be able to drop it, and if he didn't, oh well. "Is Ms. Evelyn Acosta home? I only have a few questions. I won't take up a lot of time."

The young woman's brows furrowed in a dubious frown. Andrei watched indecision, anxiety, and grief play over her features before she grudgingly opened the door. "If you upset her even more, I'm booting you out myself."

"I'll remember that, Ms....?" Andrei let his voice trail off in question as he stepped inside and offered her his hand.

"Wanda. I'm Robin's twin sister." She shook it briefly as he murmured his condolences, before turning to lead him down a short hallway. Andrei heard the low hum of conversation before they came to the living room. Family pictures covered the walls, some formal, many candid. They looked happy. A smiling couple with two girls, though the ages varied. And more pictures of what seemed to be grandkids.

One in particular caught his eye. An imp of a little girl with a baby tucked on her lap. Dark hair, gray eyes. Dean's missing little girl. From the way she held her baby brother so carefully, Andrei thought she must be as good of a big sister as Ileana had been to him.

The couches and chairs were full of people who went silent when he appeared. He had the abrupt sense of being an intruder on a very private time, above and beyond his normal feelings of exclusion. A sea of dark faces looked toward him with expressionless demeanors that accused without words.

It reminded Andrei of the time that drunk *gadje* had stumbled across their camp when he had been twelve. The man had been sent on a dare by his friends to see if he could score a date with Andrei's cousin before they left town again. He may have been drunk, but he wasn't entirely without wits. It hadn't taken him long before he picked up on the air of animosity and turned tail to run.

Andrei wasn't turned that easily, and he met each stare with silent acknowledgement. Wanda walked over to an older black woman with a careworn face. "Mama, this is Mr. Cuza, a private detective working for Mr. Marshall's family. He wanted to talk with you a moment."

Andrei nodded toward her. "Ma'am." She was darker than her daughter, with tired eyes and more iron gray in her hair than black, but she sat in the chair, straight and proud, every inch the matriarch of the family. "I'm very sorry for your loss."

Inadequate words for what she was going through. A mother shouldn't have to bury her daughter, and he should've had the opportunity to grow old with Dean. That was the way the world should work, even if it fell short too often. Inadequate words, but they needed to be said.

"Thank you, Mr. Cuza. We can talk in the kitchen," Evelyn said as she stood up and addressed the other people on the couch. "Excuse me."

Andrei sensed a stir in the air, and an image of a woman flickered next to Evelyn. It disappeared so fast that he only had an impression of dark hair and an even deeper sense that he was intruding. He glanced at Wanda as she walked out of the room and noted the similarities. So Robin was hanging around too. As he turned to follow Wanda and Evelyn to the kitchen, he felt air touch the back of his neck, a brush of fingertips and a hot zip of electricity. He stiffened and bit back an exclamation of surprise. The last thing he needed was every ghost in the area to start visiting him. He had enough of them that were family.

Covered dishes sat on the counter in the kitchen, and when Wanda opened the fridge to pour them all some tea, Andrei saw more dishes in there. He felt almost immediately at home here, despite the grief and fear that hung heavy in the air. In some ways he supposed he wanted to share it with them. Despite the sadness, it was so much like being at Dean's parents' house. This was a place where the extended family cared for its own, whether by blood or community.

"I'm sorry to intrude on you today, ma'am," he said, thanking Wanda as she handed him a cold glass of tea. "As I explained to your daughter, I'm a private detective, representing Dean Marshall's family."

"We've already told the police everything we know." She searched his face with penetrating eyes. "You said Mr. Marshall's family hired you?"

Andrei hesitated; something told him this woman was astute at picking up lies and that she would have nothing to do with him if she thought he was lying. "Not exactly, Mrs. Acosta. I'm doing this for free with Dean's family's approval and knowledge."

Wanda prowled restlessly along the counter, wiping at spots that didn't really need cleaning while her mother continued to study Andrei. "Why are you involved, young man? For justice or revenge?"

"Really, Mama, why does it matter?" Wanda asked with stark bitterness as she tossed the sponge into the sink. "He's one more person looking for Inez and Tristan. I'm all for any help we can get."

"To be brutally honest, Mrs. Acosta, your missing grandkids won't get the national attention that other kids would," Andrei said, meeting her gaze. "They should already be all over the news in every state. Yes, I'm doing this to find Dean's killer, but I know he'd want those kids found. He'd be the first to send me out. Besides, I have a pretty good track record at finding missing people, especially little ones."

Evelyn remained quiet and Andrei let her think it out, biting back a sigh of relief when she finally nodded. "Please, call me Evelyn. I'll tell you what I told them, but it isn't much. Robin was on her way here, to start her life over again. Her and Blake tried to make it work, but he seemed to get more and more unhappy after Inez was born. He'd wanted a son, not a daughter."

"He was a jackass. I never understood what Robin saw in him." Wanda joined them at the table. "And it pissed Robin off that he couldn't see how wonderful Inez was. I think that's when she finally decided to wake up and realized what a loser she'd married."

"He wasn't that bad. He's their father, remember that," Evelyn said with a sharp look at her daughter. "He always said that one day he would buy her a house on the beach. But Wanda's right, he never was the same after Inez was born. Started working weird hours, stayed away from home more than he was there, and she finally got fed up. He fought her leaving, though, and she stayed a bit longer and ended up getting pregnant with Tristan."

"She believed in him long after everyone else knew he wasn't going to go anywhere," Wanda cut in. "Believed him enough to let him put a wall between us and them so we couldn't see what was going on until she was truly miserable. He got more possessive after Robin got pregnant again, and she finally kicked him out."

Andrei took out his notebook, turned it to a fresh page, and began making up a new list of the pros and cons of Blake Olsen being the killer. The police would nail him quick if that was the case, and it definitely was a check in the plus column that the kids were still alive, but that meant Inez probably witnessed the murders, and he'd seen too many shattered little faces on children who shouldn't have seen the things that they had.

"Do you have any idea where Blake is now?" Not arrested already or brought in for questioning, because Justin would've called him. "I heard that Robin filed a missing person's report on him."

"Dead for all we know," Wanda said. "I'm pretty sure he was doing something illegal. I found drugs at their place, right before Robin left him. I wouldn't be surprised if he got on the wrong side of some of those people he ran with."

"I need to know everything you do about his disappearance. When did it happen?"

"Oh, it couldn't have been long after Tristan was born. The divorce was still being finalized. I think he gave up on the idea that she'd change her mind and come back to him." The lines of grief and age etched deeper in Evelyn's brow as she thought. "Maybe mid-June. I'm not sure how long he was gone before Robin realized or how much longer before she let us know."

"She was scared though," Wanda said in a low voice. "She tried to hide it, but something had spooked her."

Andrei frowned, making another notation. If the killer was somebody who Blake had pissed off and they'd gone after Robin too, then those kids were as good as dead or sold off. Resolve hardened in his gut. He wasn't going to believe that until he found positive proof.

"Robin was coming from Richmond, correct?" Andrei waited for their nods before continuing. "Was she supposed to leave yesterday, or did she suddenly decide to come early?"

"She wasn't planning on coming until she found a job here, but she kept moving the date up." Evelyn wrung a napkin, knotting the fabric in her gnarled hands, and Andrei laid his hand over hers in a soothing gesture. "We encouraged her to come quickly. I didn't like the thought of my baby being down there all alone and hurting, trying to care for a newborn on her own."

Andrei asked a few more questions, organizing his thoughts as he went. There was a certain amount of relief in burying himself in an investigation. Shoving emotions aside was far easier when he had a puzzle to work out. The calmer he became, though, the more upset Evelyn got, and he decided that he had enough information to go on when tears filled her eyes.

"Don't cry, Evelyn," he said, summoning up a smile as he squeezed her hand. "We'll all work to find your grandkids for you. Would you happen to have a picture of Inez and Tristan that you could let me borrow?"

"I've got it, Mama." Wanda hurried from the room.

Evelyn tightened her hand on his with a surprisingly hard grip. "Tell me the truth, young man, I can take it. You think my babies are still alive?"

"Yes, ma'am, I do. If he wanted to kill them, they'd be dead already. In the meantime I want you to get the news out there as much as you can. Call the networks, talk to the reporters, get the image of your grandkids all over the place if you can. The more the word is out, the harder it'll be for him to move about."

"You keep saying he. What makes you so sure it's a man?"

"Justin told me that Dean defended himself. He wouldn't have lifted a hand against a woman. Maybe to save the kids, but I don't think it would've occurred to him to do it for himself until it was too late."

"You sound as if you knew him very well."

For a moment, a profound depression swept over Andrei. He couldn't get used to people referring to Dean in the past tense. Every time he thought he'd steadied himself, something would remind him of the intensity of that aching hole inside of him, and his emotions threatened to rise up and drown him.

Luckily Wanda chose to come back at that moment. "Here," she said, handing him a smaller version of the picture he'd seen in the living room of Inez holding her brother. "And I didn't think it would hurt to have a picture of Blake either, just in case."

Andrei lifted the other photo up to examine the happy couple. The woman looked like Wanda, not an exact copy, so fraternal twins then, but a beautiful smile lit up her face. Both she and the man behind her had their hands on the swell of her stomach. The stamp date on the picture was from five years ago, so it had to be before Inez was born.

A flicker caught his eye, a touch of air, and Andrei lifted his head, gaze already searching for Dean. He stood by the table, blood spreading across his shirt, his image wavering in and out until he turned solid with a rush of air that almost yanked the picture out of Andrei's hand. A sick, cold feeling settled in Andrei's gut. Dean didn't look at Andrei or acknowledge him. He stared at the picture in Andrei's hands, rage and fear chasing across his face. "Run, Inez. Run, sweetheart."

Dean's voice sounded so harsh and distant that Andrei barely recognized it.

He touched the photograph, leaving a bloody fingerprint on the man's chest. His gaze clashed with Andrei's as his lips moved again. "Andrei, I'm sorry." With another flicker he vanished.

"Are you okay?" Strong fingers squeezed his hand hard enough to hurt, and Andrei once again focused on the now. Evelyn stared at him, her dark face creased in worry. "Mr. Cuza? If you'd gone any whiter, you'd've passed out. Get him some more tea, Wanda."

"I'm… I'm fine." Andrei laid the photograph down on the table and clasped his shaking hands together. He stared at the bloody fingerprint, his eyes burning from the intensity of his gaze. This was the fucker who had killed Dean. There was no doubt in his mind now. Hate rose up hard and hot and consuming.

He examined Blake Olsen's features. The man was handsome in a pale way. His hair was a fine blond, his eyes an Icelandic blue. The way he touched Robin's belly seemed more possessive than protective. He'd be in disguise by now. So Andrei concentrated on the little things that would be hard to hide. Blake had a long face, and his jaw tapered to a point. His eyes were a little wide-set. Hair and eye color could change, but the shape of his face would stay the same.

"What is it?" Wanda asked as she set his refilled glass in front of him. Andrei's heart pounded when she picked up the photo, but she mustn't have been able to see the mark Dean left because her expression didn't change.

"Does Blake own a camper truck?"

"No, he never struck me as one to rough it. When they went on vacation, they always stayed in hotels." Evelyn took the picture as well and handed it to Andrei with a mystified expression. "He loved her. I know he did at the beginning. I have a hard time believing he'd do anything to hurt her or those kids."

Andrei didn't bother to argue with her and get her worked up and upset. He'd tell her when he had proof. He gathered the pictures together and rose, clasping Evelyn's hand. "Here's my number." He handed her a business card. "Call me if you think of anything new or if you just need to talk and you want to know if I've made any progress.

If I don't answer, I promise I'll call you back as soon as I can. In the meantime you get the news about your grandkids to every media outlet you can. Harass the reporters that come to your door. Make a post on Facebook and Twitter and places like that. Anything to get their faces out there and people keeping an eye out for them."

"Do you really think you'll be able to find them?" Evelyn asked, clutching the card in her hand. Andrei looked between the hope in her eyes and the skepticism in her daughter's.

"I swear it, Evelyn."

Chapter Six

ANDREI had left at the worst possible time to head down to Richmond on a weeknight. Rush hour traffic slowed his progress to a crawl, and by the time he reached the other city, the sun had almost disappeared from the sky, taking what remained of his control over his temper with it.

The small house that Robin had lived in before her death didn't lie in the worst part of Richmond, but the area still didn't inspire much confidence. The neighborhood was surrounded by pothole-ridden, dying shopping centers, railroad tracks crossed behind the park, and the chain-link fence to keep kids from wandering onto them sagged despondently in several places.

The houses on the side of the street were a mixed lot; some showed evidence of care while others had been boarded up. Andrei passed Robin's house, noting the pots of flowers she'd hung on the porch and the recently mowed lawn, though one of her neighbor's was covered in weeds.

He wasn't sure what he'd find there, but he hoped it would be some clue as to why Blake had chosen to kill her now as opposed to any other time. If it had been because of the divorce, why not when she kicked him out? The fact that she took his son out of state might be a possibility, but why disappear beforehand? There were far more questions than answers. But those answers would give him a feel for the man he hunted.

Andrei parked around the corner and strolled around toward the back of the house. It was dark back there. Robin hadn't left one light on in the entire place, which meant either break in and maybe get caught because a flashlight could alert neighbors or wait till the morning.

He couldn't wait. Each delay meant that Dean's killer got farther and farther away.

Andrei slipped through the shadows toward the back door. As he fumbled in his pocket for his lockpicks and small flashlight, the back door popped open with a soft creak, and he felt the soft caress of air against his cheek. Andrei's heart lurched and sped up. A warm murmur filled his ears as he was struck once again by Dean's presence.

"Thanks," Andrei whispered and tugged a pair of gloves on as he ducked under the police tape and shut the back door behind him. The tiny beam from the flashlight revealed an utter disaster. It looked as if Robin had started out neatly packing and organizing before she'd been interrupted. There were boxes stacked with notes on the cardboard stating the contents and the room; other boxes had been torn open, their contents scattered.

"Okay, now what spooked you? Or did somebody else come here looking for clues?" Andrei murmured to himself. He went through the house room by room, looking for anything out in the open, but a quick search revealed nothing. Several times he heard rustling noises, but when he went to investigate the sounds, he turned up nothing. He decided to chalk it up to Dean trying to help him as well before his own nerves stretched too tight.

Andrei returned to the living room and stood in the center, turning around in a slow circle. The worst of the chaos had been in the bedrooms. Clothes left half hanging out of closets and dressers; cabinets ransacked and left open. He hadn't been able to find any trace of violence. Chances were if the police had found any clues, they'd have tagged and bagged it already.

He had the insane urge to break something, to add to the chaos around him by making a little of his own.

He had a big fat nothing. And Dean would be stuck here for an eternity if he didn't get his head out of his ass and track those kids down. Fine, Robin's place had no clues. So he'd use his strengths and go out to talk to people. Blake might've been running drugs, and there were places in the city notorious for that. At least it was a place to start.

Andrei slipped out the back door, leaving everything the way it had been. The hairs on the back of his neck lifted, and he whirled around, reaching for the gun at the small of his back. An old man stumbled back with a squawk of surprise.

He caught the man's arm before he fell down and hurt himself, and gave him a moment to steady himself before releasing him. "What do you think you're doing?" the old man blustered, his bushy brows drawing together in a fierce glower. His sparse hair was pure white, and liver spots marred his skin. He looked like a bag of bones spit out of a graveyard. "I've called the cops already. You leave her alone. You can't keep coming around here sneaking about like this."

"I'm not who you seem to think I am," Andrei replied in a calm voice, noting the lights now blazing at the house next door. "I'm a private detective."

"That's what the other fool said," the old man snorted, and Andrei froze in the act of reaching for his wallet. "Perverts, that's what you all are. Peeking through windows at a woman with her babies."

"Gramps!" Andrei looked over to see a boy in his midteens heading toward them, hair flopping in his face. "Are you nuts? The doc's gonna kill the both of us."

"I'm fine." The old man tried to bat his grandson's hands away as he found himself steered toward his own house. "That doctor doesn't know what he's talking about. Call the police. I caught this man breaking into Robin's place. He's made a wreck of it. Poor woman's going to be so upset."

"Here, let me help," Andrei said and took the old man's other arm as they guided him over the uneven ground between the houses. He must not have heard what happened to Robin, and the pleading look the grandson gave Andrei told him that he wasn't to find out either. "Robin left to go stay with her mother."

"See, Gramps, you don't gotta worry about her no more." They ushered him through the door and got him settled in a comfortable armchair that looked almost as worn out as the man. "Just sit here and I'll bring your meds."

"What's your grandfather talking about?" Andrei asked in a low voice as he followed the young man back to the kitchen. "Was someone hanging around Robin's place?"

"Gramps is nuts. He's always watching out the window and calling the cops for stupid shit." The kid dashed about, gathering water and a bag that rattled with medication. "I'm sorry if he bothered ya. I just left him alone for a minute."

"That's not a problem. So you never saw anything out of the ordinary yourself?"

"I already said that, didn't I?" Now the kid cast him a dirty look as he impatiently pushed too-long hair out of his eyes. "Thanks for helping him, but you gotta go now. He just got home from the hospital, and I've gotta get him settled."

"Two more things and I'll be out of your way. You're doing a good job." Andrei reached into his pocket and pulled out a business card. "I'm Andrei Cuza, and you are?"

"Martin." The kid's eyes widened as he looked at the card. "You weren't fucking around, you really are a private detective. Did Mrs. Olsen really get killed?"

"I'm afraid so. Now if your Gramps says anything else about somebody hanging around, you write down the details and give me a call, okay?"

"What's in it for me?" Martin asked, casting Andrei a shrewd look through his mop of hair.

Andrei looked around the bare kitchen and then at the lines of strain around the boy's eyes and mouth. From the looks of things, it seemed like it was just him and his granddad eking out a living on the old man's Social Security check. Something poked his back, and then Ileana popped up from around the corner of the counter. "Dean says ta give him some cash or else."

Andrei bit his tongue on the retort that came to his lips and pulled out his wallet again. He fished out a twenty only to get another hard nudge in his back. Ileana watched him with a hand over her mouth to hold back her giggles and her eyes sparkled. "He's got a grizzly bear grrr face."

Dean was a bleeding heart sucker. Andrei pulled the rest of the cash out of his pocket and laid it on the counter without a word. It might be the very last time he got to indulge Dean. "Satisfied?" he said to both the kid and Dean.

"Yep." Martin scooped up the money and stuffed it in his pocket. "Call you if Gramps mentions the weird guy at Robin's house. No problemo."

"Just so you know, if there was somebody and it leads us to her killer, there might be a real reward involved." Andrei had the brief impression of Dean's fingers on his hip, a faint squeeze, and then it dissipated. He tried drawing his scattered thoughts back as Ileana fiddled with a coin on the table, making it spin in circles.

"My second question, how well did you know Blake Olsen?"

The kid's eyes immediately shuttered, and he turned away once again, picking up the tray that held his grandfather's meds and water. "He had a bad temper, didn't like Gramps cuz he caused trouble for him sometimes, so mostly I stayed away."

"Do you know where he liked to hang out?"

Martin shook his head and made a beeline for the living room. "Nope. Look, ya gotta go now."

"What about those people he was friendly with? Where could I find them?"

"Try Gilpin Court or maybe Churchill. Now will you go?"

"IT'S so weird, I mean, I knew Andrei was good. Dad said so and it takes a lot to impress him. And he never had to scrounge for a job, but I don't know. I never pictured this." Dean stood across the street and fidgeted as Andrei talked with another group of thugs. It drove him out of his skin to be standing here when Andrei was over there, even though he knew logically that he couldn't do anything if Andrei did get into trouble.

"Those are some very bad men," Ileana whispered, pressing against the back of his leg. It reminded him uncomfortably of Inez, and he wondered what she was doing at this moment. Was she scared and crying for her mama, or did she sleep?

"I know, Poppet." Inez had better be sleeping. It was too late to be up. Speaking of which, Andrei should be in bed himself. It had been thirty-six hours since he'd been shot, and Andrei had barely slept at all in that time. He was going to push himself until he collapsed.

"Make him stop, Dean. He listens to you."

Andrei listened when he wanted to.

"I can't. He tenses up when he senses me near, and the last thing I want is for him to get tense around those dudes. They look trigger happy already. And Andrei's got to be stirring things up with his questions."

Actually, Andrei looked right at home. He hung with those guys with no evidence of any self-consciousness that Dean could see. He'd stopped long enough to grab a hotel and change into his jeans and worn hoodie. Even his posture had changed. Dean had to admit that it looked a little unsettling to see Andrei in this light. No wonder he didn't have any qualms about heading into the Baltimore ghettos.

Dean breathed a sigh of relief, and Ileana bounced around him with a laugh as Andrei broke away from the group and angled down the street toward his mystery van, as Dean had dubbed it.

"Come on, Poppet," Dean said, taking Ileana's hand. "Let's hope he got what he wanted this time. He's been at this for hours." From street corners, to biker bars and back again, Andrei had trolled them all with a relentless persistence. Blake didn't stand a chance.

He lifted Ileana into the van and winked at her. "Do you remember our new game?"

Ileana giggled, her eyes sparkling as she bounced on the seat. "Yep! It's a fun game."

"Good." Dean didn't understand why Andrei couldn't hear him or why when he did manage to make himself heard, all that came out of his mouth were apologies or pleas for Inez to run. At least he could sometimes touch Andrei and on occasion be seen. And Andrei always seemed to know when he came close. As he slipped into the seat next to his partner, Andrei's shoulders tensed, and he half turned toward him. The same torn expression crossed his face as if Andrei both longed to pull him close and push him away.

Dean looked away, his chest heavy and his throat aching. He knew why Andrei reacted that way, but it didn't make it hurt any less. He felt the warm clasp of Andrei's hand against his own, felt the squeeze of his fingers.

"I've got a name, Dean."

Dean drew in a shuddering breath and turned toward Andrei. Even as he opened his mouth, he knew the wrong words were going to emerge again. He struggled against it, fought to say the right ones. "R-run, In—Inez. Run, Inez. R-run s-s-sweetheart. An-An-Andrei, I—I'm s-sorry."

Frustrated, Dean turned away from the stark pain in Andrei's eyes and looked at Ileana. "Why does that keep happening?" Whenever he tried to talk directly to Andrei, to make him hear, the words got all fucked up. He could murmur to himself all he wanted, knowing Andrei wasn't hearing, or talk to Ileana without a hitch.

"Those were your last thoughts." Andrei turned to look sharply at his sister. "It's stuck in a loop. I kept singing Mum's lullaby."

"Well how the—" Dean stopped himself before the curse came out. "How do I make it stop?"

Ileana shrugged and picked at her turtle's shell. "Not sure. I think it gets better once you accept that you're dead."

A shock went through Dean, and Andrei pressed his lips together until they went white. Andrei turned back around and started the van without a word as Dean's thoughts churned. Accept it? He had a hard enough time even acknowledging it, even believing he'd died had been a stretch.

Accepting it would mean facing that it would be a very long time before he could be with Andrei again, or his family. Accepting it would mean giving up his dreams of one day adopting a kid or five and buying a house in a suburb made for families. Dean scrubbed a hand through his hair and stared moodily out the window.

Dean could sense Ileana's unhappiness from the backseat, but when he turned around to reassure her, she had disappeared. He sighed; oh well, he'd cuddle her later on when she showed back up again. It wasn't her fault. He'd asked the question, and she'd given him the honest truth.

At least Andrei looked as if he were heading back to the hotel. It was too late for the bars to be open, and the streets were deserted. Dean still wasn't sure how Andrei had managed to sniff out the last group.

"Are you still there?" Andrei murmured with a faintly embarrassed expression on his face. "I feel like an idiot when people think I'm talking out loud to myself. And I can't tell if you're here or not."

Dean touched his shoulder in silent reassurance. "Go on." Even knowing Andrei couldn't hear him, he was compelled to answer him. He tried to summon up a smile, though Andrei continued to stare straight ahead. But he tensed when Dean touched him, and he heard something, even if it wasn't words he could understand.

"Okay, so we know Blake Olsen is the man we want. He's the missing kids' father, so that might buy us a little time, but I'm not one of those who believes they're safe because of that and the fact that he hasn't killed them yet."

Dean crossed his arms and glared out at the night. Every time he thought of Inez and Tristan with that man he got so fucking pissed that the urge to tear Blake into tiny shreds became almost overpowering. The window next to him began to rattle violently, and a gust of wind punched the side of the van. Andrei swerved with a startled shout.

A faint howl arose in the distance, an eerie, alien ululation that somehow managed to convey an unnatural hunger. Not so much words as impressions seared into his brain of a lusting, desperate appetite so depraved it could never be satisfied.

The howl shocked Dean so badly that his anger fled and with it the window stopped misbehaving. "Oh Christ."

"Dean, for godssake, chill out before you drive me off the bridge into the James River."

"Sorry," Dean muttered, clutching the door handle until his heart stopped racing. It was crazy. He shouldn't react this way. He was not a man prone to violence. It was like his mind was still caught in the moment just before he died and he couldn't grasp that extra step between what he had been and what he was now.

Besides, Andrei could be hurt, so it looked like Dean would have to start exercising some control over his emotions. Easier said than done.

Silence settled between them as Andrei drove. Dean was beginning to think he wasn't going to pick up where he had left off when Andrei started to speak again. "Blake disappearing beforehand and hiring a private detective tells me that he really thought this whole thing out, from killing Robin to kidnapping his children. But the timing of the murder and how you got caught up in it makes him dangerously unpredictable."

Dean supposed that made sense. Blake couldn't have been intending to kill Robin along the parkway. He'd lost control and reacted like a rabid animal. He sure as hell had seemed like a rabid animal when he'd come after Dean. There had been no reasoning with him. "So what's the next step, after you've slept for the rest of the night?" Andrei looked positively haggard.

Andrei pulled into the hotel parking lot and stopped the van. He turned toward Dean, his gaze searching the space as he looked right through him. Dean leaned forward and cupped Andrei's cheek, his heart flipping as Andrei closed his eyes and leaned into the touch. "I miss you, Dean," he said in a broken whisper.

Dean couldn't speak past the tightness in his throat. Didn't matter anyway given the circumstances. He didn't know how much Andrei could feel, but he'd take anything. He slid closer, his heart pounding. He paused, his lips just hovering over Andrei's, overcome by the moment. Then he leaned in and kissed him. Andrei stiffened, making a strangled sound in the back of his throat.

He didn't pull away though, and Dean pressed his advantage, stroking his thumb over Andrei's high cheekbone. It wasn't the same. The pressure of lips against lips was fainter, and he could only imagine how it must look from outside the van, but Dean didn't care. It was something, some little bit of contact that he craved so desperately. Andrei responded, his lips parting on a broken sob.

Dean slipped his arm around Andrei's waist, deepening the kiss. The electric sensation and faint pressure transformed into something far more potent and real. Dean could taste him, feel the stubble on his chin rasp against Dean's jaw. He could sense the heat and life inside Andrei, and he craved more.

Andrei sank back against the seat with a soft groan. He looked up at Dean with dazed eyes as Dean straddled him. Tears spiked his dark lashes, and Dean kissed them away, tasting the salt on his lips. It lit a fire inside of him, fed by Andrei's moan as he lifted his lips for another kiss. "Don't stop."

The sound of his voice broke through the haze of passion and need. Dean ran his hand through Andrei's hair. If he had looked haggard before, he looked almost gray with fatigue now. His eyes were dull and his touch weak. Dean opened his mouth to speak, but the words got lodged in his throat.

"No," Andrei protested, reaching feebly toward him as Dean slid off his lap and opened the van door.

Dean caught his hand and kissed Andrei's knuckles. His partner needed to be in bed, passed out for the next twelve hours at least. He manhandled Andrei out of the van, bracing him when he staggered as if he were drunk. What the hell had happened? Andrei had been tired, no doubt, but now it was almost as if he'd taken a handful of sleeping pills on top of the lack of sleep.

Dean guided Andrei up to his room and let him fall across the bed. He took Andrei's shoes off, but his skin crawled at the thought of touching the guns Andrei carried on him. He didn't even have to see them to know they were there. He could sense them at Andrei's ankle and the small of his back, cold and dark. It made Dean's chest hurt thinking about them, and he had to clamp down on his thoughts before he started bleeding again. Andrei did not need that to be the last thing he saw before he slept.

Andrei groaned and fumbled for the holster at his ankle first. He set it on the dresser, gun still nestled inside, before struggling out of his hoodie and the second holster. "Why'd you stop?" Andrei turned sad, tired eyes on Dean, and he was stricken to see a few threads of silver in Andrei's black hair.

"You n-need to sleep, b-babe," Dean said, the words fighting to come out as they tore at his throat. He stripped the rest of Andrei's clothes off down to his boxers and got him under the sheets and blankets. Andrei's hair stood out against the white of the pillows and brought out the dark circles under his eyes. He fell asleep almost immediately, leaving the lamp on by the bedside.

Dean stood next to the bed staring down at him, fear and confusion putting his thoughts into such a tangle that he couldn't unravel them. This had been the outcome he'd hoped for. Andrei clearly wouldn't wake up until late morning at least. Only this was not at all what normally would have happened.

Andrei should have argued with him every step of the way. Dean kicked the dresser, making it thump, and Andrei didn't stir. Frowning, he went to make sure the blinds were shut tight before unplugging the clock and flicking off the lamp. Andrei should've tried to kick his ass for sticking him in bed like an invalid.

Dean sighed and gave in to his own longing. He got naked and crawled into bed with Andrei. A pain ached in his chest that had nothing to do with being shot. A splintered, empty throb that eased a bit as he felt Andrei's arm come around him, the familiar position brought a bittersweet smile to his lips.

He'd figure out later on why Andrei had gone so wonky when Dean had kissed him. Right now, he just wanted to soak in the feel of Andrei's body nestled against his own, of his partner's breath on his neck, and Andrei's leg tangled between Dean's. The memories would have to last him for a very long time.

Chapter Seven

ANDREI woke up with a throbbing in his temples that reverberated through his skull and an ache deep in his bones. He rolled over with a groan, throwing an arm over his eyes. Then memory struck like a lead weight on his body, and his throat closed up.

Dean had been murdered. He was gone and Andrei was on the trail of his killer. When was this nightmare going to end?

Darkness swamped over him, and Andrei turned to bury his face in the pillow. Sleep called with a siren's lure. He craved the oblivion of being passed out and not hurting anymore. Not facing the idea of being alone. He couldn't ignore it. Dean needed him to find those kids, and he needed to shove everything down and bury himself in this investigation. Maybe when Blake bled out himself, Andrei could rest.

He must've gotten thoroughly shit-faced drunk last night because he couldn't remember what had happened after he'd gotten Scott Metcalf's name. He'd meant to see what he could find out about him online and check Dean's credit cards to see if there had been any activity on them. But he must've passed out, and he certainly felt the throes of a hangover minus the bad taste in his mouth.

He opened his eyes and found the room to be near pitch black. The faint line of light around the window said that it was morning. "Fuck." A glance at his watch brought another curse to his lips. Dean had done this to him somehow. He'd slept half the morning away.

"That sneaky cocksucker." Andrei sat up and looked around the room. Dean was nowhere to be seen, but the room had a coffee pot and a packet to brew at least a cup. He ignored the quick sting in his eyes, the twist of his heart, and the ever-present ache. He had a job to do.

After a shower and the coffee, Andrei felt more alert, and memories of last night began to filter through the haze. Dean holding him. Dean kissing him. And what energy he'd had left had disappeared under the blaze of cold fire between them. "When I get my hands on you, Dean Marshall...." Somehow he had been whammy kissed.

Andrei grabbed his laptop, headed across the street to a little café, and ordered more coffee. Just in case Dean showed up, he asked for an omelet too. He didn't actually have to choke it down; if it sat there, it should make Dean happy.

It didn't take him long to check the credit statements, and to his surprise there had been activity on them. If Blake had planned his own disappearance and Robin's murder, he should've been too smart to use the stolen credit cards of a dead man. Andrei continued his electronic searches and discovered that Blake had a juvie record that had been sealed.

As he took a sip of his coffee, the plate with the omelet slid in front of him. Andrei glanced around, but he didn't even see a flicker of Dean out of the corner of his eye. He didn't have to; the napkin on the table fluttered with an eddy of air that gave away his presence. Andrei's stomach rebelled at the thought of eating, so he nudged the plate back out of the way and turned toward his computer screen.

The plate returned and a fork clattered onto it, drawing the attention of a man sitting in the booth next to him. Andrei gave him a weak smile. "I'm not hungry," he said under his breath. "Knock it off, Dean. I've got something here I need to track down."

This time when he turned to his laptop, the lid slammed shut, and the laptop slid off the table onto the booth opposite him. "Hey." Several more diners turned toward him, and the plate began to rattle in front of him, and a wind stirred his hair. His ears hot, Andrei snatched up the fork before it began dancing. "You win," he hissed.

Immediately, calm returned to the table, and Andrei took a bite of the omelet with ill grace. "Christ, you nag worse than a woman," he muttered. He could feel eyes on him from all around. It reminded him uncomfortably of what it had been like as a child whenever Ileana would do something out of the ordinary and remind his clan how he broke the rules by talking to her. All those uncompromising, judging stares. He had to steel himself from shrinking back.

Dean appeared across from him, somehow managing to look both stern and apologetic at once. Andrei's heart lurched at the sight of him as he immediately felt guilty for his irritation. The last time he'd seen Dean this clearly, and not just little scattered glimpses, Dean had been covered in blood. There was no trace of any injury now, much to his relief.

"Was last night real or a product of exhaustion and wishful thinking?"

Before Dean could indicate either way, Andrei's phone rang. He glanced down at the ID, and a tense thrill caught him up at the sight of Justin's name. He wondered if he could con Justin into a little exchange of information.

"Are you calling to check up on me or to give me some news?" Andrei asked, leaning back from his half-eaten plate. Dean ignored it, his eyes intent on Andrei's face as if he was just as hungry for news.

"Where the hell are you?"

"The Pancake House, having a very late breakfast. Where are you?" Andrei handed the plate to the waitress as she came by, and ignored Dean's glare. He'd eaten half, far more than he'd intended.

"In Baltimore, where you're supposed to be. I thought you were going to St. Mary's."

"I did, and Dean's mom wants to know when you're going to release him." Andrei couldn't bring himself to say more, not with Dean sitting right across from him. He felt bad enough about leaving the details for Dean's funeral in her hands, even if she had insisted.

"As soon as I know, I'll call you." Justin's voice went from testy to resigned. "Since I know you're not doing what I asked you to do, do you have anything for me?"

"As a matter of fact, I might." Andrei retrieved his laptop, his hand tingling as Dean touched it. "Somebody used Dean's credit cards yesterday. They bought a shitload of baby goods, kid's stuff, drew out cash, and no activity since then. I'm about to e-mail everything to you."

"We'll catch this guy. With the mistakes he's making, we'll have him before you know it."

Justin had to be operating under the assumption that it was a random killing for money, and Andrei didn't know how to tell him that he knew the identity of the real killer. Justin would never believe in ghosts or in anything he couldn't see or touch for himself. Besides, Andrei needed to find Blake first.

"Keep me in the loop, Justin. Whatever you find, I want to know."

"I will, now are you going to tell me where you are?"

Andrei hesitated as he brought up one of the programs he used to run background checks. "I'll tell you if you promise to look into a name for me. Scott Metcalf. He'd most likely be in Richmond. He might drive a Ford sedan, older model, and he might have a private investigator's license."

"Dammit Andrei, you shouldn't be in Richmond. Come home."

"I promise you I will, once I track this guy down. It's important, Justin. He may have been sniffing around Robin Olsen's place before she died. A neighbor saw him a few times."

"And you didn't report this to the police down there?"

"I'm not a complete imbecile," Andrei growled. "The neighbor did, but he has a reputation for calling the cops about every little thing that happens in the neighborhood, so I don't know if they took it seriously or not. Maybe he's just senile, but it won't hurt to look into it."

There was a long silence on the other end, and Andrei held his breath until Justin grudgingly spoke again. "You're right, it can't hurt. I'll see what we can dig up, and you get your ass home."

Andrei didn't dignify that with a response. He hung up the phone, ordered more coffee, and buried himself in his research. Dean had disappeared sometime during the conversation. He had to be really gone this time, because there were no more strange happenings.

What if that had been the last time? Andrei swallowed hard. He was never going to get over the ache of missing him.

"ILEANA," Dean called as he searched among the makeshift tables and awnings of what looked to be some kind of small fair. She had to be somewhere around here, or he wouldn't have been drawn to this place when he'd thought of her. Wherever this place was, it had to be pretty far from Andrei, because he could only sense him dimly. It was almost as if he had a tether to his partner, a silver thought, attenuated by the distance between them.

Dean wandered down the booths, all of them manned by people who bore more than a passing resemblance to Andrei. They had his black hair, golden skin, and sharp, hawklike features. It made him uncomfortable to think he walked among the same people who had abandoned Andrei as a teenager. But where else would Ileana have gone if not back home?

He spied a flash of red and yellow between several women who crowded around some glass cases that held jewelry. "Ileana?"

The little girl turned around to him, her face a tragic mask of heartbreak. Dean felt a little pang of empathy and held out his arms to her. Ileana ran to him without hesitation, and as he lifted her, she wound her arms around his neck. "What is it, Poppet?" Dean asked, smoothing a hand down her dark braids. "What's got you so upset? Last night? You didn't mean anything by it."

Hot tears wet his neck as Dean carried her over to the mess of vans parked behind the tents. He found a partly uncluttered picnic table and sat down with her. "You an'… an' Andrei are m-mad at me," Ileana hiccupped, the last part coming out as a wail.

"No, we're not and if you'd stuck around, we could've told you that." Dean sat her back and dug in his pocket for a bit of tissue so he could wipe her eyes. "You were honest with me. I'm just having a hard time admitting that I'm going to have to give up everything." Even now he couldn't say he was dead out loud. It just didn't sound sane.

"Everything's different," Ileana said miserably, laying her head on his shoulder. "I don't understand. Papa's got white in his hair, and Andrei and Sergey have gotten bigger, but I'm still small. And nobody wants me around anymore. Not even Andrei. He doesn't want you around anymore either. I thought he loved us."

Dean laid his cheek on her hair and rocked her gently. "He does want us around, very much, but he wants us to be safe and happy more. That is love, Poppet. He knows how much it upsets you to see everything change and not know why. Maybe we're really not supposed to be here." And that hurt to admit, but it seemed like every time he turned around he was smacked in the face with that truth.

As soon as the words left his mouth, Dean sensed the change in the atmosphere. He shut his eyes and held tighter to Ileana. If he didn't see the portal to the other side, he wouldn't have to refuse, right? It wouldn't count against him.

"Why did you stay?" Was the whole world littered with spirits wandering about? He hadn't seen any others. Or maybe he just hadn't recognized them.

"Andrei needed me. Who else was gonna take care of him and make sure that he ate or held him when he was scared or upset so he could go to sleep at night? And who was I gonna play with? He was my best friend."

Dean blinked back tears. Boy did that sound familiar on every single point. A gleam of light caught his eye, and he turned his head to see a door to one of the vans aglow. He turned his back on it as it started to open, and gave Ileana a hard hug. "I have a few questions. You think you can answer them for me?"

Ileana cast him a wary glance through red-rimmed eyes. "Maybe. What kind of questions?"

"Questions about what it's like to be a ghoulie-ghostie," Dean said with a grin and tapped her on the nose. "You're the ghost specialist around here."

"I am?" All traces of unhappiness vanished as her little face became animated. "Is that kinda like being a princess of the ghosts?"

"If that's how you want to look at it, then sure," Dean said with a chuckle. "Okay, first question. Can you help me and Andrei find the missing kids? You seem to move about a lot easier than I do. Maybe if I were to find a picture for you, you could...." He trailed off as Ileana shook her head.

"Neither of us can unless we're tied to them. Most of the ghosts I met were tied to a place or to someone they loved lots and lots. We could walk around and look for them, but I don't know where to start looking. After we found them, then we could get a taste of their energy. That would help us find them again. That's how I found you. You and Andrei have been together so long that I learned you. I knew Andrei liked you lots, so I didn't want you to get lost."

Well, that had been a long shot at best. "What do you mean, a taste of their energy?"

"You give them big hugs, and... I don't know... you taste them. Sometimes it makes you hungry, but you don't want to taste too much 'cause then they fall down. Weird huh? But after you've tasted them, you could always find them."

Sometimes Ileana's answers were too confusing. "Okay then, next question. Andrei sees you a lot more clearly than he does me. And he can talk with you and even touch you. You're more... solid to him, I guess is how I would explain it. Is that all because I'm still adjusting to being...." *Dammit, Dean, it's just a word.* "To being, you know...."

"Dead?" Ileana offered.

"Yes, Poppet, because I'm dead." There, that hadn't been so bad. Dean swallowed around the tightness in his throat.

"I dunno. I think it's both your fault. It's like you're both trying to do things different and can't...." Ileana's face screwed up into a grimace of concentration. "It's like you can't meet. He's moving that way, and you're moving this way. And you're waving at each other from far away."

Dean supposed that made sense, only he had no idea how to get them synced up so he could communicate with Andrei. If he had only a limited time left with him before having to say good-bye, he didn't want it filled with frustration.

It was a sinking realization. He was going to leave Andrei behind. His heart rebelled at the thought, but he knew he couldn't handle sitting back and watching Andrei get old on him. Or move on. And Andrei wouldn't be able to move on if he lingered, and that wasn't fair either. None of it was fucking fair, and it filled him with an impotent helplessness that made him want to pound his fists on something.

Being around Ileana though forced Dean to see that Andrei's fears for him were very real. And he knew Andrei well enough to know he'd blame himself for Dean's unhappiness. Even if Dean made the decision to stay on his own. Maybe there was some way he could take Ileana with him so Andrei didn't have that burden on his soul anymore. Then neither he nor Ileana would be alone, and Andrei wouldn't be either, not if Dean knew his family.

They wouldn't abandon him like Andrei's had. He watched some of the people at the booths and wondered which one of them was Andrei and Ileana's mum and dad. Anger surged hot and potent inside of him, and the sky around them darkened. Tent flaps gusted in the sudden strong breeze.

Once again a howl rose and then yipped sharply in the distance. The cries carried with it the sounds of gnawing on flesh, hungry moans that brought to mind maggots and fetid rot. The unnatural shriek, the way the ravening sounds sent icy tendrils of fear into the deepest part of him, made Dean shudder. The sound came from far away, but the impression of it had crawled, squirming into his brain like worms in the earth.

Ileana straightened with a cry of fear, and her stuffed turtle tumbled to the ground. She fisted her hands in Dean's shirt and shook him. "Stop it! You'll call the Jackal Wraiths! Please, Dean," she sobbed, looking around wildly. "Stop it."

Dean tamped down his anger, and the sky brightened again. Most of the fair shoppers had continued to go about their business, but one or two looked in their direction, concern darkening their expressions. He couldn't really be affecting the sky outside of this limbo world, but somehow they had sensed it anyway.

Dean drew in a shaky breath, trying to dispel the sense of wrongness that clung to his skin even after the sounds had disappeared. "What're you talking about, Ileana. What're the Jackals?"

"They hunt us. Those of us left behind. They're drawn to anger. The stronger the anger, the easier it is for them to find us. Once they catch your scent it's almost impossible to lose them."

Was this threat real or just the figment of a little girl's frightened imagination? Dean thought of those howls and shuddered again.

"Ileana, what happens when they catch us?"

She clutched at his shirt, terror on her face as she looked around. "Mum's looking for me. I gotta go."

"Oh no you don't, not this time." Acting on instinct, Dean pulled her closer and wrapped her up in his arms. "Stay with me, Poppet."

He glanced over and saw a woman stalking in their direction, her lips tight with anger. He gathered up Ileana and hurried away. She may be human and alive, but there was something menacing about her. "Who's that?" he whispered in Ileana's ear as he carried her into the crowd of shoppers.

"Mum. She's got the sight. Andrei doesn't like me coming here because she once tried to get Father Gregor to banish me."

Dean didn't have any idea what she was talking about, but he could always ask Andrei when he ever figured out how to talk to him. "Okay, you were explaining those Jackal Wraiths to me. It sounds like they're important, so you'd better finish telling me. What happens to us if they catch us, and how do you know when they're coming?"

Ileana trembled in his arms and pressed her face against his neck. "They eat us," she said in a barely audible whisper that made the hairs on Dean's neck stand up.

Dean set her down once they emerged on the other side of the fair. He wanted to dismiss this as just the imaginings of a child, but his instincts warned him against that. He shook Ileana's shoulders gently. "Why didn't you ever tell Andrei about them?"

"Because they can't see him. And I was afraid if I told him the Jackals would know and would eat Andrei too. 'Cause you know, Andrei gets super mad sometimes."

There had to be another ghost Dean could talk to, one who had been old enough when they died that they could reason better. It all sounded like a child's made-up story, but Ileana's fear was very real, and Dean had seen enough weird shit in the last couple days that he was ready to believe anything. How much of her fears were drawn from those creepy howls over hard facts?

"Do you know of anybody who can tell me more about the Jackal Wraiths? Somebody we can talk to?"

Ileana's brows knit together. "I can take you to *Puri Daj*, but she won't like you."

"I can deal. Who is she?"

"She's Old Mother. She's like my grandmother only far, far older. She was grandmother to my clan back when we still roamed the Old World."

Okay, so a couple-hundred-years-old gypsy. That would mean she'd be extra hidebound and set in her ways, but it also meant that she would really know all those rules about limbo that Dean needed to know. Andrei spoke sparingly of his life before he met Dean, and what he had told him let Dean know that this woman would not want to speak to him at all.

"Is there anyone else we can talk to? This world has got to be full of ghosts."

Ileana shook her head. "I can only visit and talk to family."

Family. That gave Dean an idea. "She's not going to like me because I'm an outsider."

"*Gadje*." Ileana hugged him around his waist. "But I don't think of you like that."

Dean hugged her back. "I know, so you'll just have to convince her I'm family. If you can see me, then I must be, right?"

"You're so smart." Ileana's face lit up. "You are family, which means you're in her book, and she can't argue against that. Doesn't mean she'll be nice, though."

"Like I said, I can handle that. How do we find your Old Mother?"

Ileana slipped her hands in Dean's. "Close your eyes and think of me super, super hard. No peeking 'til I say."

Dean did as she said and concentrated on Ileana, the feel of her tiny, warm hands, how expressive her eyes were when she was sad or happy, the chiming sound of her voice. He felt a lurch and closed his eyes tighter. Ileana's hair smelled like sunshine and flowers. He pictured her sundress with its panels of red and yellow as everything around him seemed to spin with the disorienting whirl of a very drunken stupor.

"We're here!" Ileana crowed. "You can open your eyes now."

Dean fell to his knees, his stomach heaving in spasms—at least it was empty. That was the only plus. He'd be the only ghost in the history of the world to upchuck. How frickin' embarrassing was that?

"Dean?" A hand shook his shoulder. "Dean, are you okay?"

He opened one eye, drawing in a shuddering breath when he saw solid ground. "Ileana, I love you, I really do, like my own sister. Don't ever do that to me again."

"Don't be silly." Ileana laughed like he'd said something hilarious. "Come on, it's going to take a long time to make *Puri Daj* say it's okay to talk to you."

She had a point, and Dean wanted to get this over with so he could get back to Andrei as soon as possible. He looked around in confusion at the collection of campers, vans, and mobile homes. In their midst stood an old-fashioned painted wagon, complete with a wagon tongue for hitching horses.

"Is that where she is?" he asked as he pulled himself back up and pointed to the wagon.

"Yep, she has to follow her book. She's been here so long that all of her other ties have been destroyed. That's the only one left, and she can't go far from it."

"Ileana, you're not making much sense. What does a book have to do with anything?" Dean asked as he took her hand.

"You're tied to Andrei; some spirits get tied to places like the house they lived in or objects they loved. All of Old Mother's children died forever ago, and her real *vardo* was destroyed. All she has left is her family Bible. Even that was damaged when the Nazis tried to burn it."

Dean found himself fascinated by the history as Ileana tugged him toward the ornately wrought wagon. No, *vardo*, that's what Ileana called it, and he remembered Andrei using the word too. He would've loved to have the chance to examine it in closer detail, but Ileana had already scampered up the steps.

"Wait. What happens if a spirit loses all of their ties?"

Ileana gave him a blank look and then shrugged. "I don't know. Nothing's gonna happen to Andrei."

Dean bit back everything that he wanted to say before he scared Ileana or made her cry. He needed to find a way to take her with him when he passed on. The thought of her wandering around alone, without any ties, scared him almost as much as it did Andrei.

Ileana paused with her hand poised to knock on the door. "Now remember, don't let her hurt your feelings, 'kay? She's jus' old. She don't mean all the things she's gonna say."

Dean had no doubt the woman would mean every word, and he didn't give a flying fuck what she said, just as long as he left with the answers he needed. He winked at Ileana and gave her hand a gentle squeeze. "I think I can handle it, Poppet, just as long as you don't stop holding my hand."

Chapter Eight

ANDREI smelled the sickly sweet rot of death as soon as he let himself in through the apartment door. He cursed under his breath and stuck his lock picking tools back in his pocket. Interrogating Scott Metcalf would not happen in this lifetime. The man's body lay on the couch, hands, feet, and mouth duct-taped together. His skin was gray, spattered with blood and worse.

It was hard to tell if he'd been worked over or not before he died. Whoever had killed him had shot him in the face. Andrei used the tip of a pen to ease up the man's shirt. Contusions mottled his stomach and along his ribs. Andrei let his shirt fall back into place. He'd bet good money the killer had been Blake Olsen. The timing fit too well. This man had been dead for at least a couple of days.

"Looks like you took the wrong job," Andrei said under his breath as he scanned the room. He had to make it quick before either Dean or Ileana came looking for him. There were some things that they shouldn't see.

After a few minutes of searching, he found Scott's laptop under a newspaper and a half-empty pizza box. Flies buzzed unpleasantly, darting about as he powered it up. He'd dearly love to take it with him so he could do a thorough search, but he'd have to live with what he could download onto a flash drive. He was pushing Justin's patience with him enough.

Old superstitions crept into his thoughts as he waited. Andrei muttered a prayer for the man's soul and kissed the crucifix around his neck. Blake had abandoned Scott like this, just as he'd abandoned his wife and Dean on the side of the road. There would be quite a few spirits waiting for him, demanding recompense when Blake met his due.

Andrei did a quick search of the dead man's hard drive and downloaded the folders onto his flash drive. Justin had told him that Scott had several priors, both for breaking and entering and for forgery. Andrei banked on there being something in these files that might lead him to Blake. His skin crawling, Andrei finished what he had set out to do and shut down the computer again.

A quick look around the rest of the apartment didn't yield that much more information. The man had the right equipment for forging documents, so it was a fair bet that Blake was running around with a new identity.

Andrei paused in front of the dead man. He itched to cover him with a blanket, to give him at least that much respect for the dead whether the man deserved it or not. He didn't know him, so he wasn't in a position to judge. Covering him would fuck up the crime scene, and he'd already interfered enough. The best he could do was call the cops when he left with an anonymous tip.

"I'm sorry, man," he murmured.

The man's face had been destroyed. To shoot someone in the face like that when they were bound and helpless, that took some serious rage. What had this man done to make Blake hate him so much? He'd been beaten pretty badly before he'd died; whether it was to get information or just because, Andrei didn't know. Andrei could understand killing a man that represented a loose thread. Blake couldn't afford to leave Scott behind when he could point the cops in his direction. But this display of sadism had Andrei fearing for the kids' safety. He'd believed Blake wouldn't kill his own kids; now he wasn't so sure.

It was just one more incentive to hunt the bastard down as fast as he could. A man who did something like that had to have a past. His sealed juvie record and what had been done to Metcalf gave Andrei some idea of what that past could hold.

Andrei slipped out of the apartment again, and his skin stopped crawling after he shut the door on the body. At least there was still no sign of Dean. He had no idea where his partner had disappeared to, and Andrei hoped it stayed that way until he left the area. Dean wouldn't be happy to see the kind of neighborhood Andrei was in; he hadn't missed the worried look on Dean's face last night when he'd caught a glimpse of him or the way that Ileana had attached herself to him.

It warmed him a little inside to realize that the two people he loved most in his life were actually getting a chance to know each other.

Andrei pulled out the disposable phone he'd bought and left an anonymous tip as he reached the van. Adrenaline still pumped through him, giving him energy despite his lack of sleep. He wasn't sure how many hours he'd gotten last night, and coffee would only last him so long. Andrei pulled his thoughts away from that. He did not want to think about going to bed alone.

Besides, he still had to find Blake's dad and get the man to talk to him. The drive didn't take long and took him over the river into a middle-class neighborhood. There was no answer at his house, and Andrei debated whether to confront the man at work or not. Urgency made the decision for him.

Andrei slid his gun into the glove compartment and locked it up before making his way inside the bank. It was one of the nicer ones with polished floors, armed guards, and a petite woman who greeted him with a smile.

"I want to speak to your bank manager, Mr. Olsen, regarding an important business matter," Andrei said, and after several minutes of insisting, he found himself ushered into a well-appointed office.

"May I help you, Mr....?" Richard Olsen had the same pale blond hair that his son had, only silvering at the temples. His jaw was long, tapering to a point at his chin, and his gaze was sharp as he took in Andrei's appearance before narrowing his eyes in distaste.

"Andrei Cuza," he replied, holding out his hand. After a moment, Richard shook it and with an air of resignation, gestured him toward a chair.

"How may I help you this afternoon? Are you looking to open up a new account?"

"I'm with a small private investigation firm in Baltimore. I'm looking for your son, Blake. I understand he's been missing for a few months now."

"I don't know where he is. I haven't seen him." The man's eyes slid to the side as he picked up a stack of papers. "Now if you'll excuse me, I have some work to attend to."

"Not just yet." Richard Olsen knew something, and Andrei refused to let up until he got some information. "Were you aware, Mr. Olsen, that your daughter-in-law had been murdered?"

Olsen's eyes hardened as he reached for his phone. "That woman is no longer any relation of mine. She took off, taking my son's kids with her. If you don't leave now, I'm calling security."

Andrei rose, took the phone, and set it back down in its cradle. "You don't want the scene I'll cause out there. I'm only asking for a few minutes of your time. Your grandkids are missing, and Inez saw her mama get shot," he said in a cold, hard voice. The man flinched, and Andrei knew he scored a hit. "Do you know why your son had Robin tailed?"

"She had no business leaving him and taking his kids as well. Blake always wanted a son, and she quit and walked away from him as soon as she became pregnant with Tristan, just like his mother. It wasn't right. Some may have said that he hung onto her a little hard, but you can't blame him. A man has a duty to hold onto what's his."

Like hell Andrei couldn't place full blame on Blake. He knew all about how it felt to have a mother up and leave, but Blake still had had his dad at least. Though, with the anger in the other man's eyes, that probably hadn't been a good situation. Still he couldn't imagine hunting down and terrorizing Dean if he had ever decided to leave him. That wasn't love… it was ownership.

"He'd never hurt those kids." Olsen believed that, it was clear in his expression, and that eased Andrei's mind somewhat.

"What about Robin?"

"No, of course not." Once again the man's eyes slid away. "My son's a good man, whatever you think. That bitch broke his heart, and he up and left. He didn't have anything to do with her death or their kidnapping. You just leave him alone. All he wants is to put the pieces of his life back together again."

"So you don't think he's dead like everyone else seems to?"

Rage flared in Olsen's eyes, and his voice rose. "I didn't say that. You're putting words in my mouth. I don't know where Blake is. I don't know if he's okay or not. I haven't heard from him in months."

"He has a history, doesn't he? Of hurting women." Andrei threw that out there in the hope of getting some confirmation, another bit of the puzzle that he could give Justin. "He roughed up girlfriends who tried to break up with him."

Olsen's face turned white then red as his mouth thinned into a hard line. "Those damn records were supposed to be sealed. You can't use that against him. Those girls lied about my son."

The door opened and the petite woman from the front stuck her head in. "Is everything okay, Mr. Olsen?"

"Yes, everything's fine. Please show Mr. Cuza out." Olsen gathered his composure and shot Andrei a hard look, daring him to make a scene. "We're done here."

"Of course, thank you for your time." Andrei turned to go and then paused, giving Richard a hard look of his own. "If you hear from your son, you might want to tell him that his ex-wife was murdered and his kids are missing." Richard paled as the woman gasped. "I'm sure that him being a good dad and all he'd want to know."

He left, leaving Richard Olsen sputtering behind him. Okay fine, time for the next plan. He needed to get his hands on the man's cell and house phone. Sooner or later Blake would call him, and Andrei wanted to hear and record every minute of those conversations. He didn't care if the evidence got thrown out in court or not, just as long as Blake paid in the end.

Without a thought, his hand drifted to his cell phone to text Dean his whereabouts. He often did that when an investigation shifted him from one location to another. It kept Dean from worrying too much. He froze and then started the van with a soft curse. Time to kill that habit.

THE woman who glared out at them from the wagon had the most wizened face Dean had ever seen. Her skin was deeply lined, and the hair that peeked out from her folded, colorful kerchief was a snowy white. Her gaze was no less keen though, no matter her age. "You, get inside," she snapped, pointing a gnarled finger at Ileana, and then the eagle-eyed gaze turned on him, and she spat, just barely missing his foot. "And you, leave now."

"He comes too, Old Mother. He's family," Ileana replied, sticking her chin out at a stubborn tilt. "And he needs your help."

Dean had no idea what the protocol was in a situation like this, but he figured one of his charming smiles would fall flat, so he opted for a nod instead and hoped that his nerves didn't show. The old woman creeped him out.

"No *gadje* belongs in the family. Who would allow such a thing?" Old Mother's eyes widened in incredulity, and she grabbed Ileana's arm, hauled her inside, and slammed the door in Dean's face.

Dean grabbed ahold of his temper and shoved the door open, forcing himself inside. The old woman turned away from where Ileana cowered in the corner, and her expression grew dark. "Don't you dare lay another hand on her," Dean snarled, stepping between the old bitch and Ileana. "I don't care what you think about me, but she's your great whatever granddaughter, and you'll be nice to her."

The wagon rattled ominously, the air shivered, and Dean could feel the force of her rage, far more potent than his own had been. Ileana moaned and pressed her face against Dean's side. "Please *Puri Daj*, please don't bring the Jackal Wraiths to us."

The woman controlled herself with an obvious effort. "If you don't wish to be gobbled up, then leave. I'll not tolerate an unclean man in my home."

"But he's family, I swear it," Ileana said. "I went to his wedding, so I saw it with my own eyes."

The old woman gasped and sat down, clutching her skirts in a white-knuckled grip as Dean winced. "Actually, Ileana, it was a commitment ceremony. In the eyes of the state, they didn't consider that a wedding." Even if his heart said different.

"You said the words to each other in front of a holy man," Ileana argued. "That counts and I bet you're in Old Mother's book."

"No daughter would go against her father's wishes and marry a *gadje*," the old woman snapped.

Ileana's brows drew together in confusion. "What daughter? Dean married my brother, Andrei. And I know he's in your book even if they kicked him out of the clan, 'cause you showed me."

The woman turned white, then red, and she shook her fist at Ileana. "You should not say such vile things, Ileana."

"Look, I get it," Dean cut in before another argument could start. "You're older than the damned dinosaurs and your brain is stuck in your own time, so I'm not going to take offense at that. I'm not working on a lot of time here, so the sooner you answer my questions, the sooner I can stop polluting your trailer."

Dark eyes narrowed and her voice quavered with constrained fury when she spoke. "Ileana, you will leave and you will take him with you. Don't return until his taint is gone."

"You promised that you'll always help family, and we need your help," Ileana insisted. "You promised."

Dean watched the struggle on the old woman's face and felt a touch of pity for her. It must be overwhelming to be caught between all the traditions and world you knew and one that kept changing beyond your understanding. To have one vow contradict another. Is that what waited for him if he stayed?

The old woman's gaze shifted to the corner, and when Dean looked as well, he saw the book. One of those old heavy tomes of a Bible, the cover cracked and blistered by fire, the pages singed. Dean longed to ask how it had survived the Nazi's fires, but that may get a little too personal for the Old Mother to answer.

"Just check your book. If I'm in there, give me an hour of your time. If I'm not, I'll leave. I promise," Dean said in a calmer tone. Ileana could just ask the questions without him. He didn't hold out much hope that he'd actually be in the book, but this wrangling back and forth got them nowhere. "It does record every birth, death, and marriage of your descendants, right?"

The woman pressed her thin lips together, and her eyes were hard, little black coals hot with anger. "I will check and then you will leave, *gadje*. Do not return again."

"I swear it," Dean said and mentally crossed his fingers, praying that Ileana knew what she was talking about.

The old woman stalked over to the book and caressed the cracked and scorched leather with gnarled hands. "Ileana, if I remember aright, you are the daughter of Emil and Mariana Cuza, yes?"

"Yes, Old Mother. I'm the eldest. I have two younger brothers, Andrei and Sergey." Ileana walked over to the woman as she opened the pages with reverent fingers. "Father Gregor baptized us all."

"Yes, yes," the woman muttered with impatience in her voice. "I know where to find you now." She paused on a page and ran her finger down the entries. Dean inched closer, intrigued in spite of himself. He didn't really think he'd be in there, but still… this was a list of all of Andrei's family and that alone drew him.

The woman froze at the same time Dean saw the entry. *Andrei Michel Cuza b. March 10, 1974 m. Dean Patrick Marshall.* And there below was the date of their commitment ceremony, June 2, 2001. They'd just had their ten year anniversary not two months ago. Dean grinned, uncaring of the stinging in his eyes as Ileana broke out in a whoop of delight.

"See, I told you!" She threw her arms around Dean's waist and squeezed him tight. "You are family."

Dean hugged her back, his mind racing with excitement. Just wait till he told Andrei. Laws may come and go, but it seemed as if the universe at least had a sense of balance. Or at least, a wicked sense of humor.

"I know it wasn't the answer you wanted," he said to the woman gripping the book in her white-knuckled hands. "But we had a bargain, and Ileana told me that you swore to help family, so I know you'll speak true."

"Three questions," she spat, glaring up at him, her entire body stiff with indignation. "I'll answer three questions true and give you the answers I know. Is that a deal?"

"It is, but only if you agree to give me as much detail as I want. You can't try to foist me off with quick, pat answers. I'm just as anxious to be out of here as you are to have me gone. So the quicker we can get through this without games, the happier we'll both be."

"Agreed," the old woman said after a moment of struggle on her face. "We can talk outside. You've been in my home long enough."

Dean resisted the urge to roll his eyes as she swept regally out of the wagon, Ileana skipping behind her. Oh well, it was too stuffy in here anyway. Dean couldn't imagine a whole family dwelling in such a tiny space.

They sat waiting on a log nearby, the woman looking off in the distance, her eyes fixed on some faraway spot as she ignored the sight of him. Dean stretched out on the ground, another log against his back. Crazy old bat. If he didn't need answers so bad, he'd be content with just leaving her.

"First question, what are these Jackal Wraiths Ileana told me about? The creatures that eat ghosts and follow strong emotion. Are they real and can I fight them? And yes, that counts as one since it's all on the same topic." Dean wouldn't let her squirm out of her oath.

The old woman started and looked at Dean with frightened eyes, all trace of hostility gone. She hadn't expected that question. She slid a protective arm around Ileana and leaned toward him. "The Jackal Wraiths... they are very real. If you've attracted their attention, you must leave. Now. Before you put her in any more danger."

The last word cracked like a whip, not out of hate this time, but true fear. He'd been hoping that the howls he'd heard had been brought on by a combination of Ileana's own imagination and the ordeal he'd been through.

"I haven't and I want to make sure it stays that way." Dean tugged up a piece of grass and twirled it between his fingers in an effort for a nonchalance he didn't feel. His shoulder blades itched as if someone stood behind him with a knife ready to plunge it between them.

"If you keep control of yourself, then you should not have a problem with the Jackals." Old Mother gave Ileana a sharp look. "I've been trying to get this one to understand that for many years now."

"It's hard for her," Dean said, wincing as he thought of all the times Ileana let her feelings run crazy. "She only understands so much. But she seems to think it's mostly anger that gets their attention."

"That is the most potent for them and affects our surroundings the most; the bigger the disturbance, the greater the attraction. Anger and hate will call them the fastest. So have care, young men are often passionate." She sniffed and looked away. "The Jackals are what keep our numbers down. Sooner or later, everyone succumbs."

"What happens if they catch you? There's really no way to fight them?" There had to be a way. Everything had a weakness.

"No. They can only be diverted if stronger prey calls to them." The old woman glowered at him. "Attend to me, and you had better etch my warning into your bones. They hunt in mated pairs and cannot be fought. Once they have a taste of your soul they can follow you anywhere. They slip through cracks in time and show up where you will be. They prolong the hunt purely for the pleasure of the fear it raises in their victims. And once you're done, once you've fought and run past any strength left, they divide you between them and devour you. Is that spoken plainly enough?"

Dean felt the prick of his hair rising on end and the rough wood of the log digging between his shoulder blades as he pressed back against its support. "Yeah, I think I got it. No trying to play hero and keep my temper in check. I think I can manage those. These creatures, can they hurt the living?"

"They hunger for the living, yet cannot touch those whose souls are still attached to their bodies. A living person would have to exist both in the real world and in limbo and their rage and hate would have to be potent enough for them to compromise their soul to attract the Jackals. The only other way the Jackals can touch a living being is if their mind is gone. Madmen leave themselves very open. They don't link with them often because they lose some of their power. I think they'd only do it if it would give them a chance at stronger prey. So your... Andrei is safe. You would be safe if you moved on through your door."

"I can't leave at the moment, but when I do, would it be possible for me to take someone with me?" Dean's gaze slid to Ileana, and the old woman followed as she caught his meaning. Gnarled fingers stroked the little girl's hair, and her expression softened.

"I have heard of such a thing happening only once. I believe it was a success though I cannot say with any certainty." Dark eyes gripped Dean's own. "If someone would try with this one, then they would have my gratitude."

"Try what?" Ileana asked.

A quick shake of the old woman's head warned him, and Dean gave Ileana a wink. "Try and keep you out of trouble, Poppet."

She grinned and came over to him, wiggling into his arms. "I'll try harder not to be trouble, and then we can stay together, right?"

"If I have anything to say about it, I'll keep you right by me. I don't mind that you wander off, you know this world better than me. But can you hear me when I call to you?"

Ileana shot the old woman a guilty glance and lowered her voice. "Yeah."

"Then just come when I call so I don't have to go searching for you. Deal?"

Ileana nodded with a happy sparkle in her eyes and turned her attention back to her stuffed turtle. Dean was grateful for that because he didn't want her paying too much attention to his third question.

"How come Ileana can talk to and touch Andrei as easily as if she were still alive? She told me that the reason why I can't speak to him normally is because I haven't accepted my death." It seemed to get a little easier each time he forced those words out. This time the hesitation didn't grab him by the throat.

The old woman plucked at the fringe on her shawl. "Ileana and Andrei were both very young when she got sick. The young have their heads filled with possibilities, and they're much more accepting of strange things, especially when loved ones are involved. They were able to speak to each other so easily because death had little meaning for them and because they wanted to."

Dean looked down at his hands, absently fiddling with the band on his finger with his thumb. "I know I'm having a hard time accepting it, and I also know that Andrei wants me to go. He's afraid of me being stuck like Ileana."

"As well he should be. Some stay by choice, others out of ignorance, but the consequences either way are far-reaching."

Dean shifted and glanced down at Ileana to make sure she was still lost in her play. "Last night I was able to touch him for a short period...." He trailed off as the old woman's gaze sharpened. "It affected him, he seemed almost drunk afterward."

"Talking to and touching the living is a matter of will, but the living suffer for being touched by the dead. You ask why Ileana can interact with Andrei so easily. After she died and came back, she stuck by his side and her desire was so great that she was able to touch him. Andrei became very ill. Ileana unwittingly took a measure of Andrei's life force. It wasn't until after he recovered that he became immune and was able to touch her back with ease."

"I made Andrei sick?" Ileana turned toward Old Mother.

"Yes, though I doubt either of you remember it after all these years. It takes a significant amount of energy to create that bond so you can touch them at will. Now that you have, Ileana, you do not have to worry about hurting him again. The price has already been paid."

A chill settled in Dean's stomach followed quickly by another wrench of keen loss. Well that explained everything. He'd just have to make sure he didn't touch Andrei again. He wasn't going to hurt Andrei just for the sake of kissing him again, or holding him in his arms. Every time he was tempted, all he had to do was think of Andrei stumbling around that hotel room disoriented and how quickly he'd passed out once his body had hit the bed.

That kiss hadn't been enough of a transfer that he could touch him easily now, so it meant that any more would drain him again. Who knew how much it would take, and Dean was a lot bigger and older than Ileana.

"I understand, thank you." Dean didn't know how much time had passed since he'd left Andrei, but the urge, the need to see him again had become an itch he could no longer ignore. "I know you didn't want to help me, so I appreciate your honesty."

A visible struggle crossed the woman's face, and then she shrugged. "You're family and I stick by my word. You should know that you're not going to be able to stop yourself from being near him, trying to touch and talk with him. You're locked into the feelings and desires you had when you died. Where touching your Andrei was as natural as breathing. You'll forget my words when your old life calls too loud. You won't be able to stop yourself. The only way to protect you both is to move on."

"Understood."

"A moment more," she continued as Dean rose to leave. "I would know. Why do you stay when you know the consequences? You aren't leaving, I can see it on your face. Why not leave now and take her with you?"

"He can't leave," Ileana said, jumping to her feet and clinging to Dean's hand. "He promised he'd stay with me, and Andrei needs us. Don't go, please, Dean."

Dean stroked his hand over Ileana's hair and hugged her to him. "The man who murdered me also kidnapped two kids. Andrei's hunting him down. I need to help find those kids before they're killed too."

"And after, you'll keep your word?"

Dean hated the thought that his staying caused Andrei more pain, that he hurt him physically. It was such an abnormal, backward thought, but he had to face that reality. It wasn't safe for him here, and if walking away gave Andrei some closure and allowed him to heal, Dean would find a way to make himself do it. He gave her a slight nod, and the old woman smiled, holding out her hand to Ileana. "Come child. You will stay with me while Andrei and Dean search for this killer. It is no place for a child."

"But…." Ileana took a step toward her, casting a longing glance at Dean. "When will I see you again?"

"I'll call out your name real loud when it's safe. I promise." Dean knelt down and gave her a hard hug. He'd miss her smiles, but the emotions flying thick and hard between him and Andrei as they wrestled with their grief was no place for her. And he didn't want to take the chance of her seeing something violent. It was coming. He knew it in his gut. "You stay with *Puri Daj* until then."

Ileana went over to her, her slight body reluctant and her dark eyes, so like Andrei's, unhappy. Dean sighed, though he felt a little better when the old woman gave her a smile that he was sure would never be cast in his direction. "You could go with us," he offered, and the old woman looked at him in surprise. "I suppose numbers wouldn't matter."

"Thank you but no. My fate lies in a different direction."

"Why'd you stay?" he asked, unable to help himself.

Old Mother's spine straightened as she shot him a dark look, and Dean felt immediately as if he'd stepped his foot right back into taboo territory. "My children's children needed tending to." And with that she swept back into her home, urging Ileana in front of her, and firmly shut the door.

BACK at the hotel, Andrei brought up the contents of the flash drive with the same tense excitement he always got when he knew he was on the trail of something. The feeling was more intense this time, and his fingers trembled as he worked the keyboard. There had to be something on here that would lead him to that bastard and get those kids reunited with their grandmother. Andrei couldn't forget about Inez and Tristan in his zeal to see Blake pay for Dean's murder.

A flicker out of the corner of his eye caught his attention. "I wondered where you had gone to," he said, turning around. For only a split second, the image remained and then disappeared. Andrei was left with the impression of a woman with angry eyes and wild curls. It had happened too fast for him to get anything beyond that.

Andrei let out a curse on an explosive breath. So Robin was still hanging around too. Just great. Another ghost he could sense, who had answers, who couldn't communicate with him in the way he needed.

"Dammit, Dean, where are you?" Andrei muttered as he turned back to the screen. He hadn't gone this long without at least a glimpse of him since Dean first showed up.

It didn't take him long to find the photographs, hundreds of pictures of Robin and her children at home and around Richmond. More than enough photos to make a young woman paranoid, especially after her ex disappeared. Feeling like she was always being watched and stalked. And more than enough photos to unhinge a possessive man even if he'd hired him in the first place. Some of them had a definite sexual overtone to them. Scott Metcalf had been a sleazy bastard, and it had gotten him killed.

His phone rang, the caller ID reading Justin's name. Andrei hesitated before answering. He did not want to hear another lecture or foist the detective off with bullshit about when he would leave Richmond. But he couldn't take the chance that Justin discovered something new.

"It's me."

"We've got him. The Feds are talking to him right now." Andrei's heart lurched to a stop. "So if you haven't left Richmond yet, get your ass on 95 and come home."

"What?" A tremor rippled through him, and Andrei found himself groping for Dean's hand before the realization of loss flooded through him again. The cops had arrested Dean's killer. It was over with, and Dean would move on. "You've got Olsen?"

"Who? Olsen? Man, you need some sleep, Andrei." Justin's voice turned worried. "Olsen was the other vic, remember? You're mixing shit up."

The sick feeling returned tenfold, and Andrei sank his head onto his hand and fisted his fingers into his hair. They had the wrong man. "No, her husband, Blake Olsen, I'm telling you he's the real killer."

Justin was silent on the other end as Andrei's insides knotted up even more. Fuck, he hadn't meant to say one word about it until he had hard proof to back it up. "Look, man," Justin said in the careful voice someone used when they didn't want to further upset a man who they already thought may be unbalanced. "Come back home and we'll sort it out then."

"Fine, I'm on my way, just tell me this. That guy you nabbed, what did he have to say about the kids?"

"We're still working on it, but by the time you get here, I'm sure we'll have cracked him."

"Yeah, keep telling yourself that," Andrei said and hung up before Justin could respond. Twenty minutes later he was on the highway heading back to Baltimore.

Chapter Nine

ANDREI hovered in the doorway to the house he had shared with Dean, finding it hard to take that last step across the threshold. He had to sometime. He couldn't avoid this place forever. Clutching the manila envelope in his hand, Andrei shifted his overnight bag and laptop on his shoulder and forced himself to enter. It was just a house, a shell, nothing more, nothing to act like a pansy over.

He flipped on a radio to fill the silence and left his bags on the floor of the living room. Still clutching the envelope, he grabbed a bottle of vodka and a glass before sitting down on the couch and setting all three items on the table in front of him.

He was still numb from his argument with Justin. No matter what he had said, no matter the evidence he'd presented or the theories he'd laid out, none of it had been enough to sway the detective. Not when the DA was fully intent on prosecuting the wrong schmuck for Dean's murder and fighting with the Feds over jurisdiction. Fucking politics. God damn them all.

Andrei poured a glass of vodka with a surprisingly steady hand and sat back with his glass, eyeing the envelope as if it were a viper coiled and ready to bite him. As he lifted the glass to his lips, Dean walked through the front door and paused, frowning at him. Andrei's heart stuttered and twisted.

"Just in time," Andrei murmured before tossing back the drink. The vodka flowed smoothly down his throat, though it did nothing to fill the hollow ache inside him. "You might not want to stick around. I think it's going to get ugly."

The furrow between Dean's brow grew as he sat down on the couch next to him with an unspoken question in his eyes. Andrei could see him as clearly this time as he'd ever seen his sister. The only other time he'd seen Dean this solid he'd been kissed breathless. This time his hand shook as he poured himself another glass.

"Politics. That's why I never would've made it in the police force, *iubito*. Fucking politics. I have no stomach for that game. We've got a woman hell-bent on making a public stand against illegal immigration, so they've pounced on the first plausible suspect they had simply because of the color of his skin and the fact that he doesn't have a U.S. citizenship."

Andrei downed that glass too, not looking at Dean. He didn't need to see his expression to know that he disapproved of him drinking like this. "So the case is closed. Your body has been released so your parents can go ahead with your funeral, and they've all but given up on finding those kids. That I agree with. With as long as that sadistic bastard's had them, they're as dead as you are."

Andrei jumped as Dean's fist came down on the table hard enough to make the envelope shift. He ignored the sudden thumping of his heart and set the empty glass down. "I can't be as single-minded as you. I can't push everything aside every second in pursuit of some greater good that will make no difference in the long run. There's always going to be more perverts and murderers and so-called parents who abandon their kids. Life fucking sucks that way." All he had left in him was vengeance. And right now, even that felt so fucking empty.

He had a black hole inside of him, and inch by inch it ate him alive. Dean was dead. It had hit him like a bat to the side of the head when Justin had handed him the envelope. Andrei grabbed it off the table, tore it open, and spilled the contents out onto the polished surface of the table. Keys jangled and a ring bounced and rolled before finally coming to a stop.

Andrei stirred it with his finger, a woven white gold band that matched the one on his own hand. It seemed incredibly sad to him that a man's last moments in life could be reduced to the contents of an envelope. Dean's hand stretched out over his, though for some reason, this time Andrei didn't even feel the brief flutter of a touch.

"Andrei."

The sound of Dean's voice was so soft, a bare whisper that fluttered along all the raw places inside Andrei, a sigh that did nothing to fill the ache. He swallowed around the tightness in his throat and reached for the bottle of vodka again.

DEAN paced along the couch where Andrei had passed out cold. No sooner would Andrei wake up half-sober than he'd find another bottle of something and drink himself into a stupor again. This wasn't mourning, it was avoidance, and it did him nothing but harm. With each minute, Blake got farther away with those kids, and if something happened to them because he'd delayed hunting them down, Andrei would never forgive himself.

Not that Dean wasn't doing some avoiding of his own. Maybe he was single-mindedly fixated on Inez and Tristan and ignoring what Andrei was going through, but dammit he did not know how to comfort him, not when Andrei couldn't hear him, not when he couldn't touch him. He felt the seconds ticking away inside of him. A part of him knew that he was locked on that one moment, that one need, and unable to look toward the future until those kids were found.

He grabbed the pillow out from underneath Andrei's head and thwapped him with it to no effect. Andrei continued to snore; even in sleep his face was drawn with lines of unhappiness. The funeral was tomorrow, and Andrei had not bothered to answer any calls from Dean's family or Justin, or call them back. His mom must be going nuts worrying about Andrei, and that pissed him off too.

Dean would've shook him if he dared touch him. Agitated, he kicked one of the empty bottles, and it hurtled across the room before shattering against the wall. Andrei sat up, groping for his gun as he looked around the room with a bleary gaze. "Who's there?"

He uncoiled himself from the couch, holding the gun in a surprisingly steady hand as he searched the room again. "Dean?"

Instinct overrode conscious thought, and Dean grabbed ahold of Andrei's wrist and pulled the gun from his grip, flipping the safety back on. The thought of Andrei waving around a loaded gun in his state scared the bejeezus out of Dean. "N-need to-to t-talk." He tossed the gun down on the couch.

Andrei gasped, his red-rimmed eyes widening as he took in Dean standing next to him, and Dean dropped his wrist with a surge of guilt. Andrei reached for him as Dean stumbled back out of reach. "Touch me, I know you can." Dean's heart ached at the stark need in Andrei's eyes. "That night in the van, when you kissed me, it wasn't just my imagination. And just now, that wasn't a barely there ghost touch, dammit. It felt real."

Dean shook his head, fighting his own need to hold him, to comfort him. Ever since he'd first met him, when Andrei had been a terrified, heartsick teenager, clutching everything he owned in a single knapsack, Dean hated to see him hurting. Especially if there was something he could do to ease his pain.

"Please Dean, touch me."

"Andrei." Dean struggled to form the right words, to keep the automatic phrases of his death thoughts from emerging instead. "Andrei, I… I can't. I'm sorry. I'm s-s…. Ru-r—" He pressed his lips together to keep the rest of the litany from escaping.

"Bullshit. Fucking bullshit," Andrei snarled and turned away. His hand shook as he reached for a bottle that still had some alcohol left. "Why the fuck are you here, then? Why are you doing this to me?"

Andrei wouldn't look at him as he lifted the bottle to his lips. A week ago his hair had been completely black, and now silver touched his temples and an occasional strand gleamed in his hair. Those hadn't appeared until after they'd kissed, and Dean didn't want to see them get worse just for a moment of passion. He didn't want to almost kill Andrei as Ileana had, even if Andrei didn't remember that it had happened to him as a kid.

It was tempting, he couldn't deny that. Andrei had built up an immunity to Ileana. He could touch her without repercussions now. What would it take for the same to happen for them? What price would Andrei have to pay? It was selfish to even think such thoughts, but to touch him again… to hold him for whatever time they had left….

"I can't, it's not good for you," Dean managed to say without stuttering. He refused to be the incubus to Andrei's victim.

Andrei turned cold, black eyes on him. "You don't get to pick and choose what's good for me. What's healthy for me. You think this is it? Having you half here? I need you to move on for my own sanity, and you fucking refuse that too."

He took a step toward Dean, stabbing his finger in his direction, making the alcohol slosh in the bottle that he still clutched. "I see you out of the corner of my eye every time I turn around. I sense you even when I don't see you, hear the murmur of your voice without words. How the fuck is that good for me?" His voice cracked on the last words, and he turned away to finish the remainder of the bottle.

"Knowing what is going to happen to you if you don't move on?" Andrei whispered. "Watching you hurting and confused and knowing that there is no chance of it getting better for you because you left all your chances behind?"

Dean was very grateful that Andrei only knew the barest part of what could happen to him. If he knew the whole story, he would be freaking out even more.

"I-I will, I s-swear to you," Dean said, the words coming easier for once. "W-when you find In-Inez and T-Tristan, good or bad I'll g-g-go." It was on the tip of his tongue to tell him his plans for Ileana too, but he stopped himself. He didn't know if it would work or not, and he didn't want to raise Andrei's hopes only to have them destroyed at the worst possible time.

Andrei sat down on the couch and dropped his head into his hands. "I can't do this, Dean. First Ileana, then the rest of my entire family, and now you. All the best parts of my life get stolen, and I'm left alone."

Dean closed his eyes as those stark words tore at him. He wanted to hurt somebody as much as Andrei hurt. As much as Dean hurt. No, not somebody, a very specific person, but he forced himself to put Blake out of his mind before the anger built up out of control.

He knelt down in front of Andrei and started to reach out to him before letting his hands fall. He forced the words out through lips that wanted to stutter, concentrating fiercely on Andrei's pain, his need to talk to his partner for the comfort they both would find. "My f-family is not your family, b-babe. They w-won't abandon you. You'll n-never be alone unless you s-s-shut them out. You c-can't k-keep doing this to yourself. You g-gotta start living."

"Please tell me what the fuck I'm supposed to live for," Andrei snarled, lifting his head.

"F-for all those k-kids you've rescued who wouldn't have stood a ch-chance if it wasn't f-for you. For all the ones st-still out there. For Inez and Tristan." Andrei held his gaze before jerking his eyes away. "For m-me."

Dean reached over and scooped his band off the table. He held it in his palm and concentrated a moment, then smiled when it appeared on Andrei's middle finger next to its mate. Andrei rubbed his thumb over it, and when he met Dean's gaze again, some of the bleakness was gone from his eyes. "We'll al-always be a p-part of each other."

"That's incredibly sappy, even for you," Andrei said in a rough voice.

"Yeah, w-well. You can't bl-blame a guy for t-trying." There had to be an easier way to communicate than this. He was getting worn out, concentrating so hard. "You're sc-scaring me. I d-don't want you to do something st-stu-stupid on me, okay?"

Andrei's eyes slid to the gun that Dean had tossed aside. "You mean eat my gun?" A chill settled deep in Dean's bones, and then Andrei shook his head. "No, I'm not the suicidal type. If I was I would've killed myself when I was fifteen."

Dean breathed a sigh of relief and then rose. "G-glad to hear it. Now g-go, take a sh-shower and get cleaned up. W-we need to t-talk."

Andrei held his hand out to him, his eyes eloquent with need. "Join me?"

Temptation tugged at Dean. He'd never been able to refuse Andrei anything he needed, and he longed for it too, the chance to hold Andrei tight again, to steal whatever precious moments they had left together. He pressed his lips against the yes that threatened to come out and shook his head, taking a step back. "I-I c-can't."

Andrei's shoulders slumped, and then his dark eyes flashed as he straightened again. "You can't or you won't?" With that he rose and headed downstairs to the shower in his office instead of the one off their bedroom.

Dean sighed and resisted the urge to follow him. If he did, he knew he wouldn't be able to stop himself from wrapping his arms around Andrei and kissing him until he smiled again. Instead he concentrated, picking up the broken glass and empty bottles in a telekinetic storm of activity. While he was at it, he threw away every last bit of liquor they had in the house, including the bottle of champagne Andrei had bought to celebrate. No need to have the lure within reach.

A sound caught his attention, and Dean looked over to see Andrei standing at the top of the stairs wearing nothing but a pair of soft, worn sweatpants that rode low on his hips and clung to his thighs. He'd taken the time to shave, and his hair was a damp, tangled mess, the silver threads shining even brighter now.

Dean's cock stirred, and he was sure that was just the reaction that Andrei was going for. He loved the way that the thin, soft fabric hugged all the right places. And it was easy to see that he wore no briefs either. Dean groaned. Wicked man. Andrei was hard enough to resist without him actively trying to seduce Dean.

"How is it that you're not stuck saying the same things anymore? Your stuttering isn't as bad," Andrei asked, rubbing the towel over his hair one more time before draping it over the railing. "And I can see you much more clearly than before."

"I've been t-told that my inability to c-communicate with you was b-because I hadn't accepted my d-d-death yet." Andrei paled and Dean felt a stab of regret for saying it so bluntly. They both needed to face the truth, though. They were working on borrowed time. "And you c-couldn't see me or c-communicate with me because you didn't want to. You were b-bl-blocking me out."

Andrei considered that, his head cocking before he moved over to the couch and sank down in a sprawl. "You're probably right about me blocking you." He rested his feet on the coffee table and stretched out long legs as he turned worried eyes on Dean. "You don't blame me, do you? Knowing what you know now. I didn't mean it, I just...."

Dean sat down next to him as Andrei trailed off. "No, I-I understand. I-I wish you'd t-told me about Ileana b-before, though."

"I wish I'd done a lot of things before." Silence fell as Andrei fiddled with their bands with his thumb, first one then the other. "But you wanted to hear about the investigation, right? That's why you're here? To talk business."

Startled that Andrei didn't try to make any moves on him, Dean nodded. "Well that's n-not the only r-reason," he added. "I n-need to be with you until this r-reaches the end. I only left b-because I h-had to get answers about w-what was happening with me. St-straightforward answers. Ileana t-talks in circles."

"Well, I'll fill you in then." Andrei laced his fingers over his hard stomach and closed his eyes. Dean leaned closer, drawn in by the unguarded pose. Instinct had him wanting to slip his arm around Andrei's shoulders to draw him closer. Though they were only inches apart, the fact that Dean refused to close the distance made the gap seem much wider.

"The cops picked up Hector Delgado the other morning on a convenient anonymous tip. He had your credit cards on him, though not your wallet. A search of the vehicle he was in found a woman's purse with Robin's cards and a handgun they're pretty sure will match the ballistics report. Since Mr. Delgado is an illegal immigrant, the DA's all over it, and Justin says his hands are tied. And, though I hate to admit it, the evidence is pretty damning. Either Delgado came across the crime scene and took off with the goods or Blake passed them off to him."

"The h-how doesn't m-m-matter."

Andrei shot him an irritated glance. "It always matters, Dean. I'm not sure if Blake picked Delgado out beforehand and found a convenient scapegoat with him, but either way, I'm pretty certain Delgado has laid eyes on him. If I can get him to verify that Blake is alive, maybe I can convince at least Justin to keep searching."

"So you're n-not g-giving up on those k-kids? You didn't m-m-ean what you s-said earlier?" Anxiety sank its claws into him. Andrei had good instincts. If he believed Inez and Tristan were dead, chances were he was right.

Andrei sighed and sat up straighter. "I'm sorry about that. I was drunk and hurting and so fucking pissed off at everyone, including you, so I lashed out. When we find Blake, we'll find them too. According to Blake's father, he resented having his kids taken from him, especially his son. And he clearly had issues against women. His mom left when he was young, and I wouldn't be surprised if his dad didn't use that as a pressure point on him."

Andrei was still hurting and half-drunk; as long as Dean stuck around he'd never be able to take the first steps toward moving on. That thought filled him with a possessive jealousness. Andrei was his, always had been his, even before he realized how the other man felt about him, how Dean felt about his own sexuality. And the two basic instincts tore at him.

"W-what if I-I hadn't been there? W-what if it was my p-presence that escalated the s-situation? R-Robin might still be alive. You w-wouldn't be alone." Dean dragged a hand through his hair. He'd been so caught up in getting to Andrei, in finding those kids, that he hadn't given himself a chance to come to terms with his own actions, to face the consequences.

"You can't blame yourself, *iubito*." Andrei's gentle voice cut through his dark thoughts. "The man I love wouldn't have left a family stranded by the side of the road. And Blake proved he was willing to kill his wife. If not when he caught up with her, then later on, and her life would've been hell in the meantime. She left him, and in the mind of a man like him, that was unacceptable."

"We've g-g-gotta find those k-k-kids, Andrei. The th-thought of them being with him... I c-c-cannot leave them like that. And you've g-got to stop bl-blaming yourself too. There w-was nothing you could've d-done to help me. It was so fuck-fucking qu-quick. It's n-not your f-fault."

"Easier said than done, but I'll try." Andrei turned toward him, lifting a hand as if to touch him.

"Wh-what's your next m-move?" Dean asked as he shifted to the other side of the couch, putting even more distance between them before he did something that would haunt him. It was getting harder to not touch Andrei; the struggle to talk and keep his distance eroded his will.

Andrei pressed his lips together, a wounded expression crossing his face before he assumed a frozen mask. "Tomorrow, I'm going to be with your family." At his funeral. A chill raced through Dean. "Then I'm going to Delgado's hearing and posting his bail if he gets it."

"You're w-what?"

"I want to talk to him freely, not with guards hanging over my neck. That's even assuming they'd let me visit him in jail." Dean gave him a skeptical look. He could see a dozen holes in the plan. "I know it's rough, but I'm working on a limited time schedule," Andrei continued.

"Then you d-do think it's just a matter of time before he does h-hurt his own k-kids."

"I'm talking about you, Dean. I don't know how much time you have before you're stuck or if it's already too late. Which means I'll be spending the rest of the night looking through the data I pulled from

Scott Metcalf's computer." A look of disgust tightened Andrei's face as he straightened and ran a hand through his hair. "Something I should've already been doing instead of acting the fool."

"Is th-there anything I-I c-can do to help? You can t-t-talk things out with m-me."

Andrei shook his head. "I need to call your mom back first and apologize. Get myself something to eat and some coffee. I have to tackle this with a clearer head."

"When was the last t-time you had s-something real to eat that did not come from a b-bottle?" Dean asked as he rose to go check the fridge. "Was it that omelet the other d-d-day? The one you w-wouldn't have eaten if I-I hadn't m-made you? D-dammit b-babe, and you go on about being w-worried about me."

He didn't want to think about what Andrei would be doing to himself when he left. He sure as hell had never dreamed that his partner would drown himself in drink when he wasn't pushing himself past the limits of his endurance. The only times he'd slept were when Dean had made him or when he'd passed out.

Dean pounded his fist against the fridge, frustration rising up that he controlled with an effort. He couldn't let it get ahead of him. Old Mother's warning remained fresh in his head, and he didn't want to take the chance that she was a paranoid old woman who passed her own fears onto Ileana. There certainly weren't dead spirits everywhere, so there had to be some truth to her story about the Jackals. And the memory of those howls still made him tremble.

Before he'd been shot, he'd been a pretty even-tempered guy. Now it seemed like he was ready to lash out at everything. His fist clenched and he tapped it against the fridge, gentler this time. He had to get a grip.

"I'm trying, *iubito*," Andrei said behind him, his voice hoarse. "I swear I am. I'll make some soup or something, okay?"

It was so typical of him that a smile tugged at Dean's lips. "Just not out of a c-can. I should have some leftover ch-chicken and dumplings in the freezer."

Arms slid around him, and Dean closed his eyes as Andrei pressed close, his breath warm against Dean's neck as he laid his head on Dean's shoulder. Dean sank into his nearness, felt the sense of Andrei and his warmth getting stronger, making him crave more. "Sometimes it's so hard to remember why you should go. Especially now... being able to feel you like this... being able to talk to you. I miss you so damned much."

Dean echoed that sentiment. It would be so easy to pretend that the last few days had just been a long nightmare they'd woken up from. He reached a hand back, sinking it into Andrei's thick hair as a hand slipped under Dean's shirt to splay against his stomach. They could go back to their room and forget about it all as they made love.

Electricity slid along his skin as Andrei groaned and kissed the side of his neck. Dean turned around and spun them both to press Andrei against the counter instead. "Don't stop," Andrei gasped, parting his thighs as Dean stepped between them. His cock rose, balls aching with the suddenness and strength of his arousal. Dean rocked against Andrei's hip, rubbing against the hard length of his cock.

"Andrei...." Heat filled him as they kissed, and Andrei sagged against him with a needy moan. Dean sank his tongue into his partner's mouth, hungry for more. Fuck, he tasted like heaven.

Dean slid his hands over the curve of Andrei's ass as a brief war fought inside of him. There was a bed back there somewhere, a couch even closer, hell he didn't think Andrei would mind if he turned him around and bent him over the counter, but it would be nice to get his mouth on him too.

Strong hands gripped his shirt, then came the sound of tearing fabric and scattering buttons before Andrei stripped the rest of his shirt from him. Dean tore his mouth away with a shuddering gasp. "An-Andrei."

"No, stay with me, Dean... stay." Andrei held him tighter, fingers digging into his back. Dean slid his hands down to Andrei's thighs and lifted him up onto the counter as urgency gripped him. Andrei's cock strained against the thin fabric of his sweats and Dean jerked them down enough for it to spring free.

Dean leaned down, arms circling Andrei's waist as he sank his mouth down over Andrei's cock until his nose brushed the crisp, black curls at the base. Andrei tasted like clean skin and his familiar, salty musk. Dean ran his tongue along the throbbing vein, lifting up enough to suck and tease the flared head.

Andrei's head fell back to rest against the cabinets. "Oh God, Dean." His hips rocked, sinking his cock deeper into Dean's mouth, filling him with vital energy. His hunger grew as he bobbed his head. Andrei's moans became deeper, punctuated with desperate whimpers. He fisted his hand in Dean's short hair, the moans becoming gasps.

"Dean... Dean, please... don't stop."

A warning shouted in the back of Dean's mind, but he couldn't concentrate on it, not when Andrei was so close to coming. Andrei tightened his hand, stinging his scalp, and Dean welcomed the sensation. It made him feel alive.

The warning became alarm bells, and Dean jerked back, Andrei's cock slipping from his lips to bob glistening and hard against his stomach. Andrei sagged back, slumping against the cabinet, the dark circles under his eyes more pronounced than before.

"Dean?" Andrei panted, reaching for him, his eyes dull with need and exhaustion.

Dean recoiled in horror. "A-an-Andrei... R-Run!" He wasn't alive. He was dead, dead and harming Andrei. He had to get out of there before he did any more damage. He stumbled back another step as Andrei hopped down, having to catch himself before he slid to the floor in a boneless heap.

"Dean... what's wrong?" Andrei straightened and yanked his sweats up before taking a step toward him. "Stay with me... talk to me."

"C-c-can't." He was dead. He had to remember that. He was dead, and Andrei was lost to him. "I love you."

"No, wait!" Andrei took a lurching step toward him, and Dean disappeared, fleeing before he lost control again.

Chapter Ten

THE air had cooled some as the afternoon wound down into evening, but the sun still blazed with heat, and the open awning near the gravesite provided zero protection from the humidity. Wearing a black suit coat should be outlawed in the summer, especially in Baltimore. It did not feel like September was only a few days away.

Andrei fiddled with the rings on his fingers and stifled the slight cough that had been nagging him since he'd woken up that morning. Dean's expression had become stricken when he heard it, and it hadn't taken much for Andrei to coax the reason from him. He vaguely remembered being very ill soon after Ileana had died and his mother's fear as she sat by his bedside, cooling his forehead with damp washcloths.

At least Dean had returned. Andrei had wondered more than once through the long night whether he'd have to once again see Dean looking at him as if he was a cockroach that had crawled out of the sink. Now his rejection and distance made much more sense. Andrei would be fine, he'd bounced back before, and he'd do so again no matter how much Dean touched him. He rarely got sick, so he didn't see this slowing him down at all.

He slipped his arm about Trish's shoulders as Dean's youngest sister walked up next to him. Despite her red-rimmed eyes, a little wistful smile touched her lips. "I know it sounds super cheesy," she whispered, "but it feels like he's right here telling us all he's going to be okay. You feel it too, right?"

Andrei glanced over at Dean, who hovered near his mother and his other sister, Rachel. The clothes he'd been murdered in had disappeared, and now he had on the same linen shirt and khakis that he'd worn at their commitment ceremony. Andrei rubbed his thumb over Dean's ring and smiled down at her. "I don't think it sounds cheesy, Trish. He probably just wanted to say good-bye to everyone. Let you all know that he's going to be okay. That's something Dean would do."

He just wished he believed Dean would be okay.

Trish hugged him hard and then went to rejoin her husband. Andrei looked at Dean again, watched him brush his fingers over his mom's shoulder. He looked good. Seeing him in those clothes brought back some of the happiest memories in Andrei's life. The sun had been this brilliant the day of their ceremony, though it hadn't been so humid. The breeze coming off the bay had been a blessing, and the light in Dean's hazel eyes when he'd looked at Andrei as they said the words....

"Mr. Cuza." Evelyn Acosta stopped in front of him, her dark face lined with strain. "I'm sorry, about Mr. Marshall. You should've said you were family when you came to see me."

"Dean was my partner. I would've married him if Maryland would have allowed us." He would've taken Dean's name and dropped Cuza forever. Andrei cut himself off before his thoughts turned bitter again. "We were together a long time. I didn't think you'd have talked with me or taken my offer with the case seriously if you'd known how personal it was for me."

"I might not have." Evelyn took Andrei's hand in hers. "I'll always be grateful to Mr. Marshall. If he hadn't been there, my baby would've died alone with no one defending her or my grandbabies. I know that's no comfort to you—"

Andrei gently squeezed her hand, and out of the corner of his eye, he saw Dean drift closer. "I understand and I know he wished he could've done more. I want you to know, despite what the cops think,

I'm not dropping my investigation. And I do have a lot of experience finding children."

"God bless you, Mr. Cuza," she said in a choked voice. "That's not why I came. I was going to call you and ask, but bless you. I'm not ready to give up yet."

"Andrei, not Mr. Cuza, and thank you for coming." Andrei grasped her shoulders and met her gaze to show her the strength of his conviction. "I'm following a few leads, and I'm still confident that I can find them."

Dean smiled at him as he stopped next to Andrei. "You are amazing, babe." Andrei's fingers twitched, almost reaching to take his hand before stopping himself. "I don't think you see how you instinctively reach out to help others before you think about helping yourself."

Dean had always seen Andrei with blinders on, making him out to be far nobler than he was. A selfless man wouldn't have gotten dead drunk for the last few days. Not when so much rode on the outcome. He'd hit the bottom hard and kept on going. "Truth is you took care of me more than I ever took care of you," he murmured under his breath.

"What was that?" The expression on Evelyn's face was one that Andrei had seen many times over his life when he'd been caught responding to Ileana. That slightly uncertain look in the eye as if they wondered if he was unhinged. It was no wonder he talked out loud to himself even when he was truly alone. Better that people believed he had that personality tic over thinking he heard voices.

"I apologize. I'm working some things through in my head, and it sometimes has the tendency to slip out loud. It's a bad habit."

"I understand," Evelyn said. Andrei tensed as she glanced toward the coffin resting on the lift over the waiting hole. That wasn't Dean. Dean stood next to him, close enough to take his hand. He wasn't that cold body going into the ground. "You'll call me when you uncover anything new?"

Andrei pulled his attention back to the grieving woman in front of him. "I will. Right now it looks like he might've left the state with them, but I don't think he went too far."

"Well then, it's time I go speak to Mrs. Marshall, from one mother to another." Evelyn squeezed his hand one last time.

"I know Carole would appreciate that."

"And you take care of that cough. Some hot tea with lemon should help."

Andrei glanced at the stricken expression on Dean's face as she walked off. He would have to address Dean's guilty conscience later when they were alone. What Dean had been trying to tell him, about touching not being good for him, made sense now. But Dean wasn't going to make that choice for him. Andrei could handle a little cough if it meant that he could be with Dean fully during whatever time he had left with him. And he was too much of an ornery bastard to fall prey to a fever again.

Especially when the side effects included his ability to see Dean so much clearer now, and his partner did not stutter as much today, not unless he let his emotions get the better of him. No, they were going to have this out. One way or another, he'd get Dean to see things his way.

ATTENDING his own funeral had to be at the top of the list of the strangest things ever to happen to Dean. Forget strange, it was downright surreal. That being said, he had everyone he loved all in one place. For the moment, the urgency over the investigation took second place as he indulged in being with them one last time even if they didn't know it. Even his guilt over last night faded. He'd draw the line with Andrei later.

Justin even showed up, though he kept his distance from Andrei. Dean appreciated that he'd come, and he knew Andrei would too, once he calmed down some. For now, Andrei showed no signs of forgiveness or of letting go of his anger.

As Dean stood by each one of his family members and close friends and said his good-byes, they seemed to fade into the background, becoming a little less real. The letting go left him with a sense of bittersweet rightness. Dean took his hand off his dad's shoulder and watched the real world envelope him again, leaving Dean in the hazy, shimmering limbo. It was like watching a scene play out through a screen of water. Only Andrei now stood solid among the rest of his loved ones.

"You have a real nice family. They look like they love you lots." Both Andrei and Dean looked down at Ileana, who had appeared in between them. She grabbed both of their hands. "Swing me high?"

"Now's not a good time, Poppet," Dean said, giving her an apologetic smile. "Maybe later when it's just the three of us."

"Oh fine." She looked around at everyone curiously. "Did you say good-bye? I did, except for Andrei. We played instead, didn't we, making angels in the snow?"

Andrei nodded, passing a hand over her hair. Dean remembered all those strange gestures now. The times when he'd overheard Andrei say something in passing that made no sense, and he'd chalked it up to Andrei's tendency to talk to himself. Only now he knew the truth.

"I did say good-bye." And it had filled Dean with a sense of peace he'd been lacking before. It was good to see his family together and to be reminded that they took care of each other. Including Andrei. "I thought I told you to stay with Old Mother. That crazy old bat didn't upset you, did she?"

Ileana wrinkled her nose in disapproval. "You shouldn't call her that. It's not 'spectful."

"Yeah well." He supposed this was one of those times he should provide a good example. "You're right, but that doesn't answer the question."

"Today's a big day. I thought you and Andrei should have all your family here. I had to sneak away, though. She's been hovering."

"Something you two want to tell me?" Andrei murmured under his breath.

"I'll let Ileana fill you in. I'd planned on telling you, but things have been crazy." His eyes drifted to the archway of a mausoleum a little bit farther into the cemetery. A soft, golden light had started to gather in the center, filling the space. Once again the longing filled him, stronger this time than any other time before.

Dean found himself walking over there before he realized that it probably wasn't a good idea. With each step he felt lighter, almost joyful, and the light glowed brighter. He forced himself to stop in front of the portal, swallowing hard as he watched himself step out.

"I see you've finally accepted that you've passed on." The other Dean gestured to his clothes. "I like that, very fitting that you wear such happy reminders. Are you ready?"

Dean shook his head, his mouth dry, and he focused on the three people keeping him here. He stuck his hand in his pocket and pulled out the bit of ribbon that had fallen from Inez's hair. The lure of the light muted, giving him a chance to think. "I'm not done yet."

"Andrei can find the children without your help. You know that."

"Maybe, but he still needs me." Dean looked back at Andrei who listened to Ileana chatter on as he stole questioning glances in Dean's direction. "Andrei's more fragile than I thought. I need to help him let go."

"He needs to find his own strength. You can't do that for him."

"You're right, but I can stand by him while he does." Dean turned back to face himself. The need to go tugged at him, and the more he fought it, the heavier he felt. "Can I ask you a question?"

"I won't guarantee that I'll answer, but go ahead."

"Fair enough." Dean gestured toward Ileana and gave the other version of himself a pleading glance. "Can I take her with me? When I do decide to go with you. She was too young. She didn't understand what saying no meant."

"Her longing to stay beat out her longing to move on." The other Dean looked thoughtful for a long moment. "She may, but you do realize that if you linger too long, both of you will be stuck in limbo."

Dean grinned and spread his arms as he took a step back. It was hard, like walking through quicksand, the ground sucking at his foot. "Well then, I'll just have to make sure that doesn't happen."

"THAT money was supposed to be for the boat you always wanted," Dean groused as they walked toward the grim, fenced-off Baltimore City Detention Center. "Not for hiring a hotshot attorney for some scumbag who probably was a hoodrat friend of Blake Olsen's. That name doesn't sound at all like a hoodrat. Olsen. Sounds like a farmer. What the hell?"

"Anybody can find themselves mixed in with the wrong kind of people, no matter their background. And let's face it, this city breeds it." Andrei jaywalked across the street and Dean followed, eying the thick rolls of barbed wire on the fences. Somewhere in that uninviting stone block were the answers Andrei sought.

"Hey, it's Baltimore, hon," Dean said with a quick grin that he didn't feel.

"Richmond's not that much better either, and let's not forget the joy that is DC," Andrei said under his breath, nodding to a woman and grabbing the door for her as she approached the building. "Besides, if Delgado is cleared, then they're going to have to look at other suspects."

Okay, so maybe Dean's nerves were showing, but this really had to be the worst plan ever. Andrei had to cash in some favors to get this interview today after Hector Delgado failed to get bail. Dean knew it was going to come back to bite Andrei on the ass, hard. People at the police station and DA's office were already irked by the noise Andrei was making.

"True. I still don't like you using the boat money. You could've used the money I set aside for the new gym." It stung, after all the work he'd put into pulling that together, but once again, it wasn't like he was in a position to open it up.

"What am I going to do with a boat when I can't share it with you? And the gym money is tied up with investors," Andrei murmured as they walked up to security.

Dean cut a quick glance at him as he coughed, but he had to admit, it sounded a bit better today. Still, the new lines around Andrei's eyes and pronounced silvering of his dark hair at the temples bothered Dean, even if it gave Andrei a more distinguished air.

Andrei didn't speak as he went through the security process, and there was no other chance to talk as they waited with a few other visitors before being taken in to see Delgado. Something about the detention center set Dean on edge. So much emotion, most of it dark and intense, and Dean had to work on concentrating on not getting swept away. At his funeral he'd been caught up in saying good-bye to his family and friends, and hadn't noticed the overall mood. This was a different matter.

"There's our man now." Andrei nodded toward the security glass where a short Hispanic man appeared, darting nervous glances Andrei's way. The man's shoulders hunched as if he'd taken one too many blows and expected more. "We only have half an hour to talk with him. And I'd dearly love to know how he got his hands on Blake's gun."

Some of Dean's animosity faded as Delgado got closer and he could see the man more clearly through the limbo haze. He was young and terrified and, truth be told, the dullness in his eyes made Dean think he wasn't all that bright. There was a childlike quality about him. The man hunched even more as Andrei picked up the phone and motioned for Delgado to do the same.

"You the man that got me a lawyer to help me out?"

"I am," Andrei answered as Dean looked around the room, at the cameras and the guard. He knew Andrei didn't care if he got into trouble for interfering in an investigation, but Dean did. The DA was going to find out about this visit five minutes after Andrei left, if she didn't already know.

A range of expressions from gratitude to fear crossed the young man's face as he wet his lips and shifted in his seat. "What I gotta do?"

"I just have a few questions I want answered, that's all. I've also arranged for your attorney to come visit you later on today. Will you talk with me, Hector?"

"I wanna see my sister. Can you get her here too? I know she gotta be worried 'bout me."

"Christ," Dean muttered, disgusted by Blake's tactics. "He found himself a retarded kid and used him. I swear, when I see Blake, I'm kicking his balls up into his throat. That just isn't fucking right."

Andrei shot him a hard look. It amazed Dean how protective he was of kids and teenagers and how Andrei couldn't see what a good father he'd make. He really hoped one day Andrei would realize that, because he'd make some kid really happy.

"Okay, tell me where she lives, and I'll see what I can do, but I expect you to answer some questions in return. Got it?"

"I didn't kill that lady and man. I swear it. They said I did, but I didn't. And I don' know nuttin' about no missing kids. I tried to tell the cops, but they kept at me and kept at me. Now they say they gonna ask for the death penalty. I didn't do it. You gotta believe me."

Dean grabbed a chair when the guard was looking in another direction, sat down, and propped his feet up on the ledge to listen. He felt bad for the kid, he really did, but he wasn't sure how much Andrei could actually help him.

"I believe you, Hector, and I'm trying to help, but you've got to talk to me," Andrei said in a soothing tone. "I'm not going to let you get executed for something you didn't do. Now tell me, how'd you get that purse?"

"Some crazy white man gave it to me, and another bag too. I gave that to my sister cuz she's always needing baby stuff. He had real wild eyes, like a dog. Ever see a really mean dog? I got bitten by one like that once, and they had the same kinda eyes."

"Was he taller than you, with blond hair?"

Hector paused and when he spoke again his voice was confused. "No, sir, he had no hair. He took off his hat and wiped his head. He was bald, but he had real crazy eyes, I'm telling ya, like a wolf's."

Andrei fished out a photograph and held it up to the glass. Dean recognized it and shivered to see his bloody fingerprint still marring the surface. He couldn't see Blake's face without remembering that nightmare all too vividly. His body jerked, pain flashing through his chest, screams sounding in his ears.

With a muffled gasp, Dean pulled his thoughts away from that memory. A glance down showed he was back in the clothes he'd been murdered in, the red stain growing on his chest. He willed it away, frowning in concentration until he was back in jeans and a T-shirt. Andrei did not need to see that again.

"Yeah, yeah! That's him." Hector stabbed his finger at the glass in his excitement, and the guard looked toward him with a frown. "We gotta show the cops this."

Dean stood up, though he didn't know what he'd do if the guard decided to cut the interview short. He didn't think distracting him with a goosing would be very wise, even if it was tempting. "You might want to keep him calm, babe. If he gets worked up, I don't think they'll give you your full thirty minutes."

Andrei nodded. "We'll make sure your attorney knows, and right now I think it's a good idea if we tell her this news before we tell the cops. She can handle passing along the evidence."

Hector's gaze skipped around, and for a second, Dean thought Hector saw him, but then Dean realized Hector had looked right *through* him. Ugh. Fucking weird.

"I thought you were gonna help me!" Suspicion darkened Hector's expression, and his hand tightened on the phone. "Yer lying to me, just like the cops did. They said if I confessed I'd—"

"I'm not lying to you. Remember you already met with your new attorney. I wouldn't have paid her all that money if she couldn't help. I'm not out to get you." Andrei held up the picture. "I'm out to get him. Now I'm going to give a copy of this to your attorney, along with all the other evidence I gathered. You were set up. Blake gave you that bag and then called the cops on you."

Hector blinked and then frowned as if he was trying to process that reassurance. He worried his lip, and Dean wondered how much time Andrei was going to waste quieting Hector's fears. The minutes were speeding by. Not that Dean didn't sympathize, but given the situation Hector was in, Dean didn't think he would be ready to believe anything.

"The new attorney, she say that the INS wants to deport me if I get released. They say they gonna make me leave the country. Man, I been here since I was a baby. Where'm I gonna go?"

Dean saw the kid start to stand and move as if he were going to hang up. Andrei didn't have time to arrange another interview. He dove through the security glass and touched Hector on the shoulder. Dean shivered from the quick, hot zip of electricity and tasted Hector's absolute terror.

Andrei's eyes widened as Hector sagged back into his chair and he shot Dean another hard look. "Your attorney will help you with your immigration status too. But first we have to clear you of the murder charges. Now calm down and trust me. I've helped you this much, haven't I?"

The poor kid looked frightened half to death. "Yeah, guess so." He kept looking around him as if he sensed Dean hovering right over his shoulder, so Dean slipped back through the barrier to rejoin Andrei.

"Okay. I'm not going to stop," Andrei said in the same even, patient tone he'd been using with Hector.

"What do you want? Nobody gives nuttin' without wantin' something else."

"You're right, I do want something in return. I need your help finding the real killer. The man who gave you those bags. Once he and those kids are found, you're not going to be accused of those crimes. No matter what you signed. The lawyer I hired will see to it. She's good."

"I can't help! I don't know nothing about that dude. He said the bag was his old lady's and she didn't want it anymore. He asked if I knowed anybody who'd want it. It was a pretty piece. My sister woulda liked it. So I jumped on it. And then he disappeared."

"Do you remember the date? Was he on foot? Was he carrying anything?" Andrei shot the questions out, one after another, and Hector's face reflected his confusion.

"Hey," Dean cut in. "One at a time, okay? If he gets frustrated and freaks, that's going to be the end of this, and I really don't want to zap him again, even if it's a quick one."

Andrei nodded after he glanced over at Dean, who had returned to his chair. "I'm sorry, Hector. One question at a time."

"I should'a dumped it when I saw the gun, but I knew a guy who knew another guy who'd prolly buy it," Hector said moodily, leaning closer to the glass. "I'm in real trouble now, even if your lady friend helps me out."

"Yes, you are, but you're not alone. Now talk to me. What day did you run into that man? Where were you?"

"It was Friday, and I was hanging on the street, you know, waitin' for my friends. It was morning cuz I'd just finished eatin' when I saw him. He was getting ready to go into the dollar mart." Hector spilled out the rest of the story as Dean gnawed on his lip and eyed the clock.

Weird that Blake had chosen to stay in the area after he'd killed him. Dean would've thought the man would've hightailed it in another direction as fast as he could go. If only he'd been able to at least remember some of the numbers on the tags on that camper truck. He racked his brains for what details he could, but his attention had not been on what vehicle the man was driving.

"Ask him if he saw a truck, blue body, I think, with a dirty white camper," Dean said.

"Are there any other details you saw, for instance, what the man was driving? Did he go into the store?"

Hector shook his head after considering it, his face screwed up in thought. "Nah, I was looking at the purse. When I looked up, he'd gone."

"Did you see any strange-looking vehicles on the road, perhaps parked nearby?"

Dean glared at Andrei, wishing he'd just get on with it and ask Hector about the truck, but he ignored the unspoken request as much as he had the spoken one.

"Oh yeah, there was this weird truck with a little house on it, and it dragged another car behind it. It drove by real slow as it passed, and I thought I saw it later on when I got to my friend's car. But the cops nailed me not long after that."

"Did you see anything else, anything at all that might help us identify the truck? Did you catch the license plate?"

"It wasn't Maryland. I know what all of Maryland's license plates look like. It hadda plane at the top, like one'a those old-fashioned ones in an Indiana Jones movie, with the four wings. The truck was blue and, oh, it had some stickers on it. You know the white ones with the letters that make no sense with the black around 'em?"

"I think I know the ones you're talking about, Hector. They're for places that people visit. The letters stand for locations. Do you remember any of the letters?" Andrei asked as the door opened and another guard came in.

"You have five more minutes," the guard said and Andrei nodded.

"I'm not too good with letters. I get 'em mixed up sometimes." Hector's eyes strayed toward the guard. Dean stood up and walked toward the newcomer, ready to interfere if Andrei needed a few more minutes. "Do ya really have to go?"

"I do, but you're going to be in good hands, and I'll check on you when I can." Andrei glanced back at the guard. "Thank you for your help. If you remember any more details, use some of that money I put in your commissary account to call me. And be sure to tell your attorney the same thing."

"But I didn't do nuttin' to help. You helped me."

"Trust me, you did more than you know."

As the guard came forward, Dean asked, "What's going to happen to him?" Hector was looking at Andrei like he was an angel about to be snatched away. "Do you think he'll be okay?"

Andrei gave him a tight smile and a shrug; then Hector spoke up again, his voice excited. "Hey, I 'member one of them letters on that sticker. *X*, like on a pirate map. And maybe a *B* too. I like *B*s, like in babies and baseball and B'more."

Chapter Eleven

"ANDREI, I'm giving you thirty seconds to open up this door before I bust it down."

Andrei cursed at the sound of Justin's voice and closed his laptop. He'd been friends with Justin long enough to know the detective would follow through on his threat. "Hold on a sec," he shouted back and bolted for a pair of jeans he could yank on.

"That's what you get for going around aggressively naked," Dean snickered from the doorway to their bedroom.

Andrei didn't bother responding, and he had no plans to stop what he was doing either. Not until he'd seduced Dean right back into his arms and his bed. He'd become a nudist if that's what it took. He just needed to keep himself forefront in Dean's thoughts and let instinct and all the years they'd been together work for him.

He knew at least a bit of how it worked being a ghost. Dean was stuck mentally at his death. Whatever he'd found out since then about his touching hurting Andrei would fade as his natural inclinations took over. And all of those inclinations would lead Dean right back where he belonged. Unfair tactics maybe, but with the amount of time they had left together, Andrei wasn't in any mood for fairness.

As Andrei buttoned his jeans, Justin began banging on the door again. "For the love of...." Andrei muttered under his breath as he grabbed one of Dean's shirts to slip on. He yanked open the front door to glare at Justin, who glared right back. "What the hell is your problem?"

"You, that's my problem. Now are you going to let me in or am I going to have to force my way in?" Justin held up a bottle of Scotch. "I've even brought a peace offering."

"If you think that's going to make me forget that the police dropped the ball on Dean and Robin, you're crazy." Andrei stepped back and tugged the T-shirt on. "You might as well come in before you get the whole block curious."

"Look I'm sorry about that. I know it's been making you sick inside, and apologies aren't enough. I should've said something to you at Dean's funeral instead of leaving this unresolved. That wasn't right either. So I'm here, off duty, to help you out with your investigation. Just don't let word of it get out, okay?"

Andrei stared at Justin in surprise; in all the years he'd known the other man, he always followed the rules. It had caused more than one argument between them. "For real, you're going to help me against the DA and Fed's wishes?"

Justin winced, his wide, dark face looking pained. "Technically, I'm supposed to be here to tell you to stop interfering. She wasn't at all happy about you hiring that lawyer for Delgado and then questioning him. Especially after all the questions his attorney raised. I caught hell for it."

"I hope you're not expecting me to feel guilty." Irritated anew, Andrei pulled out two mugs and flipped the coffeemaker on. Scotch was nice, but he had work to do and a lot of info to wade through. And if he had one drink, he didn't know if he'd be able to stop himself from taking another and then another. "Did you come to lecture or help?"

"I can't do both?" Justin held up his hands as Andrei shot him a hard look. "Okay, tell me again why you think it was Blake Olsen, when everyone else, including his father, believes he's dead. I'd thought you'd lost it before, but I'm ready to listen now that you seem more rational."

"What are you going to tell him, babe?" Dean asked as he took a seat in his favorite armchair. "If you tell him the truth, he just might have you committed for observation for a few days."

"He had Robin tailed. Remember that Scott Metcalf guy I had you look up for me?" At Justin's sour expression Andrei continued. "Blake had hired him to keep tabs on her, and when Metcalf got a little too personal with some of the pictures he took, he killed him too."

"And you know this because?"

"Witnesses put Metcalf at Robin's house several times, and Blake's own cronies led me to Metcalf's place where I found the photos and some other info that I haven't been able to sift through yet. But I'm hoping that it gives me an idea for where Blake might've gone next."

Justin's brows drew together in a fierce glower. "Did you leave that anonymous tip that led the Richmond PD to Metcalf's body? You stole evidence? Jesus Christ, Andrei, you're going too far."

"I didn't steal anything, and I left everything as I found it. The police have the exact same info I do. Besides, Hector Delgado ID'd Blake as the man who gave him the purse."

Andrei found it difficult to concentrate on the task at hand with Dean sitting nearby, watching every move. He'd always worked alone before; even when he had to do his time at a larger company before going private, he'd stuck to solo assignments when he could. Now it seemed as if he'd managed to get himself two partners, both questioning how he did things.

"And the prosecutor will argue that you coached him."

"Do you really think that? I don't give a damn what she says, Justin. She wants a quick win so it'll look good on her record. Hector is an easy mark. That's why Blake picked him. I want to find those kids. When we find them with Blake, that ought to be enough for even her to see the truth."

"It has to stick for a trial. Remember that, Andrei," Justin warned, his expression grave. "Think about what a huge blow it would be if after all that, Blake Olsen walks because of a mistrial or we can't convince the jury because evidence got thrown out because it was obtained illegally."

"Trust me, Justin. I'm taking it seriously. I have no intention of letting him walk on a technicality." That wasn't even going to be an option if Andrei could help it. Blake wasn't going to get a chance to have a trial.

Dean gave him a sharp look. "What is going on in that head of yours, babe?" Andrei had absolutely no intention of answering that and was grateful that Justin's presence allowed him to ignore it. Dean didn't need to see his darker side.

"That's good enough for me." Justin sat at the table and stirred sugar into his coffee. "Now where are you going from here? Do you think he's still in Baltimore or gone back to Richmond?"

"No, I think he's done with Richmond. Why go through all of the trouble of making it seem like you're dead if you're just going to go back to where people might recognize you?"

"By that logic, why come to Baltimore at all?" Justin countered. "The place where he met Delgado wasn't that far from the kids' grandmother. She thought he was dead too."

In truth, that bugged Andrei as well. It seemed like a stupid risk on Blake's part. After killing Dean and Robin, he was on the highway already. He could've gone anywhere, and with a camper truck, the implication was that he planned on traveling, so why remain in the area?

"He's staying to see Robin one last time," Dean said and looked abashed when Andrei cocked his head in question at him. "Maybe because a part of him feels guilty or because he wants the closure of seeing her in the ground and knowing she can't take his kids from him again. He's changed his appearance enough that if he keeps his distance at the funeral, no one will recognize him. At least, that's what my heart is saying."

Dean had good instincts. That second scenario made sense to Andrei, and since he had planned on going to her funeral anyway, he'd just keep an extra eye out, maybe have Dean wander around for him. They could end this today.

"Perhaps he's waiting to see Robin buried. I'm going to her funeral this afternoon anyway, so I'll watch for him. Otherwise, I'm going on the assumption that he did leave town after finding a patsy to take the fall for him. That could be why he went into Baltimore, just looking for someone like Delgado to take the blame." Andrei winked at Dean, and the warmth of his partner's returning smile eased some of the darkness roiling inside of him.

He wanted Justin to leave so he could go to Dean and take him in his arms and assure him that it would be okay if they were together. At the same time he couldn't let himself stop, not even for a short amount of time. The investigation provided its own urgency for Dean's sake and the kids. To be honest, the war inside of him, between go, go, go and stopping to savor his remaining time with Dean, got to be more exhausting each day.

"Do you have any leads on where Blake will go next?"

"Some possibilities." Andrei opened the laptop and motioned for Justin to pull up a seat next to him. Dean rose and came to stand behind his chair as well, making the hair on the back of Andrei's neck prickle in awareness. "Scott Metcalf didn't just take sleazy pictures, he was also in the business of making fake IDs. He's got templates for a number of different state driver's licenses, including North Carolina. Delgado said that he thought that the truck's license plate had a bi-plane on it, which would fit North Carolina."

"You're going on the word of a kid who may still be the killer? Who's in this country illegally and who had the murder weapon on him?"

"They're determined to make him a villain one way or another, aren't they?" Dean murmured.

"I have to follow what leads I have because if I went your way, I'd be giving up. Now did you come to argue or to listen?"

"Fine, I'll back off. I want to help." Justin gave him a lingering sideways glance and the deep bass of his voice softened. "You know I do."

Dean leaned over and flicked Justin's ear, his face set in hard lines. Andrei's jaw dropped as Justin jumped, slapping a hand to the side of his head as he looked around with wide eyes. "Ow. What the fuck?"

"You can tell him for me to keep his eyes to himself," Dean said.

Andrei shook his head and turned back to the laptop. Telling Dean that Justin wasn't looking at him like that was useless, and he had to bite back a grin as Justin took another look around.

"Something wrong?" Andrei asked.

"No, I um…." Justin pulled his hand away from his ear, the tip turning red under his dusky skin. Dean had really nailed him. "I think a fly bit me or something."

"Troublemaker," Andrei muttered under his breath before drawing Justin's attention to the laptop to show him what he'd found at Metcalf's place.

"It's not being a troublemaker," Dean said, and Andrei felt a brief brush of fingers, the first time Dean had touched him since he'd disappeared on Andrei. "I'm just reminding him to keep his mind on the job."

Andrei leaned back, hoping that Dean would touch him again. "Evelyn Acosta said that Blake promised her daughter a house along the beach. I wanted to start by making a list of campgrounds in North Carolina, concentrating with the ones along the beach. Delgado also mentioned a sticker with an *X* on it, possibly a *B*. If he's right, it could mean the Outer Banks."

"Well you have to begin somewhere, and that seems as good a place to start as any other. When are you heading out?"

"If Blake doesn't show up at Robin's funeral, I'll leave about two or three in the morning. Hit there first light." Andrei felt that brush again, so faint that it was more an impression of fingers than an actual touch.

"Three," Dean said. "Try to get some sleep at least."

Andrei nodded, not wanting to argue about it, even though he was fairly certain that he wouldn't sleep much regardless of the time he left. Justin turned toward him, his expression worried. "Tell me you're not going to go off looking for a fight, Andrei."

"My first priority is getting Inez and Tristan out safely. I'm not going to be able to do that if I go off half-cocked searching for blood." What happened after the kids were safe was a whole other matter.

"Okay then, let's make your list."

ONE good thing about being a ghost was that it made it incredibly easy to skulk around. Since Dean wasn't going to miraculously come back to life, he might as well learn to enjoy the good along with the bad or else he wouldn't be able to handle not just the grief, but the upside down way that his view of the world had changed. Strange, he thought he'd feel different inside after he had been buried, but except for seeing people through that wavy haze, he hadn't noticed any difference at all.

Dean stood on one of the many little hills in the cemetery, trying not to let his thoughts take a morbid turn. It was hard not to think of claustrophobic coffins or worms and... ugh. *Fucking ass, just stop it.* He would drive himself crazy, and that was the last thing Andrei needed.

He concentrated on the next hilltop over, closed his eyes and felt the now familiar lurch as he moved. Or maybe the world moved around him. Either way, when he opened his eyes again, he'd shifted. There were several good vantage points around here to watch the funeral, and Blake could be at any of them.

Andrei stood below with Robin's mother, sister, and the rest of her loved ones as the preacher droned on about ashes and dust. Dean couldn't really hear him from this vantage point, but he was sure that was the topic. He should've stipulated that he wanted something nice and cheery at his own funeral. Something about sunshine and the tang in the air where the Chesapeake met the Potomac River or the hum of energy at Baltimore's Inner Harbor.

He wanted Andrei to remember all the good times and believe that one day they'd have them again when they were reunited.

A cold chill slithered over his skin and settled in his gut. Dean turned and saw a man approaching, a trucker cap pulled down low so that half his face was shielded. Dean didn't need to see his face. Dean could sense his killer now, a primal stirring in the air that made his hackles rise. He'd recognize Blake anywhere.

That fucking bastard actually had the gall to come here. The sky darkened as Dean took a step toward Blake, his thoughts racing, lips peeling back in a snarl. That gloating motherfucker.

He took another step, his hands balling into fists as blood poured out of his chest and soaked his shirt. He'd kill him. He'd rip him apart with his bare hands and—

In the distance a howl rose. The strange, high-pitched sound, almost as if it didn't belong to this universe, skittered down Dean's spine. Oh fuck, the more he heard it, the more true madness threatened. Like the howls somehow had the power to splinter his brain. He froze, until the sight of Blake's grim smirk set his thoughts on fire again. Between one step and the next, somehow Dean closed the distance between himself and his prey.

Blake stared through him, his gaze riveted on the scene below as Robin's casket was lowered into the ground. Dean hissed, stretching his hands out to throttle him. "Asswipe… run."

Blake whirled, staring around wildly, and Dean snarled again, closing his hands around Blake's throat. For a second he *focused* on Dean. Blake's face went white as he fell back with a shriek. "Andrei. Andrei—" Dean said, caught completely up in the horror of those last minutes, the rage and fear and grief.

The sound of Andrei's name on his lips made Dean pause as another howl ripped through the air. It keened and slavered, the wet, tearing sounds of flesh being stripped from bone and devoured. *Feed us. Tear your soul from your skin. Tasty bits of emotion. Hungry. Hungry. Hungry.*

Closer this time. Their voices, the high-pitched yipping, those sick sounds dug into his skin. So much closer, like those Jackal Wraiths had somehow used the same trick Dean had to move through the intervening space.

With a shout of thwarted rage, Dean whirled around so he couldn't see Blake and concentrated hard on Andrei. He flooded his head with memories of him, the sound of his laugh, the way the sunlight glinted off of his black hair, and the feel of Andrei's arms around him.

The world lurched sideways. "Dean!" Strong hands grabbed his shoulders, and Dean opened his eyes to the worry and distress on Andrei's face. "What's wrong? What happened?"

Dean turned and pointed up the hill, trying to get the words out that tangled on his tongue. "Ass-ass-asswipe...." He growled, trying to get ahold of himself. Those howls were even closer now. "He's here!"

Andrei's eyes went as sharp as obsidian as he followed the direction of Dean's finger. "I see him. Good job, Dean."

Dean fell to his knees, gasping and shuddering as Andrei took off with a dangerous glint in his eyes. He wanted to help him, needed to help, but God help him, those howls, the horrid chewing sounds filled his ears, drowned his soul under fear. They were so much closer. He had to run, calm down and lose them somehow. With a despairing cry, Dean shifted away from his partner and the murderer that Andrei chased down.

ANDREI slipped away from the funeral, ignoring the tight anger on Wanda's face and the sharp curiosity on Evelyn's. Blake had disappeared from the top of the hill, and Andrei began running. That son of a whore would not get away today. They'd be burying him next.

As Andrei topped the rise, he caught sight of a figure up ahead, his head down as he walked swiftly away. He yanked his gun out of the holster and chased him down, closing in on him with every stride.

The man looked over his shoulder and stumbled with a curse as he reached the parking lot. Andrei slowed and trained his gun on Blake. One shot and it would be over with. Dean could rest. Andrei scanned the parking lot for the camper truck and cursed when he didn't see it. Fuck, he couldn't take Blake out until he knew where those kids were.

"Hold it right there, Blake."

Blake ducked behind a car and popped up again with a gun, taking a potshot at Andrei. "Fucking, bastard." Andrei dove behind another car and rolled, coming up in a crouch. Footsteps ran off toward the left and Andrei followed, keeping low, his heart racing. He had to concentrate on apprehending Blake instead of killing him outright, more difficult and far less satisfying.

As soon as Inez and Tristan were safe, though, Blake was his. Another shot rang out and Andrei ducked. "Give it up, Blake. I'm on to you. There's nowhere you can hide where I won't find you."

"Who the fuck are you?" Blake snarled, the sound of his voice coming from several yards away. Andrei crouched and made his way in that direction. He should remain quiet, but the need for Blake to know who was going to end him overcame his stalking instincts.

"That man you shot." The gun trembled in his hand, and Andrei clenched his teeth together.

"Yeah, so what?" Two more gunshots took out the window above Andrei's head showering him with glass. "He shouldn't have been messing around with my wife."

Grief warred with rage and Andrei jumped up, rolling over the car hood as more shots followed him. Mentally, Andrei added up the bullets used and prayed that Blake didn't have another clip on him. "You stupid fucker. He was just changing her tire. He was my partner, you bastard, and you took him from me."

"Cry me a fucking river. Why don't you step out and you can join him."

The sound of pounding feet alerted him and Andrei took off after Blake as he bolted, weaving amongst the cars and cursing at the way they slowed him down. "Where's Inez and Tristan?" Andrei shouted.

A side mirror near him burst and a sliver of glass drew a line of fire across Andrei's forehead. "They're my fucking children. You're a dead man too. You hear me? You're not taking my kids from me."

The cars thinned out as they approached the end of the parking lot, and Andrei's heart froze as he heard the distant wail of sirens. Blake could not get arrested. He'd lose his chance. He charged after him as Blake ran across the street, dodging cars. A horn sounded, bearing down on him, and Andrei fell back as an SUV hurtled by him. The driver stuck his hand out the window, flipping him off.

"Son of a bitch, get out of the road."

On the other side of the street, Blake ran toward a nearby shopping complex. Cursing, Andrei followed, urgency and rage adding impetus to his feet, and he ran faster than he ever had before between the speeding cars. Blake turned and shot, making Andrei dive for cover again. His shoulder hit the concrete hard, jarring his whole body. When he rose, Blake had gone, but left a wake of staring people and pointing.

"What the hell is going on?" someone yelled as Andrei got to his feet again. "Is a movie being filmed? How fucking cool is that."

Andrei put on a burst of speed and came around the corner as Blake disappeared around another, but not before another round of gunfire that shattered a storefront window next to Andrei. "Fuck, fuck, fuck. Get out of the way, he's got a gun," Andrei shouted, pushing between shoppers who bolted, screaming when they saw his own gun. Crazy bastard. Someone was going to get killed.

The chaos slowed him down, and as he barreled around that building he caught a glimpse of Blake even farther away, ducking among cars in another parking lot. He burst out onto the little street in front of the stores and too late saw the car approaching out of the corner of his eye. He angled his body, prepared to jump, and shouted as the bumper struck him. Cursing anew, Andrei pushed himself up off the ground, and when he straightened, Blake had disappeared.

Chapter Twelve

THE howls no longer seemed to nip at Dean's heels, though he could still sense them not too far away. He shuddered and thought hard of Andrei, bringing up one of the many happy memories they shared. This time it was when they first moved into their house after leaving behind that cramped, dingy apartment near the gym. It had been snowing pretty hard, and Andrei tried to go about the move in a methodical fashion. And the look on Andrei's face when Dean had thrown that first snowball... Dean chuckled. The empty rooms of their new home had held such promise for the future, and they had been so excited at the thought of filling them.

The future. It had been stolen from them by Blake. The anger roared up again, and Dean wrenched his thoughts away. *No! Safe thoughts. Have to think safe thoughts.*

A snarl rent the air, and Dean lurched to another location with a hot spurt of fear driving him. He could almost imagine the hot air on his skin. *Run little soul. Taste your anger. Savor your fear.* The words faded as he moved away, though the terrible noise of the Jackal Wraiths feasting remained strong. He didn't want to know if those sounds were a projection the Jackals used to terrorize their prey or the sounds of some hapless victim being devoured.

Those noises stabbed into his brain, and the howls tore away all the happy thoughts he kept trying to surround himself with. Instead, they dredged up every bad memory and brought them to the forefront of his mind in vivid, exacting detail. He relived his murder over and over, and the rage toward Blake remained at a slow simmer, no matter how hard he tried to cool off.

Dean paused long enough to get his bearings, then jumped through limbo, blindly this time. Something that Old Mother said kept haunting his mind. The Jackal Wraiths could slip through cracks in time and show up where their prey was going to be. It wasn't a theory he was eager to try out. The thought of popping up somewhere and having them waiting for him kept him jumping from one point to another without a stop for rest. Resolutely, Dean pushed the Jackals and Blake from his thoughts and concentrated on Andrei instead.

When he stumbled to a halt again, his stomach roiled with nausea and exhaustion was starting to creep in. He closed his eyes and listened intently. The sounds had faded a little more. *Thank God.* The chills stopped crawling over his skin, though his heart still pounded.

This time he brought up memories of Sunday dinners at his parents' house: the taste of fresh corn from the farmer's market; blue crabs steamed and covered in Old Bay seasoning, just waiting to be picked apart; the sound of his brother teasing his two sisters until they ganged up on him for retaliation.

He and Andrei had told the whole family they'd started dating at one of those Sunday dinners. Andrei had been more nervous than him, understandably so. Dean had no doubt of his family's acceptance. As Dean's dad had put it, he wasn't all that surprised, because there had always been a vibe between Dean and Andrei, and at least Dean had the sense to pick someone who wasn't intimidated by the Marshall brood.

Dean gathered his energy and shifted again with another lurch. The Jackal Wraiths were in the distance, and their howls became more baffled. Hope surged. It was working. He just had to keep his mind clear of all the negative emotions.

He looked around to gather his bearings and was unsurprised to find himself in his parents' backyard. It caused such a bittersweet pang. Dean turned around slowly, taking in the sight of the little house on the water and storing the image deep in his mind to sustain him.

He wished he knew where Andrei was now and what had happened with Blake. He'd left Andrei to deal with the man alone. Dean's fists tightened, and he had to force himself to unclench them.

No, nothing he could do about it now. He couldn't help Andrei if he let himself be torn apart. He had to remember to keep his temper. He didn't think he'd be able to lose the Jackals again. Each brush with them only seemed to make them latch onto him more.

Dean popped over to his childhood home in Mechanicsville and filled himself with more good memories, then moved to the church where he'd first met Andrei. With each jump, he concentrated on the good instead of the bad, and with each jump, it became easier to keep the anger from taking over.

He continued to move from place to place long after he couldn't hear the Jackal Wraiths anymore, until he was absolutely certain he'd lost them. He was almost too tired to get excited about it. He just wanted to see Andrei, hold him and know he was safe. Their house was quiet when Dean appeared, and it looked as if Andrei hadn't returned yet. He sat down to wait, trying not to think of all the ways the chase could've gone wrong.

Come on, Andrei can take care of himself. Obviously better than you can. Telling himself that didn't stop Dean from worrying and wishing he didn't feel so damned useless.

As the hours dragged on after he returned home, his resolve not to hunt Andrei down weakened. The thought of Blake hurting Andrei made Dean sick with fury, and that was why he *couldn't* risk searching for him. It was crazy. He now had the taste of Blake's rancid and oily soul in the back of his throat. And he couldn't use it to find Blake. Dean had to get control of himself if he wanted to be of any help to Andrei.

The sound of the key in the door distracted him from his brooding thoughts, and Dean surged out of the armchair as Andrei came in. "What the hell happened to you? Are you okay?"

Dean crossed over to Andrei and brushed his fingertips over the cut on Andrei's forehead. Someone had cleaned it and put butterfly bandages on it; Dean wished that he'd been the one to help him.

"There you are. I thought you were going to stay beside me. Where did you disappear to?" Andrei dropped down on the couch and stretched out his legs on the coffee table, exhaustion dragging the corners of his mouth down. "Blake got away."

"I…." Dean sighed, guilt eating away at him. "There's a slight complication I haven't told you about."

Andrei scrubbed a hand over his face, then fixed his gaze on Dean. "How pissed off am I going to be about this complication?"

"Considering the mood you're already in, babe, I'd say off the scale." Dean sank down on the other side of the couch, facing Andrei, and tucked his foot under him.

"So that means the complication spells danger for you." Andrei rose and grabbed the bottle of Scotch that Justin had left earlier.

"Oh no you don't." Dean appeared in front of Andrei and yanked the bottle out of his hands. "You're not going to pickle your liver while I'm around."

"Fuck you, Dean. You don't know what it's like." Andrei sat back down and sank his head in his hands.

"No, fuck you. You think you're the only one hurting? The only one of us missing what we can't have anymore?"

"I don't want to fight," Andrei murmured, raising his head. His eyes were red rimmed and tired. "You have all the answers and are making all the decisions. I ask you to go so you'll be safe, and you refuse. I ask you to touch me, I fucking beg you, and you refuse because you don't want me to get hurt. Where does that leave me?"

Dean stared at him, at a loss for words, and Andrei took the opportunity to snatch the bottle back and down a few gulps. He didn't know what to do. All of his instincts screamed at him to take Andrei in his arms, to end this madness and give them both what they needed, but Old Mother's warning echoed in his head and froze him in place.

"So, tell me this complication of yours." Andrei set the bottle on the coffee table and settled himself on the couch again, his hands crossed over his stomach. "What else do we have to worry about?"

Dean hesitated and wished he'd kept his fucking mouth shut. Andrei didn't need to stress over something else. Only now that he'd already said something, Andrei wouldn't let it drop. So in terse words he told Andrei everything he knew about the Jackal Wraiths, the times he had heard them, and the consequences if they caught him.

Andrei didn't speak when he was done, just took another long pull on the bottle and laid his head back on the couch with his eyes closed. "You're not going to harass me to leave?" Dean asked after a long, agonizing moment.

"What's the point? You won't and it will lead to another argument, and I can't handle that right now." Andrei opened his eyes and turned his head toward him. He slid his hand along the couch, stopping just short of touching Dean. "You don't understand, I don't want you to go. I don't want to say good-bye and not know when I'll see you again. I'd give up ten years of my own life if it would buy me that time with you. We don't have that option, so at least if you go, there's the hope that one day I will be with you, and we won't be parted again."

"Soon, I swear it. You're on the trail of Inez and Tristan. As soon as they're safe, I'll go, I promise. A few weeks won't matter. And we may not get to touch, but we can see each other, we can talk, and that's better than nothing." Dean hesitated and then he decided that he had to give Andrei some hope. "I've been told that I could take Ileana with me when I go."

"Is that even possible?" Andrei whispered, and his Adam's apple bobbed convulsively. "Do you believe it?"

Dean brushed his fingers over Andrei's hand, the light touch that Andrei could feel but that didn't open that drain of his energies. "The woman who told me is absolutely committed to her descendants. You and Ileana are among them. You should've seen the look on her face when I asked. I believe her, plus the man in the doorway who keeps calling me to cross confirmed it."

Once again Andrei remained silent, and when he spoke again, his voice was hoarse. "Thank you, *iubito*. You don't know what it was like, seeing the heartbreak and confusion on her face. Her little brother had endless hours to spend with her, playing, sharing confidences, but after my parents left me, playtime was over. She never understood and it hurt her."

"Poppet has a one-track mind, but she loves you. She's devoted to you."

"What else does she have? Absolutely nothing. And the thought of me dying and leaving her all alone...." Andrei closed his eyes, but not before Dean saw the shimmer of tears in them. "Each year it got worse because I couldn't see any hope for her."

Dean's throat tightened. Andrei must've hated himself for Ileana being stuck. Even if he'd just been a kid and hadn't known the rules, Andrei would've blamed himself. "You don't have to worry about it anymore."

"I don't want you to look at me and not understand how I got old on you. I don't want to see that same look on your face, Dean, and know that you're lost too. And that one day I'm going to wind up moving on and leaving you with nothing but an endless, confusing void."

"It won't happen, babe. I swear to you. If it's the last chance I have to walk through the door, I'll go and take Ileana with me." Dean hoped that he'd know when it was the last time. He couldn't imagine that he wouldn't warn himself. "Even if you haven't found Inez and Tristan yet, I'll go."

Andrei took a deep breath and nodded. "That's all I can ask, thank you. Tomorrow I'll be leaving for the Outer Banks. Blake knows somebody's onto him now. He'll want to get out of town fast, and there's a couple hundred miles of beaches and campgrounds to search. It's going to take me days to do a thorough job. Justin's going to be keeping an eye on the paper trail from this end."

"I know. I was there when you discussed it. I guess you need to get some sleep, then." Dean stayed next to him, tracing his fingers over Andrei's hand, unable to stop as long as it didn't seem to be affecting his partner in a bad way. "Something else strange happened this afternoon. I wanted to get your spin on it."

Andrei turned his hand over, palm up, and tangled their fingers together. How many nights had they sat on this couch, watching TV or talking over the day, touching just like this? Such an easy, loving, simple touch. How many times had he taken it for granted?

"Go ahead."

"Blake saw me at the funeral. I have no idea how. Nobody else has caught a glimpse of me other than you. Not even Justin when I was screwing with him earlier. Why now?"

"I don't know. Maybe because you have a blood tie." Andrei frowned, his eyes far away as he thought it over. "But, he couldn't have seen you the whole time, or he would've picked another vantage point or left altogether."

"No, he didn't. I recognized when he did. He was looking through me, then all of a sudden it was like he focused or something. I'm surprised you didn't hear him shriek when he did."

"What were you doing when he saw you? Something out of the ordinary?"

"Attempting to strangle him." Dean glanced away and tugged on his earlobe as Andrei turned toward him.

"Run that by me again."

Dean shrugged, uncomfortable with meeting Andrei's eyes after that admission, but he made himself do it anyway. "Don't tell me you haven't thought of offing him yourself once or twice."

Something dangerous flashed in Andrei's eyes, a hardness Dean had never seen in his face before and had no wish to see again. "Oh, I understand the feeling, and I can't say that you don't have provocation. It's just not you. You're not the vengeful type."

"Yeah, well, I feel like an idiot about it now." Dean shuddered as he remembered those howls. He hadn't really believed that old woman and Ileana's stories about the Jackal Wraiths. Not really. Even though the first time he'd heard the howl it had freaked him out. It hadn't been real enough.

He'd never had much of a mystical bent when he was alive, and though he believed their urgency, he could sense it, it was hard to really picture what they were saying. But, after everything that had happened earlier in the evening. Those hours of being chased, constantly hearing those teeth and snarls, feeling them.... Those howls. Fuck. They'd eaten into his brain, whispering all the things they would do to him when they caught him. No, he fucking believed now. At least he hadn't caught a glimpse of them. He'd never have been able to escape then. The howls were bad enough; he couldn't even begin to imagine what they looked like.

"He probably sensed your intent. I'm sure most people, whether they have the sixth sense or not, would feel it when a spirit thirsted for their blood." Andrei touched Dean's cheek and sighed as Dean let himself fade before he was tempted to kiss him. "Promise me you won't act on it, though. Like I said, it's not you."

"And what about you, Andrei?" That look flashed in his partner's eyes again, and it hurt to see it. "What kind of man are you?"

"You've known me a long time. Do you have to ask?" Andrei let his hand fall as he turned away again.

"I've never seen this side of you."

"That's because I never wanted you to see it." Dean stared after him, unable to think of anything else to say to that as Andrei rose and walked toward the stairs to his office, taking the bottle of Scotch with him. "I need to finish making that list before I get the sleep you want me to get."

A SENSE of slithering wrongness jerked Dean out of a light doze. He glanced around at the gray haze surrounding him, disoriented. He concentrated on Andrei and where he'd left him passed out, slumped over at his desk where he had been making a list of campgrounds in

North Carolina. The drink had been partially to blame for his state, but Dean had cheated a bit too, zapping him just enough that he fell asleep.

Dean turned around, frowning as he stared up at the ceiling as the wrongness passed overhead. Terror froze his insides, making his mind babble until he realized that he didn't hear the howls. It wasn't the Jackals, then. He took a step closer to Andrei, his heart still pounding with fear. A rancid taste coated the back of his throat, and immediately fury replaced the terror.

Blake was here. That sadistic son of a bitch was in the house. *How dare he?* Dean was going to…. He stopped himself again, closing his eyes and thinking of Ileana, Andrei…. They needed him to keep ahold of his temper. He could do it. He forced himself to count to ten and then to twenty until he got a grip on himself.

"Andrei," he said in a hoarse whisper. "Babe, you've gotta wake up. Blake's here."

Andrei snored in response. Dean glared at him and then stared up at the ceiling. He had to confront Blake, and he had to do it in a way that wouldn't set his anger off and get the Jackals on him again. Only the thought of that monster in their home, the home he'd made with Andrei… and the thought that he had to be here to hurt Andrei made it so very hard to keep ahold of his control. And he hadn't even laid eyes on Blake yet.

He could do this. No, he had to do this. Dean closed his eyes, and instead of concentrating on Blake, he pictured his living room, and with a lurch he was there. He spun around, studying the shadows, and saw Blake disappear down the hallway toward their bedroom. Dean concentrated hard, searching for a weapon he could use without actually touching Blake.

Using his mind he grabbed his heavy skillet from the kitchen and sent it hurtling down the hallway after Blake, following the rotten taste of him. Dean snarled in satisfaction as he heard a heavy clunk and loud cry. Got the bastard. He lurched and appeared in the doorway just as Blake got to his feet again, looking around wildly.

"You don't belong here." Dean concentrated all of his energy on Blake, grateful that the effort helped him to keep his emotions in check. He took a step closer, beginning to tremble. A bottle of cologne flew off the dresser and struck Blake on the arm that held his gun. "Leave. You won't touch him."

Blake whirled around, the gun going off, shattering a window. Dean jumped back, the roar of the gun filling his mind. His chest ached as if he'd been punched in the sternum. He found himself on his hands and knees, panting, blood dripping from his chest onto their bedroom floor. So much fucking blood. The kids... where were the kids? He had to save them.

ANDREI jolted awake at the sound of a gunshot and looked around his office in confusion. Dean was nowhere in sight, and a bottle of Scotch sat on his desk. Andrei passed a tired hand over his face, lethargy making every movement an effort, and a cough tickled the back of his throat. That was it, no more drinking. All the aches from his encounter with Blake earlier in the day came rushing back.

He looked upstairs as footsteps creaked overhead. "Dean? Is that you?"

The footsteps paused and Andrei's heart began to race. Not Dean, then. He slid his hand toward the cell phone. He'd call Justin; they could have a squad car here in minutes. Then he paused and picked up his gun instead. There could only be one person up there not answering when he called. This could be his chance.

"Blake, you are one dumb motherfucker," Andrei breathed. Adrenaline chased away the lingering exhaustion in his bones and the Scotch in his blood. He eased out through the sliding glass door and took the outside stairs, crouching low. Another cough threatened and he stifled it against his arm. He made his way around to the front and pressed himself against the house as he scanned their street in both directions. No sign of a camper truck anywhere. "Dean, where are you?"

He tried not to think about those Jackals that Dean had told him about as he crept toward their front door. Dean could keep ahold of his temper. He would be okay. "Then where the fuck is he?" he muttered back to himself.

Andrei peered through the broken bedroom window and saw a shadow flicker on the wall as someone left. Glass crunched under his foot, and Andrei pressed his lips together to hold back a curse. Maybe the sound wouldn't carry.

As Andrei turned toward the front door, Dean appeared in front of him, flickering in and out, with blood covering his shirt. Andrei leapt back with a curse, his heart hammering. "Christ, Dean, don't fucking do that to me."

"An-Andrei. Andrei, I-I-I'm s-s-sorry."

Andrei stepped closer, reaching out for Dean. "It's okay, I'm here. You're here, *iubito*. Snap out of it."

"Ass-asswipe," Dean spat. "R-r-run!"

"Dean, listen to me." Andrei tried to grab hold of him, but his hands passed right through him. "You're with me."

"Run!"

Andrei gasped as a force propelled him back several feet. He stumbled, falling on his ass as Blake stepped onto the porch and raised his gun at him. Andrei rolled out of the way and scrambled to his feet, darting around the side of the house as the gun went off. Fuck, if Dean hadn't pushed him, that one would've hit him for sure. Stupid of him to let himself get distracted in a cat and mouse game with a murderer.

DEAN whirled on Blake as he came tearing out of the house after Andrei. The urge to grab Blake around the throat and slowly throttle the life out of him overcame all other instincts. "You won't touch him."

Howls sounded nearby and Dean ignored them, fury exploding out of him. He rose off the ground as lightning ripped across the sky with a peal of thunder. The howls changed to yips of excitement getting closer. His soul shivered as his mind filled with all the terrible things that waited to pounce on him. He could feel an echo of it, his essence being ripped slowly from his body, eaten piece by piece as the Jackal Wraiths slavered over him.

Dean threw all that fear and hate and rage at Blake. The trees in their yard bent and trembled as a psychic storm tore through them, taking away branches and leaves. Blake paused at the top of the outside steps leading down to Andrei's office, took aim, and fired just as the whirlwind hit him.

Twin shouts of pain pierced the ever increasing darkness. The air weighed Dean down, held him trapped as he now struggled to break free of his own anger. Andrei had been hurt. Blake was still there. *Andrei, Andrei, Andrei....*

Dean dropped, falling to his hands and knees as the storm quieted and the stars appeared again one by one. The ground was littered with debris, fallen twigs, leaves ripped apart, and the ground was turned inside out in a path straight from Dean toward the top of the stairs.

Run little soul.... The words screamed out of the high-pitched yips that seemed to come from just behind him. A burst of fear jolted Dean to his feet. He couldn't look behind him. He had to see if Andrei was safe. The horrible, wet ripping sounds followed him as he stumbled toward the stairs—ripping and chewing and swallowing. His flesh quivered in response.

"No, no, no...." He staggered to a stop at the top of the outside stairs and looked down at the bottom. Blake was pushing himself to his hands and knees, shaking his head groggily. Andrei stepped out of the shadows, his left arm hanging limply by his side, and kicked the gun on the ground out of the way.

"I'm not sure what you did, Dean, but thanks."

Andrei jerked Blake up by his shirt and pressed the barrel of the gun to Blake's temple. "I'm only asking this once. Where are Inez and Tristan?"

It was over; Andrei could handle it from there. Dean started to sink to his knees in relief when Ileana appeared next to him and grabbed his hand. Her face had drained of all color, and her eyes were huge and terrified. "Dean! You gotta go. They're coming. They're coming for you!"

Oh God, Ileana. Dean stumbled; the howls wormed into his brain, creating little pockets of madness. Every bad memory, every moment of horror filled the holes. That was true hell. Dean looked over his shoulder, frozen as Ileana continued to pull on him. Good thoughts, he had to think good thoughts, only there was no room left in his mind for anything good.

"Dean, please!" Ileana shouted.

"Dean? Ileana?" Andrei's voice came from far away, almost drowned out by the howls.

Mist slithered out from around the corner of the open door to their house, writhing and undulating. Dean stumbled back as Ileana shrieked. The mist elongated and Dean shuddered as the impression of lean, emaciated bodies seemed to appear within. He couldn't look; if he looked, he'd lose his fucking mind, and he couldn't look away either.

Hungry... so hungry... little soul... such hate... such anger... such terror. Such sweet emotion to savor.

"Oh God." Dean snatched up Ileana, pressing her face against his shoulder as jaws and teeth solidified out of the mist first. Then came the pointed ears, the triangular faces. Tongues coiled out, impossibly long, slithering as the mist moved toward them, and Dean had the wrenching, terrible sensation of that tongue pushing through his body, violating him in obscene ways, tearing away small pieces of his identity.

Dean... we know you now... Run, Dean... run and try to hide again... give us our hunt.

Ileana dug her fingers into his muscles and his shirt was soaked by her tears. Ileana... he had to get her away, find someplace safe for her before the Jackals caught up to him. Andrei would be safe too if they followed him. With a despairing cry, he concentrated on another place and disappeared with a lurch.

"DEAN?" Andrei bolted up the stairs and reached out a hand to where Dean had been just a moment before. "Dean? Where are you?"

He looked toward the house where Dean had been staring, his face transfixed with horror and his body hunched as if expecting a blow. There was nothing there. The door stood open, the ground around him cluttered with detritus from the trees.

"Dean, talk to me. Illy?" Ileana always came to him when he called. "Ileana!"

He turned in a slow circle, moving deeper into the yard, his eyes straining to see into the shadows. Nothing.

The throbbing in his arm reminded him of Blake, and Andrei ran to the top of the stairs, but the other man was long gone. "Christ!" The image of a woman flickered where Blake had been kneeling. She stared up at Andrei, her expression stark, and Andrei clung to the railing to keep from falling down the stairs.

"Robin?" Andrei moved toward her, holding his breath as a tear rolled down her cheek. "I'm looking for your kids. They're still alive. Blake is more concerned with keeping what he considers his than harming them. Can you help me at all? Give me a clue?" She had to know where her own children were.

Robin turned, pointed, and then disappeared. Andrei sagged down on the steps, coughing as the last of the adrenaline faded from his body. South. That's what she gave him. He'd already reasoned that out for himself.

His arm throbbed like a bitch. Andrei pressed a hand to the wound again, applying pressure. At least the worst of the bleeding seemed to have stopped; must've just winged him. He'd get up in a minute and make the calls he needed to make. Blake had gotten away…

again. Andrei was screwing up this investigation at every point. When Ileana had appeared and warned Dean that they were coming, he'd forgotten about everything but getting to them.

"Dean, please, come home. Let me know that you and Ileana are safe," Andrei called out.

For the second time in less than twenty-four hours, Andrei heard sirens in the distance. Justin was going to think he'd lost his ever loving mind if he found him sitting outside, injured, and talking to ghosts. Especially after the madness at the shopping center today. He tried to summon up the energy to move inside and failed.

The crazy-assed story that Dean had told him would not leave his thoughts. Dean and Ileana had seen something, and whatever it was had scared them absolutely senseless. What if.... Andrei tightened his fist in his hair and yanked as his shoulders started to shake. He couldn't think like that. Dean was clever and resourceful, and Ileana had been a ghost for a long time. They would take care of each other.

Andrei kissed the crucifix around his throat and begged in silence. Please, please, let them be okay. Dean and Ileana had to still exist. He had to have faith. Oh God, please let them be okay.

"Dean? Illy?"

Chapter Thirteen

ANDREI leaned his head back against the headrest and struggled to suppress the series of wracking coughs. His ribs ached like a bitch, and his arm throbbed as if someone had jabbed a rusty nail into his bicep and jerked it around a few times.

Maybe he should've taken Justin's advice and rested for a day before heading down to North Carolina. Yeah right. He would've driven himself crazy wondering what had happened to Ileana and Dean. When he wasn't doing that, he would've been obsessing over those missing kids and pouring over maps of the Outer Banks. At least by driving down, he was doing something proactive.

He'd rented a Jeep that he could take off-roading, just in case Blake had decided to risk not staying in an official campground. Besides, Blake knew what his van looked like now, and it would stand out amongst all the other vehicles. But after a long day of driving and searching the beaches around Corolla and Duck, Andrei had nothing to show for it. Not one blue truck with a camper and car attached to be seen, and neither Inez's nor Blake's picture had provoked any recognition.

Now it had gotten too dark to search the beaches anymore. Andrei pulled out his cell phone and dialed Justin. He stared out the windshield at the hotel with its welcoming lights that just seemed to drain the last energy from him. *Dean, where are you, iubito?*

"Where are you?" Justin's deep bass grumbled in Andrei's ear.

"Kitty Hawk. There's a couple campgrounds here and in Kill Devil Hills I want to check out tomorrow. They don't seem to be too big, but a lot of people are heading into town for Labor Day weekend, so I expect them to be full."

Justin grunted. "How's your arm?"

"I don't think I broke open the stitches or made it start bleeding again." Andrei forced himself to get out of the Jeep and gather his gear. If he didn't move now, he might just be out there till morning. "I'm getting ready to grab a room and some food. I'll take a look at it then, but I think you worry too much. The doctor did a good job patching me up."

"With you, I think I don't worry enough. Why don't you stay put, rest for a day, and I'll join you down there? I have some leave built up. We could cover more ground between the two of us."

If anyone would stop Andrei from putting a bullet in Blake, it was Justin. And he had no doubt that Justin would arrest him on top of it. He didn't want his friend to have that kind of a moral dilemma on his hands, because even though Justin would arrest him, it would screw with him.

"Aren't you in enough trouble dealing with me? I thought your chief said I was a bad element."

"What do you expect? You were involved in two, fucking count 'em, two shootouts in one day."

"Blake did all the shooting." Andrei set down his bags as he reached the lobby door and suppressed another cough, smothering it in his arm. "Okay, yes, I'll admit to being tempted to take a few after the funeral, but that was only after he'd first shot at me several times, threatened other people, and was attempting to get away."

"Please tell me you didn't bring your gun with you. You're not licensed to carry a concealed weapon in North Carolina."

"What do you think I am? An idiot?" Andrei's arm began to throb even more in countertime to the throb in his temples.

There was a long pause on the other end of the line, and then Justin said, "I think you're too emotionally invested in this case and need to back off, that's what I think. You look like you're dying from the inside out. Once you find those kids, you need to find a way to let Dean rest."

Dean. Andrei's chest panged as he picked up his bags again. Dean and Ileana had to be okay. Andrei wouldn't accept anything less. Why the hell hadn't he heard from them? "Yeah, I just need to do this, then I can let it go. Look, I'm getting ready to check in and then I'm going to crash. I'll call you tomorrow night with an update."

Before Justin could argue with him, Andrei hung up the phone. A hot shower and a clean bed was all he needed. Andrei thought of Dean and sighed as he walked up to the counter. He could almost hear Dean's pointed commentary on that. Food too.

"Checking in, sir?" The clerk looked up with a polite smile.

"Yeah, but first...." Andrei fished the pictures out of his laptop bag. "Have you seen this man, either around town or looking for a place to stay? He may or may not have two kids with him, a little girl and a baby."

The clerk studied the two pictures and then handed them back to Andrei with a regretful smile. "I can't say that I have. We get so many tourists around here they all kind of blend together. I'm sorry." Her fingers paused over the keyboard. "You still looking to check in?"

"Yeah, one room, just for tonight." He turned his face away, leaning against the counter as he began to cough. The more he tried to suppress it, the worse it became, and Andrei became uncomfortably aware of people turning to look. "Sorry, something caught in my throat," he finally managed.

"Are you sure? You look like you need a doctor." The clerk looked at him uneasily as Andrei held out his credit card and a business card.

"I'm fine. If you see those kids or that man, call either me or the number on the back. It's a detective at the Baltimore police station."

His legs trembled. Andrei couldn't remember feeling this bad in a long time. He never got sick. A good night's sleep. That's all he needed. That and maybe some soup. And more than anything some news, something about either the kids or Dean and Ileana. He did not want to fall asleep again to the silence of loneliness and more what ifs running around in his head.

DEAN and Ileana stumbled out of another jump and fell in an ungainly heap on the ground. He had no idea where they were; all he cared about was that, for the moment, the howls were distant. Those never-ending howls. He shuddered and tugged Ileana to him as she cried silently.

How long had they been running? Hours? Days? It seemed like an eternity of hell. Dean was so exhausted that every bone in his body ached as if it had already been gnawed on. Ending it now would almost be a mercy. That's what Old Mother had told him, that the Jackals tormented and chased until their victims had nothing left in them. Dread had become an ever-present deadweight in his gut, dragging him down.

He couldn't even sense Andrei anymore. He tightened his arm around Ileana as the howls lurched closer. *Hungry... hungry... hungry....* His heart leapt in fresh terror for a moment before settling back to the same dull, heavy horror. "Poppet. We've got to get up," he panted.

"I want Cougar," she sobbed. "I lost him. We gotta go back and look."

"We don't have time to look for a stuffed turtle. We need to get moving." He forced himself to his knees.

"But he's scared. What if the hungry things eat him all up?"

Dean brushed her tangled hair out of her face. She'd lost the ties holding it back long ago. What if the Jackal Wraiths ate them both up? Much worse than a turtle. He'd made a promise to Andrei to take care of her, to take care of himself and make sure they both crossed over. He wouldn't be able to keep that promise if the Jackals caught them.

He shuddered as the chewing sounds crawled under his skin, the terrible crack of bones shattering, and the slither of those tongues over flesh. Dean choked back a hysterical laugh before Ileana grabbed ahold of him. He needed to concentrate. He couldn't let the sounds get to him.

"You need to go to Old Mother. I'm sure she'll help you find Cougar," Dean said, as he'd said every single time they'd found a few moments before the Jackals closed in on them. The creatures couldn't have a link to Ileana. She never heard them unless they were almost on top of them. She reacted more out of Dean's fear than her own. Ileana had done nothing wrong. If she left him, she'd be spared this endless chase.

Ileana shook her head and clung tighter to him. "No, no, no. I'm staying with you. You're in trouble."

"That's why I want you to go. You'll be safer without me, and I can move quicker without you."

"No! You're going to let yourself get eaten up. I'm not leaving. You can't make me."

Not for the first time, Dean wished he knew of a way to make her leave and stay with Old Mother. But if that old bat, with all her years of experience, hadn't been able to keep control of Ileana, he had little hope of succeeding himself.

Ileana's head whipped around as the howls closed in on them, coming from what seemed like all directions at once. Dean searched the area for any sign of the mist that appeared first. Then he realized he was just delaying things in a last-ditch effort to conserve what energy he had left.

"I'm not going to let them get me." Dean struggled to his feet, swaying with exhaustion, and held out a hand to Ileana. "Come on, Poppet. Time to move again."

Ileana stuck out her chin and scrambled to her feet without complaint. Tears still fell from her eyes, but she wasn't sobbing anymore. "I can pick this time, 'kay? Think of me."

Dean couldn't summon up the energy to argue. He didn't even have it in him to be angry at his pursuers anymore or rage toward Blake for killing him. All he had left was concern for Ileana and sorrow for Andrei. Every other emotion had been burned away, purified from their harrowing flight.

He wrapped his arms around Ileana and bent his head toward hers as they fell into that limbo world that allowed them to jump from one place to another. The disorientation was far more acute now that they were at the end of their reserves and even here, with the wrenching, twisting madness all around them, Dean could still hear the Jackals right behind him.

Soon, little soul.... Dean screamed as teeth nipped at his heels. *Scream again for us.... Taste your fear, Dean... feast on your flesh.* A thousand needles pricked him, driving deep into his skin, his eyes. A trap closed around him, just waiting to snap shut. Dean lost all sense of Ileana, and every time he tried to concentrate on her, the howls came a little closer.

"Andrei."

Dean landed heavily on the ground, all the breath driven from his body. Nearby he could hear the sound of retching, and his own stomach rebelled. He was dead; why did he still have such human, such living reactions? He tried to roll over onto his side and managed to turn his head. Ileana whimpered on her hands and knees, her straggling hair obscuring her face.

"Ileana. Ileana...," he panted. "We... we have to go." He couldn't jump again. There was just nothing left inside of him. He'd either end up falling for an eternity or getting caught by the Jackals. Neither was an option he wanted to consider. There was only one thing left to do.

Andrei... God, Andrei. I'm sorry. I wanted the chance to say good-bye to you. I love you. If only I could tell you one more time.

"Dean... I'm scared. I've never gotten sick before." She lifted her head, her face wan and her eyes dull with exhaustion and debilitating fear.

"It's okay, Poppet." Dean pushed himself to his hands and knees, not at all surprised by the blood that started dripping from his chest to the ground. This was the end. Made sense that his body should go back to his final moments, right? "I'm going to make sure you're safe. No matter what it takes."

Even if it meant he'd never get to say good-bye to Andrei. Even if it meant knowing that Andrei would be haunted for the rest of his life, not knowing whether or not Ileana and him had been devoured. At least this way, there was a chance of seeing him again sometime, of letting him know that Dean had kept his last promise to him.

"Ileana, get close to me. Hold on tight."

"I don't hear them," Ileana whimpered as she struggled to sit up. "I don't wanna jump again, Dean. Please don't make me."

Dean could hear them... the Jackal Wraiths closing in on them. A vicious glee arose in their howls now. An obscene joy in anticipation of the pain they were going to mete out to them with slow relish. Some things didn't need words to be understood. Not when the sounds ran through him like acid pumping in his veins, burning and tearing away at him from the inside out.

Andrei... Andrei....

He had to hold on. "Not gonna jump, Poppet. Going someplace safe. The Jackals will never be able to get us there." Please let that be true. He had nothing left inside, no way to fight.

Ileana crawled over to him and wrapped her arms around Dean's waist. "But what about Andrei and Old Mother and Cougar?"

I'm ready. Do you hear me? I'm ready to go. Dean threw that thought out to his other self behind the door.

Slavering snarls and growls scraped at his eardrums. Dean moaned and tried to cover his ears, but the sounds only intensified. They were close... so fucking close, and he couldn't see that light in the doorway anywhere.

"Andrei... Andrei will catch up with us one day. And Old Mother—"

"You are the bastard son of a goat. I told you to keep your temper. I told you how important it was, and just like a young man, you ran off rashly and within days forgot everything I told you."

Dean's head jerked up at the sound of that querulous voice. Old Mother stood before him, bristling, her gaze sharp with rage. Dean bit the inside of his cheek before he said something in front of Ileana that he would regret later. "I'm handling it." *You crazy old bat.*

Ileana gasped and Old Mother's eyes narrowed. Belatedly, Dean remembered how Ileana told him that he spoke very loud inside his head. How come he couldn't read their thoughts? Why did he even worry about such a ridiculous, trivial thing now?

Please, do you hear me? I'm—

Dean's prayer cut off with a shudder as a howl whipped across his body like a lash. If he turned his head, he'd see the Jackals pouring out of those mists, gathering into jaws and shining teeth. He'd trapped himself and Ileana with him.

Please, please, please....

He pushed himself up onto his knees, searching the area for any sign of that golden glow. His heart sank dully when he found nothing, not even the Jackals, though he knew they were coming closer with each beat of his heart. He couldn't even sense that pull of longing that he got when he thought of passing on. *Good fucking job, asshole. You really did it this time.* He pulled Ileana's arms from around him and shoved her toward Old Mother. "Go. Take her with you."

"*No!*" Ileana shrieked as she twisted around and reached out toward him. "No, Dean, no."

"The Jackal Wraiths require a sacrifice. They have the taste of a soul in their jaws now and won't stop until they've fed." Old Mother clamped her arms around Ileana, caging her despite her struggles.

Run, Dean... so hungry.... Another howl whipped at him, and Dean reeled as he lurched to his feet. He refused to have it end on his hands and knees. Old Mother shook Ileana as she leaned down to whisper in her ear.

The mist began to form along a bend in a tree where a crooked branch met the truck. Long tendrils slithered down, materializing into tongues that reached for him. Dean snatched up a branch from the ground with a snarl. "Come an' get me."

Please... for the love of God... where the fuck are you? Seriously... I'll go without argument now....

"Take her and go." Dean glared at Old Mother who snarled right back at him, saying something in a tongue he didn't understand.

The Jackals leapt down from the tree, the heads on the long necks undulating, the lean, emaciated bodies weaving amongst themselves. Dean took a step back, brandishing his makeshift club as they snapped their jaws at him. Sweat trickled down his face, and his breath came in harsh pants. They were going to pounce any moment. One of those tongues was going to lash out, snag him by an ankle and drag him to them. He thought he might go mad if one of them touched him. He might just go mad waiting.

Andrei... Andrei... God I'm sorry babe, I'm so sorry.

Dean grunted hard as Ileana barreled into him and wrapped her arms around his waist. "Dammit, Ileana," Dean roared, dropping his weapon as he tried to pull her from him. "I told you to go with Old Mother."

"Look at me. Please, Dean, look at me, not at the hungry things. Dean, please."

The Jackals stiffened, their unnatural eyes gleaming as Dean tried to look away. He struggled against it, silently screaming inside. Old Mother shouted in fury and ran past him right toward the Jackals. Immediately, all their focus turned toward her as the Jackal Wraiths' horrific tongues and tails lashed.

"No, wait. Don't." Dean's arms went around Ileana without thought. And when he finally pulled his gaze away, it felt almost like something inside of him ripped away and was left behind. Ileana trembled as Old Mother started screaming, and instinctively Dean turned to help.

Ileana grabbed him by his ears and yanked his head down. "Look at me."

Dean opened his mouth to argue only to find himself caught by the intensity of Ileana's gaze. Her eyes, so like Andrei's, filled with tears. Then the world fell away as they dropped through that space, followed by the sounds of Old Mother's horror-filled screams of agony. For the first time in what seemed like forever, the Jackals didn't follow.

This time when he landed, Dean knew just a moment of blessed silence broken only by the sound of ragged crying from Ileana. He blinked up at the stars shining through the trees overhead before closing his eyes again on a rush of nausea. The world still spun. He tucked Ileana closer, too tired to offer more comfort than that. He'd just rest here a moment....

DEAN awoke with a start and Ileana jerked awake next to him. She sat up with a scared little cry. "What is it? Is it the Jackals?"

He listened hard for a minute, straining to hear anything from them, and to his relief it remained silent. Even the taint of their madness had gone from his mind. "No, Poppet. I think they're gone for good." He sagged back down and closed his eyes, still exhausted from the chase. At least he could also feel Andrei again, a faint and tenuous line, darkened somewhat, but it stretched right back to him so impossibly far away.

He'd been such a foolish jackass. He had to learn more control than he'd shown. It wasn't like him to have his emotions spin so wildly out of control, and now Old Mother had paid the price.

"Is it true?" Ileana asked in a small voice. "Do you really think she's gone?"

Dean stared up at the stars as regret swamped him. No one should go out like that. Not even an old bat like her. She'd sacrificed herself for the sake of her children's children as she had told him she would.

"Yeah, I'm sorry, Ileana. She did a very brave thing for us."

Ileana sighed and laid her head on his shoulder. She seemed to be too tired for tears. Dean passed a hand gently over her tangled hair. *"Puri Daj* always said that was her destiny. That's why she stayed behind. She knew she would be needed."

That offered scant comfort for Dean. He forced himself to sit up before he began beating himself up too badly. He didn't have time for regrets. The only way he could make it up to Old Mother would be to keep his promise and bring Ileana with him when he moved on. He touched the bit of ribbon in his pocket. As soon as they found Inez and Tristan… please let it be soon, before something else he did not want to know about crawled out of the gray mists of limbo.

"Where're we?" Dean asked as he looked around at the collection of cars, trucks, and tents. They seemed vaguely familiar, but it was hard to tell in the darkness.

"We're with Old Mother's caravan. That's where she told me to take you." Ileana stood up as well and took his hand as she turned toward the old-fashioned *vardo* standing outside all of the others. "She came for you too, even if she called you names. She said, 'Ileana child, you go to that hardheaded brother of yours and get him out of here. Don't let him argue.' And then she pushed me at you."

Dean closed his eyes as once again regret stole over him. "Come on, Poppet. Let's get her family Bible. Someone should take care of it for her, and I bet Andrei would love to see it." And when he left, he could take it with him. Maybe if any part of Old Mother remained, it would go with him and Ileana to the other side.

"Ooooh, that'll make her happy. She'd want somebody to take care of it. But we gotta be careful. We can't spill anything or turn the pages too fast or touch it with dirty fingers, 'kay?"

"I'll be very careful, I swear." Dean wished for her innocence. He didn't think Ileana truly understood the horror of Old Mother's last moments, and he was grateful for that mercy. Even the memory of those howls had the power to make him shudder. Dean clung to the faint line that connected him to Andrei. He needed his partner.

The *vardo* held a faint scent of decay as he stepped into it, and dust lay everywhere as if it had been abandoned for weeks. He hoped they hadn't really been gone from Andrei for weeks. Andrei would be freaking out if that were the case. It didn't feel like it had been that long. And something as old as this wagon probably wouldn't last long without the spirit who had dwelled there.

Dean ran his hand over the finely carved, gilded walls. "Get the book, Poppet. Then we're going to go find Andrei." Another jump so soon when he was still exhausted would probably wipe out what reserves he had managed to gather. Staying would mean Andrei would still be stuck not knowing what had happened to them, and that was too cruel. Besides he had to know what had happened with Blake.

Maybe it was already done and over with. Which meant it would be time to say good-bye. Light spilled along the wood, chasing away the dust and decay. Dean trembled as the longing to go through the doorway washed over him. He was so tired of being pulled in one direction, then another. He was just fucking tired period.

Ileana turned toward him, her arms wrapped around the huge book, her eyes wide. "You're not leaving me, are you, Dean?"

"No, sweetie, you're going to stay with me. I promise." Dean walked over to her and took the book out of her arms before she dropped it.

"Where were you when I called? I begged for you to come, and you never did." Dean looked over at the man who stood in the doorway. His own face stared back at him gravely. "I would've gone then."

"The creatures who hunted you don't belong on this side, Dean. We couldn't open the gate the moment they latched onto you. We can't risk letting even the smallest taint of them coming through and becoming a canker." He stepped out of the doorway toward them.

Dean let out a tense breath, and relief flowed through him. "So they really are gone?"

"The sacrifice has been made. As long as you don't draw their attention again, you will be safe from them." He held out his hands to them. "Are you coming?"

Dean closed his eyes against the tug and shook his head sharply. "Soon, just a little bit longer, please."

"I'm not going to be able to come that many more times. You keep calling and then refusing. You're going to lose your chance." The other Dean paused. "And break your promise."

Dean squirmed inwardly and shifted the Bible to one arm so he could wrap the other about Ileana's shoulders. "I'm taking it on faith. Since you're the one to greet me, I must say yes sometime, right? Soon, I swear. I won't think of you or call you again until I'm ready."

"You're thinking in terms of paradoxes. No such thing over here." The other Dean stepped back, and the door began to shut, taking with it the light and the longing. "Hurry, Dean."

Chapter Fourteen

ANDREI pulled over at a small gas station in Rodanthe. This was his fourth day in the Outer Banks, and he'd yet to get any leads on Blake or his kids. A couple people thought he might be familiar, and one lady swore she thought she remembered Inez's eyes, only they couldn't point him in any direction. The only thing that gave him any hope was the occasional time Robin appeared. She never said anything or stayed for long, but she left him with the impression that he hadn't gotten off track.

The visits from Robin also brought home the terrible reality that he hadn't seen or heard from Dean and Ileana in days. Every time he lay down to rest, he could hear their shouts of terror in his memory. He almost wished Dean hadn't told him about the Jackal Wraiths. Dean normally was not a man prone to anger, but these had not been normal days. Andrei couldn't expect him to keep his temper considering the stressors he kept encountering.

And Andrei was rapidly running out of hope that he'd see Dean and Ileana again. Some nights the lure of the bottle had been almost too much. Imagining himself waking up to Blake's gun in his face was usually enough to stop him from stepping over that line. If not that, then picturing Dean and Ileana returning to find him in a drunken stupor did the trick.

Tall vacation homes, lifted up off the ground on pilings, lined the narrow road. The tang of brine hung in the air and invigorated Andrei as he climbed the steps to the small shop. His cough had almost disappeared, and he wasn't plagued anymore by those bouts of weakness that sometimes came over him and left him sagging for support. That had been the only good thing to come out of the last several days.

The small store was filled with tourists getting gas and buying sunscreen, trinkets, and snacks for the day's outings. While wandering up and down the aisles stocked with locally made goods, Andrei talked quietly with the patrons, showing his pictures until the line around the register died down. Three people stood behind the counter, an older couple and a man who looked like their grown son.

"Excuse me, I need a minute of your time." Andrei didn't give them a chance to refuse as he pulled out a picture of Blake. "I'm looking for this man. He might be driving a blue truck with a white camper on top. He may have bought baby supplies or been with an infant and a little girl about five years old."

The woman took the picture and frowned. "He looks a bit familiar. I think he might've stopped in here a few days ago. Clayton, was this the guy who'd asked about the campgrounds in the area?"

"You mean the guy who wasn't interested in any of the ones we have around here?" The older man leaned over, glanced at the picture, and shrugged. "Maybe, it's hard to tell. He had a trucker cap on, kept his head down."

Excitement gripped Andrei as all his senses seemed to sharpen. Finally, a bite. "Did you talk about any campgrounds in particular?"

"Well he seemed more interested in heading farther south. I told him about Waves, which is closer to the lighthouse. But then I mentioned the RV Park here, and he liked how big that was. Lots of things for kids to do."

"How big?"

"Oh man, it covers a good fifty acres I'd say and has several hundred hookup sites. You might be able to talk to someone at the conference center about him." Clayton handed back the picture of Blake. "'Course he might not be there anymore. Some good-sized storms are brewing out in the Atlantic. It's hurricane season, and the more nervous people are packing up."

"Wait, the guy had a little boy with him." The woman pointed to the postcard stand. "He hung out over there looking at the pictures. Cute kid, real quiet. At first I thought he had lost his parents, 'cause to be honest, I didn't exactly match him with his dad. But he went right to that guy when he called."

Andrei glanced down at the picture of Inez with her bright eyes and pretty curls all done up with ribbons. The best way to hide a little girl would be to make her appear to be a boy. "Could this be the kid you saw? Hair cut short maybe or hidden under a cap?"

The woman studied the picture and then handed it around to the other two. "I don't think so. They look a bit the same, but the little boy had sad eyes. The girl looks like a sweet imp."

It was slim but more than anything else Andrei had gotten yet. "Is there any other detail that stood out to you about him? Anything strange or notable?"

"He had a kickass wallet." The younger man spoke up for the first time as he finished ringing up another customer. "The Justice League done by Alex Ross. I asked him where he got it from, but he brushed me off."

Andrei's fingers trembled as he carefully tucked the pictures back in the folder. He'd bought that wallet for Dean, knowing how much he had loved comics. It hadn't been expensive, not nearly as nice as the leather wallet it had replaced, but Dean had been so fired up over it. And now Blake was using Dean's wallet. Funny how a small detail like that only made him want to hurt Blake even more.

"Thanks, you've been a big help." Andrei handed the woman his card. "If you see this guy again, call me or Detective Mansle, but try not to say anything to him that might raise his suspicions. He's twitchy enough as it is."

"What did he do?" the younger man asked. "He seemed an okay enough guy to me. A little standoffish, maybe."

"He murdered some people, including his ex-wife, and kidnapped his kids." The woman gasped, and Andrei gave each one of them a pointed look. "He's dangerous and has proved more than once that he's willing to go after anyone he sees as a threat, so if you see him, just call the number. Don't try to engage him."

Andrei left them murmuring amongst themselves, filled up the Jeep with gas, and headed over to the RV Park. The man at the shop hadn't been kidding. The place was huge, with rows upon rows of spaces for camping. Andrei left a message for Justin about the latest development, got a map from the conference center, and headed out on foot.

The man at the center had looked at him like he was crazy when he'd asked about a blue truck, and he hadn't recognized Blake either. That didn't bother Andrei; one man wasn't likely to stand out amongst the hundreds of others, especially if he kept to himself and stayed quiet, not causing any trouble.

Andrei wouldn't be able to cover the entire park on foot with what remained of the day, but he'd have an easier time scouting without having people notice a vehicle cruising up and down. It wouldn't take long for people to start to comment, and something like that would get back to Blake quick if he was here.

The sun beat down just as hard down here as it did back in Baltimore, but the breeze coming off the Pamlico Sound reminded him of late summer days in southern Maryland. A time when Andrei had to almost reinvent himself in a way. He'd run from the first foster home, unable to adapt to all the differences in culture and expectations, and wound up in one of the many tent communities hidden in the woods of Calvert County. It had been almost enough like his clan. Andrei had been desperate enough by then that he'd let one or two people in, and that had started him on the long, slow road to adjusting to his new world.

Somehow that had led him back to Dean and his family. After his parents had left him, they'd been the first people who'd approached him where he'd been sitting in the church pew trying to figure out what he was supposed to do. Funny how life worked itself out that way, everything coming back in a circle. Dean's parents had gotten him into a different foster home, one that suited him more, and he'd ended up finishing high school right next to Dean. Not bad for a kid who'd never gone to a formal school before.

Now Andrei was going to have to figure out how to start over again. He didn't want to any more now than he had then and had as little choice. It was either start over again or lay down and give up, and he didn't know how to give up.

If he only knew that Dean and Ileana had escaped from those things chasing them. Dean was smart. He'd pass on through the doorway before he'd let himself be destroyed even if it meant not saying good-bye. Sometimes those reassurances worked. Other times they didn't because Andrei still didn't have a grasp on how the whole thing worked.

By the time night descended, Andrei had nothing but sore feet and shredded patience. He'd talked himself hoarse, questioning families with children about Inez's age in case she'd been lured out to play, talked with other men about the advantages of RVs over campers and tents. The discreet interrogation had led to a few tantalizing hints that kept Andrei hoping that Blake was still here.

He also had to come up with a way of separating Blake from the rest of the people in the park. He wanted to get Inez and Tristan out of harm's way and someplace safe so he could have a one-on-one conversation with Blake. That would be tricky, and he hadn't figured out a way to accomplish both. It was times like this when he wished he'd taken Justin up on his offer. The kids could've been safely given to him, and Andrei could've taken care of business. He didn't even care anymore if Justin knew that he was guilty.

It was too dark to search now. People were heading into their temporary homes or stretching out near the fire pits as they began cooking dinner. Andrei smelled woodsmoke and hamburgers cooking, making his stomach rumble. At least the hurricane that was brewing out in the Atlantic didn't seem inclined to race its way toward the coast. That would make his search much more difficult.

He began to jog, eager to get to the Jeep, and once there, took a quick glance at his notes before he headed out. The town was dark as he drove through it, the only lights coming from high up in the vacation homes, and heat lightning arced across the sky. He could see glimpses of families sitting around kitchen tables, sharing the evening meal, and it made the dull ache inside of him jolt.

Andrei tried to ignore how cold and empty his hotel room seemed when he returned. He tossed his keys on the dresser, turned on the TV for noise, and left his clothes in a heap on the bathroom floor. An hour later he had showered, changed into a pair of sweats, and just sat down to his still warm delivery food after having made his regular phone calls to Justin and Evelyn.

"It's good to see that you're somewhat taking care of yourself."

Andrei dropped his forkful of untasted manicotti and whirled out of the chair so fast that it crashed to the floor. Dean stood near the door, cradling Ileana. Andrei's heart leapt in his throat, choking off any ability to speak as he stumbled toward them. He pulled Dean into his arms, his breath finally leaving him on a choked sob when Dean didn't try to pull away.

Ileana curled her hand in his hair, and Dean pressed his cheek against Andrei's as the three of them held each other. He felt the drain on his energies from Dean's touch, but instead of the electric punch that left him staggering and ready to pass out, it felt like a warm trickle, as if he were running or working out. He must be getting used to it, because he could handle that without scaring Dean and making him run.

It took several minutes for Andrei to get himself together enough to risk pulling back to look at them. Ileana had dark circles under her eyes, and her hair was a bedraggled mess. Dean had new tension lines around his mouth, and his gaze was far older than it had been when he left, like he'd seen or done things that he never should have. They looked like they'd spent the entire time they were missing on the run.

"You're safe," Andrei murmured, cupping Ileana's cheek in one hand and Dean's in the other, his eyes stinging. "I couldn't stop wondering what had happened to you."

"We almost got eaten," Ileana said as Dean set her down on a chair at the small table. "And I lost Cougar. And *Puri Daj* got killed."

Andrei tried to make sense of her stream of information and latched onto the one thing he could comment on. "Cougar will find his way back to you, Illy, he always does. Once you've rested and are feeling more like yourself, he'll return."

He reached out, unable to stop himself from touching them, making sure they were real and safe. He didn't want to let them go, and yet he needed to so they would stay safe. He had a few more days with them at the most, and then he'd have to say good-bye; in the meantime, he would make the most of every moment he had left. No more anger and angst, not when he was with them.

DEAN let Andrei pull him closer and closed his eyes at the warm brush of Andrei's lips over his own. Such a simple touch and coming from Andrei, it soothed the raw places inside of him, wearing away the edges so it didn't cut so deeply into him anymore. Dean couldn't resist that closeness, and the last thing he wanted to do was hurt Andrei again. Putting a distance between them would do just that.

Andrei was strong. He was a survivor. And as long as he didn't show any weakness from Dean's touch, Dean was more than content to let it continue. He soaked up the simple, loving touches like a man left too long in the dark starved for the light.

"You guys kissy face a lot."

Dean turned toward Ileana, trying to appear unconcerned all the while wondering just how much she'd seen of them over the years. It was acutely embarrassing. "Ummm."

"That's what couples do when they're together." Andrei picked up Ileana and set her on his lap, smoothing the tangles from her hair with his fingers. "I hope you had manners enough to leave when we did. Remember our talk about privacy?"

Ileana rolled her eyes and snuggled in closer as Andrei worked from the ends of her hair up. "Duh. Watching you kiss each other is boring."

Dean chuckled and tapped the end of her nose, relief flowing through him. "And you are a little minx." It was good to see her looking so secure in Andrei's arms and the sparkle start to return to her eyes. What he wouldn't give to be in Andrei's arms himself.

"What happened?" Andrei asked quietly, braiding one section of hair before moving on to another.

Dean shook his head and mouthed "later" over Ileana's head. He didn't want to unburden himself to Andrei while she was still awake, and he desperately needed to do just that. "Why don't I finish your hair, Poppet, and we'll let Andrei eat before his dinner gets stone cold."

"Okay." Ileana slipped down after throwing her arms around Andrei's neck and giving him a kiss on his cheek.

Andrei sighed and without a word, they both scooted their chairs closer to one another. Dean smiled at the unspoken gesture. "How many days has it been?"

Andrei shot him a sideways glance, the fine lines around his eyes and mouth deepening as he tensed. "Four."

Dean closed his eyes as he fiddled with the long strands of Ileana's hair. Four days lost to them while those monsters had chased him down. Andrei touched his hand and then slid his fingers up Dean's arm. "You're here now."

"Yeah, I am." Dean smiled at him. No regrets. They had such little time left together, and he didn't want any ugliness or guilt to mar that time. "How goes the investigation?"

"Blake's at a campground in this town. I'm pretty sure of it." Andrei pulled out the map of the park and showed Dean the areas that he'd already searched. "I'll start again tomorrow just as soon as it's late enough that I can walk around without raising suspicion."

Dean stared down at the map, frustration and worry tangling inside of him. He'd be able to answer the question of where Blake could be found in a heartbeat. He could follow the putrid taste of the man and come back and tell Andrei exactly where Blake had disappeared to with those kids. Inez and Tristan would not have to spend one more night in his company.

Only, he didn't trust himself. The two times he'd confronted Blake he'd been overcome with rage, and it had almost gotten him torn apart. He didn't even think he could summon up that kind of anger right now with how worn down he was, and he still didn't care to risk it. Too much was at stake.

"Do you think Inez and Tristan are still…." Dean glanced down at Ileana, half-asleep in his arms, and let the rest of the sentence trail off.

"They are. Someone in town ID'd them. Though Blake is trying to pass off Inez as a little boy. At that age it's easy to do."

Dean breathed in a sigh of relief and rose, cradling Ileana against him. "Where should I put her? She's exhausted. I'm pretty shagged myself. I never thought a ghost could get tired, but jumping all around takes energy." And putting forth the energy to make sure Andrei could see, hear, and touch him took even more.

Andrei tossed his paper napkin on the remains of his dinner. "The couch will work. I'll get the extra blanket from the closet."

"We're not gonna leave again, are we?" Ileana asked sleepily as Dean laid her down and straightened her sundress. "We're gonna stay and be a family, right? I've wanted a family again for the longest time."

Dean smoothed his hand over her head. "We are a family, Poppet. No matter where we are." He leaned down and kissed her forehead as Andrei returned, shaking out a blanket.

Dean stepped back, watching as Andrei tenderly tucked the blanket around her. He'd always loved watching Andrei with their nieces and nephews. He had far more patience with them than he did with any adult, and it always made Dean ache because he had wanted so bad to raise kids of their own with that man. There were so many children out there alone and neglected, just like Andrei had been.

"Sing 'Nani, Nani'." Ileana twisted her fingers in Andrei's shirt as she cast him a look of appeal through her lashes that would've melted the hardest heart.

His cheeks flushing, Andrei glanced at Dean. Dean couldn't remember Andrei ever singing, not to anyone, not along to the radio, not even in the shower. And he understood why the moment the first words passed Andrei's lips. His partner was as tone deaf as they came, and he was clearly embarrassed at having Dean witness him singing. It didn't seem to bother Ileana one bit as she fell asleep with the first true smile on her face in days. And damned if listening to Andrei butcher a lullaby didn't make Dean fall in love with him all over again.

Andrei quieted as he watched her sleep and then looked at Dean over his shoulder with a wary expression. "Go ahead and say it. I know you're dying to."

"You definitely aren't going to win *American Idol*, babe."

Andrei shook his head as Dean grinned and held out his hand to help him up. "Always teasing. What am I going to do with you?"

"I think we both know the answer to that," Dean said and kissed Andrei's knuckles.

The blanket on the couch collapsed as Ileana disappeared with a sigh of air that sounded like a last breath. Andrei's brows drew together in a worried frown. "Where do you guys go when you do that?"

"I have no idea. It's some misty, empty space. She'll come back right here when she's recovered. We've been running almost nonstop."

Dean ached to touch him, to renew the loving intimacy of their relationship. He slipped his arm around Andrei's waist and drew him closer as Andrei's eyes widened. Andrei fisted his hands in Dean's shirt at the small of his back and wet his lips, looking at a loss for words. Dean rested his forehead against Andrei's. "I love you, just the way you are. I love you more today than I did yesterday. And I'm going to love you even more tomorrow."

Andrei's eyes closed, but not before Dean saw them sheen with moisture, and his voice sounded rough when he spoke. "Lie down with me? Please, *iubito*. Just hold me for a bit."

Dean couldn't deny him any longer. His time was too short, and Andrei never asked for anything with such vulnerability. He kissed Andrei's eyes and held him tight for a few moments longer before nodding. "I'll hold you." And savor every second.

Andrei drew in a shuddering breath before he straightened and gave him a shaky smile. Without a word he took Dean's hand and led him over to the bed. Dean searched his face for any sign of the exhaustion that normally came over Andrei when they touched, but all he could see was the same need to be close.

They stretched out next to each other, tangling their legs and wrapping their arms around each other. Dean closed his eyes, his head close to Andrei's. He could feel his partner's breath against his lips, smell the warm, comforting scent of his presence. Andrei slipped his hand under the back of Dean's shirt and warm fingertips stroked his skin.

"Talk to me, Dean. What happened while you were gone?"

Dean looked into Andrei's dark eyes, remembering all those times when Andrei had come back in the middle of the night, his expression bleak. He would hold Andrei just like this, touching and soothing until he could talk about whatever he'd seen or done that haunted him. It didn't matter how long it took because eventually Andrei always unburdened himself to Dean.

"Isn't this my job?" Dean laid his head on Andrei's shoulder, slowly starting to relax as Andrei hand rubbed up and down his back.

"You're the one who needs it tonight," Andrei said softly.

Dean did not want to talk about the last several days. He did not want to think about the Jackals or remember Old Mother's screams as her soul was torn apart. Even now it had the power to make him shake. Andrei didn't press. He held Dean and waited as the waves washed ashore outside the open window, and eventually the words started to come, trickling at first until the dam inside him burst.

Andrei caressed him as Dean told him about the Jackal Wraiths and the horror that the howls engendered in him, the way he was sure that the sounds were driving him mad. He nuzzled Dean's cheek, comforting without words as Dean spoke about the unnatural creatures and how he seemed to feel them without actually being touched. The way he and Ileana had been deliberately chased, run to ground until they had nothing left. Finally, Andrei held Dean tight as he whispered about the end, how he'd begged to leave and worried about leaving Andrei behind without a word of their fate.

He paused, his throat tightening as he wound down toward the end. "Don't stop now." Andrei slid his hand to Dean's side and stroked a thumb along his hip. "Get it all out."

"It's bad." Over everything else, Dean wished he could erase the end from his memory and the role he had in Old Mother's destruction. He'd never be able to repay what she had done for them. "Andrei, I...."

Dean buried his face against Andrei's neck, shaking with silent tears as the memories rolled over him. Andrei didn't speak, and Dean was grateful. What could he say? Everything Dean needed was given to him through the way Andrei held him. He felt drained, cleansed, and renewed all at the same time as bit by bit the words were pulled from him until he finally lay silent.

"I don't understand why she did it. She hated me and what I represented, the outsider lover of one of her great-grandsons. She could've saved Ileana easily and left me to the Jackals. And she didn't; she sacrificed herself instead. I just don't get it."

"I don't think you can understand why, Dean, not really, because you don't truly see your own predicament. You're too new to being a ghost. You haven't had to face the confusion and disassociation of watching things change without you and not being able to adapt to those changes. If I were to take a stab at it, I'd say that by the time she rescued you, she'd forgotten all about you being an outsider. And I'd bet that she'd dismissed us being a gay couple even faster. She just wouldn't be able to process it."

"Maybe," Dean said after a minute of thinking it over. Old Mother hadn't called him a *gadje* when she'd showed up. In fact, she'd referred to him as Ileana's brother. "So since I was in her family Bible, I became family, because that's what she knew and understood." Andrei nodded and Dean sighed. "I don't think knowing that helps."

"You'll have to forgive yourself sometime, Dean. When it's not so raw inside," Andrei murmured.

Dean lifted his head and stroked his hand through Andrei's silvering hair, pushing it back from his temple. "All I need to know is if you do, babe."

"You mean for completely ignoring everything I said and almost getting your soul fed to demons?" Andrei's voice held no rancor in it despite his words. He slid his hand to the back of Dean's neck and played with his hair. "You did what you felt you had to do. You have good reasons for staying, damn good reasons for being angry, and you're a man who keeps his promises. We have such little time left, and I'm too happy knowing that you're safe. How can I not forgive you?"

Relief swept through Dean, along with a sense of urgency. This might be his last night with Andrei. Tomorrow they'd find the kids, and he'd have to fulfill his promises, but tonight was theirs alone. "Thank you." The words were not enough.

Andrei's expression turned bleak, and he framed Dean's face. "I'm sorry too. For everything, for lashing out at you, for drinking so damn much lately. I was in a damn tailspin I couldn't get out of, and then you were gone again, and I—" His voice broke and Dean pressed a finger to his lips.

"Andrei, there's no need to say it. I understand. Bad enough losing me the way you did. I can't even fathom how you felt after finding out I was a ghost when you went through what you did with Ileana. Even knowing what I do now. I love you. We are both coping as best as we can. The mistake we're making is not doing it together. Not anymore." He shifted, pulling Andrei under him, and the sound of his partner's voice catching made his body stir.

"Dean, I love you too." Andrei pressed closer, holding tight to him. "Stay with me tonight."

"I'm not hurting you, am I?" As much as Dean wanted this, as much as Andrei needed it, he'd find a way to stop and back off if it was going to put Andrei in a coma.

Andrei shook his head as he clutched at Dean. "No, it doesn't hurt. I don't feel even a little tired. I'm getting used to it. Please, Dean, don't stop. I can handle it."

Chapter Fifteen

ANDREI stared up at Dean, clinging to him, his heart pounding. *Please, please….* If Dean pulled back now, he wouldn't be able to take it. Some days he felt like he was hanging on by a thread that could snap at any instant. Now he had Dean back, when he'd been on the verge of losing hope; he didn't know how much longer he'd have him, and he needed this, to feel him, to connect with Dean.

Please believe me. Don't walk away now and tell me that it's for my own good.

Dean smiled as if he heard him, and Andrei's heart skipped a beat when Dean lowered his head. Dean brushed warm lips over Andrei's, and Andrei felt his eyes begin to burn. He slipped his hand around the nape of Dean's neck and pulled him closer, seeking more contact. Closing his eyes, he sank into the feel of Dean's lips, drank in his taste. Nothing felt so right as Dean kissing him.

Andrei slipped his hand under Dean's shirt and splayed his hand against warm skin. The little pull of energy from him into Dean was barely noticeable anymore. Not like the drugging, wild drain from before that had zapped through him like an errant lightning bolt and left him a mess, shaking and unable to barely stand.

He slid his hand into Dean's hair as the kiss broke. Dean touched his forehead to Andrei's, and their breath mingled together. Andrei kept his eyes closed. It all felt so real. From the way Dean smelled and the feel of his thick hair between Andrei's fingers to the sound of the ragged intake of his breath and the sensation of his familiar weight over Andrei. It would be so easy to pretend that the past nightmarish weeks had not happened. That they'd just come to the Outer Banks on a whim, to celebrate Dean's deal.

"Look at me, babe." Dean touched his lips to Andrei's forehead, brushed across his cheek.

Andrei pressed his lips together and shook his head. The ache moved up to his throat, rendering him speechless. Dean moved his lips, kissing Andrei's eyes and the corner of his mouth, little, tender touches that broke the dam inside of him.

"Just give me a bit, let me pretend you're still alive," Andrei said hoarsely. "Let me pretend that I don't have to give you up."

"Andrei." Warm, calloused hands cupped Andrei's face. "Look at me. I'm real. I'm still with you. A part of me will always be with you. Even after I go through that doorway."

Andrei wrapped his arms tighter and opened his eyes, memorizing the expression on Dean's face, the love that was there, always freely offered with no rules or conditions attached. Whenever he'd felt completely lost or overwhelmed, Dean had been there, his guiding star.

"I'm not ready to say good-bye to you."

"This isn't good-bye, babe." Dean brushed his thumbs over Andrei's cheekbones, his gaze intent. "We have this time together now, for who knows how long. Let's enjoy every moment we're given and not linger on the past or worry about the future. I have you with me right now, and that's all I need. It's like our song, the one we danced to at our commitment ceremony. You remember that song?"

"I'm not likely to ever forget it." The party had gone on late after the ceremony. The lanterns had come out, the hot summer air had cooled somewhat, and lightning bugs scattered over the lawn as they danced. Everybody else had ceased to exist except for the two of them, lost in each other and their own world.

"This time tonight, this extra bit of unexpected time that I've been given to be with you, this is our time in a bottle." Dean touched his mouth to Andrei's and whispered against his lips. "This is what we'll carry with us when we have to say good-bye."

"How do you always know what to say?" Andrei asked as some of the ache eased inside him. He gave Dean a small smile and lifted his head to nuzzle against him, breathing in his scent.

"I don't know. I guess I'm blessed when it comes to you."

Andrei drew Dean's shirt off and pressed his mouth to Dean's throat. Stubble teased his lips, reminding him of how exhausted Dean had looked when he'd first showed up. He wanted to soothe that horror from Dean's mind, and with the tender way that Dean touched him in return, it felt like he was trying to do the same for Andrei.

Every caress, every kiss took on a new meaning as Andrei committed each one to his memory. Words were unnecessary as they stripped each other slowly, stroking their hands over each bared spot. Andrei pressed his cheek to Dean's chest and listened to the strong, steady beat of his heart. He didn't know how it worked, and he didn't care so long as he could hear it.

Andrei tipped his head back, and Dean kissed the hollow of his throat, tongue slipping out to taste his skin in that way that always made Andrei shiver. He pressed his lips to that spot again and then rubbed his cheek against Andrei's chest, stubble gently rasping against his skin, making Andrei come alive again as each of his senses became attuned to him. This was all Andrei needed, connecting with his other half.

When Dean slid down lower, breath tracing a path along his stomach, Andrei stopped him with a squeeze on his arm. "No, wait, together. I want to taste you too."

A smile flashed across Dean's face, and he kissed Andrei's navel, tracing the lines of his abs with a hot tongue. "My favorite position."

"One of your favorites," Andrei said as Dean lifted up onto his hands and knees and turned around, giving Andrei a nice view of his tight ass. "You have so many."

Andrei rolled onto his hip as Dean stretched out opposite him. He slid his hand along Dean's hip and felt the stroke of fingers along his stomach as Dean touched him in return. "Remember the first time we did this?" Dean asked with a soft chuckle as he cupped Andrei's balls, rubbing his thumb across them. "I didn't know what I was doing, and you were so freaking experienced. I just knew that I wanted you so bad that I wasn't going to wait any longer."

A bittersweet ache filled Andrei as he closed his eyes and thought of that afternoon. Dean had been so endearingly nervous and eager to explore at the same time. They had lain down next to each other just like this, taking their time, learning all the nuances of each other. Now Andrei knew exactly where to nuzzle, knew the scent of Dean better than he knew his own.

"I remember." Andrei smiled and leaned in closer, trailing his lips along Dean's thigh. "I don't think I ever told you, but I was so shocked and nervous myself that it was all I could do to keep my hands from shaking when I touched you."

Dean went still with surprise before looking down between their bodies at Andrei. "For real? You played it so cool."

"I'd wanted you for so long, loved you while trying to pretend that I was okay with being just your best friend. And then you said those words." *I think I like you, maybe just a bit.* And all of Andrei's carefully guarded distance had crumbled. "You can't blame a man for being shaky on the inside after that."

Dean's initial stumbling confession had led to that first, sweet kiss that had been better than all the kisses that he had imagined between them, which had then led right to Dean admitting that he loved Andrei. When Dean had asked for more, Andrei had no will at all to resist him, and before he'd known it, they'd been naked and stretched out just like this.

"No, I don't suppose I can." Dean brushed a kiss over the head of Andrei's cock, and it throbbed in answer. "I used to wish that you'd show me more of everything that you keep locked up inside until I realized that you do, I just needed to learn how to read it."

Andrei swallowed against the sudden tightening in his throat as he leaned his forehead against Dean's thigh and drew in a shuddering breath. How would he go on, day after day without him? The thought of that loneliness, stretching out without end terrified him. No, loneliness he could handle. Not having Dean to turn to, to share his life with, that was something else altogether.

Dean rubbed his lips against Andrei's thigh, giving it a gentle nip. "Stop that. We don't know what tomorrow will bring. I could be here another night or two. And I'm going to enjoy every last moment that I can loving you."

Andrei blinked back the sudden stinging in his eyes as he looked at Dean. "How do you do that, *iubito*? How do you manage to dismiss all the bad stuff and just concentrate on the good?"

Dean hesitated and the expression that crossed his face made the shadows under his eyes deeper. Andrei wished he'd never asked the question at all. He wanted to see Dean smile again. He wanted to see him writhe in pleasure and need just for him instead of being haunted by nightmares.

"That last morning... I couldn't have asked for a better last morning with you. If I could go back and relive it, I wouldn't change a thing. Ever since I woke up on the side of the road, it's been a waking hell until I walked in tonight and I saw you and I got the chance to talk to you and to hold you. Tomorrow more craziness awaits us, and the both of us are going to be in danger if you find Blake, so tonight I just want to make love with you again and again until neither of us can move. I want to remember all the good times with you, all the reasons why we love each other. I want you to look back on this night and that last morning and smile, Andrei."

Andrei slid his hand down to tangle his fingers with Dean's. He had no words to answer that, just a renewed determination to concentrate solely on Dean and push everything else to the side. Just as he always did when they were naked together. Here there was no blood and tears, no violence and rage. Right here was the warmth of Dean's skin, the scent of his arousal, and the closeness that enveloped them both.

His breath caught as Dean traveled the length of his shaft with lips that nibbled in little kisses. Desire surged right to the surface. How many nights had he begged just for this—one more chance to touch and taste Dean, one last night to hold him close?

"I love it when you do that," Andrei murmured as he leaned closer and nuzzled against Dean's sandy curls, breathing the scent of him in. He felt Dean's lips curve against his cock.

"I know. You like this even more." Dean flicked his hot tongue to tease the head and play with the tiny slit there, and Andrei's breath caught again on a wave of intense, dizzying desire. It was like every little action had been amplified.

"Dean." Andrei turned his head and laid a hard, sucking kiss against his shaft. It jerked against his lips, and Andrei was rewarded with the soft sound of pleasure that Dean made.

This was all that mattered, being with the one man who'd taught him what home and family meant.

ANDREI opened one bleary eye on a groan. His entire body ached from his bones on out, and the bed shook as shivers wracked him. He curled up into a ball, wrapping the blankets around him and ignoring the nagging feeling that he'd left something undone. Only no matter what he did, he couldn't seem to warm up, and when he finally did, he broke out in a sweat, and he tore the blankets off of him.

The cool air against his skin jerked him out of his lethargy. He wasn't at home in his own bed. He was in the hotel, after a long night of loving with Dean, taking turns making love to each other. Andrei rolled over onto his side and eyed the empty pillow next to him. At least Dean still rested, off wherever it was that ghosts went to when they were depleted of energy. He was safe for the moment, which meant that Andrei was free to turn his attention to Dean's killer. He had to find Blake before the man moved on again, taking the kids with him. Andrei sat up, every limb feeling as if they had weights attached to them.

Dean would freak the fuck out if he saw him like this. He had time to get himself together before Dean showed up again. He forced himself to his feet and laid a hand on the wall to steady himself as the room swayed. A cold shower. That's what he needed and something to take care of the fever. He'd be fine.

Twenty minutes later he felt marginally better, if still a little tired. At least this time he wasn't coughing. His stomach protested the thought of food, so he drank a cup of coffee as he watched the news. Hurricane Alice was closing in on the coast though it remained several days out, and it looked as if the storm might be upgraded to a category four. County officials were already discussing the possibility of a mandatory evacuation. Andrei cursed under his breath, a sense of renewed urgency hitting his gut. If Blake panicked and evacuated before Andrei found him, he'd have to start all over again, and he did not want to give Evelyn that news.

Andrei headed to the RV park with mixed feelings. He parked the Jeep where he left off the search yesterday and grimly began to walk the lanes he hadn't seen yet, looking for that blue camper truck. His legs were shaky, and not too long into his search, he got another attack of shivers. Even with the sun beating down on him, his skin felt like ice.

He forced one foot in front of the other, keeping his goal in mind. There were more pluses to look forward to. Today, he'd find the kids and they'd be returned safely to their grandmother. Today, Dean's killer would be punished. Today, Ileana and Dean could move on and would be safe. It was those pluses that kept him moving on when he wanted to give in, sink to the ground, and let sleep overtake him.

He couldn't let himself think of the one glaring, wrenching minus. Today, he'd have to say good-bye to Dean and Ileana. They'd be safe. He had to keep reminding himself of that. It was the only thing that made the thought bearable.

Ileana popped up in front of him, and Andrei stumbled to a halt, swaying and breaking out into a sweat. He grabbed ahold of a light pole and gave her a tired smile. She looked back to normal today, with no trace of the terror and sadness on her face from the night before. He hoped that she had forgotten that nightmare. She often conveniently forgot the bad stuff. "Hey, Illy. I see you've found Cougar again." The stuffed turtle hung from her hand as Ileana looked at him with a little frown.

"You look awful, Andrei."

Andrei barked a short laugh. "I just need a little nap and I'll be fine. Where's Dean?"

"He's waiting back at the hotel. He sent me to check up on you 'cause he's afraid that if he sees the bad man again, he'll go all grrrr face and make the Jackals chase us again." Ileana slipped her hand in his, skipping along as Andrei started moving again, one step at a time. Andrei could barely keep up with her chatter. The sun broiled the water out of him as soon as he drank. Blake. He had to find Blake and the kids.

He scanned row after row of tents and campers, downing half his water bottle when he paused to catch his breath. "Ileana, want to play I spy with me?"

Andrei thought that Ileana would jump at the chance to play a game, but instead she looked at him and cocked her head. "I think you should let Dean play doctor. Please, you look really sick. Like when you were little. Dean can make it all better."

"I can't, not yet. I promise I'll lie down and get some rest as soon as we find those kids, okay?"

Ileana crossed her arms and furrowed her little brow fiercely at him. "I'm gonna tell."

"I know you are." Andrei tapped the end of her nose. "You can tell Dean all about what a bad boy I've been after we play I spy, okay?"

"Fine." Ileana rolled her eyes and looked around the RV park. "What am I spying? Is it Dean's little girl with the pretty hair ribbons? Can I have hair ribbons like that, Andrei? Please?"

"I'll see what I can find. Do you want yellow-and-red ones to match your dress?" Andrei paused at another intersection, the lanes extending out to both the right and the left. He had grave misgivings about Ileana's help, but he wasn't quite sure that he'd be able to cover the second half of the park today. Not with as bad as he felt.

"That would be so pretty." Ileana jumped up and down and twirled in a circle, her skirt flaring out. "What should I look for?"

"Remember Uncle Eugene's truck with the sleeper on top?"

Ileana nodded, her eyes sparkling. "We liked to crawl up there and hide, and I'd tell you stories."

"Yes, we did. Well that's what I'm looking for, a truck like that, blue with an OBX sticker on the back. You think you can remember that?"

"Yeppers!" Ileana turned down the left side and skipped off, waving to Andrei as she went. "We'll find him and then you can get him good for hurting Dean."

That was the plan. Andrei watched her go off, her boundless energy seeming to exhaust him more. A spate of coughing wracked his body, and Andrei hugged an arm around his waist. How the hell had this happened? He'd been getting better, and he could've sworn Dean had not pulled that much energy from him last night. He'd even stopped feeling the loss not long into it. Dean was going to be so pissed with himself. Andrei closed his eyes and willed the coughing to go away.

"Hey buddy, you okay?"

Andrei wiped the back of his hand across his mouth and cursed under his breath as he lifted his head. Great, why not draw attention to himself some more. A young man stood there, basketball in hand as he looked at Andrei in concern.

"I'm fine, just swallowed some water the wrong way." He straightened, ignoring the young man's uncertain expression, and walked down the right-hand path. Time became a blur as he wandered up and down the lanes, and the sun rose higher, adding to his misery. Andrei was beginning to consider that it might be wiser to go back to the hotel room and take some more medicine and a nap when the object of his search appeared, nestled in the far end of the lane, half hidden behind a gigantic RV. The blue paint on the truck was faded, but the camper looked pretty new. A maroon, four-door sedan was parked on the other side.

Acute shock rippled through him, and Andrei swayed again, then sat down hard on a picnic bench. His heart raced, adrenaline pounding through him and washing away some of the haze as his focus narrowed. He couldn't go charging in there at midday; it was too public. His mind raced as he made and discarded plans. First he had to make sure that this was the correct camper truck and that Blake was inside.

Andrei rose before he drew too much attention to himself and walked a few feet away before turning to study his target again. He could circle around and approach the camper from the back, but there wasn't much cover, and he didn't trust his own body to not betray him with coughing. Of all the times to get sick. He never got sick. He'd have to risk it and hope that if he acted casual, nobody would notice him.

Then a whole other dilemma hit him. He couldn't take out Blake in the middle of the day. He'd learned his lesson the last two times he'd encountered Blake. The man would not go down quietly. And he couldn't in good conscience leave those kids with Blake until nightfall. Not when he had their grandmother and aunt waiting and praying for news. Not when the man was a sadistic fuck.

Andrei forced himself to take a calming breath. One thing at a time. Once he determined whether or not it was the right truck, then he could decide what to do. He returned to the main lane and walked up a bit before circling around. The blue camper truck had just appeared ahead of him once again when Ileana popped up next to him.

"I'm bored with this game, Andrei. And you promised that you'd go back to the hotel room and let Dean take care of you."

Andrei caught Ileana's arm and put a finger to his lips to indicate that he couldn't talk. Her dark eyes widened. "You found the bad man?"

He nodded toward the camper, and Ileana let out an excited squeal of delight. "Ooohhh, wait till I tell Dean. He'll be super excited. Punch him really hard on his nose."

"Before you go running off," Andrei said in a low whisper, keeping his eye on the windows. "Would you like to play a sneaking game?"

"Like when we went to Robin's house and Dean opened the door for you and we used the flashlight and looked all around?"

"Almost like that." Andrei crouched down next to Ileana and pulled out the two photographs he had, one of Blake and the other, Inez and Tristan. "Only this time, you're going to be my scout, which means you get to go first."

Ileana clapped her hands and thrust Cougar at him, somehow making the stuffed turtle materialize the way that she did at the strangest times. "Here, hold him, he's scared. He doesn't want to go into the bad guy hidey hole."

Andrei tucked Cougar under his arm. "I just need to know if it's the right camper truck and if it is, where Blake is inside and where the kids are. Okay? You think you can report back to me with that?"

Ileana saluted and then scampered off. Andrei leaned against a tree and stifled a cough. His sister disappeared through the door and then stuck her head right back out almost immediately. "There's nobody here."

"Are you sure?" Andrei whispered.

"Positive. I even checked the beds behind the curtain. Nobody's home." The door to the camper popped open a few inches. "Did you wanna take a look? What do we do now, Andrei?"

Andrei glanced around at the other campers and tents making up the clearing. He heard the low murmur of conversation from a firepit two stations away where a mother and daughter were cooking. A man had stretched out on a sunchair, snoring in the afternoon heat. He was the closest, but it looked like the majority of the campers were either off enjoying the park's various activities or they'd ventured on down to either the sea or Pamlico Sound side of the island to play in the sand. Probably where Blake had gone too since the car was still here. Andrei wouldn't get a better time than now to look around.

He put on a pair of gloves and crossed the space quickly. He clambered up the outside steps and was soon up in the cramped space of the camper, before easing the door shut behind him. There was evidence of kids, with a diaper bag on the tiny counter and a sandcastle bucket on the floor filled with a mix of shells and sand toys.

Ileana perched on top of the cubbyhole bed, legs dangling as Andrei opened the diaper bag. "Whatcha looking for?"

"Absolute proof that this is where Blake has been hiding. The world is full of crazy coincidences." Andrei drew items out of the jumbled mess in the bag and laid them, one by one, carefully aside so he could put them back in the correct order. Not that he thought Blake would notice, but it didn't hurt to be careful. The diapers were definitely for a younger baby. At the bottom of the bag were hair ribbons, and Andrei's heart skipped a beat. He pulled them out, a whole handful of various colors that looked very similar to the one that Dean carried around in his pocket as a token of Inez.

He drew out one ribbon and handed it to Ileana. "Ileana, find Dean for me and ask him if this feels like Inez to him. He might be able to tell for me."

"Okies." Ileana hopped down from the bed and took the ribbon. "But if you don't hurry up, I'm telling Dean you're sick, and I don't think you want that."

"As soon as I'm done here, I'll head straight back, I promise." Asking Ileana not to tell was an exercise in futility, and dire threats had never worked either, not even when they were kids. He didn't want Dean to come looking for him and then be set off. "Make sure he stays at the room, okay?"

"I will. I don't want him to get mad." Ileana hugged Andrei's waist and then disappeared. Andrei carefully set everything back in the diaper bag, then poked around a little more, listening intently for any sounds of the owner returning. He didn't have enough proof. He smothered another round of coughing against his sleeve. It felt as if a weight sat on his chest, pressing down on his lungs, and the stuffy air in the camper made it worse.

Andrei found a folder stashed in a cupboard, and he drew it out, quickly thumbing through the contents. The truck registration was made out to a James Clements. Andrei's stomach clenched as that thrill of the chase struck him. With a shaking hand, he drew out his phone and took a picture. That name was very, very familiar. He was pretty certain he'd seen that name in Scott Metcalf's files. There were birth certificates as well, made for a baby boy with a different name and a young girl. He bet that he'd find those names among the paperwork too. Blake may be trying to pass off Inez as a little boy for now, but at least he didn't plan on keeping that charade up indefinitely. Andrei couldn't imagine what that would do to a child.

Andrei was very tempted to wait for Blake to come back, but all the different ways the confrontation could go bad kept running through his head. Besides, there was no room to hide. He'd have to leave and watch the camper from a distance. Or wait and return later. Blake knew what he looked like. Andrei didn't want to risk being seen and scare the guy off now.

He returned the folder and then left the camper after making sure that nobody was about. Yet again this was one of those times where he cursed the lack of a partner. He almost wished he'd agreed to let Justin accompany him to the Outer Banks. The detective was too bound by the rules, though. He'd call the Dare County cops, who'd come blundering in and scare off Blake.

Andrei headed back toward his car. It was getting hard to think clearly, and he wouldn't be any good if he collapsed right here in the middle of the park. By the time he sat down and blasted the air conditioning in the Jeep, the sweats had overtaken him again. This wasn't an illness, not this fast acting. He tore the bandages off his arm and checked the partially-healed bullet wound in his arm, but there didn't seem to be any sign of infection. Damn. Something was seriously wrong.

When he got back to the hotel, the room was empty, and Andrei didn't have the energy to wonder where Dean and Ileana were. He fumbled open the cap to the ibuprofen, spilling the contents across the bathroom counter. Maybe he should go to one of those urgent care clinics after he had a nap, get some antibiotics. His thoughts were fuzzy and disjointed. As he fell across the bed, the walls seemed to expand and contract, reminding him of a more urgent, heated coupling in the middle of the night. He had the brief thought that the walls were breathing and closing in on him before darkness dragged him down.

Chapter Sixteen

DEAN popped back into the hotel room with Ileana beside him, and his excitement immediately turned to alarm when he saw Andrei curled up on the bed with all the blankets wrapped like a cocoon around him. Dean could see him shaking from across the room. "Andrei?"

A dry, raspy cough answered him, and Dean's heart plummeted. "Oh my God." He ran over to the bed and then froze before he touched Andrei. One more touch just might kill him. "Fuck." Dean stopped the further spew of curses as Ileana joined him by the bed.

"I told him that he needed to go see you." Ileana sat on the bed and laid her cheek against Andrei's forehead. "He's so hot. Why's he shivering?"

A sick feeling of helplessness settled over Dean, followed by inarticulate rage directed toward himself. Andrei said that he hadn't felt the pull of energy last night. How could this be happening now? He looked as if he'd aged several more years. "He's got a bad fever, Poppet. We need to get him to a hospital."

Dean dragged a hand through his hair. And how was he supposed to accomplish that? He couldn't pick up Andrei and carry him there. He sure as hell couldn't drive a car either. Somehow he needed to bring an ambulance here.

"I told him that you'd play doctor." Ileana looked up at him with expectation. "Make him better."

Dean swore, pacing up and down beside the bed. "I'm the one who got him sick in the first place. Just like you got him sick when you were little just after you became a ghost." How much could one person take? Ileana had drained him when he was just five, and now Dean had done it again.

"Oh." Ileana sat back, her brow furrowing. "Well, he'll be okay, then, right? 'Cause he was fine when he was little, and he's bigger now." Her dark eyes filled with tears. "Did I really make him sick, Dean?"

"You didn't know what you were doing, Poppet. You were just doing what came naturally to yourself, which was play with your baby brother." Unlike Dean, who had known and had still been unable to resist his instincts. He patted Ileana's braids and wiped her eyes. "Now none of that, it was in the past, and we need to figure out a clever, ghosty way to get Andrei the help he needs. Got any ideas?"

Ileana pointed toward the phone beside the bed with a look on her face that made Dean feel foolish. "Okay yes, I can call 911, but we need to let them know that he needs an ambulance and what room he's in. We can dial the phone, but how do we make them hear?"

Dean jumped as Andrei's hand closed around his wrist, gripping him with surprising strength. His touch burned and his breath came in quick, raspy pants as if he couldn't get enough air in his lungs. How had that happened? Andrei shouldn't be able to touch him unless Dean wanted him to.

"Found them. Can't...." For a moment Andrei's fierce glare faltered, and his expression became confused as his hold on Dean's wrist loosened, allowing Dean to pull free. He began mumbling and Dean leaned closer, trying to catch what he said. "Justin... get Justin... found them."

"One thing at a time, babe." Dean concentrated and then picked up the phone. He'd heard stories of ghosts talking through phones. He just hoped that they weren't just stories. He handed the phone to Ileana. "It'll sound more urgent if it's coming from a kid. They might just tell me to drive him to the emergency room. Ready?"

Ileana nodded, twirling the phone cord with her fingers as Dean dialed 911. Dean watched, holding his breath and praying that it would work. He heard the operator answer, and then Ileana burst into loud, noisy tears. "Please help. My brother's really, really sick. He's super hot and his breathing sounds funny."

Dean breathed a sigh of relief as he heard the woman answer Ileana. He left her to the conversation and went to fill up a glass of water. Andrei would need fluids. And if Old Mother was right, and she had been right about everything else, the damage had already been done and he could touch Andrei at will now and have Andrei touch him in return without further damage. That's the only reason he could think of for Andrei being able to grab him.

He eased an arm under Andrei and helped him to sit up as Ileana hung up the phone. "They're on their way. Lady said they'd be here right quick, and she tried to get me to stay on the phone. How come?"

"I think that's standard procedure, Poppet." Dean held the glass to Andrei's lips. More of the water spilled down Andrei's chin than went into his mouth. "Come on, babe, you've got to get some down."

"Mum used to wet a washcloth and put it on my head when I was sick." Ileana ran off and came back a moment later. She slopped a very wet washcloth on his head, dripping more water down his flushed face, and Andrei began to shiver again.

"Justin... Justin... gotta tell him." Andrei's teeth chattered between words.

"Hush, babe. I'll figure out a way to let Justin know. You've got to rest, save your strength." Dean eased Andrei back against some pillows that he piled up as another harsh round of coughing wracked his body. Andrei's nails were starting to turn a purply-blue, and Dean swore. "When did she say the ambulance will be here?"

"Soon. She promised they'd take care of him."

"Mum." Andrei tossed restlessly, getting even more tangled up in the blankets. "Mum, where's Illy? Where she go?"

"She's right here, Andrei." Dean motioned for Ileana to cuddle up next to her brother. "See, she's not going anywhere. Try to get some rest."

Dean resumed his pacing, clenching and unclenching his fists and listening to the rattle of Andrei's breath until he heard the welcome sound of an ambulance in the distance. *About fucking time.*

DEAN set aside Andrei's cell phone with a sigh. Justin was blowing it up with text messages and endless calls. It seemed like he had decided to finally get off his ass and to come down to the Outer Banks and investigate for himself what the hell was going on. It had taken a whole twenty-four hours' worth of texts to do it. Dean had sent him more than enough messages to let him know that Andrei had been admitted to the hospital and that the kids had been found and that he needed Justin's help. The problem was getting him to believe them.

Justin had seemed pretty pissed and sure it was a prank, but Dean thought he must've called the hospital to verify because he'd stopped arguing with Dean. He looked at Andrei, then reached out and laced their fingers together. Andrei's breathing had settled with the respirator, the IV steadily pumped fluids into him, and the machines monitoring his blood pressure and heart rate remained steady.

"You've got to get better, babe. It's not your time yet. You've got too much to do," Dean murmured, brushing a kiss across Andrei's knuckles.

"What if Andrei doesn't get better?" Ileana asked, swinging her feet as she sat in the chair next to him. "Then he could be with us too."

Dean closed his eyes as a lump of heartache and grief settled in his throat. He held Andrei's hand tighter, trying to will some of his stolen energy back into his partner. "I can't say that I haven't thought that too, Poppet, but there's something in me that says again and again that Andrei isn't done yet. Looks like we're just going to have to be patient and wait for him to join us."

He gently set down Andrei's hand and then turned to Ileana. "Do you remember where you and Andrei found that bit of hair ribbon?"

Ileana nodded, swinging her legs faster. "In a blue camper truck at the bottom of the baby's bag."

Dean drew in a deep breath, trying to calm the spate of nerves that struck him. He could do this. He could face his own anger and fear of it for Andrei, for Inez, and for little Tristan. "Do you think you could take me there?"

"But I don't know where it is." Ileana tossed Cougar up in the air and then hugged the turtle after she caught it. "It was in a big, big park with lots and lots and lots of campers and tents. It was like a real big carnival. And Andrei took forever to find it."

Dean fought for patience as he reached in his pocket and fingered the hair ribbons there. They were both Inez's; he'd known them immediately. "You just said you knew where it was."

"Nope, you asked if I knew where we found the hair ribbons, and I told you. You didn't ask me if I knew where the camper was. I only found it 'cause Andrei was there. I don't think I could find it again."

"You could try," Dean said, giving her a level look.

Ileana rolled her eyes. "So could you. You gots the ribbons. Have you even tried to use them to find your little girl? Searching for her would be better than following the taste of the bad man." She crossed her arms over her chest and stuck her lower lip out. "Do you want her to be your sister too?"

"No. I just want her to be safe with her family again, both her and her brother." He tugged on Ileana's braid. "There's only one you, and I have enough sisters at home."

Dean pulled out the ribbons and looked at them. He could sense Inez through them, dimly, stronger now with both ribbons than before. Maybe it would be enough to take him to Inez. Dean shoved the ribbons back in his pocket. He didn't know if he dared. What if he came face-to-face with Blake and went off again? Old Mother had sacrificed herself for what remained of her family. He couldn't piss on that by being reckless.

"Ileana, when you would go to visit Old Mother, you would zero in on her touch, right? Is there a way to expand that?" Dean scrambled for a better way to explain it as Ileana gave him a confused look. "For example, just say you wanted to pop up near, but far enough away that you could sneak up on her. Like that game that Andrei told me you liked to play with him."

"Ooohh yeah, that's a fun game. Do you want to do that with Inez?" The sparkle returned to Ileana's eyes as she began to bounce in her chair. "I betcha she'd like that game. It's a fun one."

"I'd like to, but I'm going to need your help. I'm afraid that if I just concentrate on Inez that I'll pop up right next to her, and if Blake is there that could be very, very bad."

Ileana's expression became solemn, making her eyes seem even larger in her thin face. "You're afraid you'll call the Jackals again. Please don't do that, Dean. That was awful bad."

Dean squeezed her hand. "I don't want to, which is why I need to sneak up on them. If I feel myself start to get angry, I'll jump back here." He'd never seemed to stay mad long once he was out of Blake's presence. "Are you ready to try?"

God, what was he doing? He'd already screwed this up once and almost gotten Ileana destroyed in the process. There was so much at stake. Did he dare? Did he even have a right to push it?

Ileana wrapped her arms around his neck. "It's okay, Dean. Finding those other kids is important, and if we get close then maybe I can help look for the camper like I helped Andrei. I might recognize it. Then once we find them, we can call the police, and they can get the bad guy. Not you and not Andrei. I think maybe Andrei might want to get him a little too bad."

Dean was amazed by her insight. That was a worry that had crossed his mind on more than one occasion. He'd seen Andrei driven to find a person before, but not like this. There were times when he saw a feral light in Andrei's eyes that made him wonder what would happen when Andrei caught up with Blake. He eyed Andrei lying still on the bed and rose to kiss his forehead. He just didn't have any easy answers.

"Let's just see if you can show me how to get close, and I'll take the rest from there. I want you to come back here to stay with Andrei to keep an eye on him. You're to let me know if he gets worse." He wasn't going to risk getting Ileana caught up in this madness again. He'd made a promise to Andrei to take care of her and himself. He wasn't going to break that last promise. So he'd better find a way to keep a grip on his temper.

"Can I help you when the big, dark man with the deep voice gets here?"

It took Dean a moment to process what Ileana meant. Justin. Well it would take a number of hours for the man to get here; by then Dean should be done with his mission, so he didn't see any harm in giving her permission. He nodded and held out his hand to Ileana. "Okay, Poppet. Let's go hunt the big bad wolf."

DEAN paced restlessly up and down the lanes of the RV park for the second night in a row. This was taking him longer than he'd thought it would. Ileana had been able to bring him to the park, but had not been able to show him successfully how to zero in and follow Inez's trail in little jumps. Between following on foot and going back and checking on Andrei often, the time had seemed to speed by.

Full dark had fallen, the moon a bare crescent in the sky, and the only illumination came from campfires, lanterns, and the warm yellow of electric lights gleaming through camper windows. He could sense the pull from Inez getting stronger—not too far ahead now—and once again his doubts assailed him. He knew that they were close, surely that was enough. Justin was a good detective. Andrei had said it more than once. All Dean had to do was somehow find a way to point him in the right direction.

He sighed; yeah, just that. It would be far easier if he had something specific. Dean drew in a deep breath and crouched down, trying to shake out the nerves. He could do this. Justin wouldn't pay any attention to his texts unless Dean told him exactly where to go. The west section of the RV park wouldn't be enough.

Dean straightened and forced himself to go a little further. He could sense both of them now: one touch was sad, confused and scared, the other cold and inflexible, rotting from the inside out. That second touch sent a cold trickle down his spine, made his chest ache where he'd been shot, and stirred the embers of Dean's temper.

He closed his eyes and pictured Andrei and Ileana as he rubbed Inez's hair ribbon between his fingers. He couldn't forget his promise or his purpose for staying. He held onto the mental image of Andrei smiling, the way the curve of his neck smelled, the feel of his body against Dean's, until the anger dissipated and was replaced with determination.

Dean clung to that calm as he steadily moved forward. The sensation of his killer grew stronger, almost overwhelming Inez's touch, and Dean had to pause again, his forehead breaking out in a sweat. Blake's aura lay on his mind like a thin coat of rancid oil. The camper sat at the end of this lane. He couldn't miss its presence even though he couldn't see it yet with the darkness and the light from fires stabbing at his eyes. It screamed wrongness.

He wished Ileana were here with her incessant chatter and spontaneous hugs or Andrei with his steady presence. Dean was bleeding again. A trickle at first, and it wasn't long before his shirt became soaked. The image of Blake standing over him came back so strong that for a moment Dean was back on the side of that sunbaked parkway, filled with that helpless desperation.

"Run, Inez. Run, sweetheart," he gasped, straining to hear little footsteps running.

Ileana appeared in front of him and immediately wrapped her arms around his waist. "It's okay, Dean, the bad man can't hurt you again."

But he could if Dean couldn't rein in his anger and the urge to choke the life out of Blake. His hands longed for the action. Dean drew in a deep, shuddering breath and clamped down on the reaction hard.

"How'd you know I needed you, Poppet? Was I thinking real loud again?"

"Yep! I heard you all the way at the hospital. You were growling in my head and calling for me."

Dean smoothed a hand over her hair. "How's Andrei doing?" He needed the distraction of conversation, something normal and good to concentrate on.

"Better. I heard the doctors tell Mr. Justin that he should wake up soon, so I left him Cougar so he wouldn't get lonely." Ileana tipped her head back and looked up at him. "Wait till we tell Andrei that you found the bad guy too. Are ya gonna use Andrei's magic phone to send him messages again? Mr. Justin didn't like that much. He kept using bad words under his breath."

"I bet that getting text messages from a ghost is very disconcerting." Dean stared back toward the camper, hung up on indecision. It was the need to see for himself how Inez and Tristan were doing that drove him forward. Just one quick peek to make sure they were healthy, and then he wouldn't push it anymore.

His heart clenched as the camper came into sight. That lot didn't have a cheery fire going with chairs situated around it and people talking and sipping beers. All of the windows had curtains pulled over them, and no sounds of children playing came from within. "I'll go peek for you," Ileana said and scampered off before Dean could stop her.

He swore under his breath and paced back and forth. Logically, he knew Blake couldn't hurt her, and it was a much better idea that she look instead of him, but inside he hated it. Ileana was just a young girl. A curtain twitched aside, and Dean's heart stopped again as Inez's little face peered out. "Oh sweetheart," Dean breathed, taking a step closer and then another as her presence filled him up, driving away the reek of her father.

Her hair had been badly shorn, as if Blake had just cut off the ribboned pigtails and not bothered to make it neater. He paused under the window and smiled as her gaze focused on him. "Hey, Inez." He touched his fingers to the window as Inez smiled back, showing off the gap between her teeth. "Help is coming. You hold on just a little while longer. I swear I'm coming for you."

Ileana appeared next to him and gave Inez a cheery wave. "The bad man is feeding the baby." She tugged on Dean's hand. "Let's go now and get Mr.—" She broke off with a sharp gasp.

"What is it, Ileana?" Dean demanded.

"Oh no, no, no, no. Andrei!" Ileana yanked her hand out of his and disappeared.

Dean sensed his connection with Andrei suddenly jerking and bucking like a fishing line. Oh my God. Icy fear struck him; Dean latched onto the fading sense of Andrei and let it pull him right back to the hospital.

ANDREI stirred, feeling as if every limb was held down with weights. He was so tired. He just wanted to sleep a little extra longer, but a sense of urgency kept nagging at him, poking and pushing. He tried opening his eyes, fighting and losing the battle. "Dean?" he whispered, already sinking back down into the lethargy that reached for him.

"Thank God, you're awake," a deep bass voice rumbled near his side. "The doctors tell me that you've been out of it since the ambulance picked you up."

That voice. Andrei shifted through his memories where the past and present seemed inextricably melded together. He was both a five-year-old child with his mum mopping his brow and a grown man... Justin. That's the man's name. Andrei batted at the contraption covering his mouth until it was gently lifted free.

"Where's Ileana? Where's Dean?" Andrei shifted restlessly again and managed to open his eyes to slits. He looked around, registering the hospital room and all the various devices hooked up to him. What was he forgetting?

"Who's Ileana?" Justin leaned closer, filling Andrei's vision with his worried expression. Lines of strain were etched around his dark brown eyes. "Are you all here? You've been mumbling for the last couple of hours, and most of it sounded like nonsense."

Andrei turned his head and looked around the room. Other than the sight of Cougar tucked against his side, there was no sign of Ileana and Dean. He could've sworn he heard his sister's voice singing to him in the midst of the delusional nightmares that had gripped him. "She's my big sister. Where are they?"

"I didn't know you had a sister. Look, just relax man. You need your rest." Justin shifted back in his chair. "Did you find the kids, Andrei?"

The kids? Andrei tried to search his memory without any luck. Something was wrong. He was in the hospital. Dean should be here. Andrei couldn't remember why, but he knew that it was vitally important that both Dean and Ileana be here with him. They could be in danger. A wisp of a memory came back to him of Dean holding him, trembling as he related a tale straight out of a Clive Barker movie. A story of being hunted by creatures that shouldn't exist.

"Where the fuck is Dean?" Andrei asked and wished he'd had the strength to put more heat behind the question.

There was a long pause as Andrei turned his head back to look Justin in the eye. Justin looked so sad and at a loss for words, something he'd never thought he'd see from his friend. "I'm so sorry, Andrei, Dean's dead. Don't you remember?"

Andrei closed his eyes as a wave of exhaustion struck him. Hot tears welled and despite his best efforts one escaped, trailing down his cheek. "They both are, but they stayed. They shouldn't have stayed. They're going to get hurt." He couldn't let that happen. He had to find some way to keep them safe. The idea of being separated for years was hard enough, but he could handle it if he believed they were happy.

"Look, they've already started evacuating the hospital, and you're scheduled to be shipped out tomorrow. Hurricane Alice is bearing down on the coast with a vengeance," Justin rumbled. "If we're going to find those kids, we need to look now, before they leave the island. Unless they already did. I got several text messages from your phone from somebody claiming that he was Dean, of all people, telling me you found them. I don't know what is going on here, but I will find out. And if someone's screwing with you, I'll get them too. Have you been harassed? Is some psychic claiming they can hear Dean or lead you to those kids? Because if that's the case, I'll arrest them on the spot, jurisdiction or no damn jurisdiction."

"Did Dean say anything else?" Andrei struggled to sit up as he tried to put together the disjointed pieces of the puzzle. He was forgetting something. Something important. There were holes in his memory and filled with fog. Movement flickered out of the corner of his eye, and the sheet on his bed fluttered, but when he turned, no one was there.

"Just texts saying that you were in the hospital, and the ambulance crew said that a little girl called 911 for you, only when they arrived no one was there. Could that have been Inez? What have you gotten yourself into?"

Inez... Inez... Inez.... Andrei's heartbeat picked up as a face came to him of a little girl with bobbing curls and impish gray eyes. Dean's little girl who had been kidnapped the afternoon he was murdered. "No, I... I didn't see her, I think. I'm pretty sure of it." He couldn't remember what Justin knew and what he didn't. But he couldn't have already found and killed Blake. He would've remembered shooting him.

Another flicker just outside his vision filled him with a sense of foreboding. Slowly, Andrei turned his head, Justin's incessant questions becoming a blur of nonsensical sound. A woman with fierce eyes stood by his bed, her outstretched hand reaching for him. Her face was distorted in a rictus, her hair was wild, and blood soaked the front of his shirt, dripping down onto the clean white sheets of his bed.

"Robin!" Andrei tried to scramble out of the way, but there were too many cords and lines attaching him to the machines by the bed. It all came flooding back in a haze of memories filtered through his fever. He'd found Blake. She flickered and then reappeared on the other side of him between him and Justin. "Robin, wait, I know where your kids are."

"What the hell is going on with you, man?" Justin surged up from the chair and shouted for the nurse.

Robin's hand closed on his head, caging him, and hot and cold arcs of energy raced through him. Andrei gasped, his body arching up, the machines beeping wildly. His heart raced, then faltered, then raced again. *Oh fuck, oh fuck.* "Robin, wait," he slurred.

He heard Justin shout again, an inarticulate sound of surprise and pain as he fell back onto the chair with Robin's other hand on his head. The energy raced even faster, Andrei's heart struggling to keep up, and he groaned, every limb twitching and jerking.

"*Leave my brother alone!*" Ileana flung herself on top of him, breaking Robin's contact. Andrei sagged back against the bed with a ragged gasp, the edges of his vision going dim. His entire body ached as if a thousand needles had been plunged into every inch of skin, every joint. Justin lolled in the chair next to him, his dark face gray as nurses and doctors poured into the room. "Dean! Help me!" Ileana sobbed. "She hurt them bad."

Andrei's heart lurched, thudding hard against his ribs, and then the darkness closed in on him.

Chapter Seventeen

DEAN scrubbed a hand over his face as he looked over Andrei again. He had no idea where Robin was now or why she'd done what she'd done, but she'd effectively fucked up the entire situation. Now both Justin and Andrei were holed up in the hospital, and he didn't know what to do next.

At least Andrei had stabilized. They'd taken him off the respirator, his color had returned, and some of the silver had even disappeared from his hair. And there had been no more instances of cardiac arrhythmia. Dean just wished that he'd wake up. They'd be evacuating Andrei this afternoon unless he significantly changed for the better or worse. Dean kept jumping back and forth between the camper and Andrei's bedside, worried that Blake would bolt soon as so many other people in the park were doing. Each time he went back, there were fewer campers and tents than before. The park would be closed down by nightfall.

At least he hadn't come face-to-face with Blake yet. Dean still didn't trust himself. He had had a few more glimpses of Inez. She always seemed to know when he approached. And so far it looked as if Blake was staying put, and that pissed Dean off for a whole other reason. There was a category four hurricane sweeping right toward them, and Blake had his kids situated right next to the shore. What did he plan on doing when the National Guard knocked on his door and booted him?

"I don't know what else to do, Poppet," Dean sighed. He glanced at Ileana who sat cross-legged at the foot of Andrei's bed, weaving a cat's cradle between her fingers. "I've tried sending messages to the police from both Andrei's and Justin's phones, but everything is so chaotic right now with people trying to prepare their homes for the storm and getting off the island that no one's paying attention."

"Silly, silly, Dean," Ileana said, her brows knitted in concentration as she danced her fingers through the mess of string. "If the bad man leaves, you'll be able to follow Inez, and you can tell Andrei where to go. If the bad man stays, then he's a stupid head."

Dean gave up trying to talk to her and sat down next to Andrei. She didn't understand why he had such a hard time following Inez's trail in little jumps, and if he couldn't do that, then how the hell was he supposed to find her again? He couldn't walk everywhere. The poor girl would be dating by the time they found her. He took Andrei's hand, grateful that there wasn't even a hint of the exchange of energy that had started this whole crisis. He could only figure that he'd passed that point with Andrei, just as Ileana had. "Come on, babe. Wake up and talk to me."

Andrei's hand tightened around his own, and Dean's heart flipped as he looked down and saw Andrei open his eyes. Not only was he awake, but there was sense in his gaze this time, not the dull, confused look that had been there the few other times that Andrei had roused. "God damn, it's about damn time." He dropped a hard kiss on Andrei's lips, and relief flooded through him. "How do you feel?" he asked as Ileana swarmed up and curled up right against Andrei's side, hugging him.

"Yay! You're awake. I thought the bad *mulo* had gotten you good." Ileana bounced up and gave Andrei a wide grin. "I yelled at her and scared her off."

"I feel like I've been lying on my ass for two weeks. I'm sore and restless." Andrei lifted his head and looked around the room. "Is Justin here, or did I just dream him? I had the craziest dreams."

"He was here, but Robin attacked him at the same time she attacked you. Now he's got an acute case of pneumonia complete with a raging fever and absolute delirium, just like you had." Dean looked at Ileana and wished that Old Mother was still around so he could pester her with questions. Andrei had started improving right after Robin's visit. He wasn't so sure that Andrei had been the one attacked. "Do you feel up to sitting up?"

"Yeah, I'm good." Andrei pushed himself and pulled off the nasal cannula from his nose up as a nurse came bustling into the room.

"How are you feeling today, Mr. Cuza?" Ileana watched with fascination and Dean with amusement as she took his vitals, plumped his pillows, and neatly dodged all of Andrei's attempts to get her to bring him his discharge papers. Dean chuckled as she ignored his fierce glower and attempted to look innocent as that glower turned on him.

"Can I at least get something to eat while I'm waiting for the doctor and for you to find out about Justin Mansle?" Andrei asked, giving up his argument with a quickness that made Dean immediately suspicious.

"I'll talk with the dietician about what's suitable for your stomach." The nurse poured Andrei a glass of water, moved the tray closer to the bed, and left with a promise to be back soon to remove some of the many devices attached to him.

"Dammit, I'm going to get broth, I just know it," Andrei grumbled as the door shut.

"That's probably a good idea. You haven't had anything in your stomach in days." Dean sat down next to Andrei and gave him a troubled look, waiting for him to argue. "Now that you're awake, you need to call the cops and let them know where Blake is."

Andrei picked up his cell phone that sat on the table next to his bed as it charged. "How did Justin know I was in the hospital?"

"I texted him. He's a little upset about it. I'm not sure how you're going to explain it to him." Dean gave him an apologetic smile. "I tried sending a message to the police too, but the last time I checked on Blake, nothing seems to have been done."

"They probably thought it was a scam since they couldn't verify who you were. How bad are things outside?"

"Chaotic and busy. Everybody's either getting off the island or battening down everything to ride out the storm." Dean's voice dropped to a whisper as the door opened again, even though he knew the nurses and doctor couldn't hear him. They drew the curtain around the bed, and Dean chafed with impatience.

"What are they doing to him?" Ileana asked as she edged toward the curtain until Dean hauled her back.

"Let's give him some privacy. Hopefully, they're unhooking him from a lot of those machines." That had to be a good sign. Andrei looked and sounded as if he'd completely recovered overnight, which was absolute insanity. However, probably one of the least insane things to have happened lately.

When the curtain was pulled back, Andrei looked thoroughly disgruntled, though much better without the cords for breathing, the cords to monitor his heart, and everything else that had made Dean ache with guilt and worry. "They said that my oxygen levels are good, my heart is normal, my lungs are clear, but they still want to ship me to new hospital for a few days for observation. Which is bullshit."

The nurse came right back and left behind a tray that Andrei eyed with disgust. "I hate hospital food."

Ileana crawled onto the bed and pulled off the lid, revealing the mashed potatoes, turkey with gravy, and overcooked green beans. "Doesn't look too bad to me."

"That's because your taste buds have atrophied." Andrei picked up the fork in one hand and his phone with the other. "They refuse to discharge me. As soon as I make this call and eat, I'm out of here."

Dean had several arguments against that plan, but held his tongue as Andrei called the police. It took several minutes for him to get through and even longer for him to get connected to someone with any clout. By the time Andrei hung up the phone, Dean felt as exasperated as Andrei looked.

"They refused to go look?" Dean asked, his heart sinking.

"They insisted that the park where we found Blake's truck is being evacuated, but I finally got them to promise to send a car." Andrei pushed the empty plate away. "They're undermanned and getting a lot of crazy-assed prank calls. And I'm not holding out much hope that they'll follow through. The timing is just bad."

"I can pop on over and see if he's still there," Dean offered, and Andrei shook his head.

"Even if he still is, I doubt they'd listen. It sounded like a madhouse at the police station." Andrei swung his legs over the side of the bed and removed the IV from his hand. "Screw waiting to be discharged or evacuated, I'm leaving now."

"Wait a second." Dean laid his hand on Andrei's shoulder before he could rise. "I know I said it was urgent, but don't you think you should take the doctor's opinions into consideration before you waltz out the door? You've been in the hospital for days."

"We don't have time for that." Andrei shrugged free from Dean's grip and glanced out his door, where doctors and nurses rushed by in a state of chaos. "We need to get out of here quick before someone comes to wheel my ass to an ambulance to take me wherever the evacuees are going. They're too busy to see what I'm up to now that they've already fussed over me. You don't understand, when I said I feel like I slept a week, that's exactly what I meant. I feel like the Energizer Bunny right now. I think Robin reverse zapped me somehow."

Ileana hopped down from the bed. "You mean the crazy ghost lady was helping you, and I stopped her?"

Andrei gave her a one-armed hug. "She helped, but in her zeal she overdid it. You saved both me and Justin." He shot Dean a concerned look. "He will recover, right?"

"That's what the docs say." Dean frowned and crossed his arms. "Your heart almost stopped. You should wait ten minutes to get a second opinion."

"Dean, when has it ever only taken ten minutes to talk to a doctor? Especially when you're in a hospital."

Dean hated to admit that he had a point.

Andrei stood up and pulled open the drawer next to the bed. "Where are my clothes?"

"I like the way you're dressed," Dean argued, ogling Andrei's tight ass through the slit in his bed gown before he caught Ileana looking at him curiously. Oh God, that was embarrassing. She had a habit of standing in a corner and being quiet until he forgot that she was there.

Ileana slid off the bed and skipped over to the closet. "Is this like a prison breakout?" She pulled it open and brought Andrei the pile of clothes that he came in.

"Something like that. Thank you, Ileana." Andrei tossed the clothes on the bed and sat down to get dressed. "Why don't you go and check the hallway and make sure no one's headed here wondering what I'm up to."

"Okies."

Andrei waited until she skipped out and shut the door behind her, and then began tugging on his jeans. "A man sneaking around in a robe and bed gown is very obvious, but a man in regular clothes isn't, sorry Dean."

"Your logic has no place in my fantasy," Dean grumbled, still eyeing Andrei to make sure that he didn't fall flat on his face. So far he seemed fine, even the sunken shadows under his eyes were gone.

Andrei stuffed his feet in his sneakers and shrugged into his shirt as he stood up again. He slid his hand around the nape of Dean's neck and pulled him closer for a hard kiss. "I'll be fine, Dean, trust me. I feel like I've never been sick. If I was anywhere near as sick as I think I was, I wouldn't have been able to stand up, okay? Robin did some kind of mojo, taking Justin's energy and giving it to me, I expect. I'm going to have a hell of a lot to apologize for when this is all through."

"You're going to do what you're going to do regardless of what I say, babe." Dean shook his head and then gave him a rueful smile. "I know we don't have time and this is important. I'll stop fussing so much."

"Dean, fuss at me all you want." Andrei stuffed his wallet in his back pocket and cast him a look that Dean interpreted as that fussing was something Andrei would miss when Dean left.

Dean gave him a smile and a light push toward the door. "Come on, before the nurse returns to the station and notices your IV machine beeping. I don't feel like watching you being chased by a bunch of orderlies."

He followed Andrei out, his nerves on edge. Dean didn't understand how his partner could play it so cool as he strolled casually toward the elevators and stairwell. Dean found Ileana near the nurse's station, fiddling with a stack of files. Just as the nurse started to round the corner of the station, she knocked them over, sending the files crashing to the floor.

The nurse cursed and stopped to pick them up as Ileana ran giggling toward them. "Did I do good?"

Andrei winked at her as she caught up to them. "Thank you, sis."

Dean ruffled her hair and kissed the top of her head. "You did very good, Poppet."

"So I take it that Justin is in no condition to help us?" Andrei asked.

"Not unless he made a miracle recovery like you did." Dean pointed toward a room. "They stuck him in there."

Andrei glanced down the hall, then slipped into the room. Justin stirred against the bedsheets, robbed of his normal vitality, and Andrei's expression darkened. "He'll be okay, right?"

"That's what I heard the doctors saying." Dean moved to the other side of the bed. "It's just going to take time."

Andrei leaned closer and gave Justin a hard, intent look. "Listen to me, you big old bastard. You will not let her ghost get the better of you. Next time I see you, you'd better be ripping into me again about my methods." He squeezed Justin's hand and then looked at Dean. "Let's go."

Dean remained silent as he followed Andrei back into the hall and into the elevator. It opened again down at the crowded lobby, mad with activity as the hospital personnel tried to impose some measure of order on the evacuation.

Andrei touched the small of his back where his gun holster usually was and frowned. "I suppose my rental car is back at the hotel."

"I may be able to move small things, babe, but a car is really pushing it. You got here by ambulance."

Andrei studied the parking lot with a narrowed gaze. "And you say the Hatteras Island is under a mandatory evacuation? What about Bodie Island? All or part of it?"

"I'm not sure. Farther north they might be able to stay put, but they're forcing the tourists out." Andrei headed out on foot, and there was a look in his eyes that made Dean think he'd come to some kind of a decision. "Where are you going?"

"To get a boat."

Baffled, Dean followed him. "Why don't you call for a cab?"

"We're never going to be able to get a cab in this madness, and the officials might even have the bridge or road blocked, and we're not going to be able to get to the hotel without a good excuse. And maybe not even then. They're trying to get people off the islands, not let more on."

Ileana scampered up next to Andrei and slid her hand in his as he turned down the street and headed toward the Pamlico Sound side of the island. "Oooh, are we going on a boat ride? I've always wanted to do that."

"Babe, I don't think you're going to have any more luck chartering a boat today either." One thing was for certain, Andrei wasn't even remotely sick anymore. He hadn't paused once to cough or catch his breath, and that eased some of Dean's worry.

Andrei cast him a sideways glance and didn't answer. It didn't take them long to reach the sound, since it lay less than a mile away, and Andrei didn't seem at all winded. Dean didn't know how he did it. The homes along this side were large, some already shuttered against the storm, and most had private docks jutting out into the somewhat calmer water of the sound.

"I like that boat," Ileana said, pointing to a sleek blue-and-white speedboat a few houses down. "Can we go out on that one?"

"That boat belongs to somebody, Poppet." Dean turned his attention back to Andrei as Ileana stuck out her lower lip. "I don't think you need to worry about Blake disappearing on you. I've been keeping an eye on his camper off and on, and so far he hasn't moved. And now that my connection has gotten stronger with Inez, I should be able to find her again even if they had left."

"That's a relief to know. I thought you were trying to avoid Blake because he sets you off." Andrei gave him a worried look as he turned in the direction of the boat that Ileana had pointed out. "Are you okay?"

"I haven't actually had to face him yet," Dean admitted, and the idea still terrified him. "I've still felt a bit of the uncontrollable anger, but I've been fighting it. Sooner or later if we're rescuing those kids, I'm going to have to face him. So I tested it often while you were out of it. Tested and pushed. I think I'll be okay." He didn't have a choice.

Andrei paused and went down toward the pier holding the speedboat. "I think you're right, Ileana. That looks like the perfect one. Dean, I've changed my mind. Would you pop over to the park and see if it's empty or not while I see what the owners of the house are up to?"

"They're not going to let you borrow the boat on the eve of a hurricane. Not to some guy who just walks up to their house."

"Come on, I've got a trustworthy face." Andrei gave him a grin, and Dean felt a trickle of foreboding. He was up to something sneaky. "Please, Dean. It'll help to get a quick idea if Blake is there or not. But don't go any closer or try to get a glimpse of him. I don't want you to risk it."

For a split second, a defeated expression crossed Andrei's face, and he didn't look at Dean. "I'm sorry, Dean. If they're gone, we're going to have to start all over again."

Dean took Andrei's other hand and squeezed it lightly. "You didn't do anything wrong; you're only human. If we're going to start blaming ourselves, how about laying some on me. It was my touch that made you sick in the first place." And he was so very grateful that he didn't have to worry about that anymore, because he couldn't seem to help himself.

"You don't have anything to apologize for, *iubito*, not to me."

Dean couldn't figure out what was going through Andrei's head, and he had to admit that his partner had a point. There was no reason to try to figure out how to get to Hatteras if Blake had taken off again. "Just to ease your concern, I haven't heard the Jackals once when I peeked in on the camper before. I'll be careful. Don't do anything crazy while I'm gone."

"Me?" Andrei arched a brow and gave him a tight smile. "Hurry back and keep me out of trouble."

"Fine," Dean sighed. "I'll be right back."

"I LOVE him, but he's amazingly naïve sometimes," Andrei said after Dean disappeared. He hopped down into the boat and started to poke around, searching for a spare set of keys. He needed to get out on the water before Dean realized what he was up to. Dean was the son of a DC cop. He would not understand the occasional need for underhanded tactics.

"Dean's gonna be awfully mad at you," Ileana said as she knelt down on one of the seats and leaned over the side to trail her hand in the water. "He's gonna give you his grumpy face."

"Not mad as much as he's going to be shocked and horrified. But the owner is being irresponsible. Look at how far the water has risen. This boat should've already been dry-docked and stuck in the garage. I would guess that the owner is young, probably a bit adventurous, and is thinking of taking this beauty out later for a little wave jumping." He winked at Ileana as he untied the moorings. "I'm probably saving his life."

"I don't think he's gonna believe you."

"Yeah, me neither. That is a bit of BS." Andrei pushed the boat away from the pier and looked at Ileana. "Want to help me drive the boat?"

"Ooohh really?" Ileana was off the seat in a flash, abandoning Cougar. She came to stand by Andrei, wiggling in excitement. "What do I gotta do?"

"First, will you start the engine for me? Like you used to do in Dad's old truck when I wanted to borrow it?" Andrei grinned as the boat roared to life, and Ileana clapped, doing a little pirouette at her success. "Good job, now just come and stand between me and the steering wheel." He showed her where to put her hands as he eased the boat away from the pier and out onto the water. It would be a very choppy ride, but Ileana wouldn't mind at all. "Ready?"

"Let's go!"

Andrei opened the throttle as Ileana whooped in delight, and he couldn't help laughing with her. It was so good to be out of that hospital and doing something. Not thirty seconds into the ride, Dean appeared next to him with an outraged expression. "You stole the boat. Really, Andrei? That was your plan? Are you trying to get arrested?"

"I eased your conscience. Now you had absolutely nothing to do with helping me steal the boat." Andrei tightened his hands on the wheel as spray shot up while the boat skipped and hopped across the waves.

"What about her?" Dean threw up his hands as Ileana laughed in delight. She wasn't paying any attention to their argument; instead she was riveted by watching the water zoom by as she helped Andrei at the wheel. "What are you teaching Ileana? Isn't that like aiding and abetting or contributing to the delinquency of a minor?"

Andrei cut a quick glance toward him, softening inside. Dean would've made such a good father. He wouldn't have let Andrei screw up the way his parents had screwed up with him. He would've protected their kids.

Dean cocked his head, his eyes narrowing. "What are you thinking?"

"That I love you." So much that it ached and felt so good and right at the same time.

Dean shook his head, but the irritation fled from his hazel eyes as he sat down on one of the benches. "You know what, it's not worth arguing over. There were a few campers left at the park, including Blake's truck. Most of them look as if they're packing up and heading out. Blake's camper seemed quiet, so I'm not sure what he's up to."

"Well, we'll figure that out soon. Even if he does hit the road between now and when we get there, I doubt he'll get too far," Andrei replied.

"And it was weird. It was harder to jump this time. Like a wind tugged at me, trying to pull me off course. That hasn't happened before."

Ileana poked her head out from around Andrei's arm. "It's the big, big storm. All that energy mixes up with ghosty energy. Little storms don't bother us, but big storms can, and the big one is coming fast. It can make the things in limbo stronger too, but it's not safe to try to control it. It's too much." She slipped away from Andrei, came over to Dean, and whispered loudly in his ear. "I tole him you'd be mad about the boat."

"It's okay. I plan on enjoying this boat ride. Look, Poppet, see those birds swooping down?" Dean pointed toward the shore of Roanoke Island at the flock of pelicans as Ileana leaned into him. "Now watch how their beaks get all big as they scoop up the water and fish."

"Oh wow, that's so cool."

Andrei kept stealing little glances toward them as he navigated through the choppy waters. He wished that they could stay together just like this, and that he wouldn't have to watch Dean get confused and upset when things changed as they invariably would. As they neared Hatteras Island, Andrei slowed down and scanned the shore. The town where his hotel was located lay a little ways down the coast, and he didn't want to miss it.

Dean came up behind him, slid his arms around Andrei's waist, and kissed the side of his neck before laying his head down on Andrei's shoulder. A warm ripple went through Andrei, and he leaned back into Dean's embrace.

"How long till we get there?" Dean said near his ear.

Not nearly long enough. Andrei was torn between getting there and doing what he'd set out to do, and lingering in this peaceful moment before things got to be ugly. "Maybe thirty minutes. I just hope we can find a place to tie this baby up where it'll be hard to spot. If we can get the kids away from their father, it'll provide a good escape plan. I'm sure traffic is backed up all the way up Highway 12."

Unless he could think of a way to take out Blake now that would not endanger his kids. He hadn't been able to think of a plan yet that didn't either involve that scenario or Dean seeing him. And he couldn't bear the thought of Dean witnessing him killing someone.

"So you plan on bringing the boat back?" Dean sounded relieved. "Good, my dad would have your ass."

"I definitely don't plan on confessing my many crimes to your dad." All too soon Andrei noticed signs of civilization as the wildlife refuge gave way to the little string of towns on the island. He slowed the boat even more and hugged the shore until he found a likely spot to tie it up. Grabbing a cleaning rag from one of the cabinets, he did a quick wipe down of the steering wheel and all the other places he might've touched. Hopefully, it would be good enough.

"That was so much fun." Ileana held up her arms, and Andrei lifted her out to Dean. "Can we do it again?"

"Maybe, Poppet." Dean straightened and looked around as Andrei scrambled out of the boat. "I see a pizza place and lots of vacation homes completely shuttered up. The place looks pretty freaking deserted except for the line of cars on the road. You're right, trying to get out of here by car is going to be impossible. What now?"

"We stop by the hotel." Which wasn't far from the pizza place. Andrei wasn't going anywhere near Blake without his gun, and he'd rather take the Jeep to the campground. It would take too much time to walk it. Night would be falling soon, and tomorrow morning would bring the storm with it. A strong breeze already had filled the air with a hazy film of sand.

Not long later, Andrei entered his hotel room through the door that Dean opened for him. A quick glance in the safe showed him that his guns had been left alone. His stomach rumbled, but Andrei quieted it by grabbing an energy bar from his suitcase and downing a bottle of water as he ate it.

"How are you going to get Inez and Tristan away from Blake?" Dean frowned as Andrei strapped the guns on. "The last two times you guys ran into each other there was a shootout."

"I'm going to try my damned best to sneak them out of there without him knowing until they're gone." Then he'd deliver the kids to a National guardsman and go back for Blake. "If I can't, then I'm just going to have to improvise. But trust me, Dean, I do not want, in any way, a repeat of our first two meetings. He's too twitchy."

"Promise?"

Andrei caught Dean's hand and kissed his fingertips. "I promise."

Chapter Eighteen

THE RV park was completely deserted by the time they arrived, and Blake's camper truck stood among the litter of debris left behind by the nervous tenants as they had packed up and left in a hurry. The sky had darkened even more in the short amount of time they were in the hotel, and the wind had picked up. The flag, snapping and jerking in the wind, was the only sound that broke the silence as they got out of the Jeep.

There was something eerie about the stillness, and Dean looked at Andrei uneasily. "Don't you think you should've waited in the car while I looked around?"

"There was no hiding that someone's coming, Dean, and to be honest, I don't think we're going to find anyone home. It's too quiet, and that car I saw parked here last time is missing."

Sure enough, a hail of gunfire didn't come at Andrei like Dean had been expecting, and the back door to the camper was open, banging back against the side with a steady thump, thump, thump. The place was a wreck with cabinets and drawers ransacked, sand blown in and coating everything. It was going to be a pain in the ass to clean out if Blake ever returned.

Dean looked around the camper, feeling the same frustration that radiated from Andrei. He hadn't actually been in here before, and he was glad he hadn't because it was a mess. He would've been pissed off all over again at the sight of those children in this madhouse. To make matters worse, he could feel the hurricane coming, gathering strength and speed as it bore down on the East Coast. The storm itched along his skin and made his heart race. He was pretty sure that it would hit the Outer Banks sooner than the weathermen anticipated.

He was suddenly very aware of the fragility of this tiny string of islands and the fact that the man he loved would probably refuse to leave until he had answers. "They're long gone, babe. I don't even get a glimmer of Inez in here." Dean raked a hand through his hair with a sound of frustration. "I'm sorry, I should've kept a better eye on them. I should've come closer when I came over earlier. Then you could've concentrated on evacuating yourself."

"You did what you could. Don't blame yourself," Andrei said absently as he opened a cabinet and then closed it with a frown. "He took the paperwork with him. I don't think he plans on coming back here. I wish I knew what spooked him into bolting and abandoning this truck. I get the impression that he's been gone for at least a day."

Dean picked up a piece of paper on the floor and turned it over. His heart froze as ice seized him and horror crawled up his spine. The paper crumpled as his hand clenched into a fist, and he had to force himself to relax and smooth out the page again. The eyes seized him first. Those mad, terrible eyes that jumped out from the paper and sunk into his brain. It was a childish rendering of the Jackal Wraiths, but the power in those eyes still had managed to grab him and grab him hard.

"What is it?" Andrei asked as he came over to him.

Dean tipped the paper toward him, careful to not let Ileana see. She played on the bunk bed with Cougar, seemingly oblivious to them, but Dean knew that she saw more than she let on. She had mostly recovered from her fright, and he didn't want to bring the horror of them being chased back into her mind.

"Ugly bastards," Andrei said with a frown and took the picture, studying it intently. The sky above the creatures was a big, gray, swirling circle. Dean tore his gaze away and studied the stick figures that also inhabited the picture. Two little ones holding hands and a much bigger one dressed in red. At least the Jackals weren't looking at the kids. "Poor baby girl," Andrei sighed. "I think she's got the sight, and she's connected to you."

"The what?" Dean shook his head in denial, appalled at the thought that Inez could've seen anything like the Jackals. No, he was just jumping at shadows, making connections where none existed because the longer he stayed in this limbo, the stranger he felt. The drawing had to be a coincidence. "That's crazy, Andrei."

"Crazier than you and Ileana coming back as a ghost? Crazier than creatures like that existing?" Andrei asked in an undertone as he flicked the page. "The world is full of crazy, inexplicable things. You've just never seen them before you died. It's possible for a child that young to see things from the limbo world. I did."

It made Dean wonder what else Andrei had seen that Dean hadn't. The young boy who talked and played with ghosts. The young man out on the streets, living in a tent city and scrapping to get by. And God only knew what else he saw on some of those cases of his, those things that he spoke of in bare whispers and sometimes just hinted at when he looked to Dean to ease the memories.

Dean cupped the back of Andrei's neck and gave it a squeeze. "You're far stronger than you give yourself credit for." Surprise flashed in Andrei's dark eyes.

"Coming from you, that means something," Andrei murmured.

Dean folded up the picture and stuck it in his back pocket. "I suppose I could try to connect with her again and see where they might have gotten themselves to. It's strange, but I still think they're on the island. She doesn't feel very far to me. I can't really explain it any better than that. Something is tugging me south."

"I think you're right. Blake seems to have a preference for south, and there are a few bigger towns farther on down the road. The road is less congested going that way too."

"He could've stolen a car and ditched his other one if he feels like he's being chased." Dean gave Andrei a pointed look. "Theft seems to be a popular option these days."

"Maybe. Blake's been pretty careful, except for the few times he's been cornered. But I think stealing a car on an island with only one road off that's being monitored by authorities is pushing it, even for him." Andrei shook his head. "Would it be easier to try to link to Inez from here where she was last or back at the hotel?"

"I don't think it makes much of a difference." Dean closed his eyes and stuck his hand in his pocket to hold the hair ribbon. It helped him concentrate. He needed to get close to her, but not too close that he popped up beside her. The tension before a blind jump like this, when he could appear in front of his killer, sank its claws into him.

Andrei grabbed ahold of his bicep. "Just stay long enough to get a fix on her whereabouts. Don't try looking for Blake, okay?"

"I promise." Dean tried to follow that thin tether between himself and Inez, but the line had disappeared, leaving only a faint echo behind.

Dean concentrated harder, pulling into his thoughts the way Inez had looked the last time he'd seen her, with her big, scared eyes and the little forlorn wave she'd given him. The world lurched as it always did at the start of a jump, and then something caught him. A swirling mass of sensation that tumbled him about until he didn't know which way was up or down. It was like he'd been caught up in a tornado. It ripped at his skin and clothes, carrying with it an eerie wail that sounded close enough to the Jackals to make Dean cry out in remembered terror.

He was hearing things that weren't there, brought on by his fear of the Jackals and the shock of the picture he'd found. Dean shook his head savagely. The Jackals had no reason to hunt him down again. He thought he heard someone shouting his name and, from far away, the faint sound of "Hush Little Baby" that appeared and disappeared with the roaring of the wind.

What was going on? The storm hadn't gotten there yet. It shouldn't have grabbed him like this. Vainly Dean struggled, trying to will himself out of the disorienting whirl by concentrating on Inez. When that didn't work, he tried latching on to Andrei.

He spun out of the maelstrom, was flung through the air, and landed hard on his back. Dean opened his eyes as rain struck him, an icy, sheeting deluge that stung his skin with the force of its fall and that had him soaked in seconds. He opened his eyes, shielding them against the downpour, trying to squint through the blackness and jagged lightning that tore across the sky.

Dean scrambled to his feet, searching for shelter. Vague dark shapes rose around him, even blacker against the cloud-covered night of the sky. Dean spun around, disoriented, until he realized they were the tall vacation homes, groaning and swaying on their stilts as the waves came up over the dunes to lash the pilings. Dean tried to wipe the water off his face, but more only replaced it. He shook from cold and shock as he tried to reach back for Andrei. Something had gone wrong in limbo, holding him until the hurricane struck. And he couldn't sense his partner anymore.

Stunned, Dean reached for the feel of him again, groping in the dark as his heart pounded. "Andrei!"

Light gleamed through an unshuttered window, the only point of sanity in this nightmare. A black silhouette stood framed there, a small figure that waved before the light was doused again. Dean shook his head and stumbled closer, fighting the waves that licked at his feet and dragged at him. *Which house?*

Thunder ripped apart the sky, bringing with it a jagged bolt of lightning that hit close enough for the hair to rise on Dean's arms and neck. For a moment, the air glowed white, almost blinding him, but it was enough to see that the window where he'd thought he'd seen the figure was tightly closed with the storm shutter rolled down and latched.

The whole world had gone insane. All the normal rules had disappeared.

The furious, white, undulating spray of the waves reminded him uncomfortably of the Jackals, and as if his thought had summoned them, Dean could hear them bay, rising and falling with the wind. It seemed almost like the Jackals had become a part of the raging hurricane, chaos and destruction feeding into each other and growing stronger.

Fear paralyzed Dean until another wave struck him, almost knocking him down to the ground. He staggered, fighting to keep from falling because the water would just drag him out to sea. He seemed to have no control over whether he was corporeal. The howl rose again, closer this time, and it was all Dean could do to force himself to turn around and face it. His limbs felt weighted down, filled with ice. No, oh fuck no, he hadn't done anything this time.

The burning eyes appeared first, slithering out of the shadows. One Jackal Wraith slunk out, the other following close behind. Dean stumbled back until his shoulder struck one of the pilings of a nearby house. He wrapped his arms around it to keep from falling and slid behind it, hoping that between the darkness and the electricity in the air, the Jackals wouldn't notice him.

Again and again he tried to visualize a way out of there. *Andrei.* He closed his eyes against the horror moving closer. *Andrei.* He thought he caught a faint whiff of the scent of him, oh so familiar and steadying. He felt the grip of Andrei's hands on his shoulders and heard the rumble of his husky voice, and then it was torn away again as the storm raged through him.

Dean stole a peek, not knowing if he was more afraid of seeing the Jackals again or of not knowing where they were. They stood not far from where Dean had been moments before and stared up at the same house. Their heads bobbed and wove, their tongues lashing at the air and their coiled gaunt bodies disappearing in and out of the rain and shadows.

He jerked his eyes away and forced a calming breath, then another. Their attention wasn't on him. He didn't sense them in his mind and soul the way he had before. He didn't hear those horrid sounds of chewing and flesh being stripped from bone. Their whispering voices didn't taunt him to run and promise to devour his soul. He wasn't the one being hunted, and he was not about to draw their attention with more negative emotion.

The only thing Dean could think of was that Robin had to be hovering near her kids. Given the way she attacked Andrei and Justin, she must have succumbed to what Ileana feared for him. Becoming a… what was it she'd called it… a *mulo*, a bad spirit. Dean grieved for her. Robin didn't deserve this end. She was only trying to protect her children, and he couldn't think of a single way of saving her, short of sacrificing himself. Maybe it wasn't too late. If he could find her, talk to her about keeping control, make her understand that they wouldn't stop until her kids were saved, maybe that would be enough.

He eased away from the piling, grateful that the sound of the storm completely obscured him from whatever the Jackals were watching. Strangely, they didn't give chase, not like they had with him. They didn't tear Robin away from the house and devour her as they had Old Mother. They merely watched and waited with a calm that was equally as chilling.

Dean concentrated hard on Robin and let the storm carry him away.

ANDREI finished cleaning his gun and set it aside on the table and then picked up the other one, trying to keep his mind occupied as the hours wore on. It had been easier earlier when he and Ileana first realized that Dean wasn't popping right back. Ileana kept insisting that she thought he was farther south down the island, so Andrei had packed up and headed out, picking up supplies along the way.

Dean had been gone for hours, and Ileana had taken off a bit ago too. The electricity was out at the hotel, and the wind battered the small building so hard that it shook at times. Not for the first time, he wondered if the roof would last or if the hotel would flood. The light in the kerosene lamp danced and flickered across the table, sending eerie shadows darting along the wall. Andrei wasn't going to be able to sleep without news of some kind. He hated the endless waiting that sometimes came with this job, and this kind of waiting was even worse.

Ileana appeared, soaking wet and her hair coming loose from its braids. Andrei immediately set down the gun and reached for her. "I told you not to disappear on me again," he said in a low, furious voice as he wrapped a towel around her. It was bad enough that Dean went missing. Every time she disappeared to search for him, a little part of Andrei died inside.

Ileana clung to him, her teeth chattering. "B-but I know he's c-close. I-I jus' gotta f-find him."

That made Andrei want to go out and search too, but he'd likely get himself killed if he stepped outside the door. Who knew how many victims this storm claimed already when it suddenly started hours ahead of schedule? Andrei had barely made it to a hotel before the darkness had fallen in a curtain of rain and debris that had swept in with the wind. The hotel had been deserted, and Ileana had helped him break in. That was just one more thing he'd have to answer for when this whole investigation was over. He'd be lucky if he didn't wind up in jail himself.

"Dean will find us, Ileana," Andrei said as he rubbed her hair with the towel. In moments she was as dry as if she'd never been out in the rain. He set the damp towel aside, took the lamp and her hand, and led her over to the couch. "Sit down with me, and I'll tell you a story."

"I don't want a story!" Ileana glared at him and crossed her arms. "I want Dean to come back. He's more fun than you."

Andrei picked up a brush and tried not to let her temper poke holes of old guilt in him. He needed to keep a grip on things. "I want Dean to come back too, but we don't know why he's lost or even if he's lost. You going outside isn't going to solve anything."

He began to brush her hair as the wind started howling again. It was strange; he'd never heard wind like that before. It almost seemed like a living thing, determined to tear down and destroy everything. He thought that if he just concentrated a little harder, he'd hear words in the howl of the wind. The understanding lay just at the edge of his consciousness. Andrei's instincts told him that he didn't want to understand the words.

They both jumped as the door banged opened, and for just a split second Andrei thought he heard an insane shriek, like wires bending and twanging the wrong way, setting his teeth on edge. A dark form stood in the doorway, then disappeared between one flash of lightning and the rest. Andrei's heart jumped, but he forced his expression to remain calm for Ileana's sake.

"Don't let them eat me," Ileana screamed and scrambled onto the bed, yanking the covers over her head. "I'm sorry I was mean, Andrei!"

Andrei sprinted toward the door and fought with the wind before he managed to shut it again. In that short amount of time, he was soaked to the skin, and more water had come in under the door. At least it seemed like seepage from the water collecting on the walkway outside and not the flood of rising waters.

"Ileana, I'm not going to let anything eat you." He hoped that calmed her down because he was too busy trying to yank the chair over with his foot to worry about figuring out what she was talking about. He finally caught it and jammed it under the doorknob. He would need something heavier if the wind picked up even more.

He began dragging over the dresser and breathed a little easier after he pushed it into place. "What did you see, Ileana?" Andrei wasn't sure if there was something else out there other than them or if they were both just extra jumpy tonight. If there was ever a time when nightmares became flesh, this was the storm for it.

"Calm down, Ileana, before you make your brother crazy." Andrei whirled around at the sound of Dean's voice just as a branch tore through the plywood covering the window and shattered glass everywhere.

"Where the hell have you been?" Andrei bolted for the kerosene lamp before it was knocked onto the floor. This was going to get bad. He carried the lamp into the bathroom, latching the door behind him, his blood racing with adrenaline. The walls shuddered and the roaring of the wind rose to a crescendo.

Dean walked through the bathroom door, bringing Ileana and blankets with him. "The storm's spawning tornados. And somehow the Jackal Wraiths have come with the storm. That's what Ileana was shouting about." He pushed Andrei into the shower stall and handed him Ileana, who clung to him, weeping and shaking.

Andrei grabbed his hand. "Wait, dammit, Dean, you have to go. You have to take her." His heart sank as he stared into Dean's face. He could let him go. He had to. He was ready. He had to let both of them go, because the alternative was unacceptable. He just thought that he'd have a little more time, and he'd been wrong to expect it.

Dean shook his head and crowded into the stall with the both of them. "We can't cross over while those things are around. I found that out the hard way, but at least this time the Jackals are not after me."

Dean sank down, looking white and exhausted, and Andrei scooted over to make more room for him. He slipped his arm around Dean's shoulders as he hugged Ileana close. The roaring disappeared and with it the shuddering, making the gale-force winds that remained seem almost quiet in comparison. Having the both of them with him made waiting out the storm more bearable in the flickering dark. "Are you sure enough to risk it?"

"Trust me, Andrei. I know when those monsters have their attention focused on me." Andrei felt the shudder ripple through Dean's body. "They're here and they're after something, but it isn't me. Fuck if I know what, though. I thought maybe it was Robin, but I couldn't find her."

Andrei smoothed a hand through Ileana's hair and kissed her forehead. Softly he began singing under his breath, to try to help calm her. He had so many questions. "I think I heard them too—not like you two do, but there was something in that wind." And he never wanted to hear it again. "What happened, Dean? You've been gone for hours. Scared the hell out of me."

"I wish to God I knew." Dean laid his head on Andrei's shoulder. "I tried to follow Inez and got caught up in the hurricane. There's an energy there in the storm that I've never felt before, and it snatched me right up before it had even hit shore. It took me forever to battle through the wind to get here. I'm definitely not going to be doing anymore hopping around until the storm's gone."

Andrei closed his eyes, feeling warmth start to seep back into him with the pile of blankets over his wet clothes. "I tried looking around for a bit after you left, but I didn't have any luck in figuring out where that bastard took Inez and Tristan. Ileana led me here."

"That's okay, I found them. We could walk there if it wasn't a deathtrap outside. Blake broke into one of those fancy vacation homes and is holed up there for the storm."

Andrei went still, his blood turning to ice as a cold, potent rage woke up inside of him again. Blake was still within reach. Andrei could get to him tomorrow when the island was practically deserted. There would be one more sin on his conscience, but that was a guilt he could live with. The wind rose to another shriek, carrying with it the impression of dark words, and Dean tensed beside him.

"Once the storm eases some, if the area isn't completely flooded, you should have no trouble getting to him," Dean continued after the howling eased back again. "I doubt that Blake would expect anybody snooping around. There's only one problem, and I'm not sure of a way around it."

"Can I come too, when you go get them?" Ileana asked, lifting her head. "I want to meet Inez and the baby."

"No." The last thing Andrei wanted was to have Dean and Ileana around while he dealt with Blake. "You don't need to witness a potentially bad situation, and Dean shouldn't be around Blake. I'll go by myself, as soon as the storm clears. I'll be in and out before you know it, and then we can take the kids to a public place. I'm sure there's a storm shelter set up around here where Inez and Tristan can get the care they need."

"If you think you're leaving me behind, you're crazy," Dean said in a low, hard voice. "I can handle seeing Blake, and if I feel any stirrings of rage, I'll get out of there. I'm not going to tempt fate, but I'm not going to hide either. I've been working hard at keeping control, and I'm as much a part of this as you are. Dammit, Andrei, I have to see it out until the end."

Andrei didn't respond as his mind whirled. He wanted Blake to pay for what he did, but he didn't see how he was going to be able to take care of him with Dean around. Maybe he could leave Dean to watch over the kids. It would just be another problem he'd have to deal with when the time came. One way or another, this was going to end tomorrow.

"Okay," Andrei said softly, and Dean relaxed against him.

"Thank you for not arguing with me over it." Dean turned his head and brushed a quick kiss over Andrei's lips. "Try to get some sleep. This storm's going to last for a few hours more before we hit the eye. You're going to need all the energy you can get."

"Wait," Ileana said as she sat up in the blankets. "If Dean's going, then I—"

"No," both Dean and Andrei said at the same time, and Ileana settled back down with a sulk. Andrei let her be; trying to coax her out of a mood like that would only lead to her arguing her case.

"You didn't say what the problem was," Andrei said after he thought that Ileana might be dozing.

"The Jackals are watching the house. Another reason why I don't want Ileana to come. And before you go off on a protective tirade, I promise to be very, very careful, Andrei. There's something strange going on, and Old Mother mentioned some conditions where the Jackal Wraiths can attack the living, and I'm not sure if they apply here. As far as I know, you can't see them, so you're not going into that situation alone, and that's final."

Andrei bit back a curse of frustration. He couldn't postpone going after Blake when the storm was over on the hope that the Jackals would be gone. There was just no certainty, and the situation was too urgent for both the missing kids and Ileana and Dean. "You know, I think I can count on one hand all the times you've put your foot down about something."

"Listen this time too, babe. You're not alone in this. I'm not going to let it happen."

"Okay, but when we get there, I'm in charge. Understand?" Andrei turned his head and looked at him. "No arguments or hesitation when I give an order."

Dean pressed another kiss to his jaw and nuzzled Andrei's cheek. "Understood. Now get some sleep."

The enormity of what he planned struck Andrei. "Dean...." The words lodged in his throat, all the things he wanted to say and he couldn't. *Don't think any less of me.*

His idea of right and wrong, just and unjust had gotten so screwed up, and he didn't know what he was doing anymore. There was a hard knot of anger inside of him, and the more he tried to control it, the louder it screamed to be set free. He just needed to know that Dean was going to be safe and sane. He had to believe in the possibility that they would see each other again.

"Yeah, babe?"

Andrei shook his head and kissed Dean's temple. "Nothing. Goodnight."

DEAN sensed Andrei start to drift off after what seemed like forever, and he piled more pillows and blankets around him. Even though it seemed like his partner had made a miraculous recovery, Andrei still had just been in the hospital and hadn't been medically cleared to leave either. And a shower stall had to be one of the worst places to try and get some rest.

Restless, Dean paced between the bathroom and the main room. He could still sense the storm moving through him in a way that didn't seem to be bothering Ileana at all. Maybe because she hadn't tried moving through the limbo to find someone and gotten caught up in it. Even freakier, it was like he could sense the Jackals too, even though they were being quiet at the moment. They seemed to be scouting, zigzagging back and forth between the hotel and the house.

Dean hoped it was just a product of his overactive imagination and nerves strung taut. He was so tired, stretched thin, and the longer he stayed in this place where he didn't belong, the worse he felt. It didn't seem to faze Ileana, but then again, she was only eight. What did she really understand about life and death? He peeked outside and thought he saw something slink around the corner and disappear, but he couldn't be entirely certain.

He went back and knelt beside Andrei. He was hiding something. Dean sensed it in the way that he had walled off a piece of himself, shutting off his emotions whenever Blake was mentioned, and it scared him.

Andrei was so angry and hurt, and Dean didn't want him doing anything that he would regret later on. And at the same time, he couldn't really picture Andrei doing something violent, despite the fact that Andrei had been in more than one altercation over the years. He never would've believed that Andrei would've stolen something either, so clearly Dean was a little naïve when it came to him.

Whatever it was, Dean couldn't fix it now, but he would figure it out. He knew how to get Andrei to spill his guts when he needed to. He settled down next to Andrei, curling into him and determined to get some rest for himself. Things were going to get insane in the morning. He drifted off, listening to Andrei's deep, even breathing.

"DEAN, I don't know if you can hear me or not, but I think it's getting close to the time to head out. We may not have a long window to work with."

Dean jerked awake, appearing in the empty shower stall at the sound of Andrei's voice. Thunder struck in a series of booms sounding almost as if bombs were going off. The wind had picked up again, and the kerosene lamp had died sometime during the intervening hours. Dean sensed the eyewall of the storm approaching, violent and deadly, and its energy coursed through him.

Dean followed the sense of Andrei to the main room where he was grimly gathering together a bag full of snacks and water in case they didn't make it back to the hotel. One of the plywood sheets over a window had torn free, and Dean could see the terrible downpour outside. At least Andrei hadn't been tempted to sneak out on his own after he'd agreed to let Dean come with him.

"I heard you loud and clear, babe."

Andrei glanced at him, his expression cold and remote, and it struck a shiver in Dean. For a moment, he thought he saw a flicker of softening in Andrei's gaze before it hardened again. He was all business and ready to go, and Dean didn't like it one bit. This wasn't the same look that he had in his eyes when he was off to rescue some kid from a perv. This was different.

Dean caught him around the waist and pulled him close, fisting his hands in Andrei's shirt. Andrei stiffened, not returning the embrace, and he looked away as if he couldn't quite make himself meet Dean's eyes. "What is it?" Dean asked, and Andrei shook his head.

"It's nothing, just trying to get into the zone. You know how it is."

"Yeah, I need that zone too." Dean pulled him closer and slanted his mouth over Andrei's, and his partner's remoteness shattered. He slid his arms around Dean and kissed him back, hot, hard, and possessive. Dean's tongue thrust into his mouth, and Andrei groaned. They had time. He'd make the time to keep Andrei from slipping away.

"How do you always do this to me?" Andrei muttered as the kiss broke. He buried his face in Dean's neck, holding onto him in a way that set him on fire with need and heat.

"I'm not letting you pull back from me. Not when today might be the last time I see you for a while." Dean slid his hands under his shirt. "You hear me, Andrei? Dammit, I'm going to get under your skin and put my mark on you."

Andrei's eyes widened as he was pushed back against the bathroom door. Dean paused long enough to yank off his shirt, and Andrei pulled off his own and then reached for him with shaking hands. Dean rejoiced inside and knew just how much he was getting to Andrei, making him feel, because he only trembled like that when his emotions were raging inside of him. And that was so much better than the icy remoteness.

Dean's heart skipped a beat as he crowded close to Andrei again, trapping him between himself and the door. "I love you."

Andrei shuddered and pushed against his shoulders. "Dean, wait, I can't."

"You can't or you won't?" Dean rasped, caging Andrei's wrists and pinning them to either side of his head. He knew Andrei could get free with one jerk if he wanted to, and it gave him hope when Andrei didn't. "What're you afraid I'll see?"

He didn't wait for Andrei's answer; instead he pressed closer, chest to chest, and kissed him. Andrei made a desperate sound and tore his hands free. He clung to Dean, gripping his ass and pulling him even closer. Dean slid his hand down and cupped Andrei's cock through his jeans, and it wasn't enough. He fumbled at their zippers, tugged them down, and stroked both of them together. The sensation of their cocks rubbing up against each other and the hot little licks of Andrei's tongue against his own made the urgency all the hotter.

Andrei pulled his mouth free and drew in a ragged breath. "Hurry." He turned around, bracing his arms on the door as he leaned in and jutted his hips out. "We don't have a lot of time."

Dean sensed it too, the layer after layer of thunderstorms outside that raged inside of him as well. He paused, afraid that he'd hurt Andrei if he fucked him now with all of that violent energy he wasn't sure he could contain.

"You can't stop now, dammit Dean. You started this." Andrei looked over his shoulder at him in the flickering light between lightning flashes. "One last time, before everything changes. Before you see me in a whole different light."

Dean didn't think Andrei was talking about him moving on. He jerked Andrei's jeans down around his thighs and pressed closer, his cock nestling against Andrei's tight ass, and Andrei sighed, spreading his legs as far apart as he could with the denim in the way.

"What's going to change, Andrei?" He pressed his mouth close to Andrei's ear. "What are you afraid of?"

Andrei shook his head and reached back, grasping Dean's cock and guiding it toward his entrance. "Hard, Dean, goddamn it, fuck me hard."

Dean grabbed his hips before Andrei could take matters into his own hands and push back. He was having a difficult time thinking past the heat of Andrei's body and the eagerness of his cock that longed to be deep inside of him. They had to go slow at first, at least until Andrei's body relaxed enough to really take him. And as much as Dean enjoyed the sight of Andrei bent over, arms braced with Dean's cock nestled between his cheeks, he didn't want to hurt him.

He grabbed the bottle of lube out of Andrei's open bag and kissed him between the shoulder blades as he pushed his fingers into him. Andrei hissed, his body arching and clenching around him. "No foreplay, Dean, just you."

Shuddering, Dean kissed him again on his jaw and lubed his cock, unable to resist Andrei's desperation anymore. "Yes," Andrei panted, pushing back, and they both groaned as Dean's cock sank into him. Andrei turned his head and kissed him deep as they both began to move, their bodies slapping together rhythmically.

"Harder, harder, Dean, please," Andrei pleaded against his lips.

Dean dug his fingers into Andrei's lean hips, holding him steady as they fucked. Andrei's head fell back, his throat corded with cries. Dean pressed his cheek against Andrei's shoulder, his heart aching because Andrei still seemed so distant.

He slipped out of him, and Andrei let out a wordless cry of protest. Dean jerked Andrei's jeans the rest of the way down, helping him to step out of them, and then turned Andrei around so that they faced each other. "You're not allowed to put up that wall, not during this."

Andrei shook his head, reaching for him again. "Dean, please."

Dean pushed him back on the stripped down bed and finished taking off the rest of his own clothes. When he met Andrei's eyes, his partner glanced away. Dean clamped down on the sharp spike of anger and clambered over him. "You might as well give in now and save your energy for later," Dean warned as his body settled over Andrei's again. "There's no wall you can put up that I can't knock back down, nowhere you can hide that I won't find you."

Andrei's breath quickened and tension lined every muscle of his body. His eyes fluttered closed as Dean brushed a kiss along his jaw, and his body arched into Dean's touch. He spread his thighs and lifted his knees up to cradle Dean's hips. "Fuck me again."

Dean's cock rubbed against Andrei's entrance before pushing in just an inch. He paused, fighting the urge to sink all the way home. "Look at me, Andrei."

"More," Andrei groaned, rocking his hips.

Dean shook his head and tapped Andrei's jaw with his fingertips. "Look at me. You want to get fucked, babe? You've got to be here with me."

"Damn you, Dean. Are you going to take all my defenses from me?" Andrei said it so low that Dean barely heard him over the fury of the storm.

"You shouldn't ever need them with me anyway."

Dean waited, not breathing, just holding still until finally Andrei looked up at him. His eyes were darker than normal under all that suppressed emotion. Hard and angry, desperate and needy. A man could drown in those eyes. Dean kissed him hard on the mouth, not releasing his gaze, and thrust into him. Andrei cried out and clung to him with thighs and hands, fingers digging into Dean's flesh. With each slow withdrawal and quick snap of his hips back inside Andrei, a little more of that reserve crumbled until there was nothing in Andrei's eyes but need and love.

"I'm not letting go of you." Dean slid his arms under Andrei's shoulders, holding him closer as he gave in to the pounding of the storm in his veins and Andrei's cries for more. All too soon the hot rush was over as Dean came into that tight heat, Andrei clenching harder around him with his own orgasm.

Andrei stiffened and then went limp, his muscles trembling, his breath panting as he stared up at Dean. Andrei parted his lips as if to speak, then touched his fingers to Dean's cheek instead. He hugged Dean hard, and all Dean could do was hope that it had been enough to break through whatever clearly haunted Andrei. They had no time for more.

Chapter Nineteen

ANDREI'S body ached as he crossed the parking lot to his car. Between sleeping in the shower stall and Dean's antics, he would be feeling that soreness for a while. It made him feel a little more human and a little less dead inside. No doubt what Dean had been aiming for. Sneaky bastard. Now Andrei would have to refocus on what he had to do.

"When we get there, I need complete silence," Andrei said, casting Dean a sideways glance. The soft vinyl top to the Jeep had a good sized rip in it, and the seats were soaked but otherwise unharmed. Andrei tossed the knapsack in the back. "So until we find Blake, I'm not going to be able to talk. He can't hear you, at least I hope he can't."

"I understand." Dean caught his hand before he could slip into the car. "In and out, right? This eye isn't going to last very long, and I'd like some distance between you and him before the storm strikes again."

Andrei glanced up at the intense blue of the sky over them, the sun shining down and the wall of clouds that surrounded the island in an almost perfect wide circle. The sight chilled him. "Yeah, I don't plan on making a party out of it."

He held his breath and released it in a rush when the Jeep immediately started. He didn't see any other signs of life or people stirring as he followed Dean's directions toward the house. The road was covered in sand, and he could see that at least to the north it was completely submerged under water. Nobody would be getting off over the north bridge anytime soon. "Do you see those Jackals of yours?" he asked Dean in an undertone.

Andrei hated an unknown, especially when that unknown had a definite interest in Dean. His partner frowned, staring intently all around them, and then he shook his head. "No, and I don't sense them, either."

Andrei wished he knew if that was a good or bad sign. He pulled over behind one of the houses next to his targeted one and killed the engine. His mind raced, still searching for a way to separate himself from Dean, to give himself that little bit of time that he needed to take care of Blake. He got out of the car and shut the door softly, though he doubted anyone could hear it over the pounding of the surf. He didn't see any sign of Blake's car, but a detached garage with boarded up windows sat closer to the road.

He couldn't look at Dean while he planned the death of another person, deserved or not. "Okay, first, if you could unlock the doors for me, Dean, that would be a big help." Andrei touched the gun at the small of his back to make sure that it was secure.

"Already did it." Both Dean and he jumped at the sound of the cheery voice next to them.

"For chrissake, Poppet," Dean ground out. "Did you have to sneak up on us? Today of all days?"

"Sorry." Ileana didn't look at all sorry; her eyes sparkled as she danced and spun around the puddles.

"Ileana Therese Cuza, I told you to stay behind," Andrei said in a hard, low voice as he leaned toward her.

Her eyes widened and she took a step back. "But I wanted to help too! I did good, the bad man didn't notice anything wrong at all. The kiddies are upstairs napping. They look super tired, and the bad man's in a big, dark room watching a movie. That's on the middle floor. It's a super big house."

Andrei's eyes narrowed. Blake must've gotten his hands on a couple of generators. Better and better. He'd be distracted and off his guard. A hot spike of vicious anticipation gripped him at the thought of killing Blake. Dean started and looked around with a worried frown. "What is it?" Andrei asked.

"I thought I heard...." Dean trailed off, casting a significant glance in Ileana's direction. "But I think I'm just jumpy. It was very faint."

The Jackals. Andrei looked around too, but didn't see anything out of the ordinary. Not like the mist that had been there the night Dean had gone on the run after Blake had broken into their house. But if there was even a chance that they were around, he wasn't going to leave Ileana unattended, especially with the way that she did whatever she wanted.

"Okay, here's what we're going to do, and so help me God, Ileana, you had better listen this time, or I'll have Dean hold onto Cougar in time out until you're good and sorry." That was the only threat he could think of that might make her listen.

Ileana nodded and clutched her turtle to her. "I will, I promise."

"Good, you show Dean the room where Inez and Tristan are. Dean, you said that Inez can see you?" Dean gave him a hard look and nodded tightly. "Okay, see if you can keep her from freaking out. I'm sure she's on edge with the storm and everything. If she sees me first, she's liable to start screaming. We have an opportunity here to make sure they have what they need. Tristan especially is going to need formula and diapers. So if you can help her get those together that will save us some time." Andrei glanced toward the eyewall, trying to gauge what time they did have.

"What are you going to do?" Dean asked in a tense voice. "Look at me, Andrei."

Andrei met his eyes, feeling a calm inside of him that hadn't been there since he had been told that Dean had been murdered. He was ready to confront Blake and do what he had to do. He was past regrets and second-guessing himself. "I'm going to make sure that Blake's in no position to follow us, and then once we're safe with the kids, I'll see if I can get through to the National Guard, and they can go and retrieve him."

Dean searched his face, and Andrei forced a smile. "Thank you for earlier and keeping my head straight."

Dean relaxed and smiled back at him. "Okay, let's go. Poppet, which is the better door?"

"The back one. We'll have to start at the very bottom, but he won't hear that door open. The door on the second floor is right next to the movie room."

Ileana skipped off, holding Cougar by his tail, and they followed. Andrei eased the bottom door open and listened. It was quiet, which meant that the movie room was probably at least partially sound proof. Better and better. He motioned for Ileana and Dean to go on through and then quietly shut the door behind them.

His heart pounded with a steady purpose as he made his way up to the second level. Some of the stairs squeaked ever so faintly and each time he paused, but heard nothing else coming from other parts of the house. Ileana looked as if she were enjoying the whole process. She kept flitting up to the top before racing back down again, until Dean caught her and held her hand.

When they reached the landing, Ileana pointed down the hallway toward the movie room. Andrei steeled himself, his focus narrowing on Blake and putting an end to this madness. Dean's fingers brushed the back of his neck, and Andrei froze, his heart catching. "You keep saying that I have this image of you that doesn't exist, and that's a damned lie. Remember that."

A hot, aching knot ballooned in Andrei's chest, and his eyes stung. He nodded and moved down the hallway without a backward look. He couldn't lose his resolve, not now. As he neared the room, he could hear the sounds of the movie coming from the French doors. A thick curtain hanging on the other side kept him from seeing in, but also shielded him from Blake's eyes.

At the door, he glanced back toward the stairs. Dean and Ileana had already gone up the next flight to prepare Inez and Tristan. Andrei put them out of his mind and pulled his gun from the holster at his back. The French door made no sound as it opened, but the heavy curtain stirred. The sounds of the movie exploded forth, and Andrei tensed.

He risked a quick peek through the tiny slit where the two halves of the curtain met. The room had two levels, and Blake sat on a couch on the first level, his gaze riveted to the huge screen playing out before him. Fury grabbed ahold of Andrei's gut. If either one of his children started to cry, the bastard would never know. They could sneak right on out of there and leave him hanging. That would be the wise, sane thing to do.

Maybe it was the intensity of Andrei's stare that alerted him, because Blake leapt up and spun around to face the doors. "Who the fuck is there?" he snarled, with an edge of raw panic in his voice.

Andrei swept aside the curtain and came into the room with his gun aimed at Blake. The man cursed and threw his bottle of soda at Andrei, who leaned out of the way as it flew past his head. Adrenaline and a cold rage pumped in his veins as Blake leapt over the back of the couch and ducked down. Andrei refrained from shooting; this was not how he wanted it to go, with Blake running. No, the man would feel the full enormity of the moment, just as Dean had when he'd been shot.

A hungry, chilling howl rose, and the sound made the both of them freeze. Andrei recovered first and took full advantage, darting around the couch as Blake scrambled around the other end, making for the coffee table where Andrei spied another gun. He dove over the side, landing hard on Blake and catching a vicious elbow to the gut.

"Fuck you, fuck you," Blake panted, trying to squirm free, and a savage, hateful glee filled Andrei.

"'Bout ready to piss yourself, aren't you?" Andrei laughed shortly as he pressed the muzzle of the gun to Blake's temple. The other man froze, trembling, and Andrei carefully stood up, keeping the gun trained on Blake as he leaned over and punched the button to shut off the movie.

"I've got money, not a lot but—"

Andrei grabbed the back of Blake's shirt and jerked him up to his knees, the sudden intensity of his rage almost choking him. "There isn't any amount of money in this world that's going to bring him back to me."

"Please, please don't… my kids."

"If you cared so much about Inez and Tristan, why did you kill their mother in front of them?" Trembling, Andrei straightened and pressed the gun to the back of Blake's shorn head. The sound of the man's panting, whimpering gasps filled the room. "Their grandmother will take very good care of them."

Robin appeared, blood covering the front of her shirt, her expression determined as she stared at her ex with hard eyes. Blake jolted with a sharp gasp. "Get her away from me. Thieving bitch. You left. You shouldn't have left." Andrei pressed the muzzle harder against his head, and Blake whimpered. "I swear I didn't know… I didn't know who he was."

"You didn't fucking care," Andrei snarled, as that hot, heavy feeling of helplessness pressed against his throat and eyes again. "He was trying to help. That's all. And you killed him like he was nothing! You murdered him in cold blood."

Andrei drew in a deep, shuddering breath, and for a moment he could almost sense Dean with him, looking at him with love in his eyes and asking him how what he was doing was any different. He blinked back the hot stinging in his eyes. This was different. Blake deserved death, Dean hadn't.

The curtains stirred again as a cold mist poured through. It slithered along the floor, wrapped around the furniture, and Andrei could hear the howling again, only this time it was almost a crooning song that beckoned instead of repelled. So Dean's Jackals were here, no doubt ready to pounce on Blake the moment he died to tear his soul to shreds. Andrei liked the thought of there being no peace, no appeasement for Blake even as it made him feel faintly sick inside. He remembered all too well the expression in Dean's eyes as he spoke of what had happened to Old Mother.

Andrei's finger tightened on the trigger, and the image of how Dean had looked earlier, the love and concern on his face as he tried to get Andrei to open up, came to him. Andrei froze. *No, no, no.* For once in his life he had to be strong, dammit, for Dean. His hand trembled and he cursed under his breath. "Do it," Robin breathed, and Andrei let out a choked sob.

This was the bastard who had destroyed their lives. Who had taken Inez and Tristan's mother away from them. Once again he tried to squeeze and couldn't. He was such a fucking failure. Blake sensed his moment of weakness and lurched forward, reaching for his gun. With a snarl, Andrei struck him on the back of his head with the butt of his gun, and Blake collapsed in an unconscious heap.

Andrei sank down onto the couch and buried his head in his hands as the full import of his failure swept over him. He couldn't. Not even for Dean. The mist crept closer, oozing around him and Blake as Andrei raged inside.

DEAN frowned as he watched Andrei walk away. He didn't like leaving him alone to confront Blake, and he had to keep reminding himself that Andrei was the professional and to have faith in his heart. Besides, he still didn't trust himself to be in the same room with Blake. Now would be a very bad time to go all murderous. It would only provoke Andrei more, and the Jackals were just waiting for a mistake like that.

He followed Ileana up the stairs, taking them two at a time. The storm was moving steadily along, and each moment they spent here meant they had less time putting distance between themselves and Blake and finding shelter before the hurricane struck again.

Ileana opened a bedroom door and pointed. "See, look. Did I do good, Dean?"

Dean peered into what looked like the master suite, and sure enough there Inez lay, curled up in a limp ball in the middle of the king-sized bed. He didn't see Tristan until he stepped inside and found him sound asleep in his car seat on the floor. Poor baby. Dean imagined that he probably didn't get out of there very often.

"You did very good, Poppet," Dean said in a hushed voice. "Now let's find their things, the baby bag, extra clothes, and snacks. We'll let them sleep a little longer, no sense alerting Blake if one of them starts to cry."

"Okies," Ileana whispered.

As Dean set the baby bag on the dresser, Inez stirred. He turned around as she sat up, fuzzy curls springing up in every direction. Her jeans were torn at the knee, and her shirt stained with what looked like barbeque sauce. She rubbed her shadowed eyes and then blinked up at him. "Mr. Dean? Did your boo-boo get better?"

"Hey sweetheart." Dean knelt by the bed, careful not to touch her. "I'm fine. Don't be scared, okay? My partner is here, and he's going to be coming up to take you to your grandmother and Aunt Wanda, would you like that?"

"Wha' 'bout, Tris?" Inez crawled over to the side of the bed and peered over. "Can't leave baby brudder."

"No worries, we'll definitely bring your brother too." Dean reached into his pocket and pulled out the little bit of ribbon, now a little mangled and frayed. "I saved this for you."

"Thank you." Inez took the ribbon and held it tight in her fist. "Where's Mommy? I saw her too. Is she gonna come say bye-bye?"

"I hope so, Inez, but I can't make any promises. She'll be happy to know that you're with your grandmother, though."

Ileana bounded onto the bed and waved at Inez. "Hi! Wanna hold Cougar?" She thrust the stuffed turtle at Inez, and Dean watched closely to make sure that Ileana didn't touch her. "I'm Ileana. Dean's my brother's husband, which kinda makes him my brother too. Isn't that cool?"

Inez reached out hesitantly for the turtle and hugged it to her. Reassured that she wouldn't freak out, Dean straightened to go back to the baby bag when he heard the yipping howls start up. Ileana jumped back and Inez began to cry. "The doggies are back," she wailed. "I no like them."

Dean let out an explosive breath. "Ileana, I thought you said that regular people couldn't see the Jackals or be hurt by them."

Ileana's fingers dug into the blankets as she stared at Dean with wide, frightened eyes. "Make 'em go away, Dean. Are you mad? You don't look mad."

Dean couldn't shake the bad feeling that gripped him, and he drifted toward the door. "I'm not mad, Poppet." But there was at least one angry man here—two if Blake had turned rabid again. The day that Dean had died, Blake had been running pretty cold when he shot him; maybe he wasn't the angry one.

Andrei was a complicated man. He felt so deeply but contained most of it inside, and sometimes his passionate nature exploded forth. What would Andrei be capable of when he finally confronted the man who'd torn apart both of their worlds? Dean closed his eyes as terror for Andrei gripped him.

"Ileana, have you ever heard of them feeding off a human at all?"

"Well… maybe, once. But it's just a story."

"Dammit, Ileana, just tell me what you think you know," Dean snapped, dragging a hand through his hair. Andrei wasn't an ordinary human. He saw and talked to ghosts. He was physically connected to two who were stuck in limbo—three if you counted Robin. What if that was all the extra connection the Jackals needed to feel his rage to taste and track it?

Ileana hugged her knees. "It's said that they want to, 'cause a human's soul is more po… um, pot—"

"Potent?"

"Yeah, that's it, whatever that means. But more than a spirit's soul that's already half moved on. But they can't, Dean. They want to, but they don't sense people like they sense ghosts, or they'd be feeding all the time."

How much more potent would the soul of a good man be? The soul of a man who gave in to a moment of weakness? What if the Jackals could push him into that moment? Andrei was connected to the spirit world. If there ever was a human that they could sense, Andrei was that person.

"You stay here, both of you," Dean barked and bolted out of the room. He found Andrei on the couch in the movie room, his shoulders shaking with his violent sobs, and Blake sprawled out on the floor in an ungainly heap.

"Oh God, Andrei." Dean fell to his knees in front of him, his mind spinning, his heart aching. "Andrei, no."

Andrei's head jerked up, and Dean's heart broke at the mask of agony on his face. "I couldn't do it, *iubito*. I'm so sorry. I had my chance and I couldn't do it."

Dean went weak with relief and cupped Andrei's face in his shaking hands. "Babe, you don't know how happy I am that you didn't. You aren't like him, and killing him would've destroyed some of that light inside of you. I couldn't stand to see that happen."

Andrei clutched at his biceps, holding on as the storm that had been raging inside of him finally found release as he cried. Dean wished he could give him more time and get it all the way out, but the thought of staying in this house with Blake and the kids with the storm outside and the Jackals waiting gave him the heebie-jeebies. Even now, he was careful not to look at Blake's unconscious body.

Before Dean could gently shake Andrei, he straightened and dashed the tears off his cheeks. "We should be going," he said in a hoarse voice.

Blake stirred with a groan, and that sound was enough to make the anger inside Dean twitch hotly. He ignored him and concentrated on Andrei's face instead, which hardened as he glared at Blake. "Don't even think of moving, or I'll give you another knot on your head," Andrei growled.

"Andrei, we have to hurry. We're almost out of time." Dean stood up and held out his hand to him as Andrei pulled out his handcuffs. There wasn't a sound this time, not a flicker of warning when two Jackals appeared right next to them. "Holy shit!" Dean jumped back, dragging Andrei with him and away from Blake.

"What the hell?" Then Andrei froze, looking around him with careful eyes. "Are they back? I saw the mist earlier when I had my gun to… oh fuck, I think I hear them."

The Jackals stared at Andrei with a dreadful intensity, their slavering expressions so hungry that at first Dean couldn't even speak, only nod numbly. The Jackals acted as if they couldn't even see him, but they didn't immediately pounce on Andrei either. He wished that were a comfort.

The Jackals took another step forward, paws scraping along the hardwood floors, dragging up curls of wood. Andrei tightened his hand on Dean's arm, pulling him back another step, angling him toward the door. Blake lifted his head and stared at them with rabid, naked hate in his eyes. "Go upstairs and get out of here with Ileana. I'll get the kids and be right behind you."

Dean shook his head, unable to tear his eyes away from the Jackals. "They're not after me anymore, babe. I think they want you. Besides, you can't see them and I can."

"Touch my kids and I'll slit your throats," Blake snarled. "I'll find a way to kill you again and again."

The tongues lashed out, waving snake-like in the air, one stretching out toward them as if tasting the air, and Dean jerked Andrei back out of reach. They were being herded into a corner. Another one of the tongues wrapped around Blake's legs and yanked him toward the nest of their bodies.

Andrei shouted and surged forward, reaching to snatch Blake back just as one of the Jackals turned to mist and poured itself into Blake's body through his nose, mouth, and ears. "Jesus Christ," Dean shouted and grabbed Andrei again. "Don't."

Blake convulsed and then leapt up, his actions not at all hampered by injury. He was fluid, almost boneless, and when he turned to look at them, Dean shuddered at the burning insanity and hungry look in his eyes. "Oh God."

Andrei dove for him, aiming a kick at Blake's knee that Blake blocked easily. He swung Andrei, using his own momentum against him, to send him careening into the wall. The remaining Jackal circled around the combatants. *Oh God, please don't lose your temper, Andrei*, Dean thought as he took a step forward, hands outstretched. Maybe he could zap Blake. His fear for Andrei outweighed any fury he had toward his killer. He should be able to do that safely.

Andrei and Blake exchanged a flurry of blows, his partner grunting with each impact, and Blake hardly seeming fazed at all. When Andrei went stumbling back again, he drew his gun and pointed it right at Blake's head. Blake paused, a chilling smile crossing his face. "Do it."

"Don't," Dean whispered. "It's what they want." Andrei hesitated, his gun slightly lowering though his gaze remained on Blake. "I'm not asking for him, babe. I'm asking for you."

"Mr. Dean?"

Blake whirled around and snatched up Inez before anyone could stop him. She let out a frightened wail as he pinned her to him, his hand clasped around her vulnerable neck. "What are you going to do?" he spat at Andrei. "I could rip out her throat before you get to me."

To Dean's surprise and relief, Andrei didn't go off; instead he remained steady, gun trained on Blake, his voice calm as he answered. "Blake, that's your little girl, think about that. That's your child who you went to so much trouble to get and keep safe from me and everybody else searching for her."

"Sounds like she'd rather be with your partner, like my bitch of an ex-wife."

Inez stared at him, tears streaming from her eyes, and Dean concentrated on that little face, his heart breaking for her as he closed in on Blake. Robin appeared next to him, her expression furious, and he grabbed her arm as she started for Blake as well. The remaining Jackal's head snapped impossibly around on its neck to stare at her with sudden interest.

"Don't think of him," Dean said in a low voice to Robin. "Think of Inez and how much you love her. You don't want Inez to see you torn apart." Robin paused, doubt creeping into her eyes. "We'll both grab him at the same time, and Andrei can get your daughter."

Robin cast him an agonized look and then nodded. They moved together as Blake laughed at Andrei and shook Inez hard. "Fucking bitch, couldn't save your partner, you can't save her either. Shoot me or she's dead."

"If you kill her, what's next? Tristan? Your son?" Blake paused, some of the insane desperation melting away from his face. "If you kill him too, then what do you have left?"

Dean concentrated hard on Blake and on Blake being able to see him as he and Robin manifested right in front of the other man. Blake let out a shout, and for a moment those yellow-green points of blazing madness disappeared from his eyes. "No, wait, I'm sorry."

Both he and Robin struck, latching onto his arms, and Blake shrieked, his head falling back as he squeezed harder on Inez. She wailed again and Robin screamed in rage, striking out at Blake's face with her nails as the Jackal began to howl. Blake threw Inez at Andrei and bolted. The Jackal turned toward Robin. She let out a shriek of terror and disappeared. Dean's heart ached for her as the monster loped after her.

He spun around to find Andrei holding Inez, rocking her gently and making soothing murmurs under his breath. "Make sure he's not going after Tristan," Andrei said. "I'll be right behind you. And be careful!"

Chapter Twenty

"I'VE got you, Inez." Andrei soothed the trembling and sobbing little girl as he cast a quick glance around the shambles of the room. Blake had managed to get ahold of the gun in that chaos, and the thought of playing hide and go seek in this big house during a storm with a madman had him jogging for the stairs.

He'd seen both Dean and Robin latch onto Blake. The man should've gone down like he'd been hit with an elephant tranquilizer, but if their touch had affected him at all, it sure as hell hadn't shown.

"The doggie got my daddy," Inez sobbed, clinging to him. "And Mommy's mad. The doggies are gonna get her too."

"Dean and I will figure out something, okay?" At the top of the stairs, Andrei followed the sound of a baby wailing to the bedroom where Tristan sat in a car seat. Ileana stood in front of the baby carrier, facing the door and waving a hanger around as if she were ready to beat someone with it, and Dean was shouldering the baby bag and picking up a small suitcase.

"We'd better get going," Dean warned. "That storm is picking up speed again."

Andrei nodded and shifted Inez's weight to his hip so he could grab Tristan's carrier. He hated how vulnerable he felt with both of his hands full, but there was no hope for it. "The best thing we can do is dash for the Jeep and hope like hell that Blake's at least momentarily disorientated with your attack."

"The Jackals are divided, too, so that might give both us and Robin an edge," Dean muttered back. "I'll go ahead of you and shout if I see him."

Andrei waited a few seconds after Dean bolted and followed after him. There was no way to be quick and quiet, so he settled for speed as they clattered down the stairs. Inez clung to his shoulders, her face pressed against his neck, her breath coming in fast whimpers. Tristan seemed to be making up for her quietness by yelling even louder and waving his fists in the air.

"I heard something upstairs," Ileana said as they reached the back downstairs door they had come in through. "I think the bad man is behind us."

Andrei's arms ached as he bolted across the puddle-strewn driveway toward the parked Jeep. A door behind them banged open, and a shot rang out, making both Inez and Ileana scream. *Faster, faster, faster*, Andrei chanted in his head and almost tripped over a fallen piece of debris in the road.

Dean had the doors to the Jeep wide open, and Andrei set Inez on the seat, tossing the knapsack there onto the floor. "Can you put your seatbelt on by yourself?" he asked as he set Tristan down. Dean could keep him steady until they got out of immediate danger.

"I can try." Inez knelt up and pulled down the strap.

"Here, I'll help." Ileana frowned hard at the strap, and it snatched out of Inez's hands to buckle itself. Inez's lips formed an *O* of surprise before she grinned.

"Good idea, Ileana." Dean glanced at the baby seat that rose into the air and moments later was strapped down next to Inez and stabilized. Dean snatched Ileana up and shut the doors as the sound of Blake's shouts came closer. "Go, go, go. Coming down off the porch delayed him, but not by much."

Andrei slid behind the wheel, his heart racing, and gunned it. Through the rearview he saw Blake come around the corner, moving with that same unnatural, fluid grace that he'd displayed earlier. Andrei flinched as a bullet struck the Jeep, followed immediately by another one. He cursed under his breath as he turned south on the road.

"What the hell are you doing?" Dean pointed toward the horizon that seemed hazy in the distance. "You need to go the other way. That eyewall is heading straight toward us if we go there."

"Part of that road is washed out," Andrei said with a calm he didn't feel. His nerves felt stretched taut and raw as if they'd been flayed open with a knife. "And the next town is at least twenty minutes out. I don't know if we have twenty minutes." He didn't know what he would do if the road going south was as bad.

An angry, inhuman howl came from the house behind them, and Andrei swore as he almost swerved off the road. "What the hell was that?"

"You heard that too?" Dean turned around to stare out the back window. "It sounds like the Jackal Wraiths are calling to each other."

Andrei's hands tightened on the wheel. "I can only hear the one behind us, and that's more than enough, thank you." The sound chilled him with its insatiable hunger, and he remembered the horror in Dean's voice when he'd talked about how those howls had tormented him when he'd been on the run. Andrei understood why a little bit more now and wished he didn't.

"I just had a bad thought."

"Please, Dean, keep it to yourself. We have enough insanity to deal with." The howls abruptly ceased, and that didn't ease Andrei's mind at all. Then the need to mentally prepare for any circumstance outweighed his desire to not hear Dean's worry. In the backseat, Tristan began screaming even louder. "Okay, spit it out."

"If one Jackal Wraith merging with Blake changed him that much, then what will happen if the other one does too?" Dean said, and a chill raced through Andrei. Surely this whole situation couldn't get any worse.

"I knew I didn't want to hear it."

"I hate this." Dean turned around in his seat to peer out the back window. "I don't see him yet. Ileana, see if you can get Tristan to calm down. It's impossible to think with that poor boy wailing."

Andrei listened to Ileana and Inez discuss the merits of peek-a-boo versus singing a song and glanced in the rearview mirror. The road behind them remained empty, but it twisted and turned so much that it was hard to tell if Blake followed them or not. "Got anything?" he asked Dean.

"He's still back there. I can sense him, and he's coming fast. Too fast to pull over and look for a bolt hole. I don't like this, Andrei."

"I'm not a fucking fan either," Andrei muttered under his breath as he swerved around another bit of the road that had washed out and skidded on the sand covering the other half. At this rate he was going to wind up with a flat tire from all the debris on the road. He wrenched the wheel around as Ileana made a sound from the back like they were on a roller coaster. Well at least it kept Inez from freaking out, and the baby had quieted.

They sped through the town, seeing one or two people outside assessing damage before the storm struck again, but for the most part it was almost as if no one lived there at all. Just before they hit the end of the town, he caught a quick glimpse of a car behind them.

"Tell me that's not him."

"I wish I could, babe," Dean said in a voice thick with tension.

Andrei cursed and put on as much speed as he dared with the roads the way they were. He tried to calculate how long it would take till the next town and if he dared trying to go for it. He couldn't remember if there was a long stretch of highway between here and the next. In the distance he could see flashes of light on the horizon, and the thought of being out in the open in this tiny vehicle with the kids when the eyewall hit again terrified him.

"There, turn there!" Dean barked, pointing to a side road, and Andrei took the turn hard, slewing the Jeep around.

Ahead he thought he saw the flicker of a woman standing in the road, but then she was gone.

"Why down here?" Andrei ground out, hitting the gas and trying to get out of view before Blake came around the corner. He'd probably expect them to stay on the highway to hightail it to the next town. The sea raged on their left and thundered ashore far too close for Andrei's comfort.

"That's where Robin told us to go. I heard her in my head."

Andrei snapped a quick glance at him before turning his attention back to the road. "Are you insane?" Every foot down the road brought the eyewall nearer, and he could see it tearing up the surf. There would probably be more tornadoes if the second half of the storm was as violent as the first. "The only things down here are the lighthouse and the visitor's center."

"And maybe somebody from the National Park Service who can give you a hand. All we need is to find shelter while leaving him out here. Possessed or not, his body is human, he's not going to be able to survive being outside," Dean said in a harsh undertone.

Andrei had to admit that Dean had a point. He tore into the deserted parking lot and braked as fast as he dared without slamming the kids against their restraints. He leapt out of the Jeep, his heart racing faster as he glanced toward the murderous skies advancing on them. The inky clouds roiled, stabbed by long, jagged arcs of lightning. A long finger snaked down out of the clouds, touched the ocean, and brought up a hissing, spinning stream of water.

"Holy Mary, mother of God," he muttered under his breath. If they survived this, it would be a freaking miracle.

He pulled out Tristan's car seat, the arm where he'd been shot spasming as he took up the weight. Ileana had the foresight to cover the carrier with a blanket; perhaps that would give the baby a little protection if the wind and the rain started before they reached shelter.

Inez jumped into the curving shelter of his arm and clung to him tightly, pressing her face against his shoulder. "I wanna go home."

Andrei wished he had a moment to comfort her, the time to think of the words that might ease her fears.

"Soon, Inez, I promise."

A car raced down the street toward them, struck a piece of debris, and careened off the pavement as its tire blew before it flipped onto its roof. Andrei didn't wait to see if Blake survived. He started running, making straight for the lighthouse as a reference point. The visitor's center had to be near that. He'd have to have Dean open a way in and then find a central place to hide. The sound of the eyewall approaching became a deafening roar; tree branches bowed and whipped about as debris stirred on the ground.

He tried to force his tired legs to move faster and not stumble over the uneven ground. Andrei didn't dare look behind him. If he did, he'd fall. He'd drop Inez or the baby. His arm screamed now, the dead weight of the carrier pulling on the half-healed wound.

DEAN paused and looked back at the wreckage in the hope that Blake might have broken his neck in that crash. He took a couple steps closer and crouched to see inside, but Ileana grabbed his hand and yanked. "Come on, Dean!"

Blake slithered out the half-crushed window, his body elongating and twisting out of shape. His hands curled into the ground with a clawlike motion, and his eyes met Dean's. Dean saw the Jackal Wraiths in Blake's gaze, sensed their recognition and hunger. The creatures appeared to be writhing under Blake's skin. Dean stumbled back, and he gave Ileana a shove away. "Go, Poppet!"

Blake focused his attention on Andrei, who ran ahead with the kids. He leapt forward onto all fours in one fluid movement and loped toward them with a snarl.

"Oh fuck... faster, Andrei!" Dean bolted, searching for shelter. The visitor's center wouldn't keep Blake out for one moment, so he ran for the lighthouse, passing Andrei. He glanced over his shoulder to check on Andrei's progress, willing him to run faster. Blake howled into the keening wind, and Andrei nearly tripped, weighed down by the children in his arms. Blake leaped forward again, narrowing the space between them to only a few feet. Inez clung to Andrei and screamed, the sound cutting across her brother's cries.

Fuck! Dean focused on making it to the lighthouse. Andrei wouldn't be able to run much longer. He ran right through the heavy door and wasted precious moments in trying to figure out how to unlock it. When the door swung open, he took a step outside, trying to think of something he could do to distract Blake.

The baby carrier banged against Andrei's leg, making him stumble again, and Inez cried out. Blake laughed, a high-pitched hooting sound. Dean's throat tightened with fear. The Jackal Wraiths were inside Blake. They could hurt Andrei in ways far worse than just physically tearing him apart. Blake snarled, snapping his jaws as he closed in.

"Hurry, Andrei," Dean shouted and ran toward them. "Move, dammit, move."

Andrei recovered his stride, his long legs eating up the ground, and Blake howled in fury as Dean moved between him and Andrei. "Hungry. My soul. My kids."

Dean shuddered as he remembered the hunt, the Jackals Wraiths' gnawing, empty sensation they projected onto him that never ended. He followed Andrei, who sprinted up the stairs and dashed through the door.

Andrei fell to his knees inside, holding Tristan's carrier up as he cradled Inez. "Shut the door," he gasped through harsh pants for air.

"I'm trying," Dean ground out, shoving against the door as the wind shoved back. Blake howled, and Dean heard his triumph in that sound.

"Blake!"

Dean's head jerked around, and Blake skidded to a stop as Robin appeared. She stood several yards away near the pounding surf. A pale cream sundress whipped around her legs, and her dark hair streamed in the wind. She looked beautiful, her features no longer twisted with the terror of her last moments, and the image seemed to captivate Blake.

"Come on, Blake. I'm the one you really want."

The door scraped against the concrete, and Blake turned back toward them, indecision in his mad eyes. They were closer. Dean narrowed his eyes and fought harder. The door moved another couple inches. Blake's jaws opened impossibly wide, and his tongue snaked out. His head swung, looking first at Andrei, then Robin, his body coiled and tense, torn between one prey and another. Blake slithered up one step, and Andrei jumped to his feet.

"Get away from them, you bastard," Robin shouted and ran toward him. Blake snarled and turned toward her as Andrei reached the door, slamming into it with his shoulder and adding his weight. The door closed with a hollow boom, and Dean locked it as Blake howled in rage and threw himself at the barrier.

Andrei leaned against the door, still trying to catch his breath. The loud noise from the bang of the door still echoed up through the shell of the lighthouse. Another hard thud hit the door, and Dean's chest seized with ice. He'd never forget the sight of that creature on the other side. What Blake had become… a grotesque mix of human and Jackal. His body and jaw elongated, his brow a heavy ridge of bone, and his eyes burning.

The whole lighthouse shuddered as the eyewall hit. The kids had fallen silent, tense and waiting, as the winds shrieked. Did the storm drive off Blake? Then a heavy body thudded hard against the door again, and they all jumped. The sound of claws against the metal made Dean wince and pray that the door would hold. Again and again Blake rammed himself against the barrier, and Dean felt the shiver through the frame.

"We need higher ground." Dean gestured toward the stairs. "In case the water comes in."

Or something else. Dean didn't want to say that out loud and scare the kids, though he was sure that Andrei thought the same. And if

Blake succeeded in beating the door down, Dean wanted to have the advantage of having at least a little time to prepare before Blake could pounce. A few flights of stairs and a nice landing might give him the edge he needed.

"'Kay." Andrei picked up Tristan's baby carrier as Dean eyed the bags he'd brought with a fierce look of concentration. After a moment, they slowly rose, taking much more energy than it normally would as the storm renewed its fury.

Andrei held out his hand to Inez, who had silent tears running down her face. "I know you're scared, Inez. Can you be brave for just a little bit longer for me?"

She nodded and clung to his hand as they moved up the steps. Ileana came running down, her eyes wide. "I found a good spot, Andrei. If you go up too high the lighthouse sways! And I looked out the big window at the top, but I couldn't see nothing!"

"I bet."

Andrei sounded so tired, and Dean wanted to reach out and take the burden of Tristan from him. Only he was having a hard enough time himself. The pounding behind them continued and then fell silent as they reached the first landing. That was almost creepier because now Dean had no idea what Blake was doing or where he'd gone off to.

Dean looked around the landing and nodded. It would do. The water wouldn't rise this far, and Andrei would hear anyone coming before they arrived. Andrei took Tristan out of his car seat and sighed. "He's soaked through. When was the last time that Blake had bothered to change him?" Andrei smiled at Inez. "Want to be my helper?"

She nodded and grabbed the baby bag from Dean. "Mommy says I a good helper."

Dean glanced over his shoulder back down the stairs. He wished he knew why Blake had stopped fighting the door, whether it was because he was searching for shelter himself or because he'd gotten injured.

He watched Andrei create a small pallet on the floor for the kids and change Tristan's diaper and clothes before settling down to soothe both Inez and Tristan on his lap. Dean eyed the little blanket that covered the hard stone floor and sighed. Andrei was in for even more miserable long hours than he had spent in the shower stall. Dean realized with a start that Andrei still wore the hospital ID bracelet. What a crazy couple of days it had been, and it wasn't over yet.

He'd never get the picture of Blake chasing Andrei out of his head. No matter how much effort Andrei had put into it, he'd been no match for Blake loping on all fours, his gait fluid as he got closer to Andrei with each bound. He had seemed to shift inside his skin, becoming more animal-like, and Dean had been so helpless. If zapping Blake hadn't worked, what else could he do to keep him away from Andrei and the kids?

He could only hope that the feet-thick bricks and the heavy door would keep both Blake and the storm out. But he placed no certainty on that, not with what Blake had turned into. What else was he capable of with the Jackals inhabiting his skin? And Dean had no doubt that both of the Jackals were possessing Blake now. The change in him was too profound.

Dread pooled in his stomach, and he saw the same dread on Andrei's face. The waiting to see what would happen next. He tried to hide it by talking with the kids and getting them calmed down, but it was there in the tension in Andrei's shoulders, the slight strain in his voice.

Dean caught Andrei's eye. "I'm going to go scout outside, see if I can figure out where he's disappeared to."

Andrei nodded and shifted on the blanket. "I know I've been saying this a lot, but be careful."

"I want to go too." Ileana came to Dean with a pleading look in her eyes. "Pretty please?"

Dean knelt down in front of her and laid his hands on her shoulders. "Actually, I have another job for you. Do you think you and Cougar can handle watching the stairs for me? If anything comes through that door, whether it's water or the bad man, it's your job to tell Andrei. It'll give him a chance to get a little rest." It would give Andrei a chance to get his weapon out and get the kids behind him.

Ileana looked back at her brother and worried her lip. Even she could see the exhaustion and lines of strain in his face. She nodded and hugged her turtle. "I can do that. I can do a good job."

"I know you can, Poppet." Dean cupped her cheek and gave her a smile before stealing a quick kiss from Andrei. He hated leaving them, but didn't see that he had any other choice.

Outside the storm raged even fiercer than when he'd been out in it the first time. It was impossible to see anything more than a few inches away, and the implacable energy of the storm kept threatening to pull him back in and tumble him about.

He stumbled down the steps of the lighthouse and thought he saw a shadowy figure in a flash of lightning. Stinging rain lashed at his face, the wind yanked on his legs, and Dean longed to make himself incorporeal to have a little protection from the elements. But he figured out the last time that it would be the quickest way to get snatched up by the hurricane.

Dean made his way in the direction of the dancing shadow and clenched his fists as he came upon Blake and Robin. She remained unmoving, her expression implacable and unbending as Blake lunged and missed as he went right through her. How the hell could every other ghost out here do things that he couldn't?

Blake fell to his knees and howled. Dean heard the Jackals' bafflement and rage at his inability to touch her. Blake turned back toward the lighthouse, poised to hurl himself at the door again.

"You're never going to touch my babies again," Robin shouted over the wind. "My children, my son, my daughter, not yours."

Blake spun around with a snarl, and the wind drove him to the ground, where he writhed, struggling to get up and tearing at the grass with his hands. "Bitch, bitch, bitch." He lunged for Robin again, who fell back toward the pounding surf that had surged even closer than it had been when they arrived. Dean realized her plan and smiled grimly.

Robin stepped out onto the rocks, waves frothing through her insubstantial form as Blake raced toward her, his mouth open, tongue lashing. Robin was the lure, but it wasn't enough, not nearly enough to destroy both the man and the Jackals. The Jackals needed to be distracted enough to let go of their unnatural hold on Blake's body or else he might just survive this.

Dean closed his eyes and let the energy of the storm fill him. It crackled along his nerve endings and tore through his mind. So much energy that it bordered on both ecstasy and pain. He clung with all of his strength and will on the here and now, resisting being taken over completely. "Blake!" he shouted, his voice a part of the wind. The man turned to face him with a feral snarl, and Dean pounced, pouring himself into Blake's body the way the Jackals had.

They snarled and tried to tear into him the way they had torn into Old Mother, reaching for the darkest bits of his psyche that he hadn't been able to purge himself of. He was on his hands and knees again, bleeding. He and Andrei were lashing out at each other in mutual pain in their living room. All those moments of regret that made him want to weep. Dean sensed their essences closing in around him as the dark memories grabbed him.

Then Blake's scattered, wild thoughts broke free, and he screamed, falling to his knees as his body reverted. The Jackals paused, their attention torn between him and Blake, and Dean wrenched his thoughts back to the moment at hand.

"Come get me, Blake. Finish the job," Robin taunted on the wind, stepping farther out onto the waves. "It's my fault that you lost your kids again."

Dean shuddered back, trying to pull free from Blake's body, only to find himself trapped as well within the cage of the maniac's racing heartbeat and fragile bones. The Jackals pressed closer, howling inside him now, worming through his brain and drawing up every bad memory, every moment of anger and hate and terror, forcing it on him, making all those negative emotions bubble to the surface so they could use it to rip him to shreds.

He wouldn't let it end like that. Dean stopped fighting and let the energy of the storm sweep him up. He burst from Blake's body, and the Jackals raged to follow. Lumps moved under Blake's skin as the Jackals struggled, and Robin called to her husband again. "Blake."

"Die, dammit! Why won't you fucking die?" Blake sobbed as he waded out into the waves. "Shut up!"

A wave knocked him to his knees, and Blake struggled to stand up. Then Dean was a part of the lightning that arced down, striking Blake, a part of the winds that sent him hurtling onto the shore and breaking his body on the rocks, and he was a part of the tide that dragged Blake back into the cold, unfeeling waters where the bones of so many others who had died before waited. Robin's arms came around Blake, holding him close as his body jerked and shuddered. He heard Blake's mental scream when the Jackals turned their attention to back to him and ripped into his soul as he was dying.

Dean opened his eyes and found himself sprawled out on the shore, wet sand under his digging fingers as he panted for air. Robin appeared next to him, rain streaming down her face like tears as she studied the roiling waters. When the last spark of Blake faded so did the sense of the Jackals, though Dean was sure they weren't gone for good, just dissipated until they were summoned by another angry spirit.

Robin turned to him, and Dean felt her spirit brush against his for a moment in a silent good-bye and gesture of gratitude. Then light flared around her and she was gone too. Dean longed to follow, and he had to force his thoughts away before the portal opened. He wouldn't be able to say no this time, and Ileana wasn't with him. Dean turned his thoughts to Andrei until the longing shifted.

Exhausted, Dean let go and the hurricane grabbed hold of him. He began to tumble about, his mind going dark as he became completely disoriented. He was just so tired.

Chapter Twenty-One

THE quiet woke Andrei, stiff, sore, and cold from where he leaned and dozed against the stone wall of the lighthouse. His leg had gone numb from where Inez lay on it sound asleep, and Tristan was a solid weight against his chest. He stared around, stunned, unable to comprehend for a moment that the hurricane had ended. He wasn't sure when he'd fallen asleep—sometime after the long hours of getting the kids fed and soothed. Hours after he'd stared into the dark, waiting for Dean to come back or Blake to show his ugly face.

He tensed, half-expecting the man to pop up out of nowhere. It was unnaturally still after all the hours of upheaval and commotion. He patted Inez's head and then gently shifted her down to the small blanket with a spare little shirt to pillow her cheek. Inez sported new ribbons in her hair from when Andrei had attempted to fix the ragged remains left to her. "Dean? Ileana," he whispered.

Andrei set Tristan down in his carrier and gingerly stretched and straightened, shaking his leg until the blood came rushing back. Ileana appeared at the head of the stairs and ran to Andrei, hugging him tight. "I watched and watched and watched for you, but the bad man never came. It was kinda spooky."

Andrei hugged her back just as hard, his throat tightening. "Have you seen or heard from Dean?"

She shook her head, and Andrei had to keep from swearing as worry took hold. He had been gone even longer this time than the last time he'd disappeared into the storm. He had a new appreciation for how Dean had always felt when Andrei would go off after taking a new, dangerous case.

"He's okay, though," Ileana piped up. "At least I think he's okay. I can still sense him, but he seems a little loopy."

Andrei didn't know whether or not he believed her as much as he wanted to. He needed to get the kids out of there and to a real shelter. Just in case Blake lurked around somewhere. "We'll find him again, or he'll find us. Dean is good at that. Do you know if any water came in last night?" If this part of the island was flooded, he might as well not wake up the kids.

"Nope, nothing came in, and I watched real hard." Ileana gave him a proud smile and Andrei kissed her forehead.

"I know you did. Thank you, Illy. You did a good job."

A quick peek outside showed the utter devastation of downed trees, broken pavement, and the ground littered with debris. There was no sign of his Jeep or any of Blake's wreckage in the late morning's bright sunshine. He didn't want to be gone too long or go too far away in case Inez or Tristan woke up without him. So he just did a quick check around the lighthouse, searching for any clue that Blake might be lurking around or returning. Other than a few deep scratches on the door, there was no indication that Blake had ever been there at all. Andrei went back upstairs after making sure the door was bolted and checked his cell phone's signal. They were going to need help getting out of here.

After making a few calls, he reached over to gently shake Inez awake when a stir in the air caught his attention. "Dean?"

Robin appeared, light limning her body, her expression serene. She laid her hand on his cheek with a grateful smile. "Thank you," she whispered.

Andrei placed his hand over hers and shook his head. "Thanks aren't necessary. I'm taking them to their grandmother today."

She nodded and turned away to kneel between Inez and Tristan, her hands hovering over each one of them though she didn't touch them. She crooned a soft lullaby, and Tristan turned his little face toward her as Inez stirred. She opened her eyes and smiled sleepily at Robin. "Hi Mommy."

"I love you, baby girl. You keep telling Tristan that I love him too."

Inez sat up and rubbed her fist over her eye. Andrei picked her up and cuddled her on his lap. "I will, Mommy, I promise."

Robin pressed her hand to her lips and blew Inez a kiss, who pretended to catch it, and then she faded away with a last shimmer of light. Inez looked up at him, her face solemn. "Mommy not coming back?"

Andrei kissed the top of her head. "No, Inez, I don't think she will. She knows now that you'll be safe."

"Is she like my angel?"

"Yeah. Just like your guardian angel." He touched a finger to Inez's lips to distract her. "Listen. Hear how quiet it is? The storm's over, Inez."

She wiggled out of his lap and looked around. "Gonna see Granma now?"

"Yep, someone's on their way to pick us up. Would you like to talk to her?" Inez's eyes widened and she nodded her head eagerly, reaching for the phone and bouncing as Andrei brought up the number.

"Hello?" Evelyn sounded so tired that Andrei was grateful that he could lift at least one burden today.

"Evelyn, it's Andrei Cuza." Andrei grinned as Inez clapped her hands. "I have someone with me who really wishes to speak with you."

"You found my baby?" Incredulity flooded her voice, and Andrei didn't wait to answer, just handed the phone over to Inez, who began talking excitedly, her words tumbling over themselves in her eagerness to get them out.

It felt good to watch her little face, bright with animation. It would feel even better when he handed her over to Evelyn. He could live for moments like this.

Ileana took the opportunity to nestle in beside him. "How much longer before we can be home?" she asked with a sigh. "I think I'm ready for the adventure to be over."

"Soon, Ileana, very soon, I promise."

Andrei took back the phone and reassured Evelyn that her grandkids were okay and that it would take some time to get back home, but that he would make every effort to make it as soon as possible.

"What about Blake? Do the police have him in custody?" Evelyn asked. "I'm not going to feel like Inez and Tristan are really safe until he's locked up."

"I lost sight of Blake during the hurricane, but as soon as the kids are with you, I'll resume the hunt for him." Jail wouldn't hold Blake now, not with what he had become. The only way the kids would be safe would be if he was dead. This time the thought brought with it no sense of anger or vengeance. It was just something that had to be done.

It took a bit of time to reassure her. In the meantime, Inez tried to speed up the process by shoving things into the baby bag before sitting down and trying to tie her own sneakers with the tip of her tongue poking out of the side of her mouth.

The resiliency of kids never ceased to amaze him. In the long run, he was pretty sure that she would be just fine. He changed and fed Tristan and made sure that Inez had something to eat and drink as well while he waited for the sound of help to arrive. "For the love of God, Dean," he muttered under his breath. "Where are you?"

"Mr. Dean? He outside," Inez said, pointing down the stairs. "I show you."

Andrei exchanged a puzzled glance with Ileana, who shrugged. "She always knew when he was close before." She concentrated fiercely, her brows knitting, and then her eyes lit up. "Yep! He's outside. Want me to go tell him to hurry up?"

"No, we'll go together. We want to be ready when help arrives." Andrei gathered everyone up and carried what he could stuffed into one bag, leaving the rest behind. Inez was full of energy, holding onto his hand as she hopped down the stairs and chattered on about her grandmother and Aunt Wanda.

She pulled him toward the middle of the expanse of lawn between the lighthouse and the visitor's center. It made Andrei feel very exposed, walking right out in the open with the baby in his arms and Inez clinging to his hand. Andrei looked around warily for Blake until the sight of a still form made him forget everything else.

He ran over to Dean, relief sweeping through him in a rush when Dean pushed himself up to rest on his elbows and looked at him with bleary eyes. "I should've known you'd be napping. You look like hell spat you out," Andrei said with a relieved laugh.

"Charm and flattery are not lost with you. I was planning on getting up and going to see you after a few more minutes in the sunshine." Dean winked at Ileana and smiled at Inez, who hopped up and down, pointing at him.

"See, see, tole ya! Hey, Mr. Dean."

"Hey sweetheart." Dean pushed himself up to a sitting position and ran a hand through his hair, making it stick up wildly in all directions.

Andrei sank to his knees and hugged Dean hard. "I swear, you've been making up, hardcore, for all the times you've said I've worried you. What happened? Where's Blake? Are you okay?" Andrei had never seen him look so exhausted, not even when he'd come back from being chased by the Jackals.

"He's gone, baby, gone," Dean crooned and then chuckled wearily. "And never coming back. He may wash up on shore sometime in the future, but I doubt it. I'm beat. Let me tell you, Poppet, don't ever go riding on the energy of a hurricane, okay? Worse than a bucking bronco. Not that I ever was fool enough to try that, just a hurricane. God, I'm never doing that again."

It was over. Andrei sat down, stunned, and patted Tristan on the back when he fussed over being jarred. It was over. Blake was gone. He couldn't hurt anyone else. Andrei didn't know how he felt about that. Numb maybe, tired, a bit of relief. He looked at his partner and his sister. Dean and Ileana could move on.

Andrei bit his lip, looking over his shoulder at the steady thwap-thwap-thwap of a helicopter approaching. "Are you leaving now?" He wasn't ready. He wanted just a few minutes more that wasn't filled with danger and desperation. Just a few minutes with Dean in their home where he could give them a proper good-bye. Or was this just another excuse, another reason to hold on when he needed to let go for both of their sakes?

Dean squeezed his hand and then stood up. "I'm seeing this through to the end. Let's not think of good-byes until the kids are settled." He thrust his chin out toward the helicopter that was circling the meadow and lowering, searching for a place to land. "What's with the air rescue? What happened to the Jeep?"

"There's no road left, and God only knows where the Jeep is. I'm glad I insured it. In fact the man told me that we're lucky we're not under several feet of water. Other places on the island didn't fare so well." Andrei covered Tristan's head with a blanket and took Inez's hand as the rotor blades whipped up a wind. "Come on, let's go home."

DEAN sat in his favorite armchair and watched Andrei reassure Dean's parents that he was fine. At least he'd been able to talk Andrei into a little bit of hair dye to get rid of the worst of the silver that had still been left over after Robin had reverse-zapped him. Some strands still threaded his black hair, but at least it didn't look as if he'd aged twenty years in the last two weeks. And he had lost several pounds while he'd been in the hospital. Dean knew his family; they were going to fuss over Andrei until they were satisfied. It was good to be assured that they weren't going to let Andrei slip out of their lives now that Dean was gone.

It was odd. Dean knew his parents were there, though he couldn't really see them, or make out what they were saying to Andrei. They were indistinct, nothing more than a warm sense of light and peace and love. It was even more pronounced than the phenomena that had happened after he'd said good-bye to them at his funeral. In fact, the whole world was becoming more indistinct and gray, and it was getting harder to see anyone but Ileana and Andrei in the twenty-four hours since they'd been home.

Seeing Inez and Tristan in their grandmother's arms and waving to her had been the last big thing. After that, everything had gone hazy. He was tired. Beyond tired. It was like the storm had taken everything vital out of him in that last final battle, and he hadn't missed those worried looks that Andrei kept giving him or the little whispered consultations with Ileana, who seemed baffled.

Dean had done everything he'd set out to do when he stayed behind, everything but say good-bye to Andrei. And for the first time since waking up on the side of the parkway, he had faith that Andrei would be okay when he left. And God, how he needed that faith.

Andrei said his good-byes and then shut the door, turning toward him. "Looks like I'm going to be busy. Now that Justin is out of the hospital I have a lot of explaining to do, and the Feds are still not fully satisfied. And I'm told by your parents that I have to attend Sunday dinner this weekend."

Dean grinned, remembering many such times. "Is Dad breaking out the grill and the boat?"

"Yep, and your sister is making one of her pies." Andrei patted his stomach.

"You lucky dog."

Andrei knelt in front of Dean's chair, taking his hands and curling their fingers together. Dean smiled at him and tugged a hand free to cup Andrei's face, studying him, memorizing every bit of him, the sharp line of his nose and jaw, the way his dark eyes looked so warm and loving. "You look tired. Like you're slipping away on me."

"I have one final promise to keep," Dean said, and Andrei's gaze darkened.

He closed his eyes, conflict moving across his face, yearning and fear. "You'd better not have come up with another reason to stay, Dean."

"I haven't."

Andrei's eyes flew open again, liquid with emotion, and Dean sat up straighter and leaned closer to him. "Does that mean—"

Dean laid his fingers against Andrei's lips.

"Soon. I have a few things that I want to say first." Dean paused, trying to gather his thoughts. This was going to be the last time he'd get the chance to get through to him. "Andrei, I wish you could see yourself truly, that you could see yourself the way I do. You say you're not strong, and yet you're giving me and Ileana up so we'll be safe without a whimper of protest out loud. You didn't kill Blake, though you longed to, because it was the wrong thing to do. You say you're not a hero, but you went out and rescued Inez and Tristan though you wanted to lie down and die too." Dean squeezed his hands. "It may be the harder thing to do, but I want you to live for me."

"Dean, I'd do anything for you," Andrei whispered. "I'll admit that I thought about dying. When I was in the hospital, between bouts of delirium, I knew that all I had to do was stop fighting to live and then I could be with you and Ileana. I could move on with you both...." Andrei trailed off and shook his head. "I just couldn't do it, there was something in me that wouldn't give up, that couldn't leave those kids behind."

"I'm not surprised," Dean murmured. "You never could stand the thought of not helping a kid when you could."

Andrei drew in a breath and shot Dean a pleading look. "I'm going to take up that offer with Joshua Norton, help him hunt down child predators and rescue the kids abused by them. I'm still needed here. And you know, Inez's fifth birthday party is next week. She'd be awfully disappointed if I didn't come."

"You don't have to explain it to me. Hero." Dean smiled and touched his forehead to Andrei's. "It eases my mind to hear you making plans." Making plans without him, and that had to be done sometime. There was barely anything left of him here, and the limbo was closing in around him. He didn't have Ileana's childlike innocence or Old Mother's strength of purpose to cling to.

"It hurts to do it." Andrei hesitated and then squeezed Dean's hands back. "And it feels like a relief too."

"I know, babe."

Ileana came into the room and skipped over to them, wrapping her arms around Andrei's neck. "Is it time for the song, Dean?"

Dean felt a shock ripple through him, then a sense of rightness. It was time. Andrei would be okay, and Dean had accomplished everything that he'd stayed behind to do now that he knew that Andrei would be able to move on after he had some time.

"What song?" Andrei asked, looking between the two of them. "What are you two up to?"

Dean smiled and stood up, holding out his hand to Andrei to help him to his feet. "I wanted one final dance, so I dug out our old record player and LPs with Ileana's help. Do you have it ready, Poppet?"

"Yep." She ran over to the kitchen table where the box sat and picked up one of the album covers.

"Good lord, where did you find that?" Andrei turned surprised eyes on Dean. "I thought we lost it in the move."

"We still had that small stack of boxes stored away untouched in the garage. We got so busy that we forgot about them."

Andrei chuckled with a shake of his head. "A lot was going on then."

"Ready?" Ileana called. "I'm putting the little stick thingie down now."

Moments later the sound of Jim Croce's guitar filled the room. "Remember this song, babe?"

Emotions chased across Andrei's face, and then he let out a rough laugh. "How could I ever forget it?" He held out his hand to Dean, a hand that trembled faintly. "Dance with me one more time?"

Dean pulled Andrei into his embrace, sank into the sensation of Andrei's strong arms around him as they swayed together. All the other times they'd danced to this song filled his mind, and he drank in Andrei's presence. He could sense the doorway opening behind him, and this time instead of fighting it or trying to pretend it didn't exist he let the sensation of coming home steal over him in slow degrees.

"I'd always loved this song as a kid," Andrei said against his ear, and Dean felt his lips curve. "And when you told me in high school that you loved it too, I knew you were meant for me."

"All the way back then?" Dean chuckled and kissed the line of his jaw. "You were a patient one."

"Still am." Andrei's arm tightened around his waist, and he paused as something tugged at Dean's shirt.

"Can I dance with you too?" Ileana said, looking up at them both with a wistful expression in her eyes.

"Absolutely, Poppet," Dean picked her up, half holding her as Andrei slipped his arm around them both.

"You are a part of this family," Andrei agreed. The three of them stayed together just like that until the record ended and started skipping.

Dean looked over his shoulder at the light spilling out of the doorway and felt the call down to his bones. The other Dean appeared in the doorway and smiled. He didn't speak; he didn't need to, and Dean nodded in acknowledgement. When he turned back to Andrei, his partner stared at the door and a look of awe entered his eyes.

"It's time, isn't it?" he asked in a hushed voice.

"Yeah, babe. It's time." Dean touched his fingertips to Andrei's lips, drawing Andrei's attention back to himself. They stared at each other a moment, neither saying a word, and then Andrei kissed his fingers. Dean let his hand fall away, and he looked at Ileana. "Are you ready?"

Both he and Andrei had explained it to her. He still wasn't entirely sure that she understood, but she had agreed to come with him and that was all that mattered. She'd be safe now.

"Wait a minute." Ileana wiggled to be let down, then ran over and left Cougar on top of the coffee table. "Ta keep ya company." Then she grabbed Old Mother's family Bible and brought it over to Dean. "We're taking this with us, right?"

"Absolutely, Poppet."

Ileana hugged Andrei around his waist. "I love you, Andrei."

Andrei picked her up and hugged her hard one last time, holding her close. "I love you too, my Illy girl. You take care of Dean the way you took care of me, okay?"

"Uh-huh, I'll make sure he plays real good." Ileana squeezed his neck and kissed his check. "I know lots and lots of games."

"Yes, you do." Andrei kissed her temple and then looked at Dean, his heart in his eyes. "I've been thinking and thinking about what I wanted to say to you at this moment, and I realize that there's nothing that I haven't already said."

Dean smiled, knowing exactly what he meant, and stepped forward to kiss him lingeringly. "I know. I love you, babe. Try not to get into too much trouble while we're apart, okay?"

"I'll try, but I make no promises. I love you too." Andrei glanced toward the golden light and the longing filled Dean with an achingly sweet need. "Do you even know what is waiting for you on the other side?"

Dean looked back at the doorway and the reflection of himself staring back at him. "No, but I do know this: it's a beginning, not an end. We'll see each other again. When it's your time, I'll come for you."

"I'll be waiting, *iubito*."

Andrei set Ileana down, and Dean held out his hand to her. She curled her fingers around it, her eyes starting to sparkle. All of Dean's cares and worries fell away, making him lighter. As he stepped forward through the doorway, he felt his reflection take his other hand and they started to merge as the light flooded through him.

Epilogue

DEAN walked through the small house, pausing as he had years ago to lay his hand on the shoulder of his sister, to reach out to his nephew all grown up now with his youngest kid in his arms. The house was full, people coming and going, stopping to talk to the man propped up on the bed that had been brought out into the living room to sit by the bay windows.

The colors were so vivid now, not like when he'd left this world. Only now he understood that he'd really only been a hiccup, an echo of himself. Not anymore; moving on had helped Dean find himself again, all the scattered pieces had come together. And now, after so long, he would see Andrei again.

Sunlight gleamed on Andrei's silver hair, and his nose had become even more crooked and battered over the years. His face was creased, his eyes were even more deep set than before, and his eyebrows had become entirely unmanageable, standing out like hedgerows on his forehead. He looked older than his years, the energy he'd lost by touching him and Ileana had never been fully recovered. Still, he had the power to make Dean's heart flutter, and anticipation coiled in his stomach. Andrei's eyes were closed, his breathing deep and even. Dean wanted to run to him and at the same time nerves held him back.

What if Andrei didn't still feel the same way about him?

It had been so long, and Andrei had filled his life up more than Dean could have imagined. He might not have fallen in love again, not like he had with Dean, but he kept his promise and lived life. The evidence of that stood with all the people in the room. All those kids he'd rescued and who had become part of his makeshift family. It was patently clear how much Andrei was loved.

A woman had her chair pulled up beside Andrei's bed, and she twisted around as Dean moved closer. Her gray eyes widened in recognition as she looked right at him instead of through him like everyone else in the room had.

"Oh my God, it's you," she whispered, her hand coming to her mouth. "Mr. Dean."

Dean looked closer at her—the short cap of dark brown curls over a well-shaped head, the smooth light brown skin that crinkled at the corners of her eyes—and he couldn't place her until he looked into her eyes again. "Inez." He grinned and came closer, stopping by her chair. She had a pretty plumpness about her, and her stomach was gently rounded with her unborn baby.

Inez looked between him and Andrei, her eyes darkened with tears. "I never had a chance to thank you."

"They were never needed." Dean touched her shoulder, and she brushed her trembling fingertips over his hand. "You look good, Inez. Seeing you all grown up wow, it's unbelievable. I'm glad Andrei stuck around with you."

Inez bit her lip and leaned toward the bed. "He's been so tired, and he still wouldn't stop fighting. If it's not one thing plaguing him, it's another."

Dean looked at Andrei, who started to stir with a sigh, and Dean's heart and stomach began flipping again. "I don't think he knows how. He's not a quitter."

"You've come for him, haven't you?" Tears spilled out of her eyes as Dean nodded. "Well you take good care of him, then, promise me."

"I will."

Inez stood, leaned over, and kissed Andrei's brow before gently tucking the blankets around him. She looked one last time at Dean, searching his face before moving off. He swallowed hard and came to stand by the bed as Andrei stirred again. His eyes opened and he looked around in confusion before focusing on Dean.

Their gazes met and a jolt zipped through Dean. Nope, his feelings for Andrei had not faded. All sense of sound and movement about the room disappeared, and Dean's heart stopped as he waited for a response from Andrei.

"Oh how I've missed you, *iubito*," Andrei breathed, his dark eyes lighting up as he stared at Dean in wonder.

Dean's eyes stung, though he didn't bother trying to blink it away, not when there was a similar wetness to Andrei's eyes. He sat on the edge of the bed, cupped Andrei's cheek, and leaned forward, touching his forehead to his partner's.

"You're looking good there, babe."

Andrei's body jolted with a wracked, suppressed laugh. "Beautiful liar."

"You were wrong about not being a good father. I knew it. Just look at all these kids grown up and safe," Dean whispered and brushed his lips over Andrei's. His chest ached and his throat tightened at his Andrei's nearness. So long, but they didn't have to be apart anymore.

"I did pretty okay, didn't I?" Andrei stirred and struggled to lift his head enough to look around at them. Dean sat on the bed and supported him. "They're not mine, at least not that way. You could say we all unofficially adopted each other. I just listened to them when they needed it." He stared up intently at Dean and slid his fingers into Dean's hair.

"You know, every time you talked about a case, I heard, I listened," Dean whispered.

"And I felt you," Andrei said. "It kept me going during the times when it seemed like there were more monsters than angels. I looked at the stars and thought of you. How's Ileana?"

"She's waiting with Cougar to say hi." Dean pressed another kiss to Andrei's lips and then rose. Andrei's eyes closed and his breath came out in a sigh of surrender. Dean held out his hand to Andrei and a tremor raced through his body as his heart started flipping. "Are you ready?"

A younger hand reached out to his and laced their fingers together as Andrei's spirit rose. A brilliant smile crossed his lips as he turned toward the doorway. "Always, *iubito*."

MARGUERITE LABBE has been accused of being eccentric and a shade neurotic, both of which she freely admits to, but her muse has OCD tendencies, so who can blame her? Her husband and son do an excellent job keeping her toeing the line, though. Together with Fae Sutherland, Marguerite has found a shared passion for stubborn men with smart mouths. With her solo work she often likes to explore darker themes as well.

When she's not working hard on writing new material and editing completed work, she spends her time reading novels of all genres, enjoying role-playing games with her equally nutty friends, and trying to plot practical jokes against her son and husband.

Visit Marguerite's web site at http://www.margueritelabbe.com.

The Triquetra Trilogy

ALL
BETS
ARE
OFF

MARGUERITE LABBE

From LABBE & SUTHERLAND

http://www.dreamspinnerpress.com

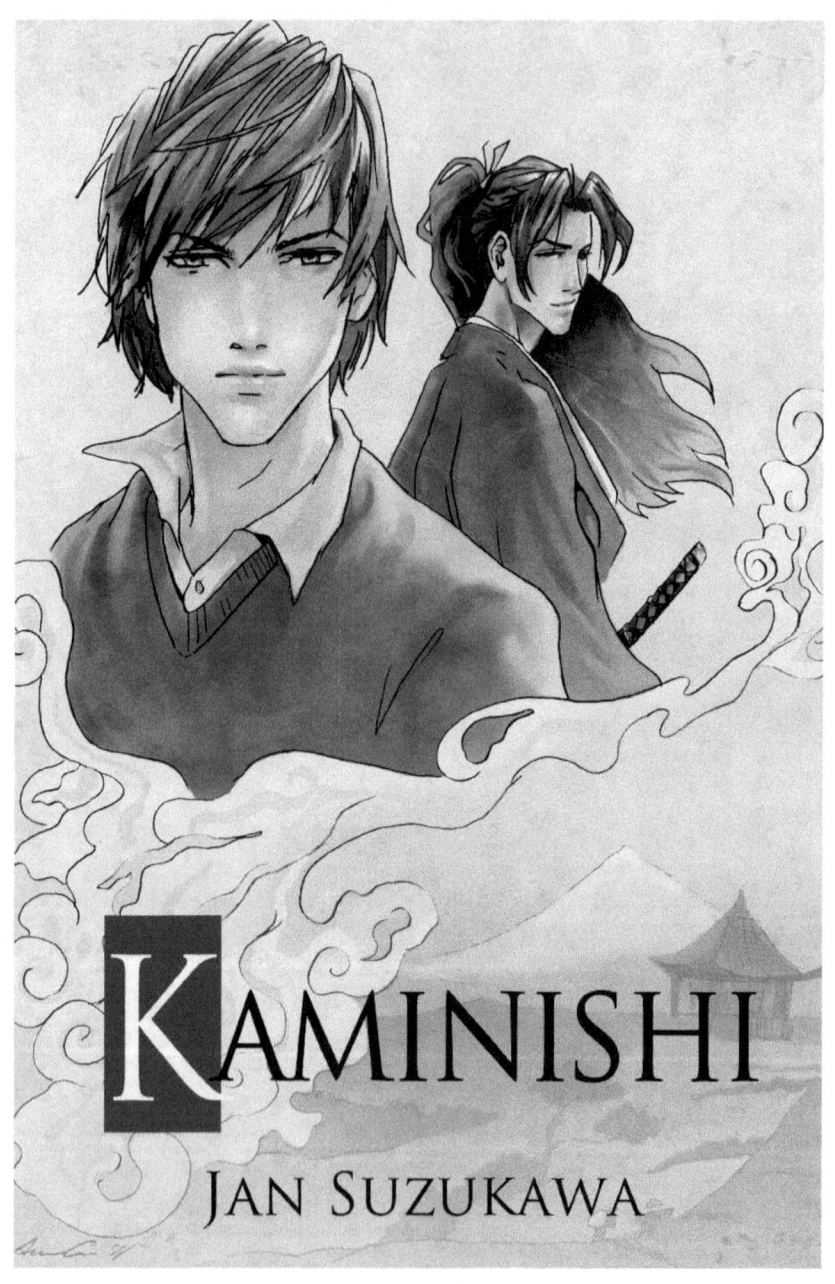

KAMINISHI

JAN SUZUKAWA

Also from DREAMSPINNER PRESS

'Til DARKNESS Falls
PEARL LOVE